TWO-FACED WOMAN

By Alex Fiano

GABRIEL'S WORLD ▫ BOOK TWO

∞

WHO WILL CATCH YOU WHEN YOU'RE FALLING?

Two-Faced Woman by Alex Fiano

Second book in the *Gabriel's World* Series
Copyright 2013, 2019 Alex Fiano
Distributed by Troublemaker Press
ISBN-13: 978-0-9969943-5-4

To the Gabriel's World audience: I thank those readers worldwide who have taken an interest and liking to Gabriel and Joel and the Gabriel's World stories, my friends who have supported *Gabriel's World*, and my unpaid intern FRO. – A.F.

∞

Gabriel's World offers a compelling community cf queer and allied characters, in stories that explore the extremes and complexity of good and evil.

Welcome to our World:
Homepage: GabrielsWorld.com
Email the author: gabrielsworld@outlook.com
Twitter: @gabrielsworld
Instagram: gabriels_world_queer_fiction

Gabriel's World: It's Time for New Heroes

MYSTERY/THRILLER/QUEER FICTION

Reader Extras: Gabriel's World now has recaps on the *Gabriel's World* website for the chapters of each book. The recaps offer chapter summaries, commentary, trivia and other insight & info, going into the plot and characters in-depth. Read Recaps of the chapters on the Gabriel's World website: bit.ly/2wUy6dJ

Books by Alex Fiano

The Hanged Man

Two-Faced Woman

The Book of Joel

Dead for Now

Hardcore

Previously in the *Gabriel's World* Series:

The Hanged Man – *What would you sacrifice to do the right thing?*

New York City private investigator Gabriel Ross faces this elemental question in the first *Gabriel's World* book. After seeing Gabriel confront a bigot in a controversial viral video, attorney Raymond Booth wants to hire him to probe a disturbing incident at Raymond's charitable foundation. As Gabriel is otherwise publicly scorned and losing clients, he's keen to take on Raymond's case. But then Raymond disappears. Raymond's sister Toni hires Gabriel to find the missing man. Gabriel turns up evidence of abduction—and then Raymond turns up dead.

Gabriel's obsession with the case pulls him into the mystery Raymond wanted him to solve. Gabriel has help from journalist Alex Barclay and Gabriel's former boyfriend Joel McFadden...leading to complications in his personal life. Gabriel begins unraveling a sinister secret connected to the foundation-a cabal tracng back to the origins of Nazism. Gabriel endeavors to uncover the conspiracy without losing his license, freedom, or life.

∞

PREFACE ♦ TWO-FACED WOMAN

Under the sky is perfect enjoyment to be found or not? From the Dao text *Kih Lo*

∞

AUTHOR'S NOTE: The discussions and interpretations of the sacred texts within this story reflect the author's learning and perspective. The use of the texts is intended to demonstrate great respect, dignity and love of the topics.

THE *I CHING* (or Yijing) is Confucian and Daoist, having evolved from the Zhou Dynasty in China. It is 64 *gua* that represent 64 situations in life. The *gua* used for the chapters have been chosen carefully. As the *I Ching* is meant as an oracle for divination, casting for the *gua* in one's situation may result in a moving *yao* or line, one that has extra meaning depending upon if it is yin or yang, and on its place within the *gua*. The moving lines have also been determined with care. The views reflected here are more Daoist. Daoism as a philosophy refuses categories and careful order.

∞

"Virtue is not as fascinating as evil." — Michael H. Stone, *The Anatomy of Evil.*

"It's everybody's fight." — What Viola Liuzzo told her family, before leaving to participate in the 1965 civil rights march from Selma to Montgomery, AL. Liuzzo was shot and killed by members of the Ku Klux Klan while she was transporting marchers to their homes.

PRELUDE ♦ 64 ANTICIPATING COMPLETION (WÈI JÌ)

Water over Fire: Life has provided setbacks. A new cycle is coming. One may still feel lacking in some way, but that is the necessary prelude to take responsibility to facilitate the new cycle. The fourth line (yang/nine) moves in this reading. Yang in a yin line means some difficulty in the journey, but the person should try to raise strength and fortitude.

∞

Saturday, November 27, 2010

GABRIEL IS BACK in the warehouse in Westchester. Joel is on his knees and Ethan Nelson pointing a gun at Joel's head, about to fire.

No, this can't happen...I rescued him. You're dead.

Gabriel tries to lift his Sig Sauer and hit Nelson across the head —like he did in in the warehouse, in August. But he can't move.

Nelson then turns and stares at Gabriel.

"I was going to kill your boyfriend."

He points the gun at Gabriel.

"I think I'll just kill you."

He pulls the trigger.

Gabriel doesn't feel the bullet hit his chest, but he falls backwards, away from Nelson, away from Joel.

Falling down further. Down into Hell.

Cold.

Blackness.

Alone.

∞

"No!"

My eyes open. I'm gripping my sheets.

I sit up slowly. The adrenaline throbs in my head and my chest. I'm covered in sweat.

It's a dream. You're alive. Joel is alive. Nelson is gone.

I feel nauseated now. The Xanax.

It's three in the morning. The bedroom is dark, but not entirely. A small lamp is on. I don't remember turning it on, but I also don't remember getting undressed and getting into bed.

I get up to go to the bathroom. A glimpse of my reflection in the wall mirror startles me. A 36-year-old man, in decent shape (when I don't work I exercise, when I don't exercise I work) but who hasn't been eating well or sleeping very much. The reflection looks haunted.

I turn away from my double and start to leave my bedroom. Then I see the broken door frame. The wood around the lock is cracked and splintered. What the fuck?

Archie, my black and white tuxedo cat, is walking with me. He stops to look up.

Joel kicked the door in. Remember?

I don't remember, and yet I know it happened.

"But Joel doesn't do things like that," I tell the cat, who's washing his paw. "We were working."

Well, Joel was working —taking care of some reports for me. I wasn't supposed to be doing anything. That was the compromise I gave into with Alex.

The nausea overcomes me and I run for the bathroom. Since I haven't eaten anything that I know of in 24 hours, it's just dry heaves.

As I lean on the sink to leverage myself back up, I see the Xanax bottle in the wastebasket. Empty. It had held at least 24 out of a 30-count prescription.

Archie jumps on the bathtub rim; his tail snaps back and forth as he watches me.

You had just collapsed by the bed. "Here is as good as any place. I just don't want to think anymore." That's what you were saying to yourself.

Then a loud noise —that would be Joel kicking in the door. You're a private investigator, you can make deductions like that.

And some moments later, Joel shaking you. "How many? Tell me!"

"Four..."

My deductive powers tell me Joel flushed the remaining Xanax down the toilet.

I go back into the living room.

Everything in here room is calm. Case files are stacked neatly on the writing desk. My cigarettes are on the coffee table with my lighter on top of the box.

Another memory. Sitting in the side chair, while Joel's talking to me, and I'm trying to open the pack of Camels. I can't do it; my fingers won't work. So I crush the box and throw it on the floor.

That box isn't anywhere around. The one on the coffee table is new, but the cellophane is off. Someone went out to buy it.

I light up a cigarette out of the new pack.

I'm not in Hell. Not the supernatural one anyway.

The dream starts coming back to me. Nelson. *He was in my client's apartment. Raymond Booth. Nelson was strangling Raymond in front of me, and I couldn't move. I could only watch him.* That was the first part of the dream.

I move to the kitchen for some water, and open the window to feel the night air of the witching hour. Freezing cold, but it cools the sweat.

The Xanax is wearing off and now I won't sleep again. I go back to the living room.

Joel has completed the reports. I flip through them. He must have finished all this while I was passed out. Watching over me.

My personal cell phone is near the cigarettes. I check to see if anything is on the phone that could offer some illumination.

The last text, to Alex, says —*me too.*

What?

I scroll up to previous messages. I see the ones from the morning that I *do* remember. Alex asking me to not work for the day and just clear my head, so we could get past our argument. Then later in the morning reminding me I said I wouldn't work.

He also sent a text in the afternoon suggesting that he come over last night, instead of tomorrow, to talk. I don't remember that one, or the reply underneath.

—*Can't. Veronica has an emergency I need to help her with, nothing bad. I'll see you Monday.*

I didn't write that. Veronica, my best friend, didn't have an emergency yesterday. However, I catch the scent of her perfume in the apartment, and I see an empty pack of her brand of cigarettes, American Spirit, in the living room wastebasket. She was here.

Archie tries to jump in the wicker wastebasket, to snag the pack. *Of course, she was here. No doubt Joel called her and asked her to come over and help watch you. They put you to bed. Deduction.*

The text under that one says, *All right. Tell her hi. I love you, okay?*

—me too

I stare at that last text. Joel typed that, and the one about Veronica. To keep Alex from coming over and walking in on me passed out.

Archie comes over to look at the phone. *That's why the reply doesn't say 'I love you.' 'Me too' is the most Joel could make himself type.*

Archie navigates the coffee table, stepping around the pack of tarot cards. Those remind me of Toni, Raymond's sister.

In the dream, after killing Raymond, Nelson stabbed Toni in the back and dumped her outside my apartment door. I open the door to see her there, staring up at me with frozen eyes.

But Nelson had drugged Toni. Made it look like an overdose, and left her in an alley in Brooklyn. I never saw her there. Well, dreams don't always make sense. He hadn't strangled Raymond by hand with a garrote, either.

And then the last part of the dream, with Joel. And there, the dream was accurate. Nelson had kidnapped Joel, taken him to the warehouse, and held him there to lure me in. He was going to kill us both, but I had managed to get in the warehouse without Nelson knowing, and knock him away. Nelson is gone. Mr. Zest, professional troubleshooter for the Tertullian Society, took care of that. I doubt Zest has these kind of dreams, although he claimed he and I were simpatico.

Remembering the dream with Joel triggers my recall of the rest of the afternoon yesterday.

I'm wandering around the apartment. I can't concentrate, I can't read. I'm supposed to be relaxing because Alex and I are trying to get over our fight. About my working too much. And whom I work with.

And Joel, studying the files on the computer fraud case, looks over at me.

"What's wrong, Gabriel? Really?"

"Nothing. I'm fine."

"No, you're not. It's what went on this summer, right? It's been three months since Toni's funeral. I know you were more shaken up about that than you said."

"I suppose. I thought I was handling it. But two clients died. I feel like I could have done something..."

"Stop saying that. Stop with the guilt. Nobody could have handled that case better than you."

"I almost got you killed, too."

"Don't think about that anymore. Is that why you aren't working? So you can let all the demons in to visit? Nelson's not going to come back and shoot me. It's over. Not the first time I had a gun to my head, anyway."

I'm trying to open the cigarettes then, and stop, crumpling the box and throwing it. That shocks him enough to leave the files and walk over to me.

I look at him. "What happened to you before?"

"I shouldn't have said anything. Forget it. Just something that went down when I was younger..."

For a moment, I don't know what is real —if Joel is alive, and I'm just suffering, or if he's dead and this is a dream.

I want to just forget everything. Forget. I'm exhausted but I can't stop thinking. And my phone buzzes with another text. It's not Danny, my other best friend. He's still angry at me. It's Alex again, checking up on me.

I can't work, I can't bring my clients back to life, I can't bring my mom and my uncle back to life, and I can't placate anyone who's living right now.

I just want to be out.

And even though Joel is talking, I get up and lock myself in the bedroom. Find the bottle. A half tablet didn't do it when I got the prescription. Or a whole, or even two. Let's double-down, then. Wait for it to hit.

Pounding on the bedroom door.

Listening to Joel's voice on the other side, but not responding.

"Come on, I'm sorry about that." ...

"Fuck...Gabriel? Open up." ...

"Goddamn it, open the door!" ...

"Gabriel? I'm sorry...please. I know you're going through a bad time. I'm here for you. Please don't hide. Come out and talk to me. Or let me in. Something." ...

"You're scaring me. Please. Open the door." ...

"If you don't open it, I'll break it down." ...

And this is where I walked into the movie.

I lie on the sofa, with the TV on. Should I call or text Joel or Veronica, or Alex? Maybe the safer thing to do is nothing.

Archie settles on the pillow next to me. His expression seems both affectionate and stern.

You can put it off for now, brother, but you know you have to make changes.

∞

ONE ♦ 64 ANTICIPATING COMPLETION (WÈI JÌ)

Fire over Earth. A radiance of energy returns like the sun rising over the Earth. It's brilliant, but also has some subtlety. A superior person is cultivating virtue and enlightening himself. Stability is important in this, to balance yin yang in firmness and flexibility. The sixth line (yang/nine) is moves in this reading. The person must in essence conquer himself, to be aware of internal dangers as much as external dangers, and to regain control.

∞

From The *New York Scene's* Thin Blue Line column, by Carl Mankiewitz, November 9, 2010

The *Scene*'s favorite unruly private investigator Gabriel Ross recently clashed with the NYPD after protesting the stop-and-frisks and arrests of some LGBT youth. The kids were breaking the law by being on the streets with condoms —first degree same-sex, right Commissioner? The Fuzz says having condoms means intent to prostitute and God knows even if true, that's surely more urgent a crime than gun and drug violence in the city. Add to that the fun of throwing teenagers into the Tombs so they can be further abused.

Ross says his lawyer Jim Pollan managed to have all potential charges dropped after a public fuss arose with bystanders and cell phone cameras. *This* time. Not all the kids in this city are lucky enough to have people stand up for them when the cops want to waste time.

Having been called in to help with the *ad hoc* protest, I then asked Ross his opinion about the plea deal for assistant medical examiner Samuel Ides. Ides was indicted for falsifying an autopsy report in attorney Raymond Booth's death in July. This happened after the discovery that New York Foundation for Art and Culture director Ethan Nelson (who killed himself after murdering siblings Raymond and Antoinette Booth) was a long-time con artist. The info about Nelson was submitted to the *Scene* via an anonymous source.

You all might remember that Ross had insisted Booth was murdered and *not* the victim of an autoerotic accident as the police claimed. Ross was roundly ridiculed by local press (except for us and the *Herald Standard*) but vindicated when Nelson left a note confessing to Booth's murder and the murder of Booth's sister Antoinette, after she confronted Nelson with evidence Ross had obtained. Although Ross claimed to have left the case once having enough evidence to challenge the official autopsy, the fact he was right about the murder has led to better press for the unfairly-maligned investigator.

Anyway, I asked Ross about all of this and all I got was "No comment." Such modesty. Instead Ross wanted to talk about the NYPD's need for training on LGBT issues. I asked him if he was confident that 'Giuliani Time' would somehow turn into a *Star Trek* episode where we all *just get along*....

From The New Jersey *Union Tribune*, November 24, 2010

The *Union Tribune* has learned of new developments in the Leonard Mathers murder case in Elizabeth. The woman accused of murdering Mathers, Sophie Faulkner, has changed counsel. Her close friend and local business owner Giselle Greenspan spoke to the *Tribune* saying Faulkner's previous counsel was incompetent, and that she had hired attorney Michaela Connor to handle the case. Greenspan has asked that anyone with information about the case please contact Connor, who has an office in Newark. Faulkner is currently being held in the Union County Jail on murder charges. Ms. Connor stated to the *Tribune* that the charges against Ms. Faulkner "seemed dubious" and that her investigator would be working on obtaining evidence to clear Ms. Faulkner.

Ms. Connor confirmed that her investigator is Gabriel Ross, a private detective licensed in New York and New Jersey. Ross was arrested this past summer after a conflict with notorious preacher Mel Bunton, whose group the Fundamental Righteousness of Baltimore protested a military funeral in Buckston. The group is known for its homophobic and anti-Semitic rhetoric throughout a ten-year history of protesting funerals. When asked if Ross's case detracted from the Faulker investigation, Ms. Connor said the charges against Ross had been dropped and that he was an exemplary investigator.

As reported previously Leonard Mathers, 42, was found on August 23rd buried in Ms. Faulkner's backyard. Ms. Faulkner was arrested on September 10 after 'touch' DNA allegedly matching Ms. Faulkner's was found on a hammer underneath the body. Mathers apparently died from blunt force trauma — including several blows to the head cracking the skull —in addition to several other bones broken. A source in the Elizabeth police department said it was one of the "most vicious murders seen here in some time." The relationship between Ms. Faulker and Mathers is uncertain, although they seem to have known each other for several years. Stan Cooper, the prosecutor handling the case, has declined to comment on any possible motive but did say substantial evidence supported Ms. Faulkner's arrest.

∞

Mom...

She stares at him from her position on the street, in front of the park. Her feet are a couple inches above the ground. She wears a bright white shroud wrapped around her body, reminiscent of a toga.

Don't wear that, he says from where he's standing opposite her across the street. *You're not dead. Come with me.*

She holds her hand out. She's a tall woman, with dark blonde hair and ice-blue eyes and strong angular features. He's forgotten what seeing her in person is like because all he has now are photos.

She speaks but he can't hear all the words. *Help me, baby...being tortured.*

Where, Mom? Where are you? Who's doing this to you?

You have to help. Don't turn away from what you need to do.

He can't take this. He runs across the street which gets wider as he attempts to cross it. Cars he can't hear or see well swirl around him. He's going to get her, carry her back, and not let her be tortured.

He's closer to her now, so close he can smell her perfume. He sees the faint lines in her face. Lines that deepened so much when she suffered from the invasive disease that killed her. He's confused that she's dead and yet here. But she's standing here, looking at him with her concern, her love, and reaches for his face. *Don't turn away, Gabriel. Don't let them make you go underground.*

I won't. He puts his hands out, feeling the white sheets of the shroud billow around him. When he embraces her, her body is warm. She touches his head as she did when she was in the hospital, when he would lay his head on her chest and tried not to cry. He used to do the same thing as a child to get comfort from her, and he does so again now. Her voice is over his head. *Help them, Gabriel. They're being tortured.*

His arms are around her tight; for a moment she feels solid.

Then she's gone, and he's fallen to the street. He looks up at the sky, indifferent blue with no sense of where she's disappeared.

Beneath his head, he hears howling underground. People are being tormented, impaled, on hooks, beaten, set on fire.

∞

THEN I WAKE UP in shock. Cold and sweating, shaking...

∞

Monday, November 29
Union County Jail, Elizabeth, New Jersey, 9:15 am

Work is a blessing these days, to avoid being in my own head. Right now, I'm sitting across from an accused murderer who looks like a kindly aunt.

Sophie Faulkner is a rangy five feet seven. Her arms and legs are taut but she is a little soft in the middle. She is white, and has short dark brown hair threaded with gray slivers. Her eyes are intelligent, brownish-gray, and she wears black frame glasses and no make-up. Her features are strong and pleasant.

Sophie sits in a gray metal chair at the end of a Formica-topped table. Stress lines are on her face from the experience of arrest and jail. The jail interview room is plain and depressing as is nearly any jail interview room across the country.

Three of us are visiting her in the jail at Elizabeth Plaza in Elizabeth, New Jersey. I'm with Michaela Connor, Sophie's defense counsel; I call her Mikki. Michaela is 35, black, short and curvy. She wears a gray suit and her braided hair is piled on her head with some braids hanging loosely. A close friend of mine, Michaela's also hired me several times to help her on cases—and gotten me out of trouble more than once. Also present is Dr. Peter Adler, a psychologist Michaela hired. Adler is a fiftyish tall white man with a faint southern accent.

Michaela has visited Sophie before. She introduces us. "Sophie, Dr. Adler is going to talk to you so we can get a diagnosis on your psychological state, to help with your defense. This is just an initial visit; he'll be back. And this is Gabriel Ross. He's a private investigator working for me and he'll be going over some background information and looking for further evidence to help you."

Sophie nods. "Sure. I appreciate all this." Her voice is pleasant, middle-class New Jersey. "I don't understand how this happened, but I want to do whatever I can to fix it."

She seems lost now. Michaela gives me a knowing look. She thinks Sophie is likely innocent; if so, that's a problem. The criminal justice system is set up for the guilty—for prosecutors to process as many plea bargains as possible. The innocent are, to put it not-delicately, fucked. I feel for Sophie. Her situation seems like mine in metaphor.

As Dr. Adler begins questioning her, I glance over my notes. Sophie owns her own small house in Elizabeth. She works as a home cleaner, organizer, and seamstress; she has for twenty-odd years.

According to what Michaela knows thus far the murder victim Leonard Mathers was a long-time acquaintance of Sophie's. She was not involved with him romantically. He sometimes helped her with work around her house. In fact, he had been helping her in landscaping her backyard. Some of the backyard had been dug up for planting bushes. Leonard had been dumped in one of the holes, and covered loosely with dirt. She had discovered him when she went out to work on the bushes.

An alleged DNA match on the apparent murder weapon is enough for the murder charge. Sophie said the hammer found under Leonard's body had been in her garage; it was one of her tools. So naturally it would have her DNA on it. We still have to wait and see if the county prosecutor is going to a grand jury for an indictment. But in the meantime, Michaela is challenging both the recent DNA test and calling into question when the DNA could have been placed on the hammer.

Adler is here because Sophie's former defense counsel told Mikki over the phone, and I quote, "Good luck with this fruitcake." He didn't explain further.

A psych eval isn't always part of a defense investigation, but Michaela picked up indicia that Sophie may have at least some memory-related issues. So, Adler is interviewing her to see what might be going on. As we wait, Sophie answers Adler's questions calmly.

He does elicit that she sometimes doesn't remember certain times of day, or even long periods. Then Adler questions her about possible drug use. She's insistent that she doesn't use illegal drugs or even much prescription medication.

He sighs and tries another tact. "Have you had sleeping problems, Ms. Faulkner? Hm?"

"Um, not often. Sometimes, at certain times I mean...sleeping isn't really the issue here."

"Ms. Faulkner, stay with me now okay? I need you to really *focus* here, and pay attention to the questions like a good girl."

Turning away from him, I roll my eyes at Michaela. She in turn raises one of her eyebrows at me, and her gaze stays on my face. I meet her eyes. She is warm for her friends, businesslike for her adversaries. For me, always a little extra based on the friendship we've slowly cultivated, involving not just work but also love of philosophical and political discussion and learning new things together in our off-time. I've even gone to some LGBTQ+ meet-ups with her as her wingman, and I'm not very social. That is the beauty of our being with each other. But that time to get to know one another over the years also means she reads me very well. Despite the fact I think I look pretty normal today.

She writes on her legal pad — *What?* We're at an angle that Sophie can't see us writing, which might be disconcerting to her.

—*He's being a prick*, I write back.

Michaela had asked me over the weekend to help her out with the case, and I'm feeling like I'm getting into the groove of where to go with the investigation. A new case gives me a sense of purpose, activates my curiosity and challenges me to find the evidence. Ordinarily, someone like Adler wouldn't bother me especially as I'm not going to be dealing with him outside of today. I've learned to professionally ignore personality problems. But I don't think that his condescension is going to elicit much from Sophie, and it just irks me.

Michaela frowns at me. *His reputation is good,* she scribbles. *We need to find any mitigating or exculpatory circumstances.*

Adler's tone gets sharper suddenly, interrupting our note-passing. "Ms. Faulkner—what is going on, hmm?"

Sophie is staring off into space focused on something invisible to our left. I'm not a practicing psychologist in any sense but I've studied psychology, and more importantly I have interacted with many persons having certain mental conditions. I'm thinking she has some form of disassociation.

I note this on Michaela's pad. And now Sophie is trying to concentrate on Adler again.

"Ms. Faulker, did Leonard Mathers make you angry in any way?"

She turns back to him slowly. "No, I told you that. When he was with *me*, he was always very pleasant. Not just *me*...I liked him, and also...well, we got along."

She emphasizes the 'me.' That stays with me for some reason. Something I heard a long time ago from another client. That person had similar speech patterns to Sophie. I consider that Sophie does not live with anyone, isn't involved. Yet she mentions how Leonard Mathers dealt with her as if he also interacted with someone she knew. And the memory thing. Perhaps it's not disassociation after all, I think. I speak up, interrupting Adler's question. "Who else did he get along with, Ms. Faulkner?"

Adler looks over his shoulder to frown at me. I ignore him.

Sophie focuses her big brown eyes on me. She scrunches her eyebrows. She doesn't want to answer.

Adler shifts his frown between Sophie and me. "Excuse me, I need to finish this."

I ignore him. "Ms. Faulkner, did someone *close to you* also know Mathers?"

Adler's mouth falls open at my insouciance. But Sophie's nodding. She's meeting my eyes, and I feel she understands what I mean. Michaela watches both of us intently. She gives me a lot of rope in terms of dealing with people, which I value. The fact that she hires me to work in Jersey even though I live in New York says a lot, although I'm licensed here as well.

"Yes. Edward did."

Michaela frowns. The name Edward hasn't turned up yet in the case. "Who is Edward, Sophie?"

Sophie casts her eyes down. "Edward, well, he's close to me. Like Mr. Ross says. But he's very discreet. He wouldn't necessarily want me to talk about him. Giselle said it wouldn't be a good idea either."

Michaela and I briefly exchange glances. She asks, "Would Edward have killed Leonard Mathers?"

"No. He'd *never*. He liked Leonard too."

Michaela is trying to keep up, while the situation has become clear to me. Michaela starts writing on her pad while talking. "Is Edward a friend of yours? Boyfriend?"

Sophie is now looking very hesitant. "Edward is...He fixes cars and bikes. That's what he likes. Leonard rode a Harley, and Edward worked on it. That was all right with me."

It seems to be all she wants to say. I'm still thinking about the person I met who was like Sophie. That was when I was working with my late mentor Manny, Manuel Smith. I began my career working in his private detective agency. One of our clients had the same affect as Sophie. By affect I don't mean stupid, zoned out, dull or anything like that. Just that sometimes she's somewhere else, as was my client. It was one of the most profound client experiences I ever had.

I lean forward, folding my arms. "She doesn't have memory loss, she has time loss. Ms. Faulkner, can I speak to Edward?"

Michaela looks puzzled but I touch her arm in reassurance. Adler sighs loudly. Sophie focuses her attention back on me. "Edward isn't here."

"He's listening, though?"

Michaela and Adler both give me strange looks. Sophie turns her eyes to the ceiling, then back at me. I keep going. "Yes, he is, I think. He's listening and you could put in a word for me to help out the situation. What do you say, Ms. Faulkner? We need Edward's help here."

Sophie's listening to me intently—and I sense she's not the only one listening.

I continue, encouraged. "I understand if he's reluctant, just as Ms. Greenspan is concerned, but also I understand your relationship with Edward and I don't judge. He must be familiar with Elizabeth too, right?"

"Yes...."

"I'm from New York, but I know the city of Elizabeth pretty well; we may have been in the same places. I'd like to have his opinion about Leonard Mathers."

Sophie blinks several times. "What is it do you do, Mr. Ross?"

"Call me Gabriel. I'm a private investigator, working with Ms. Connor. Anything said to me is confidential as it would be with her."

"I don't think..." Adler starts to speak, and I raise my hand to him, annoyed. I don't care what he thinks right now. His face gets red and he shoots Michaela an angry glance.

Sophie's focused on me. "You can call me Sophie, please. You said you know Elizabeth?"

"Yeah, and the area around here. I play softball in Warinanco Park sometimes with my friend Bob Jarvey."

"Bob? We know Bob..." Sophie tilts her head back like she's thinking. After a couple minutes Adler grunts and motions for Michaela to speak in the back of the room. I wait a little more, feeling something developing, but since Sophie isn't moving, I join them.

Adler snaps his book shut. He deliberately doesn't look at me. "...She may have depression and generalized anxiety disorder. She may be on the autism spectrum..."

I instantly tune out this bullshit and look back at Sophie. Her head is still tilted up. Beside me, Michaela is shaking her head.

"I have to leave; I'm helping a client in Paterson in a couple hours. Maybe you could speak to her again soon? I think something serious is going on."

"I'll speak to her again, of course, but she's not being very cooperative."

While I turn to glare at Adler, a chair rattles behind us sharply, interrupting the conversation. A different voice speaks up.

"What do ya want to *know*, Gabriel Ross?"

A deeper, measured, intense voice, with a hint of wryness. Our attention is brought back to her. Sophie has changed. Her glasses are off and sit folded in the middle of the table. Her bearing has changed as well. Sophie had been sitting leaning on the table holding her hands together, and her eyes moving from person to person.

But the person in front of us now is leaning back in the plastic chair, shoulders straight, and eyes half-lowered. One hand is on the table, the other gripping the ankle resting on a leg. She's looking straight at me but she isn't Sophie any more.

His eyes track me as I go back to the table. "Edward."

Edward doesn't nod. His acknowledgement is to briefly raise his eyebrows and half smile. He has a different energy than Sophie, simultaneously more laid-back yet more focused. His expression carries a touch of the sardonic. Michaela and Adler haven't moved since he spoke, stunned. I sit down in front of Edward.

"I appreciate your speaking with me." I hold out my hand.

He takes it, nodding shortly, looking me over. "You understand, don't ya? Okay, yeah. I know Warinanco Park. She likes to go there in the spring."

"It's not far from your house, I think. Sophie said you work on bikes."

"I'm good at fixing cars and hogs. It helps with the mortgage. No one bugs me when I work on machines, so it suits me."

Dr. Adler suddenly speaks behind me. "You say your name is Edward?"

Edward just looks at him with what seems to be vague contempt and doesn't answer.

Adler asks a few more questions without response. Edward ignores him and turns back to me.

"I'm not talking t'him. He thinks we have a mental disorder. He has no idea what's goin' on."

I nod. "I knew someone like you years ago. He helped the other self, the other inhabitant, in his system, as you help Sophie. You protect her?"

"Yeah, sometimes I do. But we're different. I'm not here just to protect her."

"I know. You're a separate person."

"Exactly. And there's nothing wrong with her, but she's a romantic, likes those ditzy novels. Sometimes city living here takes street smarts. You have to fuckin' get a *clue* to survive. People don't often get it—Sophie and me, so we're not currently *involved* with anyone, ya know? But that's okay, we get along. She checks out now and then—doesn't always like to know what's going on when I'm out. I have to deal with all kinds of people who give me their cars to fix, but I can do it where she can't. You say Bob's your friend?"

"Yes, Sophie said she knows him."

Edward nods slowly. "We knew him pretty well. Good guy. But he doesn't live here anymore."

"No, he's a counselor in Paterson now. So, what happened with Leonard Mathers?"

"Honestly, I don't know. He could be a fuckin' space case sometimes. We liked each other okay. He talked a lot to me because I didn't judge him either. He wanted someone to listen. So I *listened.* I worked on his Harley, and he'd spend hours going about some weird fuckin' theories on life—he was into magic and the supernatural and he was hipped on classical music —no, really he was into opera. He'd explain every opera recording in existence. But he always paid me good for my work, and didn't try to get with Sophie, ya know what I mean? He'd ask my advice about his occult theories. So he was all right. I didn't kill him. I don't know who did."

He suddenly rolls his eyes back, and then stares at me. "You understand about needing to be someone else sometimes, right? I have to leave, because you're gonna leave. Sophie has to have recovery time after I take over. We don't want the guards here to find out about *us.*"

"I understand. Edward, do you have any idea where we could start in finding out who *did* kill him?"

Edward stretches. "Jeezus, I wish I could smoke in this hellhole...well, he was into something new when he disappeared...some new quest. I didn't really ask questions. One place you could start with is Wildemore. He used to work there long ago, but he liked to hang around the place long after it closed. I think he was sleeping there or something..."

The interview is over, as Edward stares up at the ceiling. We wait until Sophie is back. She's a little stressed, as if Edward showing up was revealing too much. Nonetheless, she's functioning okay.

When we walk out from the jail to the street, Adler starts postulating theories to Michaela.

"She could be faking, but she'd have to be really good."

"She's not faking."

He glares at me. Granted my tone is a little sharp. I'm having a hard time with moderation these days.

"What are *your* qualifications in psychology, Mr. Ross?"

"I've had actual experiences with persons who have systems of selves. She's not faking."

"If you mean dissociative identity disorder, she *may* have it. I don't know it will work as a defense; people tend not to believe in its existence. But if we can find out when she was sexually abused, maybe we can show Mathers triggered something, look for any instances of breakdowns..."

"You think she's *Sybil?* Few multiples are sexually abused. They're more likely to be abused because they're multiples than the other way around. She and Edward seem pretty damn functional to me."

His face gets red. "Excuse *me*, but whatever misguided cultural sensitivity you think you're promoting is not going to help her. The body of literature on this condition, what there is, connects strongly with sexual abuse."

"When it fits the psychiatrists' needs, sure it does. Excuse *me* for assuming psychiatry has some interest in humanity and the truth."

I move away from them to go to my car on the street. I think things over while seeing in my peripheral vision Adler continuing his conversation with Michaela. I hear his voice getting angry-whiny, and tune it out.

I notice the sky seems like it wants to snow. I imagine the grey clouds bursting open and baptizing us with cold, white ice.

I'm trembling a bit. Whether from talking to Sophie and Edward, or Adler, I'm not sure. Maybe it's from my own ghosts haunting me. Edward reminding me of working with Manny, dead over five years now, rattled me.

I turn on my Camry to get the car warm; my David Gray song collection starts. *The One I Love.* A song that seems to be about love, except the protagonist is dying. My mother died around this time in 2003, seven years ago. I still feel the unreality of it. The dreams about her lately intensify that feeling. As well as the other dreams I'm starting to have, all involving death.

I have to switch out of David's songs to a mixed playlist, but the music continues to seem melancholy. I close my eyes and wait.

Suddenly Michaela is getting in the car on the passenger side.

She looks up at me. "Can we check on if anything is new in the press on this?"

"Sure." I take out my iPad from my backpack on the back seat, and start it up.

She picks up the iPod connected to the car stereo. "You have a bunch of new music."

"Joel put new playlists on all my computers. You know he likes doing that. Anyway...nothing new on here at the *Union Tribune* or anywhere else, it looks like."

"Good. I was afraid her condition might have leaked. Shall we go, then?"

I start to drive her back to her office in Newark, so she can prepare for her Paterson client.

Michaela's checking her Blackberry for voice messages and email, but I feel her eyes on me.

I remember Adler and my lack of tact with him. "Did Dr. Know-it-All quit?"

"No. He's not happy with you, but he's staying with the case. I convinced him of the good deed in doing so. At least he believes this condition exists, which helps. By the time we finished talking he was rather excited at the prospect, because it's rare."

"He's an asshole. Edward won't talk to him."

"Maybe not. Gabriel...I understand your righteous anger, but I'm limited as to who I can use."

"I get tired of people's identities being decided for them. And in Sophie's case, her personalities being decided for her."

She reaches over and puts her hand over mine on the steering wheel. "I felt like you weren't...um, yourself today. What's going on?"

Her touch is always meaningful. I know she could have fired me or given me hell, regardless of my success with Sophie and Edward. She doesn't get close to many people, as I don't. Because I respect her, I feel special that she has developed the bond with me. That sometimes puts tension on a working relationship. Her concern over me can't conflict with the concern for our clients being represented zealously.

I light up a cigarette from my pack of Camel Light Wides. I'm supposed to be quitting, but life has been somewhat fucked lately, at least in my mind. She knows why that is to a certain extent. Not everything.

I try smiling. "You know I get along with everybody."

She rolls her eyes. "Yeah, everybody except anyone in a position of authority. We need Adler. Better take a crash course in diplomacy."

I make an effort to shift into a livelier mode, that I've been thinking of lately as *cover-up mode*, and give her a wicked grin. "I'll start with you my dear, and concede to your legal acumen or kiss your ass, whichever comes first."

Michaela laughs, showing her slight overbite. "The day I see you kiss *anybody's* ass... maybe Alex's—he's pretty hot, I'll admit. What's going on with you two, anyway?"

I pause for a moment to drag on the cigarette. At a red light I shut the iPad down and change the iPod to a classical playlist. A concerto grosso.

"Hey, Mr. DJ, I asked you a question."

"He just got his promotion to editor. I was afraid my notoriety would hurt his chances but he made it. He's going to class himself out of being with me."

"That *won't* happen, sweetheart. He'd be an idiot to let you go. On the other hand...you're close with Joel again. He's working with you practically full time now."

"You know he's good at that—*almost* as good as me at certain tasks. He'll help me on this, too, if you don't mind."

"Certainly not; I *know* how well you two work together."

A little hint in her voice. I glance at her and she returns my smartass demeanor to me with a grin. Except in this case, I can't laugh it off.

She continues, "And he's as hot as Alex, in his own charming way...knowing him and you, I have to ask, do we have some sort of soap opera thing going on here? Enquiring minds want to know."

"Nothing to know, baby. I don't think I'm 'hot' enough to handle that, anyway."

She falls into laughter again. "Oh you are, which is why you're getting in trouble in the first place, love. I suggest you be careful before you're in over your head—if you aren't already."

I try to smile along with that, and don't do very well.

Her expression turns to concern again. "And you look really, really tired. Are you sleeping okay?"

The answer to that is no. But I'm not getting into it. Stupid, but I don't like to acknowledge anything that may have implications for my work. "I'm fine. I just don't like jails."

Her voice turns skeptical. "Something's bothering you, Gabriel. What is it, really? Are those two putting you in a bad way?"

"Too much on my mind; but I can always fake my death I suppose." It's a bad joke and she doesn't go for it.

She puts her hand back on my arm. "Dammit, I have to get some work done. I've got more files to handle or I'd *make* you talk to me more. I'm worried about you. Are you okay with this case?"

I feel an instant of panic that she might change her mind about me helping her. "Yes, I am. I'm already feeling righteous for Sophie. Don't worry; I just need to clear my mind."

Michaela watches me for a minute. "You're sure. Honey, it's okay if you need to beg off."

For a moment, I have to really consider it. I feel the gravity of her words. I'm declining into darkness in so many ways, but I still feel whatever energy I have for work. It gets me going, makes me engaged where otherwise I'm withdrawn.

Alex has resolutely said he thinks I shouldn't take any more cases for now; and Joel said that he'll be there for any cases I need him on.

"I'm sure I'm okay."

"Promise you'll talk to me if things get bad. In the meantime, are you following up on what Edward told you? And Sophie said she knew Bob, and that Edward knew Bob..."

"Yeah, that's a break. And I'm going to look into Wildemore. I'll want to talk to Edward again for sure."

"Now...you aren't working too hard, are you?"

"I'm fine. That's why Joel is helping, because of the work coming in. It's a good thing. You know about private practice, there's no happy medium."

"Don't overdo it, now. I know this time of year is not easy for you. Don't take on anymore for a bit."

"Gotta eat, Mikki."

"I know, but you gotta live, too. Find a way to back off before you burn out. In the meantime, I'm having the DNA re-tested. Whether or not the prosecutor files an indictment, we need to get the defense started. The police are supposed to be releasing Sophie's house this week. I'll let you know when."

"I'm going to try to go to Wildemore tomorrow."

"That's a good start. But you need to pace yourself. I see the difference in your eyes, darling. It almost makes me hesitate to ask the other question—especially being none of my business, but I'll ask anyway. Your look when I mentioned Alex. Trouble in paradise?"

"I see you are now offering criminal defense and advice for the lovelorn."

"You're not love*lorn,* you have too much of it. We're friends, right?"

"Yes, you can ask what you want. And I do have some challenges, I suppose."

"I thought so. He still wants you to move in?"

"That was ridiculous. Not going to happen, anyway. I'm not leaving my place. Alex gave that up, finally. My apartment isn't the Upper West Side but it's mine, know what I mean? I'm not living in someone else's place...anyway, we had kind of a fight last week. He seems to think I'm spending too much time working; but what it really is, he wants me to quit my profession altogether. That's the new thing he's nagging about. Go back to school, he's got connections, that type of bullshit."

"Huh. And what exactly are you supposed to do?"

"Not sure. He's known me for four months, and while I admit some wild stuff happened in the summer, he doesn't seem to know me well enough to get that I'm not an office boy. I don't care how glamorous it is." I smile at her. "Really, can you see me at an office meeting, Mikki? Schmoozing up the boss and board members?"

She has to laugh. "No. After a week, you'd be spraying graffiti on the walls."

"I don't know why he's on that kick, except he's been introducing me around lately. I met his mom and dad, nice people. But I suspect they kind of feel that I'm not, *ahem*, sophisticated enough."

"You? The Nero Wolfe of the East Village?"

"Too bohemian. Think about having to introduce me. And this is my son's significant other. Uh, he's a private enquiry agent. That's right, a dirty filthy peeper. The kind Raymond Chandler used to write about. No, I don't think that'll impress Martin Amis or Partha Dasgupta."

"Yeeouch. Someone's got class issues."

"If you mean me, of course. If you mean him, I didn't think so...but...well, his parents have it to a degree, which is funny considering he and his dad are both journalists and the British media is a free-for-all. I know he gets flak from some of his writer friends from the UK. I don't have the money/party/glamour thing. You know, some snotty fucker's got to pull out his phone at Le Bernadin, and claim Bono just texted him for advice about the IMF."

"Alex strikes me as the type who can stand up to that. Did you really *go* to Le Bernadin?"

"Once. We went to Masa once, too, but that was enough. I don't fit in with those places, and I hate him buying dinner when it costs as much as my rent. The thing is he could stand up to them but he agrees with them. His friends think what I do is useless because no cache, no high-profile, not that much money, practically no thanks. *I* don't give a fuck, but...he thinks I could do better."

"What do *you* want?"

"I'm doing what I want." This is true. Even if it's given me some hell, it's who I am.

"Then that's that. You don't let people tell you what to do, right?"

"Doesn't stop the kibitzing. Not to mention, he doesn't like me working with Joel."

"Have they even met?"

"Not really. I like it that way."

"Ah. Joel is helping you more because you're taking on more work. And therefore, you're around Joel more often. I see."

My face turns a little red in spite of my trying to will it not too. "He's been helping me since he came back. And he doesn't make allusions to me being a Dickensian guttersnipe; he supports my career. And for whatever reason, he doesn't want any payment. Who am I to turn it down?"

She shakes her head. "You don't. If anything, he means a great deal to you."

"He always has...wait, what are you getting at?" I think about what I said to Joel at the wake for my client Toni Booth a couple months back. *Joel, I care about you, but I'm not going to let you fuck up my life.*

It seems like an eternity ago when I said that; and the words seem strange—like a satire of a prayer.

"I'm getting at what's going on with you. I saw what it was like when you and Joel came over to my place the other day."

I light another cigarette. "I thought what we were doing was watching a fine documentary on the noted civil rights activist Bayard Rustin."

"*I* was, you might have been, although you couldn't concentrate. But Joel was watching *you*. He couldn't keep his eyes off you."

"Don't know what you're talking about. He's my friend and associate."

"Please. Keep telling yourself that. I ain't stupid. The boy doesn't play by Robert's Rules of Order. Ask Danny or Veronica. How are they doing, especially Veronica? Are you talking to them, or playing hermit?"

Danny and Veronica are my best friends. I've known Danny since we were 15, in a Bronx high school together. Veronica and I met at a private investigators and security personnel conference at the Hilton New York ten years ago. We hit it off so well, by the second day we ended up blowing off most of the presentations to joyride outside the city.

I smile, picking up on her hint of interest in Veronica. "I talk to Veronica almost every day. I was just over last night to fix up her apartment, security-wise. She's had some things going on; I don't want her to worry about me. And she has dual loyalties to Joel, so it's not easy because she doesn't want either of us to feel bad. Danny...you know what he thinks. He and I just had it out, too. I suppose I should do something about that, but he pissed me off."

"So you fought with your boyfriend and best friend last week."

"Yeah; makes me feel so special. Remember I said all kinds of reasons to want to fake my death?"

"Overdramatic. But...maybe the problem isn't just your refusal to acknowledge what Joel feels; maybe you don't want to admit how you look at *him*, either."

"What?"

"Let me lay it out for you. Joel looks at you like Dante looked at Beatrice. And you look at him like Jack meeting Rose."

"A *Titanic* reference? *Really*, Mikki?"

"Damn right. Because it's where you're headed if you don't get a handle on things." She's pleased with herself and I look suitably pained at her analogy.

Having stated her case, she drops the subject—thank God--and talk turns to holidays. I'm vague on that, not sure what I'm doing, if anything. I hadn't given it much thought. She wants our circle of friends to get together to do something festive. I try not to show the thought fills me with dread. Being around a lot of people, or even a small group—too much. Visiting my father on the pretense we have any relationship—too much. Figuring out how to have a holiday with Alex without leaving Joel alone—too much.

We've reached her office building. As she gets out, I nod along with everything she admonishes me to do without listening. "Pretty hot" Alex is having dinner with me, and I need to get in a better mood as this is the first night we've been together since our 'disagreement.' I wonder briefly what Edward's doing right now. I'd rather think of that than Michaela's helpful analysis of my love life. Jesus!

I play around with the iPod, finding opera to get me in the mood for the case, since Leonard Mathers was an opera buff. *Tosca, Vissi d'arte.*

So back to work, thank God for work. Edward mentioned Wildemore. It's a now-defunct mental hospital that has all the ambiance of Staten Island's notorious Willowbrook mixed with the Amityville Horror house (movie version). Some time ago, patients in the institution were moved after a local reporter found over a hundred violations of state law in patient care and safety. The facility was shut down, and it's a state junk heap now, surrounded by barbed wire. All kinds of rumors surround Wildemore: ghosts, killers, UFOs, secret government experiments, even chupacabras maybe. Sometimes teenagers go inside to hook up or smoke dope, or pretend they're Ghostbusters.

I'm definitely going to be visiting the place. I can't say I'm surprised I'm going to break *into* a mental institution. But like everyone else who visits, I will not go alone.

∞

TWO ◆ 46 ASCENDING (*SHĒNG*)

Earth over Wood: One is advancing upward slowly. Like a tree with roots in earth, reaching upward like a mountain. As with happens in growth, support is needed. Credibility, knowledge, and character is needed as well, to help with the hard work involved. The sixth line moves in this reading (yin/six). The person may be pushing himself or herself to success in such a way that brings psychic vertigo —the person is in danger of exhaustion with nowhere to go.

∞

KENT VARNEY IS STANDING across the street. He sees Kent watching him, just like his mother did in the previous dream. Once again, he tries to cross the street, to meet Kent. This time the street does not widen, but it does seem to sink beneath him as he walks. Still he's able to cross eventually and crawl up on the sidewalk.

Kent, I'm sorry.

You're always apologizing, Gabriel. It's not necessary. Did you kill me?

No, but you wouldn't have died if you hadn't have met me.

You really believe that? What makes you carry this guilt, Gabriel? I'm not sad. I had to make my life meaningful and I did. Are you doing that?

He looks up at Kent and can't find an answer. *I don't know the definition of meaningful.*

Socrates said being true to yourself. Using your intellect. Not just saying the words, but living them. Make your life meaningful, Gabriel. I'm not here in vain. Understand that, and don't live in vain.

Can you forgive me for what happened?

Kent looks sympathetic. *I'm not the one who needs to forgive you.*

They look up to see a white figure moving around them. The face of the figure is vaguely malevolent, like a Noh play mask of a supernatural character.

Kent says, *Klesa-Mara, that which is afflicting you.*

A form of Mara, the demon who tempted Buddha. A Mara as mental state.

Remember, Gabriel, the roots of the Klesa as said in the sacred Abhidharma-kośa...

Attachment

Anger

Ignorance

Pride

Doubt

Wrong view

As Kent lists them, each root extends from Mara as a black tendril, smoke-like. Vibrating negativity, pain. The tendrils reach for Gabriel, winding around his body.

No, I don't want to be this way.

But it's all mental, Gabriel. Unskillful emotions.

The tendrils engulf him; he's drowning in smoke. He feels Kent touching his hand. *You can change this, you can drive them away.*

∞

**From the editorial page of *The New York Herald Standard*
November 19, 2010**

The *Herald Standard* is pleased to announce Alex Shenoy Barclay has been appointed to Politics Desk editor following the departure of Marilyn Boxliter. Mr. Barclay has a distinguished career with the *Chicago Sun-Times* prior to his work for the *Herald Standard* as a Metro Desk reporter. Mr. Barclay was born in Kent, United Kingdom, and has a Master of Arts, as well as a Master of Science from New York University. He has reported from around the world on global political and criminal affairs. Mr. Barclay's father Martin Barclay is a senior producer for the British Broadcasting Company World News TV and his mother, a native of Mumbai, is a professor in political science at the University of Essex.

∞

November 29, Continued
Alphabet City, Avenue A, 6:45 pm

  Alex is late. He's been busy lately with this promotion thing. Alex is British on his father's side, Indian on his mother's. Alex's life experiences include fancy prep school, attending an Ashram as an adolescent to study the sacred Vedas, and interviewing despots in war-torn countries. I'm dark Irish descent, a high school drop-out with a GED and CUNY Midtown College dual undergrad degrees. My experiences include surviving childhood, taking on impossible cases, and managing to stay alive in spite of how many people I piss off.
  Alex owns a condo on the Upper East Side. I live in a rent-controlled apartment in the East Village with a lease I literally inherited from my late uncle Dominic in 2005. One or another of Alex's large English and Indian families is always flying over and visiting him. My only living relatives are my father and half-sister, and we'll spit on each other's graves from the afterlife. Alex is 37, and is often described as distinctively gorgeous; I'm 36, turning 37 in February. I've been referred to as not bad, doable, and "...you kind of look like that one guy in that one band."

I'm on the phone with my friend Bob Jarvey, the one with whom I play softball in Elizabeth, the one Edward and Sophie knew. I had tried to sleep a little after getting back from Jersey and doing some other work, but the dreams were too much, so I decided to get up and call Bob before Alex arrives.

I'm supposed to be making dinner. But four or five cigarettes into the conversation I've kind of sunk to the floor by the open kitchen window, hoping the cold December air will revive me before Alex gets here. I have a recording of *Carmen* in the background, in some semiconscious attempt to get in touch with Leonard Mathers.

"You know Wildemore?" I talk through my cigarettes. Bob lived in Elizabeth when he was an addict. He had been trained as a carpenter, but the addiction became most of his life. Bob was able to get himself out of that life, and became a counselor to formerly incarcerated persons. I happened to meet him during one of my cases in Jersey several years ago and we hit it off as friends instantly. He's still a counselor for a nonprofit in Paterson. Although he's clean, and a decent person, he still has his troublemaking side. We've had some interesting experiences hanging out.

"That place of the Damned? You planning to visit?"

"Actually I am. That's the connection to Leonard Mathers' case. As I understand, Leonard liked to hang at Wildemore."

"He lived there, more or less. Even after it was closed down."

"And that's why I want to visit. See if I can find a reason why he was killed. We don't think Sophie did it."

"I can't see that either. Not Sophie. She's hearts and flowers type. And you met Edward? He's cool. A little foul-mouthed."

"Unlike you, yeah. It was quite shocking."

Bob laughs. "Good that you and Michaela are helping on this. So you want me to break you in to Wildemore...you going to take Joel along?"

"He's out of town a few days, something to do in Europe with the estate of his friend."

"Is that right...Well, you two hooking up again yet?"

"*Jesus*, Bob...is that all anyone can think about?"

"I know sexual tension when I see it. I guess your Buddhism keeps you behaving, or something like that. Me, I have other altars I pray to, if you know what I mean. For a while, I thought maybe he and Veronica were an item. Our boy likes girls too, and I would be so envious of him if he was all up in her business..."

"No, they're just friends. We're all friends. With Veronica I just haven't been there for her as much as I'd like, so he's stepped up."

"I can step up too, if she needs a strong arm. I'm serious about that. Now you, you've been working a lot lately in Jersey again. I mean, I'm glad to see you more often, but you sound tired."

"Yeah, Michaela noticed too. That's the thing--one must work to earn money to pay one's rent and feed one's cat."

Said cat, Archie, hears the word 'feed' and comes up to see if any treats may be forthcoming.

Bob chuckles in his slightly raspy voice. "I know the sound of someone with too many balls up in the air, so to speak. You're *tired*, man. You'll get your balls in a vise."

"I haven't really....processed everything that happened this year like I should, I think."

"I hear you. You need to though, before it burns you out. How's the license thing going?"

The preacher whom I assaulted (when he wouldn't stop insulting my dead friend and her family) filed a lawsuit, criminal charges, and a complaint with the New York State Division of Licensing Services against me. The assault charges were adjourned in contemplation of dismissal, and were dismissed officially in October. The lawsuit was also dismissed for improper pleading, but that's been appealed—a legal tangle likely to go on for some time.

"They cleared me. They said it wasn't the wisest course of action, but it was on my own time and I was provoked. To quote Bill Murray, "So I got that going for me—*which is nice.*""

"That's the *fact*, Jack. It was a bad time this summer. You got past it admirably. But take it from one who knows, Gabriel. Many ways to anesthetize one's self. I liked speedballs and Bacardi 101. You work."

Sure. When I work, I don't think. I need to get back to meditating, like I used to. But the prospect of having free time to just think inspires dread.

"I know. I'm trying. So is tomorrow okay, man?"

"Tomorrow's as good as any, in the morning. I have a bunch of evening clients these days."

"Can I pick you up?"

"Don't have to. I'll meet you at Warinanco and we'll drive over in your car, if you don't mind."

"Sure. Hard to get in?"

"No problem trespassing. No guards, and it's too cold for teenagers to be fingerbanging inside. See you around ten?"

"Ten's good. Take care, Bob."

Then I stare at my silent phone after I hang up. I start thinking about what I plan to do tomorrow. Archie pads up and rubs against the phone. When he doesn't get much of a response from me, he wanders off to patrol the perimeter. My mind similarly wanders, wondering about the dreams I've been having.

Eventually I realize that someone's standing over me. Alex. The icy breeze coming in the window swirls his long hair back from his face, reminding me unpleasantly of the smoke tendrils in my dream. He's frowning down at me.

"At first I thought you must have stepped out. But here you are. What's going on, love?"

His tone is cautious. Archie has come back, and flops next to me, purring. I pick him up. "Um, I was just talking to Bob, and thinking. Lost track of time."

"I see." He glances around the kitchen. The concept of eating somehow got lost in my head.

He gets down on his knees. "Christ. You're freezing." He touches my arm, with the goose bumps raised. "Shaking too. Apparently, you're interested in getting pneumonia."

"No, just appreciating the fresh air."

"You're a nutter." He puts his arms around me, and I realize how cold I actually am.

"Come on, now." He pulls me up, but I'm nervous. We haven't really talked since the fight other than his offering to come over. I look for something to do. "Let me get going here. I'm sorry I forgot about dinner."

Alex keeps his hands on me, roaming in a way that betrays his attraction despite our awkwardness.

"Don't worry about it. Although I like to see you domestic."

I straighten up and look at him insolently, activating cover-up mode. "Typical Brit classism."

"Cheeky Yank bastard." He puts his hands on my face. "I'll have to take you into the drawing room, then, for a good talking to."

He starts kissing me.

A few moments of this and I almost forget. I want it to be anesthetizing, like work is. And yet I feel anger rise in me nonetheless, underneath it all. I had thought I was over our fight, but the anger is making me numb. As if the cold from outside penetrated my psyche, creating a core of ice inside.

He doesn't notice, speaking in my ear. "I'll order us dinner, all right? I don't want you distracted. We have to get past this row."

"I'm past it." And with that lie, I go to the sofa. He calls somebody and orders something. I check my phone for emails, feeling nervous again. Then he's taking the phone out of my hand.

"I know you've been working incredibly hard to get yourself together and I'm impressed with your resilience, but you're doing too much."

"While it lasts, I need it."

"You should keep to a one-person operation. And I'd help you out with that. Pay your rent for a few months or something, so you could take a break." He's moving his hands over me while talking, massaging my neck and shoulders in a sensuous manner. Positive reinforcement, I suppose.

Except that doesn't work with me. "Alex, baby, do I go to your office and tell you how to do your job? 'Cause if I did and that gave you the impression you could do likewise, I was on crack that day, okay?"

He gives me an exasperated look. Then he focuses on the bedroom door frame. It's still busted. I have not bothered to fix it. Really, I've been ignoring it because of what it represents. His face shows surprise and concern. "What happened with *that*?"

For a moment I can't answer. "I locked myself out by accident."

"And you couldn't pick it open? One of the useful skills out of your work."

I ignore that dig. "I panicked. Archie was inside and I just had a bad moment." I look away while I'm talking.

"Have you seen a doctor lately?"

"What the hell? What's with the damned questions?"

He brings on what I've started to call lately (to myself) his 'authoritative' voice. "Because I had to come in and find you hiding underneath an open window in 30-degree weather. You aren't sleeping well, either. And you're having a few such 'bad moments.' As much as you pretend otherwise."

I don't want to think about sleep. "I'm *fine.*" I say this in a tone that suggests trouble if he continues the topic.

"What about just a couple days off?"

Now I roll my eyes. "I just did that, didn't I?"

"Maybe you need more. Is anything so urgently pressing? We could figure out how you can handle your business so you don't need the expense of your...friend."

My irritation rises, conflicting with my intentions to have a better night. I am happy to see him; I did miss him. But something else is here now and not something good.

"That isn't a problem for me. He doesn't do it for the money."

Alex is still being affectionate with me but his expression subtly changes. "Really? How charitable of him."

The row is in danger of coming back. "This is my business concern. *That* discussion is over."

"Certainly. Nothing wrong with your ex suddenly showing up in town to help you out at all hours with your work...for free, I suppose, because of some mysterious magical source of income. And nothing wrong with you spending more time on these jobs than on us."

I reach for my cigarettes and meet his eyes while lighting up. Like he isn't a workaholic at the *Herald Standard?* Whatever. I don't like arguments, accusations, drama. It's why I'm not dealing with Danny right now, although I should.

"You're putting me on the defensive when it isn't fair. I told you, Joel used to work with me and no reason why he can't now. I don't know about his money situation but I do appreciate the help, because I work in the type of business where I need to take the jobs when they come."

I feel the tension of being split into two people right now. Then the affection in Alex's eyes gets to me and I relax some. That makes him more comfortable in turn.

But he can't let things go. He wasn't like this when we first met. Not exactly. But after he said he was falling in love with me, this life-changing bullshit started. First subtly, now regularly.

"Did you think about school, any? Something you'd like to get into?"

"No. That isn't on my radar."

"Just think about it. I know you still take classes at Midtown now and then but what about NYU? I can pay even for some and..."

My expression stops him.

"Okay. I see I've reached your limit of tolerance in my trying to be thoughtful."

"You don't get it. I don't need that kind of thoughtful right now."

I let him continue working his hands on me in spite of my irritation. Better than talking. He smiles. "You're *so* tired. I want to put you to bed right now, not fuck you. Just a couple days off at least?"

I do my own cost-benefit analysis. Joel's out of town anyway. Maybe Alex will be placated with this compromise.

"All right, I'll take off after something I have to do tomorrow morning. So can we shut the fuck up about this already? *Least* seductive conversation I've had in my life."

He takes the cigarette from my hand. "You think I can't seduce you right now, rude boy?"

He kisses the side of my neck. The anger is still in me, and confusion. I think about what Michaela said. Suddenly his hands feel strange to me and make me shiver. He mistakes that for something else and finally pulls me down, crushing the cigarette out in the ashtray by the sofa in the determined way he has. I realize I'm not ready for this as he moves his hand between my legs, but in defense I start to split into two realms. My body, feeling his arousal through his expensive clothes, reacts in spite of my mind being somewhere else. Things go on almost without my mental input. But inside I feel like one of those wooly mammoths encased in ice, thousands of years old.

∞

Afterwards, in the bedroom he falls asleep curled next to me. I'm still lying in bed awake. Sleep is a devil; sleep is too much like death. I get afraid if I sleep, I won't wake up. And what I see in my dreams is leaving me shaken when I wake.

I watch him sleeping. We wouldn't have met except for my getting involved in Raymond Booth's dangerous case. Because of that investigation I was shot at, beaten up, and nearly blown up.

Both Alex and Joel helped my work to find Raymond's killer. Then after serious threats to my loved ones' health, I told everyone I knew I was giving up the case. Except Joel.

The investigation led to a sinister group called the Tertullian Society. The Society was started shortly before Hitler's rise to power, and had some ideological influence over him. It went underground after World War II was over, but didn't disappear—in fact it has become immersed in global financial and political dealings. I'm not sure exactly what they do in the world today, but I know for certain they exist. The investigation of the Tertullian Society took me to a very dark place. Joel has already been to those places which is why I told him the truth. Not only because he's been there, but because he could go there with me.

Kent Varney, a former journalist, gave me his voluminous notes on the Tertullians and related conspiracies. They had fucked up his life years ago when *he* had investigated them and then when he became involved in my own investigation, they had him killed. The danger is still real and I can't let them know I have those notes or that I'm still researching. I have a hint as to the identity of one of their New York big shots, and someday I'm going to find him.

Alex doesn't have sleep issues. I watch him awhile and this is the kind of moment I can take enjoyment in. His hair spread on the pillow; his body relaxed. I lie against him and think about the notes. I haven't done much with them lately; working has taken my attention. But I don't want to give up that project. Not when a man died for it. Part of my inner turmoil is figuring out how to continue. I feel I need to talk to Bertrand Herrmann, an expert on Nazis who helped me understand what needed to be done before.

At least this keeps me from thinking about sleep. I ease out of bed, slip on some boxers and go to the second bedroom, which also functions as my office-cum-library. I have the notes, nearly a foot thick, in a locked bottom desk drawer.

Kent wrote much of the notes in Gregg shorthand, which I don't know but I'm learning bit by bit —a form of linguistics, semiotics. The notes aren't really organized; just archived as information, interviews, leads on seemingly unconnected stories involving murder, fraud, government, finance. A conspiracy theorist's bonanza.

Archie comes in to sit on the notes, as he believes he owns everything in the place. *You doth protest too much. He is free to question why Joel is working with you.*

"Shut up," I tell him.

I've memorized the shorthand code for Nazis. Since the Tertullians originated from Nazis I'm still interested in Nazi connections. Section by section, I flip through the pages looking for the symbols. I have my laptop with me and I jot down dates and mark pages for follow-up.

Wait, here's something. A note that a former German officer who claimed he wasn't a Nazi —at least, wasn't involved in war crimes, is somehow connected to the Banca Mediterraneo Centrale Internazionale. BMCI. Big Money Crooks International, it was called in the 1980s, as the center of an embezzlement and money-laundering scheme linked with some Italian political groups.

I remember somebody had died in connection to the scandal fallout. I'll want to research that further.

I sense more than hear a presence behind me. As I look over my shoulder, I shut the laptop. Alex is standing in the doorway. He walks around naked a good deal —well, usually after we've been intimate, which is okay with me. But I can't take pleasure in it because I don't want him to know what I'm working on.

"And this is?" He arches one eyebrow.

"I just couldn't sleep. I thought I'd work a little."

"At three in the morning? This is what I'm talking about, what it's doing to you. For fuck's sake, come back to bed."

"All right."

But I wait until he leaves before I put the notes away reluctantly. In bed with him, he caresses my head. Inside though, I'm agitated that I gave in. Ordinarily, this might be a time when I could extend intimacy to telling him my fears, my weaknesses, my problems, my demons. I could tell him what I'm doing and why. What I didn't tell him during the summer.

But I don't tell him. Because in the surrealness of the early witching hours, I can allow myself to recognize what I *can't* tell him. What I don't tell *myself* in the daytime.

Archie's eyes glow at me in the moonlight, from where he sits at the foot of the bed. *Hiding things, are we? Oh, yes, you're the great pretender.*

Since I can't sleep well, I'm up early. I've made coffee and fed Archie, so I can open my laptop on the kitchen counter to see if anything's urgent. I go to one of my email addresses; I share it with Joel. *Grosbonange.* Joel chose that, based on a conversation I had with him regarding an old Voudon rumor about Jim Morrison's soul being stolen. The Gros Bon Ange is the life force part of the soul, as opposed to the personality part of the soul. Morrison's was supposed to have been captured by evil forces. I love stories like that.

I had intended this email address to be a secure way of the two of us discussing my cases when we're not together. We leave messages for each other in the drafts folder. But somehow, the purpose drifted away from work topics —he's over here all the time anyway. Instead, we started using these drafts to discuss —or vent —about issues we won't do in person. Such as why he thinks Alex is wrong for me, and I should get back with him. After this summer, I had told him I didn't want to talk about that anymore. But the email communications have acted as a loophole I find myself participating in.

When I met Joel, I saw him as an artist. He had a past as a sex worker but the artist was developing, and enraptured me for the two years we were together. I was concerned for his safety in the nether world of escorting. He had stopped the work, but not entirely. He would take it up again when he was afraid we were getting too close. At some point towards the end he gave me the impression he had stopped for good which gave me a brief, exhilarating hope for the future, because I thought he trusted me. But he hadn't, and I felt that it was a betrayal.

Or maybe I was wrong to think that, I don't know anymore. For some reason, my conviction about what happened between us then has shifted. Always disconcerting when history written in stone suddenly is fluid like water.

I set a rule with myself this after this summer —you're involved with Alex, you love him, you can't go back to Joel. So talking about it doesn't do anything but make life more complicated. But the email messages have given me a chance to say what's on my mind, to pour out my mixed feelings. Also, for him to express what he can't say face to face.

His smartass exterior is not his real world, but his defense. With a step removed we can be brutally honest. He and I carry around anger, and not just at each other. Somehow ours is making us closer, if such a thing can happen. It winds around us together like ectoplasm, mixed with other more complicated feelings.

But we don't discuss the emails in person. A strange dual existence. With each other so much is unsaid verbally. In writing, too much is said to talk about in person. Those messages, what happened to us this summer, and our working together have bonded us even tighter than when we were actually a couple. Clearly, Mikki and Bob have picked up on that.

Today he has a message for me. Just to let me know he's okay in Amsterdam. I've had to teach him little courtesies like telling a person one's flight landed safely. I'm pleased about that but for some reason, I can't think of what to write back. That didn't used to be a problem. I can always talk to him. Now I'm unsure. And a song suddenly starts. Lady Antebellum. *Need You Now.* Off the playlist he created.

Alex has come into the kitchen while my attention is occupied. I hand him a cup of coffee which he takes to the dining table.

While tying his tie, he starts talking about what he's going to do today. A casual conversation but he reveals his secret concern in a nonchalant, apropos-of-nothing tone.

"And you're working today, but just the morning."

"Yeah."

"Alone?"

"With Bob."

He comes in and refills his coffee. Then he turns and goes back to the dining room. "Not your other friend, then? Strange I've never run into him here."

I shrug. Neither Alex nor Joel will call the other by name. Alex refers to Joel as 'your friend' and Joel refers to Alex as Harry Potter. In October, they briefly spoke on the phone—Joel answering when I wasn't able to at the moment, due to a very difficult situation. Joel's brief exchange with Alex didn't go well; Alex gave me hell afterwards because Joel wouldn't let him talk to me. I'm not waiting urgently in anticipation for a repeat of that, I can tell you.

"I'm sure you will." Inside I think...*not*.

I change the subject and tell him a little about the case with Sophie Faulker and the possible connection to Wildemore, which I'm visiting with Bob —without mentioning I'm going to trespass.

"Is something pertinent there, or are you just going for fun?"

"Both. I like going to these creepy places. I feel like they have ghosts. That might be inspiring."

He has a small smile as he finishes his coffee. "And don't forget, after this, you're not to do anything else for the rest of the week. Just rest today. When I get out the office, I'll take you..."

I don't hear the rest of it because I'm now fighting my ire. I just nod at the appropriate places and struggle with my demons inside. I'm almost relieved when he leaves.

I then turn my attention back to the case. And I think about Paul, the client Manny and I worked with. Paul and his other self Matthew. They reminded me of one of those dolls that changes into another when its skirt is flipped up.

Enough. I have to go to work. Time to visit Wildemore.

∞

Tuesday, November 30

Bob's assistance has on occasion been invaluable when I have work in New Jersey. Bob is a fifty-ish white guy, medium tall, dark hair, fairly nice-looking. He is also one of the most ribald persons I know, though he's trying to cut down on working 'pussy' or 'dick' into every sentence. He likes card games, sports, the Beatles, and black humor, as do I.

It's a fine rainy day when we meet up at Warinanco and drive over to Wildemore, so no kids are on the grounds. The building is an imposing Romanesque structure that is slowly crumbling from neglect. One main building faces the empty street. Two wings stretching back for several hundred yards. Five floors high in the main building, three in the wings. The lower two floors have boarded-up windows. A tall barbed wire fence gives the impression it's protecting the grounds from trespassers.

It was a state hospital which was bought later by a private interest later gone bankrupt. The state probably has control over it now for tax liens. I had found out no one wanted to buy the building or even the land because of bad vibes.

The fence is perfunctory. It's an abandoned building no one cares about, so no one is bothering about real security. At the back of the facility several holes in the fence offer easy access from the woods behind the medical building. Bob and I are dressed for hiking and cold rain, and make our way to the main building without too much trouble. Bob is amused by the fact I carry both my (properly licensed in both states) guns, a Sig Sauer (back holster) and a Glock (ankle holster). All I'm saying is that after what happened in Westchester County a few months ago, I don't make trips like this unarmed.

The double doors at the back of the western wing are padlocked, but my picks take care of that. We go inside, and I turn on my Vulcan halogen light. The place is dark and cold. It might as well have *Abandon hope all ye who enter here* inscribed overhead. The walls are covered in graffiti. Bottles, cigarette butts, blankets and other garbage litter the hallways. The tall ceilings seem to ring with the screams of those subjected to electroshock or water therapy.

Bob shudders. "I've seen better junk shooting galleries."

"God, what did Leonard do in this place?"

"He was kind of a handyman here. Go figure, he stayed in the place even after it was closed down in the Eighties. He invited me once or twice, but I declined—even if Angie Jolie herself was giving it up in here."

"I thought you liked ScarJo."

"I do, man. You should see the nasty stuff they do to each other in my mind to amuse me. Pure Sapphic pleasure, interrupted only by fighting over who gets to give me head."

I ignore that. "Anyway, I'd like to see the things he might have had here."

"He said he stayed in the East Wing. He believed places have magical energy in certain shapes and directions. He always said east was magical. West is death and east is rebirth. And this place was supposed to be haunted, that would intrigue him. I think that's why he came here. The east wing is the haunted one, so people say."

"Yeah? Let's start there for fun."

Even with the light, getting to the other side takes some time, to avoid holes in the floor and debris. The west wing is dark, and smells like a morgue.

I had found plans for the building online, and found out that each wing has a separate basement area with storage rooms and utilities. It adds to the strange vibes of the place. One of the rumors attached to the hospital is that patients who died under electroshock or brutality by the staff were dissected and buried somewhere on the grounds.

The east wing does seem to be much lighter, less stifling to the psyche. Leonard had clearly kept it cleared of the garbage, unlike the other side.

Something scuttles from us as we round a corner. "Jesus, was that a rat, or a wild boar? Anyway, what about Mathers himself? What kind of guy was he to get murdered?"

"Well, you know why people get murdered —money, cover-up, jealousy, husband catches his old lady sucking another dude's dick. But I don't know...Leonard was kinda off in his own thing. He was big into bikes and the occult. I think he might have caught something from the inmates, you know what I mean?"

"Yeah. Anything in particular? I heard he liked opera."

"Man! Like isn't the word. He was into it like you get into JFK assassination theories. He thought it could bring in other dimensions to life, or something like that. Been a long time since I last talked to him, you know? But he could be pretty intense, like you."

"I appreciate the comparison. Not the first time I've been called crazy."

We come to a niche with a small door. The rusted metal sign on it says, "Maintenance." Bob taps it. "I think this used to be his area, where he kept his tools and whatever. He didn't have a problem being underground."

This door has been locked with a thick chain and an iron-shroud spool pin padlock. Which I can pick, due to experience and practice. Once this is done the door shows us a staircase leading to a basement area. Blackness is beneath us like a lake.

Bob points at my lamp. "I hope that thing has a good battery."

"I have a spare in my pack, are you kidding?"

But it turns out the basement is not bad at all. To the right is a door leading to what was the serious underbelly of this side of the hospital —pipes, boilers and so on. But the anteroom we're in is clean and looks pretty pedestrian. Tools and supplies —shelves of food, a couple chairs, a small stove and refrigerator. Bob checks the lights and surprisingly, they work. Leonard must have rigged some wires.

A door leads into a second, smaller room.

We have to stop and take it in.

After expecting horror, we're shocked by beauty and warmth. Walls are covered with chalk and paint drawings, interspersed with posters and pictures. All of operas.

Don Giovanni. La Traviata. Mefistofele. Pagliacci. Tosca. Aida. La Bohème.

Theater-style curtains frame the walls. The paintings reflect the posters' emotions. Especially with the women. Whoever painted these, maybe Leonard, turned the female characters into angels and muses and goddesses. Around the edges of the paintings are strange symbols that look occultish.

We spend some time examining each one. Leonard also wrote on the walls under the posters and images information about each opera and what he felt was most important about them. I start to think a music student could learn more here than in a year of college courses.

A fairly expensive portable CD player rests on a table next chest against the far wall. On the other side of the chest is a single bed. CDs are stacked carefully. I can't remember the last time I opened one of my CDs rather than play an iPod, but Leonard must have preferred this. The lights here are softer, and the room has a strange, warm glow to it. I don't see anything bad here. I see a room dedicated to emotion, beauty, love. His secret grotto. I suddenly feel very impressed with Leonard.

"Seems like a shrine, doesn't it? I see what you mean about him. He came to this place..." I look around. "And lost himself in his dreams."

"Candles, too. And writing on the floor."

"Not a pentagram, but mystery symbols. I need to photograph these."

The costumes and poses are already over-dramatic by nature. Now they're like mythological figures frozen in time. You might expect them to move. I find them fascinating. The stars of the opera caught in dramatic poses, singing words of passion. His fondness for women, powerful female characters. Yet I feel like someone's missing; I can't put my finger on who.

I take photos of everything and then turn my attention to the chest. The flat rectangular chest seems like a personal item, not hospital issue. Someone, presumably Leonard, has painted some words on the top. I move the CD player and CD cases.

L'amour est enfant de Bohême, Il n'a jamais jamais connu de loi.

Um. Something about the words is familiar, but I don't know much French. I take another picture.

I'm getting used to this room, and getting a feeling for Leonard's mind. While I take a cigarette break, I text Alex my photo of the French words.

He responds:

—*Secret message about yourself?*

—*No, translation needed please; work related.*

—*What kind of work, I'd love to know. It means: Love is a Gypsy's child, it has never, never, known a law. You've heard it before, love.*

Now I recognize the words. Lyrics from *Carmen*, the opera I was playing last night. Of course. *Habanera*, the song where Carmen declares that no man can keep her captive; she will always be free with her affections. Ah, Alex's little crack about a secret message about myself. Funny.

And that's who's missing. Carmen. I look around, but don't see Carmen represented on the walls. "He has *Carmen* here but not on the wall. Seems odd."

"Maybe he had different ideas about her."

"Of Carmen's power?" I consider the chest. It's also locked. I use my picks on it carefully and lift the lid. The inside has a faint scent of cedar mixed with other exotic incense. Bob and I take things out that had been packed carefully. Chalk and paint, books on music, and clothes. A costume, a Gypsy costume. It looks very old, like from a turn of the century production. A couple of old posters for Carmen rested on it, rolled up.

"I remember Dominic taking Danny and I to a Metropolitan Opera production of *Carmen*. We weren't into it at the time, but he explained the beauty of the music, and also said it was a life lesson of passion spurring someone into tragic actions. He went into a long explanation of Aristotle's *Poetics* and how the opera served as catharsis to show human emotions, connect with them, and get people to think about their actions in life."

Bob laughs. "Didn't you say the *exact* same thing when you and I saw *The Dark Knight?* Including the bit about Aristotle? I see where you got it from."

"No comment. I hate it when you call me out." I start examining the trunk's contents more closely.

"Did he buy this for decoration?" Bob gently shakes out the dress, meant to cover a full-figured woman. Peasant skirt, low-cut blouse, head scarf. "Or did he cross-dress? I don't remember him saying he did that, and we were pretty honest with each other..."

"I think he did more than that. If he wanted something to come to life..."

"Lay out her clothes, Carmen would come to life."

"I've seen worse hobbies."

"I've *had* worse hobbies." Bob laughs again.

Two other things in the chest. A manila envelope, marked *Escamillo*, which contains a leather-bound notebook. The notebook looks pretty old, but it's been written in recently.

Escamillo, the bullfighter and rival for Carmen's favors.

The notebook has some more rambling writing and symbols — good, more coded information on top of my Tertullian notes. But I'm taking it with me. He pasted a CD cover on it—for a 1977 recording of the opera with Placido Domingo and Teresa Berganza. I tuck the manila envelope with notebook in my bag. We repack the trunk with respect, extinguish the candles, leave and lock the room, and leave the building. I drive Bob back to his car and then return to New York.

Later I call Michaela to update her on the discoveries. She's interested, and we agree to keep the shrine to ourselves. It's not information that is exculpatory for Sophie—for now—and Sophie has not yet been indicted, so Michaela isn't going to tell the prosecutor as yet.

Michaela starts to hang up then tells me to hold on. "I almost forgot—I want you to look into something. Sophie's friend Giselle Greenspan is paying the lion's share of the legal bills. She'd like to talk to you."

"Okay. I'll call her."

"I've spoken with her. She's known Sophie for years, and knows of Sophie having multiple..."

"Selves."

"Right. The things people don't feel they need to tell their defense counsel. But she's nice. You'll see her contact info in the file. Anyway, how did you know about Sophie—that she is like she is?"

"I've told you about Manny. He investigated a case for a man named Paul. Paul had another self, Matthew. Sometimes Matthew would talk to us. Manny told me that multiples are more than just a mental issue. He told me to always look for more than a surface explanation for anything. I got to like Paul and Matthew both, and they were separate people. But sometimes when one wanted to surface, he'd look blank—zone out like Sophie was doing."

"And you don't think abuse is involved?"

"That's a commonly-held idea, but doesn't pertain to most persons. It's just another way to live, on the continuum of ways to live. After I met them, I did a lot more reading on it. Not clinical material, but narratives from the persons themselves."

She laughs. "You know too much, Gabriel. Maybe Adler should consult *you.*"

∞

Wednesday, December 1
Canal Street, 9am

Chinatown. The fifth floor of a nondescript building.

The double wooden doors have Chinese characters. The man outside the door is Caucasian but knows the characters.

He's dressed in jeans and a long jacket over a white shirt. A small stainless-steel Buddhist prayer wheel is on a chain around his neck. He carries a knapsack, and takes out a thermos and small ceramic cup.

The man rings the bell to the door, a literal bell hanging on a chain. The tones of the bell ring in the man's head.

After a minute, the door opens. A Chinese man in his fifties looks out the door, then steps into the hall. The older man is dressed in a loose dark gray t-shirt and chinos, and barefoot. The two men hold each other's gazes briefly. The visitor then casts his eyes down and bows his head. The older man waits without expression. The visitor gets on his knees. He opens the thermos and pours tea into the ceramic cup. He then offers the cup to the older man, a *Shifu*, or teacher, of Baguazhang and Daoism.

The visitor speaks with difficulty, his face getting a little red. "*Shifu*, I have come to ask your forgiveness for being disrespectful, and to ask that you take me back as a student."

The teacher contemplates the other. Then he takes the cup. "Come inside."

The kneeling man, now looking relieved, rises and follows his teacher.

He stands respectfully as the teacher drinks and regards him.

"I rather didn't think I'd see you again, Gabriel," the teacher says finally. "What was your problem?"

The teacher, Zihao Chiang, is 5'10, muscular, and has graying black hair and a thin beard, and wears glasses. He was born in Hong Kong, educated in England, and has lived in New York for 15 years. He's something of a loner with several interesting past careers in China and Europe, including instruction in Daoism and martial arts. He's hinted at having worked in intelligence in some capacity. He doesn't advertise his teaching and is somewhat outside the community—as is his student, who found him somehow a few years ago.

Gabriel swallows hard. Where to start. "Master Chiang, I know I wasn't...I don't know what to say. I guess my problem was false dignity, what you taught me about pride standing in the way of character."

"It's more than that, now. You have darkness surrounding you. Not the natural darkness of yin, other darkness—that of ghosts. You're lost in it."

Gabriel glances at him with a plaintive expression. "I know, *Shifu*. I have nightmares. I don't know what to do about it. I'm surrounded by death."

Chiang listens carefully to the words and studies the man's posture, breathing, aura. "You're in a crisis."

He has mixed feelings. But he sees that Gabriel is already looking better just from being here, having made the effort to humble himself.

"And if I did take you back?"

"I will obey and respect you, and I will not disappoint you."

"Is that so? Tell me then, what is the *Wude*?" In Daoism, *Wude* are the aspects of ethics.

Gabriel tells him in Chinese and English. Gabriel doesn't speak Chinese, but he's spent some time learning some words and concepts in Daoism, along with some Japanese terms in Buddhism. The ten aspects of *Wude* are Humility, Respect, Righteousness, Trust, Loyalty, Will, Endurance, Perseverance, Patience, and Courage.

Chiang raises his eyebrows. He knows Gabriel has the words. But does he still appreciate the meaning? "Which do you need to refine?"

"All of them."

"Why does your *Xin* overcome your *Yi*?" Meaning, the emotional mind over wisdom mind. When this student strays, the *Xin* takes over and leads him to trouble.

"I don't know, sir. It's always been that way. It's why I need discipline, why I need to listen to another."

Chiang's voice becomes softer. "And is your teacup still full?"

Teacups are highly symbolic. Gabriel offering the tea to his teacher was a means of supplicating himself for forgiveness. If a student arrogantly feels he or she has nothing to learn, the student is said to have a full teacup.

"No, *Shifu*. It is empty."

Chiang walks around the younger man, who stays still, eyes cast to the floor. "You forgot about me, and your discipline."

"I was angry."

"And?"

"It went against the Dao. My *Qi* is corrupt." *Qi,* or *ch'i,* the life force of the cosmos, according to Daoism.

"*Qi* cannot be corrupt, only misled, misdirected. Do you still want to be a man of honor?"

"Yes, *Shifu*."

"Your actions of late are questionable. I've read about you. I did not forget you. You have been involved in something terrible. I see that. But I do not believe you were terrible yourself. I know you better than that, even though your last words to me were full of rage."

Gabriel doesn't reply, his eyes still downcast. Chiang sighs. He has his own commitment to mentor those who need it. This student has always been different. Chiang always felt Gabriel was worth the extra trouble because he truly took in the principles on a spiritual level. No, not just that. Something else. If one believes in reincarnation, and Daoism allows for that, he and Gabriel knew each other in a similar relationship. Chiang has always felt they had a longer relationship than just the time they've known each other in this life. It was one reason he accepted Gabriel as a student. Chiang mentors very few people.

That instinctive feeling means he must let Gabriel back in. The younger man has destiny to choose. If he is not careful, choosing wrong will kill him fast.

He stares at his student who is keeping his eyes on the floor, trying to measure his breathing.

"Gabriel."

The younger man finally lifts his head. Enormous pain and loss haunts in his eyes. Chiang can practically see demons flying around him.

The teacher keeps a calm demeanor. His student needs this. "We have work to do. You need to begin the process of clearing your mind. Go home. Every morning and evening for the next two days at the same time, burn a stick of incense. Concentrate on the incense. Do not speak, look at, or think of anything else but the burning stick, from the moment it's lit until the moment it dies out. If anyone is around when the stick is burning you cannot talk to them. When you have finished with this exercise, come back Sunday morning. I would ordinarily have you do this for a week, even a month."

He gets up and paces the floor, then turns back to Gabriel. "However, I can see we need to work right away. You need to heal."

Gabriel listens intently. Shadows fall across his face, and not from the light. He turns his gaze to his teacher, as if the older man were holding up a bright candle out of the darkness. "Thank you, *Shifu*."

"If you fall back again, you will likely be irreparable. Because of your commitment to *Wude*."

Gabriel closes his eyes. The test, such as it is, is both extremely difficult and very benign. He knows the opportunity he's being given to return to his mentor is rare, rarer than his being accepted as a student in the first place.

"Yes, Master Chiang. I will return as you have directed."

The teacher returns the empty cup, and leads Gabriel to the door. Then he walks to the windows facing Canal Street and looks down. In a minute, his student steps out the door and surveys the street. Gabriel's posture is relaxed, subdued. He spends several minutes looking at all areas of the street —the throngs of people walking, the cars, and the cadence of activity. He's observing the flow, and that which diverts from the flow.

Chiang watches the man observing, breathing, finally moving forward into the flow, as if he was always part of it. He is observant and respectful of others, does not make himself an island.

A hopeful sign for Gabriel, who has lifetime of work ahead. If he can cultivate himself. If he can conquer himself.

Lake over Mountain: Two persons influence each other —one provides foundation, one provides nurturing. They mutually influence each other, but can't be selfish. They should act in harmony, without prejudice, sincere, and even humble —or communication is stymied. The third line (yang/nine) moves in this reading. That means one is ready to move but should be patient for the other.

From *NYCultcha.com,* The Ethics Page: *Controlling Identity*

—Gabriel Ross, November 1, 2010

Gabriel Ross is a NYC-based professional investigator who writes on ethics for NYCultcha.

In ancient Eastern mythology, the immortal Lan Ts'ai Ho switched genders, represented as both male and female. Avalokitesvara, the male bodhisattva of compassion, is portrayed as female in China as Guanyin and Japan as Kannon. These personages demonstrate recognition of the fluidity of gender in ancient Eastern cultures—which also had an integration of homo- or bisexuality.

So if cultures thousands of years old can easily recognize the existence of transgender persons, why can't New York State? Despite advocacy by legal bar organizations and lawsuits against New York City and New York State, the New York State Department of Health insists upon a stringent and onerous requirement for Trans persons to have their state birth certificate to be changed to show their true gender.

Strangely, the NYS DOH doesn't have these requirements in a law or regulation, but apparently just policy—demanding that an applicant furnish: a surgeon's statement concerning the gender reassignment surgery (describing in detail all of the procedures performed), a psych report documenting "transsexual criteria," and a physician's statement on hormonal treatment (Thanks go to my lawyer friend Jim for getting that information, which isn't given on the DOH website). Even then the information given is "reviewed" by the agency in an arbitrary decision-making process to determine if an error in gender was made in the certificate.

These hoops don't exist for a driver's license or a passport. Trans people already face workplace discrimination, exclusion from single-sex schools, and scorn from those outside LGBT community —and sometimes from inside. For many, disclosure of their transgender status is dangerous and/or can lead to difficulty in obtaining insurance, benefits, employment, credit and more. Most trans persons do not have gender reassignment surgery. For one thing, the cost is prohibitive. So, easier criteria to obtain a changed birth certificate would be an enormous help, but there's the DOH, playing its own Kafkaesque determination of other people's lives and identities...

∞

Friday, December 3
Alphabet City, Avenue A, 11:27 am

AT FIRST JOEL is afraid Gabriel's taken another Xanax cocktail. When he lets himself into Gabriel's apartment, Gabriel is lying on the floor between his coffee table and stereo system.

Then Gabriel opens his eyes.

"Hey." He removes his John Lennon-style reading glasses but doesn't get up.

Joel takes off his jacket and hangs it on the coat rack.

The TV is broadcasting another James Bond marathon on BBC America. Gabriel isn't really watching it. Nor is he reading, although a book is under his head. He's in a rumpled t-shirt featuring The Clash, and boxer shorts. Joel has to restrain an urge to strip him and burn the sweat-stained tee.

Joel's short hair is dark blond, his eyes sort of a changing grey-blue-hazel; he usually has a goatee, although he looks good with or without. Gabriel rarely tries for facial hair; it comes in heavy and tends to make him look a little crazed. So the fact he hasn't shaved in a couple days is not giving him a sexy Sonny Crockett vibe, but more a demented-neighbor-in-a-tinfoil-covered-basement vibe.

Archie comes up to greet Joel. He picks up the cat and scratches its head, while considering what to do. He at least expected Gabriel to be working, and he needs Gabriel's help for a friend.

"What's going on," he says finally.

Gabriel doesn't answer. He reaches to get his cigarettes and light one, giving Joel the once-over. "New shirt?"

"Picked it up in Amsterdam."

"Linen; it looks nice on you."

Joel moves closer to Gabriel, aware that Gabriel's eyes stay on him. He's not looking at the clothes Joel wears, he's looking at Joel wearing the clothes. That subterfuge has grown thin now, regardless of the flutter in his chest Joel feels when he catches Gabriel doing this. But he's not giving in this time.

Gabriel blows out smoke slowly. "That coat's new too. And you don't usually wear a watch."

"It was Jan's. I'm wearing it for a while."

"Tag Hauer. He had good taste."

"Yes, he did. What the fuck are you doing, lying on the floor like a zombie?"

Joel's tone is sharp enough to make Gabriel frown. Good. He'd rather have Gabriel irritated than somnambulistic.

"An apt metaphor." Gabriel sits up with the cigarette, glaring at Joel. However intense his gaze is, though, he can't out-stare Joel this time. He finally drops his eyes, looking at his cigarette instead.

Joel can't help but feel for Gabriel when he senses the pain running through him. "Come on. You can feel sorrow, but not guilt. And we're supposed to be working today."

"I'm taking a break."

"Taking a break." Joel walks over to the chair nearest Gabriel and sits on the arm. "Is that what he mandated for you?"

Gabriel frowns at him again. His face gets a little flushed. "You have no right to say that to me."

Joel leans down, meeting his eyes.

"If anyone has a right to, it's me."

Gabriel can't respond to that. Joel reaches out and touches his hair briefly.

"I need you. Your help. A friend of mine has a serious problem. I only trust you to take care of it. You can't give up who you are because he doesn't like your occupation."

"I'm not." Gabriel gets up. He puts his glasses back on and picks the book up off the floor. A Philip K. Dick anthology.

"You didn't respond to my email, when I landed in Amsterdam. I was worried about you."

"I texted back."

"Yeah. You were "fine." Bullshit answer." Joel takes Gabriel's glasses off and finds a cloth in a drawer to clean them. "You need to take care of yourself."

Joel had gone to Amsterdam to take care of a legal matter relating to Jan, a friend and former client of his who had died shortly before Joel came back to New York City. He's debated during his return flight whether to tell Gabriel about developments relating to Jan's estate —developments that affect Joel significantly. But that particular subject is a conversation for another time.

Joel places the cleaned glasses back on Gabriel's face, acutely aware of the magnetism that sparks when they're close.

Gabriel is too, but he makes an effort to pretend otherwise. "What's the issue with your friend?"

"Her name is Geneva Lennon. She found out something strange about her family, and needs someone to investigate. She's cautious, due to the nature of the case, and she's trans. I know you're cool with that. There are organizations and lawyers and whatever who could help, but I didn't want her hurt. I want you to do it. She asked me to check and see if you could talk to her today; she's coming into the city later."

"Okay. I'll talk to her. You don't introduce me to many of your friends. Like Isabella, the one who got you yesterday."

He sounds almost jealous. Last Sunday Gabriel drove Joel to the airport as he had planned, without mentioning what happened on Friday. Pretending nothing happened. Gabriel said he was going with Michaela to visit a new client in Elizabeth on Monday, and he might need Joel's help. He also offered to pick up Joel when he returned and when Joel said his friend Isabella was taking care of it, Gabriel seemed disconcerted.

"I will. She's going to have some kind of showing for me. I meant to tell you."

"You *meant* to tell me?" Gabriel smiles and glances at the painting Joel had created for him four years ago, which hangs on the apartment wall near the door. It's a mandala in shades of blue, with ancient symbols and patterns Joel had researched.

Gabriel met Joel in a Goth bar near NYU, around four years ago. Gabriel was there looking for a girl who had stolen from his client. Joel was not Goth, but he had a friend there bartending, and he liked to sit in the bar and sketch. Gabriel had seen him sketching angels and demons, and commissioned him to paint the mandala. When Joel brought it over two weeks later, he didn't leave the entire weekend.

Joel rarely promotes his art, but his skills have been noticed nonetheless and he's sold some work, and done several projects on commission over the years.

Gabriel crushes the cigarette in a nearby incense holder that contains several crushed cigarettes. "Really? Seriously? This time you're doing it."

Joel finds himself smiling in response to Gabriel, who now genuinely appears pleased. "Yeah. Some sculptures that I've made multimedia. But she's also taking paintings."

"You didn't tell me you were doing sculptures."

Joel feels a little discomfited. As much as Gabriel's hedging gets to him, he has his own bad habits in not sharing.

But Gabriel's attitude has changed. Hearing about Joel's plans has awakened him.

"Okay, Blackbird."

Joel watches Gabriel go over to his Yamaha keyboard, which he rarely plays. "Call Geneva and tell her we'll meet her this afternoon. There's a café off Houston. *Homme Infernale.*"

The layout of the apartment, which faces Avenue A in the Alphabet City neighborhood, is living room first, the stereo/TV is against the wall to the left of the front door as one comes in, and the partly open kitchen and dining alcove are to the far left. Gabriel's bedroom is to the right, with a bathroom between that bedroom and the spare bedroom/office in back. The keyboards are to the left of the writing desk that's next to the sofa.

Gabriel starts playing Beatles songs, making some dust rise in the sunlight from the window. Joel is temporarily astonished by both Gabriel using a nickname for him he hasn't heard since they were together, and that Gabriel is playing when he hasn't in so long. He has talent, which he doesn't work at honing. His mother taught him to play and that affects him.

Joel calls Geneva, while watching Gabriel. He confirms meeting with her around four. And then he pulls up a chair next to Gabriel. Gabriel stops, uncertain as if confused by his own mood change.

"Play some more—but not the sad ones."

That gets Joel a smile. "You remember."

"Nothing sadder than a sad Beatles song, nothing happier than a happy Beatles song, nothing trippier than a trippy Beatles song."

Gabriel plays *Blackbird*. The one that inspired him to call Joel that shortly after they met. Although he never said it, Joel was always fiercely enraptured with that nickname. Enough that he doesn't get after Gabriel for lighting up again while he plays.

"I was thinking to play some other songs, but I can't find my music books."

"We'll get more from Jason." Joel takes out his phone and begins texting their friend, who owns a used bookstore in the West Village.

Gabriel stops for a moment, and picks up an old notebook off his desk, and hands it to Joel. "You want to help me on the case I have with Michaela? Take a look at this."

Then he goes back to the keyboards. Opera. *Barcarole*.

Joel makes his voice casual. "I guess I'll force myself to help you."

"That's very kind of you to force yourself. Would you text her too, and tell her? She's okay with it."

He explains Sophie's case to Joel, while Joel has some back and forth on his phone with Michaela. "She says to tell you *Titanic* is being re-released? What's that about?"

"It's some kind of joke from her twisted sense of humor. Never mind. I'm trying to figure out if Leonard Mathers might have in any way indicated who killed him or why he would be killed."

Joel turns the pages of the notebook. "Pretty stream of consciousness."

"I was comparing the symbols with the ones in my book on occult iconography."

"Magic symbols, to invoke something."

"Yeah. I started with the last pages, figuring that this would be closest to when he got killed."

"Drawings of a Devil."

"Maybe it represents somebody."

"The other stuff in the book...It's like the shorthand in Kent's notes."

"I thought the same thing."

"Repetition means something. If it's code, the repetition will be the key to understanding it."

"You're right, of course."

"No question. It's why you're begging for my assistance." Joel smiles as he takes a sketch pad out of his backpack, and opens to a clean page.

Gabriel retrieves his occult symbolism book. He sits on the floor next to Joel on the sofa, and they start going through the notebook, page by page. Joel draws the symbols and Gabriel notes where, how often, and in what context the symbols are used.

"What is above is what is below." Gabriel almost sounds like his old self, going on about some obscure topic or another.

"Say what, now?"

"The principle of *tabula smaragdina*."

Joel laughs. "Oh, of course. I remember from first grade."

"Don't give me a hard time."

"I'm always in awe of what you know, even if it's utterly incomprehensible."

"Not if you read Umberto Eco."

"*Him* again. I remember you reading and talking about him endlessly. If Eddie Izzard and David Gray have a rival for your heart, it's Umberto Eco. I think I saw a pin-up of him in this month's *Philosopher's Beat* magazine."

"You finished being a pain in the ass today? What I was getting at is what you said before. Patterns. Most of the operas this man was interested in focused on women, and he had posters of women. So does he have women as symbols?"

"According to this book, women can be represented as swans or sphinxes. And we have eight swans. You notice there's a certain line of other symbols with each. I'm curious about that."

Gabriel reviews the notebook against the sketch. "Two of the swans are decapitated. And he calls them Hypatia, maybe after the ancient philosopher in Alexandria."

"But no blood. A cross bearing fruit, and tears." Joel checks the book. "Like this one. Sixteenth Century engraving, meaning sacrifice. Fantastic. I'd like to borrow this."

"Sure. These swans, or women, were sacrificed. Hypatia was sacrificed, in a sense. She stood up to powerful people and was stoned and tortured by a mob of fanatical Christians. Does that mean these women were killed?"

"He has other symbols with the six live swans. A sword of some kind, ship and fish. The ship and fish mean night crossing—it's in the plate in the book. The plate next to it has the sword. The sword is the archangel."

"God, this is like an alchemical allegory."

"I was thinking the same thing. Or an episode of *Twin Peaks*. It's reality in mosaic form."

"Can you draw all the swans together?"

Gabriel watches him draw, while lighting up.

"I thought you were quitting." Joel's tone is now sharply disapproving.

"Gradually."

"We'll talk about that. The sacrificed swans aren't first or last. They don't have the ship and fish. Night crossing and an angel. A hero. These other women were rescued from something."

"Rescued. If these women were real maybe that's why he was killed. Here we have a case of woman with another self, who's accused of killing a man with a dissociative mind."

"No one said it would be easy." Joel glances at his watch. "Close to four."

"God, let's get going. Hold on, I have to shave."

"Really? I didn't notice. I'm going to study these other symbols. I think they're a code too."

Gabriel's phone buzzes again while he's in the bathroom. Joel can see it from where he sits as he puts his shoes back on; it's from Alex, saying he can get out now if that's good with Gabriel.

When Gabriel comes out, Joel is reviewing his drawings. Gabriel checks his phone but doesn't respond. "You ready?"

Joel gets up. Gabriel's phone buzzes again, but he ignores it.

A few minutes later they arrive at the café to meet Geneva. Geneva Lennon. She gave herself John's last name and Joel knows that starts them off with that love in common. Gabriel has a big poster of John in the apartment, also inherited from Dominic. Geneva is tall and thin, but has good body tone, dark olive skin indicating multiracial heritage. She has long dark hair under a multicolored Sixties-style scarf and dark eyes with eyebrows shaped to frame the strong bone structure in her face.

"I met Joel at an art store uptown. He helped me find some pencils I needed when the clerks weren't around."

"Joel said you restore art, like posters? Was it movie posters?"

"Yes, I do all kinds, but movies turn up most often. I also do evaluation. And handcrafted bookbinding —like if someone's favorite book has fallen apart, creating a new spine and personalized cover."

"Oh! I'd love to see that, I love books."

"Joel told me about that, actually. We'll see if we can't get you some kind of book set up sometime, with a special cover. He said you read so much your books fall apart."

"Some of them." Gabriel laughs. "Not always intellectual ones."

Joel adds, "He has more books than furniture, and more posters than clothes."

"My kind of man! I love the work. It's pretty solitary, but I do meet-ups with other artists. I was raised in Long Island and moved back here when I split up with my last boyfriend, but turns out I don't fit in here anymore. Still, my apartment isn't far from IKEA, and I live in *that* place. Now with the work, I like the concentration. You'd understand, Joel said you were into Zen. He talks about you all the time! I happen to need to be in the city today anyway, meeting with a client later on to evaluate an old poster of *Dracula*, an original."

"That's gotta be neat, to see those originals."

"I know some people who sell originals, I can hook you up."

"Excellent. But we're not keeping you from your work?"

"No, I'm balls to eight...I mean, I'm good. And this is important."

Gabriel smiles at her. "You were in the military."

"Army, yes. When I was young, 20 or so, I tried real hard to de-feminize myself in the most macho way possible. But on my passes out, I'd check into a motel and dress up like I was Claudia Schiffer and go out on the town. Hope I wasn't clocked by the locals or run into a soldier buddy. The training kept me in good shape, anyway. Were you military too? You know the lingo. I fall in the habit when I'm stressed."

"My father was Army, so I'm as familiar as one who was not actually in can be. I understand about the stress. I keep wishing I was on the island in *Lost*, I'd stay there."

Geneva laughs. "I like you already. Here's my problem." She takes a set of papers out of a burgundy folio. After flipping through documents, all encased in plastic sleeves, she hands Gabriel one of them.

It is a New York State certified original birth certificate in the name of Cesare Horton.

"You know why I wanted to talk to you? Joel showed me what you wrote in that online magazine about New York State's obstacles in changing gender on birth certificates. I liked your spiritual allusions and your impassioned stance."

"Thank you." He smiles about that while looking carefully at the certificate. Cesare was born October 7, 1976 in Rochester, NY. Cesare's parents are Christopher Terrence Horton and Alouette Valle Horton.

Joel says, "I told you he knows everything. Gabriel used to call himself, what—the traveling automaton."

"Autodidact. An automaton is a robot." Gabriel catches Joel's grin, and sees he knew that and is fucking with him. Gabriel keeps his expression neutral.

Geneva is amused at their exchange. "I had the surgery. My father's life insurance helped with that, and I found a good surgeon. I underwent various blood tests and obtained a therapist's clearance. So with all that, I sent in the information to the Department of Health."

She picks another plastic-sealed document. "I received this in return."

The letter is addressed to Geneva, from the DOH. Joel reads over Gabriel's shoulder...*we are unable to process your request, as the information you have provided us, and the information we have on record, do not match.*

Reflexively, Gabriel looks at the birth certificate again.

"At first, I couldn't find out what they meant. Understandably they don't want to discuss confidential information. But finally on the phone, they told me that my parents aren't on the original certificate, going by its record number. Not only that, the last name does not match the birth date."

Gabriel takes a minute to roll this information around in his head. "Christopher and Alouette are not on the certificate. And they have a Cesare, but it's not Cesare Horton."

"Yes. I didn't really have any suspicion I was adopted. Dad was mixed race, and Mom was white. But something nagged at me, I can't say what. Just things as I was growing up. But this was the only certificate I had. And the DOH won't tell me about the original—who are listed as parents."

Gabriel takes out his iPad and gets online. "I have a couple of decent databases; let me take a shot."

Joel talks to Geneva quietly for a minute, off topic. He knows Gabriel is following a gut instinct. Geneva is watching him anxiously.

Gabriel starts explaining what he's doing for her benefit. "Birth certificates aren't available anymore to anyone who just asks for one—you have to prove you are the actual person, or be closely related. Of course, that's to prevent identity theft. But 35 years ago, getting a birth certificate of a deceased person was not that hard. My first thought is to confirm the situation through some newspaper records. Most people have birth and death notices published."

"How can you search for it?"

"I'm using the original birth date and the first name of Cesare. Rochester is in Monroe County—I used to work in Rochester during college. The Monroe County Library system offers a genealogical records and life records database. Hold on, I have something."

He takes the information and checks it against his other databases. Geneva is more anxious than ever; she can tell he doesn't have good news.

Gabriel keeps his tone soft. "Cesare was Cesare Venezuela. He was born on October 7, 1976, in Rochester, to Maria and Jacopo Venezuela. He died five months later."

Geneva is still for a moment, then her face falls. "That means..."

"Your birth certificate is fake. I'm sorry about that. Really."

Tears come to her eyes. Gabriel takes her hand and Joel puts his arm around her.

She squeezes Gabriel's hand and uses some napkins as tissues. "I don't know what to say."

"This would be devastating to anyone." Joel pulls her more into his space.

"I had to know, but now...what do I know? My God, I don't know who I *am*. How did this happen?"

Gabriel picks up his coffee, still holding her hand. He has a comforting, strong nature that people often rely on, and Joel sees her doing that in how she squeezes his hand and keeps her eyes on his. Joel is gratified about how Gabriel treats her.

"I would guess Christopher and Alouette were able to get that certificate—easy to do in the Seventies—and then used it as the basis for a forgery. It's really good, and it's fake certified. I'm just surprised you hadn't found out until now, although you don't often need a certified birth certificate. Do you have a Social Security number?"

Geneva nods. "Yes, and a passport, before I had the surgery. And later, I was able to change the gender on my passport. When I went in the Army, they didn't have a problem with my birth certificate. How could that happen?"

"The passport agency would just want to see the certificate, they wouldn't double-check it. The Army wouldn't have a reason to be suspicious. Once you have the SSN and the passport that takes care of most life requirements."

She drinks some of her coffee now, and closes her eyes. Absorbing the situation. Identity is such an amorphous thing.

She meets his eyes. "What now? What can be done to find out what happened?"

Gabriel frowns, thinking. Joel watches him carefully, and Geneva even more so.

"You mentioned your father had died. What about your mother?"

She shakes her head. "They're both dead."

"How long ago?"

"Mom died five years ago, cancer. Dad died last year. He was a good deal older; he had a heart attack. The insurance money and their little retirement money helped my decision to have the final surgery."

"Did they love you?"

"Yes, for sure."

"That's the most important thing to hang on to, because we would need to trace your past. Really, *their* past—your parents. I want to be sure—you're ready to do this?"

"Yes. Certainly. I'll have to deal with how I feel about them keeping this from me on my own, but...Gabriel, I guess I know who I am, but I don't know who I *was*. I wouldn't care, but I need that birth certificate. Can I hire you to find out what happened?"

"Of course. We don't know what we'll find. I'm only telling you because of past experience. I know you're in a difficult situation and I want to help."

She takes out a shiny blue leather-covered checkbook. "I understand. I *have* to do this, now that I know it's fake. I've been through a lot, but I need to know what happened. I don't have a choice but to go forward. I'm glad I talked to you. Joel was right. I think you have empathy for women and trans persons. That helps more than working with some stranger."

Gabriel explains to her what a retainer with him will have, and what he needs from her. "I'll do what I can to help you with this, Geneva."

She looks into his eyes after writing a check. "He means it, Joel. He is different."

"Of course. I wouldn't have you talk to anyone else. And I work with him. We're a team."

Geneva catches the looks that go between them. "I feel so much better knowing something's going to be done."

"Good. Try not to worry. I'll keep you updated. Hopefully it won't be long, but stuff in the Seventies can take some time to dig up."

"Okay." She squeezes his hand again. "I'll get my papers together and fax them to you. Let me know what else you need."

She takes off, after hugging both of them. Joel goes over the situation in his mind.

"Why would parents fake a birth certificate?"

Gabriel studies his empty coffee cup. "Parents are such problems sometimes, leaving us genetic and non-genetic legacies. It's not going to be for a good reason, I know that already."

The two of them give study each other. Gabriel would like to forget about his father's mostly judgmental, occasionally hostile existence. Joel's parents would be more fit to sweep for mines in Afghanistan. They know how each other feels.

They go back to Gabriel's apartment. Decompressing.

Gabriel glances at his incense holder on the kitchen counter that separates the living room from the kitchen. "I have to do something for a few minutes."

"Okay. You want me to leave?"

"No, but I can't engage while I'm doing it. Or have any distractions."

"I got you." He lies on the sofa. Gabriel goes over to his incense holder and lights it. Waits. Concentrates.

After he sees that the ritual is over, Joel sits up. "What was that about? Zen?"

"Something like that."

"Okay, that's cool. So, with Geneva's case, where do we start?"

Gabriel sits near him on the ottoman. "Rochester. I'm going to see if her parents turn up there. But I might get most of this online."

"Damn, I was hoping we'd have a road trip."

"Five hours on the New York State Thruway, what a thrill."

"I appreciate you doing this. You'll do good. I can see you're intrigued. I just hope it isn't too traumatic."

"I hope not either; but digging in a person's life is a daunting task."

∞

Friday, December 3, *Continued*
Chelsea, 8:07 pm

"I haven't seen you lately, Mephisto. You've been hanging with your *strange*.'"

Chris is slouched on the sofa in Joel's Chelsea sublet, watching Joel go through boxes of art stuff, transferring said stuff to other containers to take to his new studio in Chinatown. Chris shows up casually at Joel's place like Joel shows up casually at Gabriel's.

"He's not 'strange.'"

"Yeah, but you've been tight with the private dick these days. Tell me what's up."

Joel looks at Chris. Six-foot, basketball-player physique, short but wild black curly hair, classic sultry eyes, and 3-day beard. He somewhat resembles a young Tim Curry. Chris identifies as genderqueer in the sense of not having a set gender. For now he uses male pronouns, although he's considering otherwise. Chris wears heavy eyeliner, several post earrings in each ear and some in his eyebrows. He has on a tight lace camisole under a tank top, and very frayed jeans. On his neck and other parts of his body are tattoos, mysterious symbols and bi/genderqueer colors. Joel has designed most of Chris's tattoos, although Joel does not have tattoos himself.

Chris is the same age as Joel, 32, and works in IT and sometimes in underground computer projects. He and Joel met as teenagers in the city in an ad hoc hackers meet-ups. Chris is one of the few souls truly close to Joel.

So they can speak very bluntly to each other. Joel says, "You couldn't care less."

"You're wrong. I like him, although you haven't taken me over there since you've been back. But he was always sweet to me. And he treated you good when you were together. I remember once he was at one of our little get-togethers and so out of his element. But he never showed it. You sat on his lap, and he put his arm around you just so. Just so. Not casual, not sexual, not possessive, but something else. I said to myself, "That chick's all right.""

"He still does it. It's unconscious."

"Oh, that's why you still keep after him. Someday, like in *The Matrix*, he's going to wake up and realize the truth that he's head over heels. You're different these days, Mephisto. Open up like I'm your therapist."

Chris is guileless. He acts almost solely on instinct. But he's loyal and true and has been through an evolution of life with Joel. Joel suddenly finds talking is a relief. He tells Chris about their day together. At least up to when Gabriel finished his incense thing; Joel stayed around another half-hour and then left, as he knew Alex was coming over.

"You know what a reverie is?"

"Yeah, like being zoned out."

"No, more like deep concentration. For a few moments, once he was through meditating or whatever, he was looking at me like every border between us was erased. I kept thinking, "*Come on, come on, Gabriel. Just say it. Just reach out.*""

"Deep, man. But he didn't do it, I guess. You sure you saw it?"

Joel's eyes flash anger. "I *know*, motherfucker."

Chris doesn't react to Joel's glare. "Just checking. We see what we want to see sometimes, no?"

"No. I don't have illusions. Gabriel is not in a good way these days. He can't talk to Harry Potter about what's going on in him, but he can do that with me. He's still guarded about that. I understand that—he's afraid to admit what he feels."

Chris is still lying on the generic sofa in Joel's sublet apartment in Chelsea. Joel hasn't bothered with decor since most of his attention goes to his art, and he still has a mindset to live moment by moment. Seeing Chris on the sofa actually makes him consider that he should do something different. The furniture was scrounged for him by the tenant, an acquaintance who's now working in music production in Ireland. Joel buys very little other than clothes, food, and electronics. For the first time he considers having a place on his own rather than subletting, and actually setting it up with the sort of style he'd like to see...maybe the loft he just leased. The thought is strange, like he's shifted into another realm.

"You're having some serious issues."

Joel folds the flaps of the boxes. "No *shit*. Granted, I thought it would be over with Harry Potter sooner than this. I was wrong."

"Is your own Personal Jesus worth it, Joel? Seriously? I don't remember you being hung up the first go-around."

"I was; I couldn't even admit it to myself until he was gone. And you don't know...he saved my life. But that's not why I feel the way I do. It's just something I wake up with, go to sleep with."

"Talk to me about that—him saving your life. What happened?"

Joel flashes upon that afternoon August. He can't remember everything, but he was overpowered by Ethan Nelson, taken to a warehouse in Westchester County. Nelson had a gun to his head, waiting for Gabriel. Using Joel as a lure. Somehow, Joel knew Gabriel would get past that trap. Even feeling death that close, he knew Gabriel would find him.

Gabriel grabbed Nelson, disarmed him and jammed his own gun to *Nelson's* head...for a second Joel thought Gabriel was going to shoot Nelson in the face—the anger was that strong with him.

Gabriel didn't pull the trigger. "Mr. Zest" talked him out of it for a better plan. Not one to Gabriel's personal sense of ethics, but one that ensured Joel's safety. Gabriel in essence walked away to leave Nelson for certain death. Nelson was a psychopath responsible for God knows how many other deaths, but Gabriel's decision was only done so he could take Joel out of there. Joel knows Gabriel does not regret it, but it's part of what he carries in his internal hell.

None of this is information that can be shared. "I can't talk about that. But it really happened. He really, literally rescued me. But he held back from us getting together..."

"And you think this all this intensely-interesting sitting around staring at each other is going to work?"

Joel picks up a box to take out and smiles grimly. "I don't know what else to do. I tried talking to him after...well, when I started working with him again."

"The cliché of the day is *nothing ventured, nothing gained.* Maybe he needs a little push. But you said he tells you things. How much of *you* does he know about, anyway?"

"Enough. He knows I was thrown out and why. I didn't give details. Some other stuff here and there."

"You ever tell him about anything really deep? Like about Jennah?"

"No. I don't want to. Why *would* I? Why is that important?"

"You don't share yourself well, Mephisto. That's why he got pissed at you in the first place, right?"

Joel stares at Chris with a hard look. Chris is not deterred at all, giving it back to him. Bringing up Jennah is hard for Joel. But Chris has a purpose. He senses a connection in the feelings Joel had for the woman who now lives in the museum of Joel's heart, and what he has for Gabriel.

"I mean, you're beautiful, man. You're gossamer. But shit, that grows old after a while—the Man with No Name pretense. Especially if the *past* is why you have trouble with him now, you dig what I'm sayin'?"

"Actually, I don't. Enlighten me."

"Enlighten. That sounds like *him.* Mr. Poet. Mr. Sensitive Guy. You're talking like him now. Lost your street edge, gonna get all fancy on me. Lord Byron can handle you, I guess. Me, I'd of kicked your ass to the curb long ago. You're acting like a lovesick teenager. You're over thirty now, man. Time to grow up."

"And do what?"

"Talk to him like an adult. Be there for him, share yourself. Show him you're a new man and you give him more reason to turn to you."

"I'll think about," Joel mutters. Inside he's terrified at the thought. Share and risk be rejected. Or *not* share, and lose him to the Wizard Editor and Intrepid Reporter who's over there right now.

That thought burns him. "I'm going over again Sunday. Come with me. I might be willing to start something..."

∞

FOUR ♦ 53 DEVELOPING (JIÀN)

Wood over Mountain: A relationship grows —slowly, carefully, after being still for some time. Like a tree stretching upward and downward. The fifth line (yang/nine) moves in this reading —three years have been spent waiting for good fortune. Advancement must be carefully cultivated.

∞

He's on his knees at a street. It could be the street in DC where Kent lived, it could be the street in front of his apartment building. It's as black as a starless night. Flat and smooth. He takes out Chinese coins to engage in I Ching and throws them in the street. The coins show difficulty, danger, death.

He dodges between cars to pick up the coins, goes back to the curb and throws again. The same signs show up. The engraving on the coins turn to demons waiting for him. The demons hiss in the palm of his hand. Then he has to suddenly roll out the way of a giant tractor-trailer that suddenly appears the street. The demons on the coins tell him he's Death, and he will join them.

As he comes back to the curb, Master Chiang waits for him with a cup of tea.

No matter how many times you throw, you have to respond to what turns up eventually. It's the only way to fight it.

∞

From the Rochester, NY *Times Gazette*

Alouette Jacqueline Black and Christopher James Southworth
were married May 25, 1969, at the First Methodist Church in a
double-ring ceremony.

∞

Saturday, December 4
Alphabet City, Avenue A, 10:45 am

I HYPOTHESIZED THAT Geneva's parents probably kept their first
names, and were likely from Rochester. First names are easier to
remember, as are the details of one's hometown. It's worth a shot,
and I search for these two names together in old news stories.

I find a marriage notice for Christopher and Alouette
Southworth in the Rochester *Times Gazette.* No more articles follow,
but in my background database I find their last known address (1976)
in Chili, a Rochester neighborhood. I know Rochester pretty well.

One way to find out about people is look for their neighbors.
A genealogical database gives me the neighbors at the time of
Geneva's birth. Campbell Arris was one of those neighbors. I think
about what I'm doing. Working, when I promised I wouldn't.
Sophie's case. Geneva's case. The Tertullians. Maybe I could look for
Amelia Earhart too. Well, fuck it. I said I was making my own
decisions. Mikki's worried over my exhaustion, but I'm worried over
keeping my business going. I'm worried over losing my sense of self.
I'm not letting Alex pay for me to slack off. So I'm working.

Campbell is in his sixties now. When I track him down, he
remembers the Southworths and is willing to talk to me.

"They were nice people. They didn't stand out one way or the
other, except being a mixed-race couple at the time. But I could count
on them for a favor, like watching my kids or taking in the mail if I
was out of town. I think he was in accounting and she did something
in health care."

"Did they have kids?"

"No, they liked kids but didn't have any. I don't know why,
and it wasn't polite to ask. But now that you mention it...just before
they left —and they left all of a sudden—a baby was in the house. I
remember talking about to my wife."

"A baby. You mean that Alouette wasn't pregnant."

"No. She was a real thin woman. Couldn't have happened; we saw them in passing nearly every day for around five years. Right before they left, they were in the house a lot—like they had taken time off of work. And we heard a baby crying. We thought about asking — maybe they were adopting or taking care of a relative. But, you know, not our business."

"What do you remember about them leaving?"

"Let's see." I imagine Campbell casting his mind back 35 years. "It was summer. The city was having a tough time. Crime was kind of high that year, so we kept an extra eye out on the neighborhood. My wife Louise and I were talking politics —Ford made it both fun and painful to do that. We heard the car start up next door—it was pretty late, 10 or so. I saw Chris run out of the house with suitcases. She came right after and we saw the baby in her arms. We thought maybe they had to go to the hospital. But with the suitcases? Well, they left before we could go out and ask. Never heard from them again."

"What happened to the house?"

"They rented; another couple moved in a month or so later."

"Campbell, did anyone come looking for them? Anything unusual at all happen after they left?"

A pause over the phone. "Damn. I have literally not thought about this in years. The day after they left, a man was snooping around the house. Tall guy. Young. He looked like bad news. We called the police when we saw him, and he took off. Then we saw him again in the daytime. Watching the house. He had short blondish hair, black eyes, a real cold look about him. I saw him as I was coming home from the doctor. I saw he had a scar on his neck—like someone had tried to cut his throat. That's mostly why I remember him."

After finishing this conversation, I do some thinking. Why would a couple disappear with a baby and give the baby a fake birth certificate? Why would they change their names? This has to be something illegal and almost certainly involved the baby. They left Rochester, ended up in Long Island, and kept a low profile. I can't find any mention of them elsewhere under their old names. Under Horton they led a quiet life, few records. But Long Island probably doesn't matter. The secret is in the birth, in Rochester.

∞

The next thing I have on my agenda, after taking care of some routine business, is go back to Elizabeth to speak to Giselle Greenspan, Sophie's friend. I meet her at a boutique she owns in Elizabeth. It features natural fabric clothes, artisan jewelry, hair, body and cosmetic products, and some household decorations. Most are handmade or with tags saying part of the money goes to a rainforest or collective somewhere. From the signs in the store, she also holds yoga, meditation, reiki, and feng shui and past-life regression classes upstairs from the store.

She's around 40, petite, with long blond hair entwined in wooden beads, and large brown eyes. I like her smile right away, when I introduce myself. Nice to get something different from suspicion.

"So *you're* the investigator. I saw Sophie yesterday. She likes you. She said Edward did too. Did you say you know other people who are like her?"

"Yes, I did. And that led me to read more, especially narratives from people who have other selves."

"I appreciate that. Too many misconceptions are out there. My brother is multiple. My parents do not understand. He and I are only a year apart. He and his system told me what was going on. But Mom and Dad, they haven't a clue. They've been trying to force medication and institutionalization on him since we were teens. I've fought them on this constantly. They even tried religious conversion therapy."

"God, I'm sorry to hear that. How is he holding up?"

"Good. He helps me here, and he has his own place. He's functional. Not as much as Sophie and Edward, because he's had to battle psychiatrists and psychotropic medication for so long. But we're working on it. I've gone with him to support groups. This is how I met Sophie. She's been a role model to him. We just became close."

Giselle leads me to a back office. It's windowless but large and nicely decorated with posters and inspirational signs. I take a chair and she offers coffee from a Keurig machine. While she makes it, she says, "I just wanted to meet you and check in with you."

"I understand. And Ms. Connor is an excellent attorney. She isn't going to be insensitive about the issue."

"Wonderful." Giselle claps her hands, showing fingertips done in a French style, but with the tips purple. "The other attorney assumed Sophie is insane. He was very rude. I can't see how he can defend someone when he won't even try to understand what the person is about."

"Most of the time defense attorneys are overworked and under pressure. But that doesn't excuse his being rude. Did you have any specific questions you wanted to ask me?"

"Not so much. Sophie...I can't imagine what she's going through in jail. Edward might handle it better, but I'm visiting there as much as I can. I'm paying most of the legal bills, but I'm not trying to interfere with what you're doing. I feel I have to take an interest in what goes on. I've advocated for better treatment for people with system of selves —I'm on some discussion boards, I have a Facebook page, and I talk about it to groups whenever possible. I have a media guide as well; I wrote it with the help of people in the support group, as well as Sophie, and my brother Jacob. Knowing how much people need to stand up for themselves if they're different...I have to feel comfortable that someone's looking out for her interest."

"We are. I can't tell you everything going on because of the nature of a legal investigation, but I can assure you I'm her advocate. And Edward's."

"Thank you. I know it's just begun. We're in for the long haul. From talking with Ms. Connor I feel you are working to demonstrate that she's innocent, not just preparing a defense. I'm glad you feel she isn't a murderer. If this becomes an issue at trial, she'll just be vilified. I think of other people who have selves...I don't want them to go through what my brother did. Forced medication, religious condemnation...you know what I mean?"

"Yes, I do."

She meets my eyes and smiles. "You do. I looked at your website and some stuff you wrote online. I guess you do know."

I don't say I'm gay on my business website, but I make a point of stating I'm LGBTQ-friendly. People make the connection. "Did you know Leonard?"

"I had met him a few times. He was a kind, sweet man. He liked Sophie a lot, and considered Edward a friend."

"Can you think of anyone who might possibly have wanted to kill Leonard?"

"No, and I have thought of it a lot. Anything I heard in the past few years, anyone I might have seen at Sophie's house in passing...but no. Leonard didn't inspire those feelings in people. Maybe this crime was random, like a robbery...what are you planning to do next, Gabriel?"

"Some tasks that are standard for defense work. Looking for witnesses. I have to also examine Sophie's house and the alleged crime scene. But I might have some other leads to follow, and if I discover more as I go along, I'll be on those as well."

"All right. I wanted to go into Sophie's house, to see if everything's okay, but the police won't let me. When are you going?"

"I'm going to Elizabeth on Monday. The house has been released by the police. I'll let you know if I see anything that requires attention. And if you think of anything I should know —because sometimes things just pop up later, just call me."

"I sure will! Good luck, I hope you find something."

I'm in a pretty good mood when I leave. Giselle has a natural way about her to cheer people, very genuine. We seem to like each other.

And somehow she makes me think of Toni Booth, my former client. Toni advocated for her brother Raymond like Giselle is doing for Sophie. Although Toni was also blonde and 40ish, Toni had a very different personality, and was not as together as Giselle. Toni was hell in a handbasket. Giselle is comforting, and Toni was provocative.

But I miss her.

∞

Sunday, December 5
Canal Street, 9:00 am

Chiang lets his student inside the studio. They sit down on a mat to talk.

"What did the incense do for you?"

"Concentrated and calmed my mind. I appreciated the incense for what it was, its smell, its sight, its purpose. It's a simple thing of beauty."

"Let me see your palms."

Gabriel lifts his hands from his kneeling position.

"You still have red, but it's getting better. But your eyes are haunted. You know your *Qi* affects others, yes?"

"Yes, sir."

Chiang sighs. "*Xin* again." He walks to a shallow ash box of fine sand four feet by four feet and drags it in front of the student. He uses a long-handled stick with a thin spatulate end. He smooths the sand with the stick.

Despite his melancholy, the younger man has a reservoir of anger that interferes with his abilities. Chiang wants to see if he'll react. "Gabriel. Draw the *gua*."

The *gua*, or trigrams, are the eight Daoist symbols of reality, in three lines broken or unbroken.

Gabriel leans over the box, and with his finger, begins tracing. Three straight lines.

"What is it, *Xuéshēng?*" Meaning, student. He knows Gabriel is as familiar with the *gua* in his mind as the tattoos on his body.

"*Qian*. Heaven."

Gabriel then draws all eight *gua* Trigrams, clockwise, in a circle. Finishing with *Dui*, Ocean. He then sits back on his heels, waiting.

Chiang contemplates the diorama for a brief second. Then he uses his spatula to wipe away the circle. "Do it again, better."

Gabriel glances at the destroyed work, hesitates a moment. Chiang's eyes are on him intently. Chiang had made his voice deliberately contemptuous. Gabriel looks down at the sand again, then starts drawing the symbols. Chiang has him recite what each Trigram is again.

Upon completion, he sits back. Chiang again reviews the work, and again wipes it away. "Do it again, *better.*"

Gabriel turns red on his face and neck while the Chiang clears the sand, but leans over to begin the circle.

The process occurs a third time, and fourth. By the fifth time, Chiang doesn't wait for the circle to be completed but begins wiping it away half-done. "Do it *again*, better."

Chiang watches him. The drawings were wiped away so quickly that grains of sand fly up and stick on Gabriel's face. Gabriel clears his throat, staring at the sandbox.

"Yes, sir. I'll do it better." This time, his voice is more gentle and sincere rather than forced.

Finally, Chiang lets the drawing stand. "Good. Get up, now. Take off your shirt."

Chiang walks around him. Gabriel is much more relaxed in tone, waiting. As Chiang had intended, the ridiculous drawing exercise was to engage Gabriel in both the harsh discipline of Zen and the demanding concentration of Daoism. It woke Gabriel up, brought him out of his misery, and gave him something to focus on besides himself. Eastern spirituality is about lessening the ego and focusing on others.

Part of the evaluation is the physical *Qi*. By any other standard, Gabriel very fit. But Chiang sees his color is off; he's pale. Too thin in places. Shadows on his face as if reflected from his mind. Chiang observes that Gabriel has new scars on his body —on the bottom right of his jaw, under his ear, and knife scars on his right arm and his chest.

"You've been in a couple of fights since I saw you last. When was the last time you fought before that?"

"Sparred with someone, like at the gym?"

"No, fought. Seriously. I mean, before what happened this summer in New Jersey, and when you were attacked on the street."

Gabriel thinks about it. "Three years ago, on the subway."

"What happened?"

"A couple of men came up to Joel and me and started harassing us. Talking to them did no good. We were ready to leave the train, but they acted as if they were going to prevent that and go further —making threats. So I disabled them enough for us to go."

"So that was three years ago. And then this year, all hell breaks loose. What happened in New Jersey?"

"What they were doing to the family was wrong. I wanted to tell these terrible people to stop. I know they weren't going to listen, but I had to say something. I acted rash."

"You're a protector."

Gabriel shrugs. "If you say so."

"*Xuéshēng,* if I'm telling you this it's for a reason, not to see your false modesty. You know Hinduism and the concept of dharma. It is the same here. The Dao works through you; it's why you're drawn to this work —it's your nature. But you don't do that well in listening to other people. Especially what you told me when you stormed out of here back in March. Nonetheless...you came back. *Qian Xu.* What does it mean?"

"Humility."

"You don't capitulate easily. Few can get that from you. How many men have you obeyed?"

Gabriel bows his head deeper. "My uncle. My mentor, Manny. Yourself until I was disrespectful. One other man, recently. I consider him a teacher of sorts."

"What does he teach?"

"History. How to fight monsters. He knows far more than I, so I would listen to his instruction."

"I would hope so. You cannot fight monsters until your *Yi* can balance your *Xin.*"

"I understand."

"Not yet. You are in a typhoon of your own making; feelings struggling against your spirituality, your discipline. What about your boyfriend, Joel? Do you listen to him?"

"Sometimes. We're not together anymore. But he's still close to me."

Chiang shakes his head. "More discord. Put your shirt on. We're going to go over basic movements. You need your mind focused. Something is chained to you, dragging you down. What?"

"People died."

"Did you kill them?"

"Not directly. Most were connected with a case this summer. My clients were killed by an evil man. He tried to kill Joel and me, several times. This evil man...he died too. I couldn't stop that because I had to save Joel. And a couple months ago, in a different situation, a man was stalking me because of the preacher I hit in New Jersey. He wanted to kill me in revenge, because my being gay was evil to *him.* He came close. He was going to shoot me in the subway. But my friends helped me and stopped him. He fell in front of a train by accident. I didn't want it to happen."

"I know. You're carrying that around with you. A traditional idea in Chinese thought is that the dead are still living in some sense. You are picking up on that. Just as Daoism is about harmony in the universe —that what affects in Earth affects in Heaven and vice versa — it is about harmony with the different levels of existence. The dead drag you down only if they are hungry ghosts. Were these persons loved?"

"Two of the good persons were, by their relatives. I don't know about the third, but I respected him. I honestly don't know about the bad ones."

"Respect the good ones. Reach out to them now and then with offerings. Don't let them be hungry ghosts. The bad ones may try to insinuate themselves in you, so you have to watch your back."

A hungry ghost is a person who has died and crossed over without anyone caring for him or her in the afterlife. These ghosts can come back to the world of the living and cause trouble, severe trouble.

"I will."

"After we go through the movements, go home and be peaceful. Mourn if you have to. Remember and respect, as a spirit can have even greater influence than when he or she was living. You have a lot of strength. So when you do good, it's remarkably good. And when you fall away from that, people notice more."

"It that a compliment, sir?"

"No. You're a problem. Average people have it a lot easier. Average good means average bad. You, however, have a purpose. And because of that I'm worried."

Chiang sees that Gabriel wants to respond with something sarcastic and is holding himself back. To make him focus again Chiang starts to walk away, then turns and hooks his foot around the younger man's ankle, yanking him prone.

Gabriel doesn't stay down long; in an instant he's on his feet and in a defensive posture. Chiang comes up close and the two men circle each other. Like a cat, Gabriel is instantly focused on prey. His physical discipline activates his mind.

Chiang spends a half-hour sparring with his student. Backing off, coming back to attack. Watching Gabriel tune in to his instincts until he's able to tell what Chiang's going to do before he does it. His student is not just supremely observant of people, but is able to pick up on the vibrations others put out.

"Do you feel that? Engaging with the universe. That's why you're different. You were drawn to this path. You either go with it and use the best of your abilities, or you get out *now* and create a different person. It's up to you. But now, in thinking about it, I doubt you can rid yourself of your emotions, your sensitivity. It's part of you, there for a reason. Instead, raise the level of your other instincts to match. You need to feel in touch with the nature of the Dao again, to harness the *Qi*."

Gabriel nods.

"Pride, guilt and anger will be your challenges. And refusal to trust and listen to others. That's why you left. You felt I wasn't good for you anymore. You turn red when you hear the truth. I'm not going to beat you with it. You came back. Now is the time to listen to what else your body can tell you about reconnecting with the elements, because you were meant to be a protector..."

∞

I want to get some other tasks cleared up, in order to do some serious work on Sophie's case, and Joel is coming over to help. It's only around 11 when I get back from Chiang, but I suddenly feel exhausted and lie down on the floor next to the stereo.

I fall asleep right there without meaning to. My dreams replay Chiang's words. When I wake up a couple hours later, I know Joel's here because the apartment looks cleaner. He likes to pretend I'm more slovenly than I am. I'm not slovenly at all in spite of my current fugue state. I'm just surprised I slept through his arrival and activity.

I hear Joel talking in the other bedroom, which sometimes serves as an office. I get up, shaking off the heavy feeling of daytime sleep, and turn on the stereo. Time to do something. I go in the other bedroom to check.

Joel is sitting at the desk in the room, which is situated between bookshelves on one side and the bed on the other. He's smoking and holding a book open on the desk. I'm surprised to see Joel's friend Chris here as well. I've seen him once or twice since Joel has come back, but Joel never brings people over to my place.

Chris is slouched on the bed, but sits up and swings his feet over to the floor as if he's doing something wrong. I hold up a hand. "Hey, take it easy."

"You didn't expect me, Marlboro Man."

"Don't call him that." Joel puts out the cigarette. "He's got to quit smoking."

I tune that out and stay with Chris, who seems afraid that I'll be angry he's here. "It's okay, you're with him. He has run of the place."

"*Run* of the place?" Joel narrows his eyes at me. "Like a dog?"

He looks agitated. I reach out without thinking and run my fingers down the side of his head. When we were together before and he was upset, I could do that and calm him down, reconnecting him.

"More like a cat, with supremacy of space. It's a compliment."

His eyes change, listening. I don't realize I'm just still looking at him until Chris speaks behind me.

"Letting him take over, really."

I turn back to Chris. "I need him here. Nice to see you, Chris."

His posture eases somewhat. "Well, you look good, Copernicus. Been discovering things lately?"

Chris's conversational habits take getting used to.

I have to wonder what they've been talking about. They have an air of conspiracy. Together, they're like the teenagers they used to be, hackers and street persons.

Joel's still scrutinizing me. "You're different today."

I find myself running my hands through my hair, glancing away. "I went back to Chiang's studio. To see if it would help."

He nods slowly and leans forward. "That's good for you to go back. Everything okay...otherwise?"

I take out my cigarettes. "Everything's fine." I ignore his clear disapproval of the cigarettes and sit on the bed, which used to be my bed when I stayed with Dom as a teenager many years ago. "Relax, Chris. You're welcome here."

"Why are you so good to me, boss man?"

I half-smile. Chris, now sitting next to me on the bed and leaning his long, angular body back against the wall, turns to stare at Joel, who glances at him then turns back to me.

Joel's expression is more direct, questioning. "We could do some more work if you're ready. But speaking of Chiang, where's your Daoism books? Did you put them somewhere else?"

"Threw them out last spring."

The reprimand is evident in Joel's eyes. He crosses his legs and taps the desk. "You *never* do that."

I glance down. This isn't something I'm proud of. "I was angry. I had a problem with Chiang, which is why I left. Hopefully that's over."

"So now I'll get Jason to replace them."

"You don't have to."

"I'm arranging things with him about your music." Joel closes the book, *Focault's Pendulum.*

"You like that book? And you don't have to replace mine. That was my own sin."

"Doesn't matter. I do it because I want to." He turns the book over to look at the back cover. "Yeah, it's deep. I was reading some to Chris. We wanted to look into more about the stuff Eco talks about. Damn, who's this singing?"

I can't help but be pleased he always recognizes the good ones. "Lisa Stansfield. *Affection.* I'm deeply ashamed I forgot about her. This album goes back a few years, but she's terrific."

From my controls in this room—which he set up so I could run the stereo from any room in the house —I run through some samples of the songs on her great collection.

"Yeah, I like that. I'm going to listen to her more later on."

"You'll really get into her. You like Toni Braxton; the two of them on the stereo is a great way to kill an afternoon."

Joel holds my gaze while we listen. He says, "I've studied that book on symbols. I think I know what Leonard was saying. Let me show you."

He leads me back to the living room; Chris stays on the bed dozing. Joel opens a sketch pad and the book. "He's definitely trying to speak with them—the women."

Joel shows me how he's drawn and redrawn the symbols together, laying the sheets of sketch paper on the living room floor. Each swan has a line of symbols, simple ones. Crosses, circles, triangles pointing in different directions. "They match a list of graphics in the book, forms of a mystic doctrine. At least in the book. Leonard used them for code."

"Alphabet substitution?"

"I think so. He must have had this same book or something similar. He connected the symbols with letters. I started with the vowels, that's always easiest. So I figured out a straight line up and down, what's called 'Active' here, he uses as an A. A circle, called 'Infinity,' he uses as an I. A dot, 'Unity,' U. But no obvious E or O. The problem is there's 25 symbols in the book, one short for the 26-letter alphabet. I had to figure out which letter was missing. He has a square, Quarternary, accompanied by a backward slash and '2.' Two letters back from Q is O. So once I saw that it was a little easier."

He shows me his final version of the alphabet. "I think it's right because it turned out to be names. He has '2000' right above them. I don't think he's writing about 2000 women, so I'm guessing it was the year."

Sonja Tadej. Iva Kalinowski. Julia Randjeiovic.

"The notebook is at least that old, so yeah."

"These names could be Balkan, or Central European. Also, those back pages, the writing there translates to, *The Devil has returned*. I got that far and then I had to take a break."

I look at his translation. "Holy Christ. You scare me."

"Why?"

"What you can do. It's amazing."

He looks away and smiles. "Not that different from computer coding."

"But you could see it. I can't do logic tests and codes. Even the Gregg shorthand is hard for me. Not where my intelligence lies. But you can see it. I can tell how it unfolds in front of you."

"Well." He sits up from where he's on the floor with the pad. "We complement each other's strengths."

"That's the best kind of working together."

"You have no idea. Let's see what the rest of this is."

I follow his work in decoding. More names.

Natasa Poldrugac

Darja Madzarevic
Stephania Ivanisevic
Flavenka Vucinich
Velinka Maluta

The names are connected with addresses, two of them. No numbers but a short description of a house. "Gin house," Madison and Alina. "Live house," Flora and Kilseth. Those names are streets in Elizabeth. The women's names, however, don't correspond to anything I can find immediately online. But I add checking out the streets to my agenda for Monday.

"And this Devil," Joel says. "The one who came back. It's someone who's connected to the women. I got that from what he wrote and drew here, going back and forth in the pages. And now the Devil, or the Devil's double, has returned. I don't know what that means. Figuring out how he writes is exhausting. But he had a pattern. He used different pens to mean different things, different timelines. And he is—was—connecting something this year with what happened in 2000. He keeps going back to the old pages and adding notes. He says the Devil's double is "haunting" him. And that's the last entry in the notebook, in his code. He's not good at writing dates, but he refers to seasons. The Devil was back this summer."

I review Joel's notes and begin to see the pattern of what Leonard was getting at, feel more of his personality. "The Devil was around a lot this summer. But this person haunting Leonard is connected with painful images. Symbols of pain and deception: thorns, nails, knives, a Janus face. Someone who hurts women, hates women. Leonard's trying to say the women need to be protected. Let's hope that the Devil here is real person. Maybe it's the person who killed him."

Having thought all this out, we take another break. Chris wanders back out where we are and looks over my collection of graphic novels. Joel starts going over other cases with me.

I hear a click and then realize Chris has taken a picture of us with his phone. "You two look cute."

I realize Joel and I are standing very close, and our voices have gotten progressively lower. Joel puts his arm around me; I feel his warmth acutely. "Take another one," he says.

Chris snaps that one. "Now I want one with him." He comes over and puts both arms around me.

After that, Joel glances at the ceramic yin yang figure on one of the bookshelves. "I can't believe you threw those books out. You *had* to have been mad."

"I thought I was going the wrong way at the time. Whatever."

Chris looks interested. "So what was in these books?"

"*Dao Te Jing*, some other texts, the *I Ching*."

"I remember that." Joel takes his pad, stays on the floor and starts drawing the *gua*.

"I thought you did tarot," Chris says.

"I did both. My Mom taught me tarot. I got back into it this year. But I was drawn to *I Ching* years ago. Just...shit happened."

Chris watches Joel drawing, and curls next to him, half sitting on him. Joel tolerates it like one would an impudent cat. "What is it, the *I Ching*?"

I get down next to them. "See, each line, or *yao,* is either yin or yang. Solid is yang, or nine, broken is yin, or six. You engage in finding the lines using stalks or coins, I use eight coins and a chart—or I did. Anyway, each line builds up the *gua*, or hexagram."

"Six and nine. Oh, that yin yang symbol, right? It's like a six and nine. Like on your arm." He points to the tattoo of the yin yang symbol on my left upper arm, set in a sun.

"Yeah, that's right. It connects with numbers. Nine is the topmost odd number, so yang is foremost because it's assertive. Six is middle, and yin should be midlevel because it's placid."

"Sure. It's what *I* would do. What any right-thinking person would do. But this is fortune-telling, isn't it? The Bible's against that, but I don't read the Bible. Can you read I Ching for me?"

"Well, I don't have the coins anymore, but if Joel draws a hexagram for me at random that'll work."

"So he's your oracle? I remember you talking about that once, oracles. I looked it up, even. Yeah, I like that. He's your oracle."

"If that helps, sure. Do you have a question you'd like answered?"

Chris seems to think carefully while Joel draws. "Okay...can I ask about myself or someone else?"

"Whatever you want."

"Uhhh. All right. So, like...what is the truth? Of the situation. Yeah. What is the truth of the situation?"

I look to Joel. "Let's see what you drew."

He's a little hesitant, but shows me. I reach behind me to a bookshelf to light incense in a holder there. It helps me think.

"It's Cloud over Heaven. A little more yang than yin. The gua represents raindrops from heaven. It's called Waiting, or Need. It represents patience. Heaven is always strong—it's all yang, as you can see. Water is danger sometimes. So something strong is needed, or something is strongly needed, or both. But patience is necessary for it. It's like waiting for the clouds to fill with rain and dispense—feeling the energy of the storm. To deal with it you need to build up your strength, build your confidence. It's what overcomes the danger."

Time for a cigarette. I forget how much concentration I put into that. Joel and Chris are silent for a minute.

I change the music, and then Chris makes me go with him to sit on the floor by the bookshelf on the other side of the room near the kitchen. I have some books on arcane subjects there, and he pulls them out at random and asks what they're about. Even though Chris doesn't have much in the way of discretion, he's actually rather sweet inside once you talk to him long enough. He only shows his quirkiness with people he knows. I've seen him stone silent with strangers.

I can't help but glance at my stereo clock; it's now after six. Alex is supposed to be coming over tonight.

Joel frowns. "Stop with the clock-watching. You're so anxious right now; you're making me jumpy." He does not look jumpy, now on the sofa with his feet on the coffee table, now flipping through a book on Alan Turing I recently bought.

"I'm just preoccupied." With the thought that Alex is about to arrive, and I feel like I have to cover something.

Joel's watching me while pretending to read the book. I've never explicitly told him to leave before Alex comes over because he didn't *want* to be around. And yet he's breaking unspoken protocol to stay. He knows Alex usually comes over around now. Although they've never met, they had a very unpleasant exchange over the phone a couple months ago. I was in a bad way after the incident in the subway with Reverend Bunton's crazy follower. Joel and Veronica were taking care of me and Alex called at the wrong time. I know Alex got nasty with Joel for not putting me on the phone.

Just as when I took the Xanax a few days ago Joel had covered for me, so Alex wouldn't find out what happened.

The keys turn in the lock. Alex comes inside carrying his jacket over one arm and his bag over his shoulder. He smiles when he sees me at the desk, then he notices Joel.

Joel doesn't look up at first, but finally meets Alex's gaze while spreading his arms over the back of the sofa. He has a smile of a type I can only call 'not genuine.'

The tableau holds for endless seconds. Alex then walks over to me where I sit.

"Hello, love."

I feel uncomfortable enough under the circumstances that I don't get up. He leans over and kisses my cheek anyway. Archie jumps on the table to greet him and he spends a second scratching behind the cat's ears. He nods at Chris, who nods back, staring at Alex as if he were a ghost.

I tell Alex, "This is Chris, a friend of mine." Alex nods again but doesn't say anything, which isn't like him.

Then he turns and goes back to the coat rack before I can say anything else. While his back is turned, I notice Joel scowling at him; but he drops it when he sees me looking. Chris retreats into his silent mode.

Alex then surveys the room, taking in the scattered sketches on the floor, and in a deliberate fashion finally focuses on Joel. "I don't believe we've met, really. You must be Joel."

The atmosphere in the room is on fire. Or freezing. Depends on one's perspective.

Joel speaks slowly. "Well. *Alex.* I've heard some about you. And we finally talk without you cursing me out. You have to understand I'm very close to Gabriel. I have been for a long time."

"Is that right?" Alex arches an eyebrow and adopts a slightly contemptuous tone. "A long time? I thought you didn't speak to him for a period. So what, you're reliving some kind of nostalgia now?"

I'm completely thrown off by this, but no matter. Neither is paying attention to me. I get up out of nervousness, to move to the chair at the writing desk next to the bookshelf.

Joel matches his tone. "History can repeat itself, my man. I learn from the patterns in life. Gabriel taught me that, because we're so close."

"Well, I know Gabriel's quite learned about bad character and foolish behavior, no doubt. What exactly are you still doing here?"

Joel gives him the fake smile again. "We're working, *obviously.*"

My level of discomfort has risen with their hostility.

And it isn't helped when Alex then walks back to me. His posture is casual, but his expression is somewhere between concerned and angry.

"Working? I thought you weren't going to be working this week, because you're fucking exhausted. And yet here you are on no doubt some *urgent* matter." He looks back at Joel. "And being assisted, I'm sure. Or incited might be the better word."

Now I feel defensive and at the same time smarting a little from his lecturing voice. I don't like that in front of other persons and usually he doesn't either. I start to respond with as much as calmness as I can muster, but Joel interrupts.

"I worked with him long before *you* met him, and I know him very well. I know what's good for him and what *isn't.*"

The two of them lock on each other. I feel something spilling out that I'm not ready for.

Chris's mouth is open, now staring at Joel. He seems a little confounded by the exchange which is nothing compared to how I feel.

Joel leans forward, lighting one of his cloves. Alex stares down at him coldly.

"And you think dragging him into back into work is a good idea when he's ready to collapse. When everyone else around him wants him to give it a rest."

"Why don't you ask him what he wants? Instead of trying to decide his life. You clearly don't understand at all."

"Why don't *you* quit trying to interfere in our lives. You have no business being here."

"Please, both of you stop." I get up. They look at me. This has gone too far, and I put that into my own tone of voice. "Alex, they're *my* guests. I'd appreciate your not telling them to leave. Second, I had my reasons for working. Just enough already."

And thank God, they back down. Joel slowly gets up and starts gathering the sheets with the symbols.

He says casually, "I need to get back to my studio, so he can relax about my undue influence. You want to keep these?"

"Yes, thank you." My tone comes out formal and he gives me a sardonic expression. Chris has moved quietly from the floor to go over to where Joel is now zipping up his bag.

Now I turn back to Alex. "It was just an hour, and yes, necessary. No harm done. I'm over for the weekend."

"An hour. Really."

Joel is taking the sketches into the second bedroom. "He's not lying."

And thereby lies about my lying. Jesus again.

"I didn't ask *you*." Alex takes my arm and steers me into the dining area. He speaks *sotto voce*. "He needs to leave...I don't appreciate his attitude..."

"He *is* leaving. And you weren't any better. I meant what I said. I really did not care for that." I disengage my arm from his hand. "Let it go."

"I let a *lot* go, Gabriel." He runs his hands through his hair. "Whose side are you on? He shouldn't be here, causing this sort of disruption."

"Don't do this now. I'll talk about it later." I start to move away, as I see Joel and Chris are going to the door. But Alex takes my arm again.

"You're not supporting me. You know what kind of message this sends?"

"They're leaving. Just calm down." I don't like to be grabbed that way. I step away from him and try not to be obviously irritated.

At the door. Chris hugs me again. Joel doesn't, but he puts both his hands on my shoulders and leans over to speak in a low, intimate tone in my ear. "When are we picking up on this?"

I hear double meaning in everything. I clear my throat before speaking. "Tomorrow's good. Go with me to Elizabeth, to find those addresses?"

"Of course." And practically whispering, "You cool here?"

"Yes."

He smiles. "Everything's *fine*, right?"

"Yeah." I have to smile too, but I check that when Alex comes up to the door. His voice matches his expression, ice cold, addressing Joel.

"A pleasure. Sorry you have to leave."

The look Alex gets in return for that freezing sarcasm is fiery. "The pleasure's all *mine*, Gov'nor."

"I doubt that." Alex shuts the door.

∞

"Shit...he's in trouble now," Chris says.

"Not *even*. Gabriel never lets anyone get the better of him. He'll shut that fucker *down*."

"Huh. Never lets anyone get the better of him but *you*."

Joel toys with his cloves, smiling. "Huh yourself. What do you think?"

"He's still sweet. Too nice for you, I think. You run roughage over him."

"*Roughshod*. I do not. He's just in turmoil."

"Mephisto, you played your own version of Monopoly in there. Or Stratego, or Risk. Or Hungry Hungry Hippo, something. I saw how you were, provoking him. And you were right, he's into you. When you started talking about that Lisa chick it was like you were in your own little world with waterfalls and palm trees and white sand beaches. Listening to lady Lisa, holding hands and counting stars."

"So I'm not delusional, as you thought."

"I can be wrong, it happens."

They're outside now, and go across the street to the park, leaning on the metal boundary by one of the ball courts.

Chris continues. "I thought *maybe* you were wishing-thinking, with your teenage-girl crush on him like he's a Backstreet Boy. Some guys like that hero-worship. Not our James Dean. He's stuck in his own angst. But he *cares* for you. I could see that. You were getting all intimate and he let you cross his boundaries."

"It's not just that, although I wanted you to see it —just to know I wasn't hallucinating. He's losing patience with Mr. Lord of the Manor. I saw that in their interaction—or lack thereof."

"But he *trusts* you. That has to be good, right? I mean, Jesus. You haven't seen him in two years, and when you come back he practically turns his life over to you."

"He trusts me about *work*, yeah. I proved myself with him about that."

Joel starts walking with Chris around the park, to a statue on the south side. He remembers the very first evening he spent with Gabriel, walking around the park and stopping here to talk. He glances at Gabriel's building, just visible across the park. He can see the windows but no one in them.

Chris says, "Did he tell your future with the I Ching reading?"

"I want to think what he said is true. But I'm running out of patience, too."

"Oh, the storm is coming. This *stirred* something in you. You're like that cat, ready to pounce."

Chris takes out his phone. "Here, look at the pictures." Chris captured the conversation of Joel and Gabriel with their heads close together, eyes intent on each other. Joel studies it carefully, like the Holy Grail. The he turns away, staring at the building again.

"Joel? What is it? You in pain, man?"

Joel seems to speak without being aware of it. "Him and the Intrepid Reporter about to get it on, while I'm out here. He trusts me about everything except what's between us. He's with that jackass because he's *afraid* of us."

"So just what you be doin' about it, son? Gonna wave a wand and make Lord Voldemort in there disappear?"

"Fuck him. Like you said, a storm is coming. Only the strong survive. I'm the strong one. I'm going to show him."

∞

FIVE ♦ 28 GREAT ACTION (DÀ GUÒ)

Lake over Wood: Extraordinary circumstances require the strongest skills to handle them. This has more yang than yin, so the circumstances need nourishing. The superior person recognizes the extraordinary circumstances, and the need for action without fear. Caution is needed, balance, not going too far. The fifth line (yang/nine) moves in this reading: one may need to carry a burden.

∞

He comes home to find Toni Booth in his apartment, reading his tarot cards. And smoking —so much so the ashtrays are overflowing. Archie is wandering between the ashtrays playing with the cigarettes. He worries about that. But what is she doing here?

Toni smiles at him, seeming more translucent than in life. "You don't do tarot anymore, Gabriel?"

The smoke rising from the cigarettes seems overwhelming. He finds breathing difficult.

"Yes, I just have started reconnecting with the I Ching..."

"I don't know that. I know tarot. You've forgotten about it. Forgotten about me."

"No, Toni. I won't forget you, or your son. I was accused of forgetting I Ching, too. I carry around a lot."

"Do you?" She gets up and kisses him on the mouth, like she did the day she met him. Impudent, brash, crossing boundaries. He senses she desires him, and he feels awkward in having to say no. She's dead; is it right to turn her down, insult her?

"Did you want my brother? Raymond? Do you want me?"

"I want you to be at peace. I want you to move on to a better existence."

"You pray so much. And yet, you can do more than that." She winds her arms around him, practically climbing on him. She reminds him of Voudon goddesses who visit people sexually.

"You're like that priest in *The Thorn Birds*. So devout and yet you let your desire tear your mind."

She seems to have many arms, becoming the goddess Shakti, filled with the kundalini life force, sexuality —moving her hands over him. He backs up towards the door with her still holding on to him.

"Toni, you have to move on. I can't do this." He feels her fire, her anger, her wanting. It burns him. "Watch the incense, Toni. Let it take you away."

She throws her head back and cries like an animal, wailing. It chills him, but he holds her. "I love you, Toni. I'll walk you through it. I won't leave you alone."

Her body arches, as if in death throes or orgasm. She falls backward in blackness; he holds her hand. Goes through the blackness seeing nothing but feeling her hand. He hears chanting and prayer wheels turning.

Otherworld spirits, the *Kami,* Zhong Kui, Di Jun, Kuafu...they fight with Yan Wang, the king of Hell, with the *Pretas,* the *Gaki,* the *Nü Gui,* the hungry ghosts. They fight over Toni's soul. The spirits scream at each other over their domains. He prays for her.

And a larger, unseen spirit arises like thunder. Someone's taking her away. "Be good to her," he says. "She needs compassion."

Then he falls out of the blackness, almost slapped out of it, by the larger spirit, to the street again. Chiang is there, watching him. "You survived being in the underworld. Which way do you go from here? What road do you follow?"

∞

Monday, December 6
Alphabet City, Avenue A, 9:07 am

"**WHAT DID YOU WANT** to know, exactly?'"

I'm on the phone with a Rochester attorney, David Toulouse. I had asked another attorney I used to work with in Rochester for some names of criminal defense attorneys who practiced at the time the Southworths left Rochester. She had given me a few likely prospects, including Toulouse.

I'm calling first thing, to try to get ahold of myself. I woke up drenched in sweat, and shaking. Archie was tapping me with his paw, concerned. A shower cleaned me off but didn't change the shakes. I'm hoping the calls will settle me down, before I have to go out.

I can sound normal at least. "Okay, this may sound weird, but I'm interested in finding out more about city scandals—around the mid-Seventies."

He laughs. "I hope you have a few hours."

"Well, I can narrow it down. Anything regarding children—babies, really?"

"Hmmm." I hear him moving around in a chair. "God, I haven't thought about this for a while. What did you need this info for again?"

"A case of mine. Trying to establish identity."

"What would such a 'scandal' have to do with it?"

"I can't talk about the case. As you no doubt understand."

He sighs. "Okay, let's get into ancient history then. This is more or less public information. Not as interesting as our hometown serial killer Arthur Shawcross, but bad enough. A black-market adoption ring through Bernadette McCabe. Bernadette was a respectable, conservative woman. She was considered to be something of a philanthropist for work in placing orphaned and illegitimate children. At least that's what we all thought about her."

"Were they really orphans?"

"I don't think we'll really know. But a lot of them weren't. Some were stolen. Others might have been given up, but not through official channels."

"I never found any stories about this."

"It was mostly suspicion. Bernadette disappeared. Her house burned down, I think. No records of any of these babies were found. The people she worked with left town as well. Well, one of them did. The other's dead."

"Who was that?"

"Attorney named Walt Corey. He was shady. Tried to make the adoptions look legal. Probably lots of people were not really, legally adopted because of him, but digging that up would be a nightmare. Can you imagine? Corey was kinda Bernadette's middle man. He paid off people, covered things up. May possibly have strong-armed some girls into giving up babies, or to pose as unwed mothers when couples came around to look.

"Now Bernadette's house, the one she had for show, looked real sweet. People thought they were doing the girls a favor. And Corey made them think it was on the up and up. You know how desperate people get about wanting a baby. They'll see things through the haziest, rosiest filters."

While I'm talking to him, I'm also on the Monroe County Clerk's database and looking up property records and public records. Deeds on the site go back to 1973. Putting in McCabe's name gets me an address in Greece, another Rochester neighborhood.

"I know what you mean. I feel for them, and I don't want to hurt anybody. Who was the person who left town besides Bernadette?"

"God, what was his name? He was a criminal, you know. The kind of guy you find out later is a real psychopath. I can't remember his name, but hold on."

He puts his phone down. I'm looking through news databases again, and coming up with nothing about Corey or McCabe, except one thing. Her house, the one whose deed I just found, burned down in the 1976. Just before Christopher and Alouette left town.

"I'm back. I know somebody you can talk to. Looking up his card."

"Thanks. Her house burned down, is that right?"

"Yeah! We wondered if she was caught in it, but no. Lucky no one died in that fire. I always thought the guy, the criminal, did it. Here it is, the guy I know. Peter Farabella. He was a police detective in Rochester at the time."

He gives me the number, and tells me to use his name.

"One last thing. Do you know anyone who knew Corey really well?"

"Who's still alive, I take it? Yeah, Gary Borkow. He's an attorney, too. Corey worked for him, and I think that he tried to keep Corey honest—but nobody could do that, really."

Since he has little else to tell me I thank him profusely and try the detective next. Farabella is retired and after hearing Toulouse sent me, speaks to me while he's fixing Christmas lights.

"Her boy wonder's name was Knox, Arthur Knox. I don't know where she found him. He was a real piece of work. We thought he was the one who burned down the house. I'm pretty sure he started other fires in town."

"Was he from Rochester? Do you think he left?"

"Yeah, he lived with his mother, who's also a native. He probably took off. We couldn't prove anything but we wanted to bring him in for questioning."

"What kind of guy was he?"

"He's a firebug. He seemed to be the resentful type, doing it for revenge. However, my partner and I heard he would contract out for insurances cases."

"And he was employed by Bernadette McCabe?"

"She was no prize. I don't care for baby brokers. We weren't handling missing persons or homicide, just the fire. But of course we had to investigate her background to see if that lead to the fire, which it probably did."

"Did the name Southworth come up in your investigation?"

"Southworth? No. Who is that?"

"A couple, deceased now, who might have run into Knox. By the way, did Knox have a noticeable scar?"

"Yeah, he did. On his neck. Someone had taken a try at his carotid at some point. And he was in his early twenties so he had managed to piss someone off pretty early in life."

"Any possibility Knox has come back to the city?"

"I'm not working anymore, so I don't know what's going on now. But for a while we tried to keep tabs on his mother. Terry Knox. She'd protect him to the death, just so you know. He could easily stay with her. I think he comes back here. Every time I hear about a suspicious fire, I wonder."

"And you think he was a revenge fire-setter?"

"Yeah. He was never a firefighter, understand. But he tried in his teens to volunteer. He gave off bad vibes and couldn't get in anywhere. I guessed he had resented that. We found out that after each time he tried to volunteer and was rejected, a few nuisance fires were started in the company area. These kept getting more serious."

"Anything else about the kind of fires he set?"

"I wish I could say more. We just couldn't tie anything to him. McCabe's house was torched with gas and newspapers twisted as a fuse and a matchbook set in the twist. He didn't like the *Times Gazette*, I suppose. Simple, but effective once the fumes catch. He poured it in a circle all the way around the house, so the whole house goes up."

Farabella excuses himself and I'm ready to move on. While I'm trying to track down the lawyer Gary Barkow, I also research suspicious or unsolved fires in Rochester for the last twenty-five years. Arthur isn't going to be the only firesetter in the area, but it might tell me something.

Barkow is a little harder to get a hold of. He's still working, and his office promises he'll call back. While I'm waiting, I start cataloguing the fires. First from just before Bernadette's house burning down, then after. If he sets serially, he might have done a few in that area. This is strictly guesswork. Few if any arsonists other than John Orr and Thomas Sweatt had actual signatures—specific methods of starting fires in each case —and even if the ones in Rochester did, the police aren't going to release that kind of information in an ongoing investigation.

Nonetheless, I note what little details I can find—the general address and neighborhood, if an accelerant was used. I check for follow-ups to see if anyone was caught. Not very often. Arson is one of the most difficult crimes to solve.

My business phone rings. "Is this Gabriel Ross? You said you had a very important issue. Is this about representation? Because you can make an appointment with my receptionist."

"No, sir. It's about Walt Corey."

I hear the intake of breath. From betrayal that still hurts three decades later. "Are you a reporter?"

"No, a private investigator in New York City. I used to intern for Bettina Carver in Rochester; she can vouch for me. Corey is connected to a case I'm working on, trying to track down a baby who was handled by Bernadette McCabe. I really need your help if you can, in understanding what he was doing."

Barkow breathes hard. I'm a little afraid he's going to have an attack. I hear some sounds that indicate he's pouring something. A moment later he speaks again.

"Why are you dragging that up?"

"I need to find out about him. I heard you were trying to be a mentor to him. I imagine you were very disappointed."

A pause. "That's saying it lightly." His voice has a wet quality now I recognize. The chemistry of whisky to mouth. I can practically smell it, as I did with my father. Even though the whiskey hasn't had time to have effect, mentally it does. If Barkow's like Jeffrey Ross, it won't be long before he'll be incoherent.

"How did he meet McCabe?"

"I'm not sure. By that time, he was involved in some other shady shit and had passed the point where he could easily get out. The worst was that he didn't want to. I thought of him like a younger brother. Stupid, but my brother died young. He was supposed to go to law school too and work with me, and Walt seemed so much like him..."

A pause. I feel more empathy for him, understanding the drinking. "People in town knew what she was doing, enough of us. But proving it was hard."

"She had help."

"That young guy? I have no doubt he could break arms and legs and heads. He was a psycho. I know the type well. The flaw shows in the eyes. When I saw Walt with him on the street—they clearly knew and worked with each other. I mean, Walt wasn't representing him or anything. I took him aside and asked him what he was doing. He lied to my face and said he was involved in "outreach." I started writing him off after that, and it was hard. I went back and forth—talking and giving up, until he died, and I didn't have to try anymore." I hear the glass clinking.

"Would he talk to you about what he was doing?"

"Yeah...it was confidential. I was torn about that, too. He tried to convince me otherwise. That McCabe was helping parents who couldn't have children, and the young women saved from humiliation. But he had to know the truth."

"Did he know a couple named Southworth?"

"Yeah. In-laws, I think. I met them a couple times. Just before he was killed, he told me he was worried about the man —what was his name, Knox —coming after him. He said he was trying to 'place' a baby better than McCabe could, and his in-laws were holding the baby."

"Trying to place the baby—sell it and burn McCabe?"

"He wanted more money. Apparently the baby had something special—it was from a particular family, and I would guess at that point Walt wasn't above extortion if he could figure out how. Then he was dead. I don't know what happened to the baby."

I can guess. Walt was dead, the adoption "home" set on fire. Alouette and Christopher decide to rescue the baby and raise him. The son, now the daughter, of a prominent family in Rochester.

"Any idea who that baby was?"

"I wish I did. Walt's dead, McCabe's gone —Knox probably killed her too. Now he's the only one who knows, aside from the mother."

Which means I have to find Knox.

∞

I haven't yet gotten dressed, even after the phone calls. I have to pick up Joel and we're going to Elizabeth. But I have trouble getting moving.

I'm afraid to look at myself in the mirror. I need to shave, but my hands are shaking. Eventually I just use an electric razor so I don't slice my throat.

After a shower that at least gets rid of the sweat from sleep—what's now a nightly occurrence—I try to think about what to wear. I want to make some effort to get dressed in something other than jeans and a t-shirt. It takes a half-hour to figure it out, sitting on the bed. I give up, then try again. Give up, then try again. The simple task is overwhelming to me.

I also spent a long time looking at a bottle of Klonapin. Joel doesn't know about the Klonapin. At least I think he doesn't. I have it buried in a drawer. He seems to know where I hide my cigarettes, but I don't think he searches the place. He never goes too far. But maybe I want him to find it, to call me out.

Ultimately I decided not to take it and shove the bottle back in the drawer. I'll use his presence to keep me in line today, knowing he'll expect me to be taking charge somehow.

On the drive across town to Chelsea, I try to chant to myself. "*Om Mani Padme Hum...*"

Then I give up. "Just fucking do it. Just do it. Do your job."

Joel's building is modern but not new. All over the neighborhood, high-rises are in construction—wanting to bring in the high rents from those wanting to live near the High Line, a park built on a one-and-a-half-mile section of old elevated train tracks.

I'm still having difficulty with my frame of mind. I catch a glimpse of myself in the rearview mirror. A real *Carnival of Souls* thing going on. I pick up my phone to text him, barely managing the one word.

—*Downstairs*

A moment later I get a response.

—*Really*

I look at his building. He's inside the lobby, casually leaning on the plate glass window and staring out at me. I realize I'm pretty late.

His being there startles me and I look away, pretending I'm checking my phone. Then I raise my head and give him an 'are-you-coming-or-what' expression.

He's not fooled in the slightest. I watch him move away from the window and leave the building.

I feel his scrutiny, coming from concern. I try to disregard that and update him on what I found out earlier regarding the baby brokers.

His cloves are in his jacket pocket. I take his pack out to steal one. I'm not into cloves but I've smoked enough of them for an acceptable substitute.

"You were supposed to quit."

"Yeah, I always pick the wrong day to quit smoking."

He doesn't seem to appreciate my *Airplane* reference, just continuing his disapproving look.

I do feel at least a purpose, to find out what those women are about. And some satisfaction with the progress made on Geneva's case. The idea of tracking down a mystery, a problem, always gives me energy. For work, anyway.

Inside I'm not good. I'm sure Joel realizes that. But the information gleaned from the phone calls was a step forward. Going to Jersey today, regardless of the results, is a step forward. A routine, a purpose. But I'm still shaking inside, seeing myself fall into blackness like Toni. Without anyone rescuing me.

I have Joel work with me in large part because he anticipates my needs, and when I ask him to do something he doesn't give me a hard time. He doesn't have to go with me today; he could be at my place taking care of other errands. Even more, he could be working on his own projects. But really, I need him here. I can put on the façade and get to work when he's around. I feel him trying so hard to be supportive.

But...I'm acutely aware of the other tension between us. His being there yesterday with Alex fired that tension, the one I don't want to admit to, exquisitely. So much so, the façade seems as fragile and transparent as antique lace.

He's waiting for me to respond.

I attempt to smile. "Um. Thank you. I feel like getting things done."

"And I want to help you. With that and anything else." Again, I feel his efforts, as he makes his tone of voice serious but not dire.

"You can talk to me about it. If it helps, talk all you want."

I light up the cigarette to cover my awkwardness. I don't want to talk about it. Nonetheless I feel I should reciprocate. "I don't know where to start. Um, I have bad dreams. Kent shows up, my mother shows up, Dom shows up. I'm starting to be terrified to go to sleep."

"I'm sorry."

"Thanks...Chiang is working with me."

"What does he say?"

"I have a problem with my feelings...keeping under control. I'm supposed to be disciplined in order to maintain the precepts, the Qi."

"You *are* disciplined."

I think about that, as I restrain myself from shaking. "Not as much as I need to be to recover. He's leading me to repair, to balance, to not be overwhelmed."

"This Eight-Fold Path thing, right? I remember. If that focuses your mind, and helps with what you feel, I respect that...I want to help that."

He glances up at me and I smile at him; make it as genuine as I can.

He slowly lights up as well. "And does *he* know what you're going through, really?"

I suppose Joel means Alex. "No...you know I can't tell him everything."

Joel has said before he and I have a bond from having to cross a boundary of secrets. He could say that again and I expect him to, but he doesn't. He frowns at me.

"We'll get through it."

He hesitantly reaches out to touch my hand in a comforting way. Reminding me of holding Toni's hand in the spirit world. These dreams are so vivid, I have to wonder if it's really happening. Which is the dream world, really?

After getting to Elizabeth, we spend a couple hours at Sophie's house. The police have finished going over the house as a crime scene some time back. We can see the evidence of that.

I begin my own standard investigative processes of a crime scene. Examining her backyard, taking pictures of where Leonard's body was found, taking measurements. Also checking out the rest of the house. This kind of thing is second nature to me, and starts to bring on a little more confidence. By the time we've finished I've actually lightened up more than I thought I could.

Getting in the car, my personal phone buzzes with a text. I have both a personal and a work cell on me. On the personal phone, Alex is asking how things are going. No doubt because of yesterday. Before he left early this morning, he asked several pointed questions about what I would be doing and with whom, and I was deliberately vague.

Joel's watching me. I don't respond to the text for now. I tell Joel, "I want to look into the streets in Leonard's notes. The first area is in the west side of town. I need some navigation; these aren't all areas I know."

"You want me to drive? You could handle the GPS or your Luddite map."

"*Luddite?*" I take out another cigarette, falling into a familiar, comfortable conversational mode with him. "I see we're in a frisky mood. I'll drive. It's God's will."

I see him subtly raise an eyebrow.

"What?"

"Nothing. If you can handle the driving..." He shrugs.

"You didn't know this, but *The Fast and the Furious* was based on my driving, in fact."

"Oh, do they get lost a lot in that movie?"

"You'll pay for that later." I light up as he smiles.

"Madison is coming up, that's the "Gin" house at the cross of Alina Street. Turn right."

I take the turn and slow down. We look at the plain everyday houses up and down the block. "Nothing here screams 'gin.' What strikes you about the houses?"

"Nothing much. This area is pretty nondescript. Near the railroad, airport and bus station."

"That in itself says something. We want to note what's similar about the streets, if anything. What's the next cross-street?"

"Virginia. Wait a minute."

"What?"

"Virginia. It's his code. Gin, see? Gin house. Virginia. Gin is in the middle of Virginia, and the house is between Alina and Virginia. Two-L, second house on the left."

"You're picking up on him." I shake my head. "Leonard, you riddle wrapped in a mystery inside an enigma."

I stop the car and we look backwards to the house that would be the second on the left once turning from Alina. I make a quick U-turn and go back to the house which has a for rent sign at the curb. It's actually in a little driveway that goes back some distance against a copse of trees. Set back enough that a casual glance couldn't see much.

"It's big—three bedrooms at least."

"Maybe more. It's a rental now, probably split into apartments."

I get out and take a photo of it, and write down the address to research later. "The big question is what might it have been ten years ago?"

"The same people then might not be there. What do you want to do?"

"Check the second address. If it works out, we're on to his code for sure."

Joel's going over the legal pad. "The next address is Henry, Flora Live House 4R. Coming up Kilsyth from Alina, the next Street is Olive. "Live" house. The fourth on the right."

We pull up in front. "Another big house."

"Four or five bedrooms. It's an old neighborhood, you don't see these kinds of houses anymore for single families anymore. Notice that's it's also kind of set back, like the first one."

I park the car and look around. Across the street is a five-story apartment building. Not shabby, not fancy. Well-kept on the outside. Plain brick facing. I notice an elderly black lady watching us from a second-story window. I gesture at her to Joel.

"If she's been here awhile, she may know something. Hold on, I'm going to put on the charm."

"I can think of so many things to say, but I'll just go with this: good luck with that."

I smile. "You have your skills, I have mine. Older people like me. Watch the magic."

I get out of the car and cross the street. The woman observes me approach the building and stand under her window.

"Good morning, ma'am."

"Good morning. Are you selling something? Or from the Witnesses?"

"No ma'am, I'm not. I'm doing a background check on the house across the street. Have you lived here long, if you don't mind my asking?"

"Twenty-seven years. You mean that house." She points to the house we were looking at.

"Yes, ma'am. Particularly ten years ago."

Her expression tells me something's going on. Or was. "What are you looking into about that?"

"Nothing to hurt anyone, just to help. I'm working for an attorney."

"Is this about a lawsuit?"

"No, ma'am. A criminal investigation."

Her tone gets serious. "You think some crimes were tied to that house?"

"I don't really know, ma'am. Honestly, if you have any information at all that could shed light on who was in that house in 2000, it would be enormous assistance."

She looks me over. I'm glad I actually took the time to put on a better-looking leather jacket and flat-front wool trousers. "Are you police?"

"No, private, working for an attorney. We're trying to find some pretty bad people who need to be put away."

"I see. The young man there working with you?"

I turn to look at Joel. He's standing outside the car smoking. Upon seeing us, he stands up straighter and smiles.

"He's my assistant."

"What's he smoke?" Her interest in the cigarettes is palpable.

"Djarum. Cloves...Yeah, I know. I try to get him to stop. I have Camels, though."

Her eyes light up. "I can't afford them these days. I ran out, but why don't you come on up if you don't mind sparing a couple. Your assistant can come up too."

I go over to the car, open the trunk where I have a pack hidden—much to Joel's amusement, and gesture for him to follow me. We're buzzed into the building.

Ten minutes later, after we've introduced ourselves to her, she's in essence traded and information for a couple of Camels. Her name is Annie Mallerman; she's a retired phone operator.

"This is so good." She inhales deeply. "That house...it had some bad feelings around it. The women."

I feel the adrenaline I get when pieces of a case start forming. "Women. Were these foreign women?"

"They were; I believe so. Do you know about them?"

"Only that some women, from Europe, may be involved in this case."

"I think these women were European. I didn't see them too often—the men brought them in and out at odd hours. They never said much, but a few times I heard accents or words, could be like Russian."

I can see the situation getting clearer, like a picture focusing. Not quite there, but on the precipice. "Did the women live there long?"

"Not that *I* could tell. A few months. They were hardly ever out. They weren't family, I imagine."

"And the men, what were they like? Are they still there?"

"No, sometime in 2000 they all left. The men were young, around your age. The same ones, two or three. I'm sorry I don't really know what they looked like, but maybe if I saw a picture."

"Mrs. Mallerman, I have one picture to show you." I open the case folder I have with me and take out the photo of Leonard. She scrutinizes it. "I don't remember him, no."

That's good, to me, because of the idea in my head. "Before these people all left, Mrs. Mallerman, did anything strange happen?"

"Funny you should ask, it looked like hell had broken loose over there. Early in the morning—I happened to be up—these men were running around like something terrible had happened. They cleaned out the house, yelling and cursing the whole time, and then drove off fast. Didn't see the women that day, or ever again."

"Can you tell me more or less when that was?"

"Let's see. That was spring, April or May. It had been raining hard and the ground was kind of muddy. They spattered it all over when they left. Oh, you know what? I had been watching the news, and that young Cuban boy had been taken away by the FBI people. This was the next day, and it was all over the news, if you remember."

"Yeah, I remember that. And nobody came back, not the women, not the men."

"No, never did. That is a rental house and the owner just rented it again. One of those property management companies."

Time to leave. I thank her and leave her a couple more cigarettes.

Back in the car, I start thinking; the better part of my mind is activated.

"I love watching you get information; I see you getting into it like Sherlock Holmes."

He makes me smile. "More like Jim Rockford. But thank you."

"No, not Rockford, like that guy in the Seventies who was a reporter. Chased vampires and shit."

"Kolchak? You remember we used to watch that on *Netflix*. I think that's truer than I'd like to admit that I'm like him. Always getting in trouble, almost killed, and underappreciated."

"Whereas I am just your humble *assistant*."

My phone rings. Alex again. I let it go to voicemail. "You're my *lifesaver*—you figured out his code, now we know what he was getting into...what do you want to be called, then?"

He pauses, having watched me put the phone away again. "You can call me whatever you want. So these women, I picked up on what you're thinking."

"Human trafficking. Slavery, really."

"The girls were held there. Moved in and out. That's why all the bedrooms."

"Leonard knew this. Or found it out. When was Elián Gonzales taken by the feds?"

He looks it up on his phone. "April 20, 2000."

"Close to the time of the phone call made to Sophie's house. I can't see how this would be connected with his death as yet. But it's a working hypothesis."

"Would he be that kind of guy? Involved in that shit? But she said she didn't see him."

"We'll check the other houses. We were lucky with Annie giving us that information. I don't think Leonard was involved with keeping the women captive. Not from how he drew those symbols. Maybe he found out what was going on, maybe managed to talk to one of the women. He found out their names. Something made these men leave all of a sudden. All hell broke loose, Annie said. He even might have helped the women escape—the rescued women, the swans. Human trafficking became more of a problem in the 1990s after the wars in Yugoslavia. A lot of women were lured into this by fake promises of sponsorship or good jobs."

"More stuff you know."

I half-smile. "My mother knew. She used to tell me about the Balkan women, and the unbelievable number of women who were killed in Juarez by some unknown killer or killers; these horrors were always troubling to her. I kind of picked it up from her."

"Then we're looking at the possibility that the men who were holding these women killed Leonard."

"It's reasonable doubt for Sophie, if we can construct enough of a scenario to present to a jury."

"It also means a syndicate of some kind."

"We'll see." I smile grimly. "That doesn't worry me for now."

"Could he have just stumbled on this?"

"Possible, but look how he was killed. Not gang-style, not like OC. This was hands-on. It screams personal."

"Maybe Edward knows something more. You think you could talk to him again?"

"I want to. If he's okay with coming forward and talking to me. What else?" I close my eyes. A moment later I hear the music change.

"Let's help you think; he said he liked opera, right?"

"*Carmen*. That was his special opera, I'm pretty sure."

He finds the *Overture*. I listen to it and then *Habenera*, thinking.

"Leonard...I feel he was looking for information. He had to be careful who he talked to. He was dissociative but not stupid. I saw that in his altar, in his writing. Where could he find out about women in this situation, especially what to do to help them? Maybe he contacted them. Ten years ago, not as much information around on the Internet as there is now. Maybe there's an organization in the state, in the county even, that did some work in advocacy for trafficked persons. Maybe a nonprofit or government organization."

Joel's already looking it up as I talk. "There is one, right here. Women's Freedom Network. It's in Elizabeth. Jesus—you won't believe this."

"What?"

"The woman who ran the Network ten years ago was found murdered. Hacked to death."

"What the fuck?"

He hands me the phone. I read the NJ *Union Tribune* story once through quickly, and then again carefully. April 18, 2000. Charlotte Merical, Director of WFN, was found in her apartment, stabbed and bludgeoned dozens of times. Some suspected her death was related to her work in helping victims of human trafficking. A search of her name doesn't turn up any stories of the murder being solved, no one arrested.

I look back at Joel. "Tell me this is a coincidence."

"No way. Leonard's talking to you. He left his notes in Wildemore for you to find."

That's such an unreal thing to say; I stare at him.

He meets my eyes. "I believe it. You're on this case for a reason. Now this woman. You can see what's going on. You make the connections."

"Through another dead person talking to me. Charlotte Merical, director of a nonprofit helping trafficked women, is killed the day before everyone hauls ass from a house where women are being held. Leonard was writing about women being rescued. Maybe he tries to contact Merical, and she gets killed for that contact."

"So is what happened back then connected with his death now?"

"It's a working hypothesis. His writings in the notebook were saying what happened in 2000 came back. With the Devil. We need to find out who the Devil is."

While believing Sophie innocent as Mikki does, the implications of the case are daunting. "The more I think about it, the more I feel it connects. The brutality of smashing Leonard's skull. The brutality of beating and stabbing Merical to death. The hatred of both of them. Traffickers in women hate them, see them as less than human. Leonard sounds more like he would have helped them."

"Maybe he pissed them off too. But why kill him ten years later?"

"I know. A time span like that, it's not a cover-up. It's revenge. It could be someone he knew. I have to find out more about him."

The evil of it gives me some kind of fortitude, a righteous anger. It's a challenge. Now not just for Sophie, but because something evil out there has to be stopped.

We start to head back on 1-9 toward the more industrial part of Elizabeth, on the way to the George Washington Bridge. This is where the docks and the logistics companies are located. The phone rings again. I have certain ringtones for certain people. Joel has figured out when it's Alex calling.

"Do you need to take that," he asks carefully.

I'm not going to talk to Alex with Joel in the car. "No. So listen, are you with me on this? It might get complicated."

"You mean dangerous. Of course, I'm with you. You don't have to ask that."

As we're driving, I see he gets lost in thought.

"Is something bothering you, Joel?"

"No...uh, this, um, discovery...it reminded me..."

I watch him the best I can while also watching the road. I can't tell if he has trouble saying something in particular or is just searching for something to say. But I know he's referring to his past. I want to tell him, *you don't have to say anything*. Except I sense he *wants* to.

And it's hard for him. He's told me some details on and off over the years. Compartmentalized. Just like I meet his friends in a compartmentalized way.

"There was a time...on the street. I was 15-16. I ran into somebody doing that kind of thing. Not just pimping, which is bad enough, but the rumor was he was holding people hostage, like in an apartment, and making them work—sex work. I had a friend, Grace. We were hanging together; we were *really* close...She was transgender. She stopped me from being caught by this guy. She almost got killed for it, too."

I can feel the relief he has in finishing the story, although it's barely sketched out. But for him, it was like reciting *Les Misérables.*

"I appreciate your telling me that. Grace must have been someone special."

"She was. She disappeared later. I'm not sure what happened. I just wanted to, uh, share. Not a big deal. It doesn't keep me from helping."

"You're sharing something like that is...good. I don't know the right word to describe it. You hear so much about my problems."

He doesn't respond but I see his demeanor change. More relief. He almost relaxes.

From my meeting with Chiang, I've reawakened my ability to be hyperaware. And with that, I now notice that a blue Elantra with Connecticut plates seems to be awfully interested in what we're doing. Yes. It had been on Olive Street before. I might have even seen it prior to that. Now here. The plates stick out; not so much the car, as all sedans tend to look alike. To determine if I'm imagining things I pull off to a Sonic drive-in. The Elantra pulls over as well, to a gas station next door. The driver, apparently male, seems to be on his cell phone.

"Motherfucker..."

Joel looks where I'm looking. "A tail?"

"Yeah. We'll take care of this shit." I pull around the drive-in slowly as if I was looking for a good parking place. Then I reverse, turn, accelerate and drive over the concrete abutment between the drive-in and the parking lot of the business behind it. Another street over is where the shipping companies have vast parking and loading areas. Little other traffic comes this way.

And the Elantra suddenly bounces onto the same street from the gas station side.

I turn my anger to action. "Well, *hello.* You want to play games?"

"Gabriel..."

But I'm already hitting the accelerator. My mind suddenly clears for Zen driving, seeing ahead, anticipating.

No traffic down the long road which comes at the end around a UPS plant. My Camry has more power than it looks, and I know this car like I know my hand.

He's right behind, at around 50 MPH. Around the bend and down the next empty street. I already see my next changeover. A FedEx lot is open all the way to the other street, and I drive through without stopping, swinging around a truck and some workers.

Outside the gate I turn right. I've been on this road, and I make a point of memorizing as many roads as possible, and this area of town I'm familiar with. I know this road ends in a gravel area against a fence. I go there deliberately and spin the car around, pulling up the handbrake, spitting gravel. As if I wasn't sure where I was going and panicked from being trapped. If the Elantra was tailing just for information, he would have known he was burned and sped off. His following at high speed means he has a back-up agenda.

The Elantra heads toward us, slowing as the windows lower. "Get *down.*"

He does, but keeps talking. "Should I call in..."

I'm not listening. The Elantra is coming up to us, turns diagonally about 30 yards away; the front of the car pointing to my right. He's already lifting something to the window. It's a great place for a shot—no cameras.

The Camry's nose is pointing right. I stomp on the accelerator as if I was going around his front end, to his left. He has to pull ahead to block me, and as he does, I turn sharply left and swerve around the back of his car. In the tight turn the Camry comes within inches of his trunk, lifting up a little on the right from the momentum. And we're back down the road. The Elantra driver makes a desperate shot that pings off the roof.

Then he follows, sideswiping a post.

The next step is to go to the end of the road, swing left back past the FedEx and UPS lots, and go as far as the traffic light to 1-9. I just blow through and continue north with the Elantra close behind. The Turnpike is coming up, but I'm not going there.

Joel is back up, looking cautiously behind us. "You have a plan of some kind? Going back over the bridge?"

"No. If he's trying to kill us here, he'd still try on the Turnpike. Either run us off the road or shoot out a tire if it's a parking lot. So I'm going to try to lose him."

"How—what about calling the police?"

I don't answer that. I don't call the police unless no other option exists. And by the time the police show up, we'll be dead. We can't stop. Knowing I need to protect Joel has strengthened my mind and my instincts.

I've turned right again to a side street with an underpass, and then under that to another side road heading west. The route I want 327, is to our right, but no exit to 327 is on this street. A grass median separates this street from 327, and then another median separates the eastbound from the westbound traffic. I check behind me. The Elantra is still coming up behind us. "You'll need to hold on and trust me."

Before he can ask anything else, I see the opening. Accelerate right, and over the first median. Down the wrong way eastbound on 327 for a few seconds, the strange feeling of seeing cars heading for us. Joel draws in breath sharply but I feel the road becoming my instrument.

Then over the second median and we're in the westbound lanes.

The Elantra follows, not as easily. Some cars swerve out of the way, but luckily no one crashes. The notorious 327 heading to Paterson eventually becomes a two-lane road outside of the city, a place of frequent accidents and people even driving into the houses that are close to the road. People drive faster than they should here. And I'm going faster than all of them. Using the passing lane with luck, or skill. Joel actually knows I can seriously drive, but he's speechless at the moment as I'm weaving around the cars ahead. The Elantra tries to duplicate.

Closer to Paterson is a four-lane highway, 7A, bad in its own way. While 327 doesn't have a turn-off to that highway, I know how to get there from certain incidents in my youth hanging out with a Jersey boy I had a crush on. We reach a heavily wooded area separating the highways. Except for a dirt path state officials use. I have to slow and turn a sharp right for that, then slam over to the westbound lane in the second road.

"What the hell?"

"You're about to see how well I know Jersey."

The Elantra has just missed colliding with a SUV and is gunning to catch up. A patch of traffic comes up, and he's closer. I can see him holding the gun, considering the risk. The four-lane highway we're on now abuts a drop-off on our side, with an eight-foot span and a miniscule guardrail —in some places. The drop-off is a few hundred yards of dirt and rocks leading down to the Turnpike. Going over it means landing in the middle of traffic back to New York. Not that one would be able to appreciate it by the time the car hits the bottom.

One way around the traffic in 7A, to get away from the Elantra.

I use the drop-off for my passing lane with the Elantra attempting to come up hard enough to knock us over. Even a small tap could send us spinning, so I keep my foot on the accelerator to stay ahead. I don't look at the people in the cars, in actual driving lanes to the left, who are staring horrified at us.

The Camry's wheels come close to the edge, maybe a little over. Dirt flies in the air. I yank Joel, who's hyperventilating, over to my side to counterbalance the car. Then I swerve back left, nearly sideswiping a minivan. The traffic is thinning now but I'm still on the side; the car is going dangerously fast and the Elantra driver is trying to creep to the left rear side of the fender. I pull left, scraping a little against him. The metal grinds, throwing off sparks. Joel flinches against me.

The Elantra tries to nose the Camry over the edge. I swing the wheels left again and keep my foot down, willing us to get ahead. Then suddenly a space opens in front of the traffic and I'm back on the actual highway, slipping away from the Elantra.

I grab Joel's leg as he exhales. I feel his tension and fear. "Baby, it's okay. This is going to be over in a minute."

"What you do mean by that?" The stress makes his voice gritty.

"I know exactly where I'm going."

Up the highway over 90 MPH, to another wooded stretch. Another trick.

The bend is coming up. "Seriously, hold on."

For a brief moment we'll be out of sight of the Elantra and at another dirt service road. I slow down, and Joel braces as I slam the brakes then make the turn through the woods to a much quieter road and go the back the other way on that one—east. A quarter mile up on the left is a small turn-out for sightseers—very scenic in the spring. I pull in and keep going to the far end of the turn-out, and down a dirt and gravel maintenance path not visible from the road entrance, to a space under an overpass for New Jersey Transit.

We stop there near the overpass, next to a fence that's under repair. The dust settles. Joel's clutching the dash, looking afraid to move.

"He'll have no idea." I smile at him, maybe a little wickedly. Then open my door and get out. I have to laugh, and feel a thrill of triumph, the first time I've felt *alive* in weeks. The Elantra must still be going the other way in frustration, and that gives me enormous satisfaction. No one else is around and the solitude is a respite. I lean back in the car to look at Joel. "You *still* think I can't drive, baby?"

I'm electrified with the action, energized. Joel feels this and quickly gains his equilibrium. He gets out of the car and comes around to my side. "Of course I did. Just it was unexpected that you were going to prove your *Fast and Furious* point so soon."

I laugh again. He's not as nonchalant as he sounds, but he's recovering. He comes up closer to me. I'm still flush with adrenaline and it pounds in all my nerves. Atavistic, physical. Joel shrugs off his jacket and drapes it on the car, running his fingers back through his hair, almost dreamlike. We're both sweating in the cold day, from the adrenaline.

"You sure he's gone," Joel says as he approaches me.

"Totally. We're safe, baby. He'd be here otherwise. No one knows this place. We just need to find out why he was after us..."

I stop talking, lost in his gaze. Seeing the admiration in his eyes...maybe more. Definitely more.

Joel comes up to me, puts his hands to my face and draws me to his. His mouth is imperative on mine. He presses his body against me, and in turn my arms instinctively go around him.

The feel of his mouth and body is so exotic and powerful at the same time, I'm overwhelmed. He kisses me as he used to when we were together, with a controlled eroticism that could make me drop anything I was doing to give in, like I am now. The sensation of our tongues together makes the past and present collide. The chemistry ignites between us, going to every part of my body.

Joel moves his head back. His eyes are so strong with me I can't look away. His voice is deep with sensuality. "You feel what's between us."

I have no idea what to say, what to answer. His very being is an intoxication I've been avoiding, and suddenly I'm drowning in it.

He takes my hand, draws my fingers slowly across his face as he closes his eyes. It makes me shake inside, but not like in the morning. This is an otherworldly sensation; consuming.

He continues moving my hand down his chest. Under his control, my fingers absorb his reality, his being. I feel his heart beating, feel his chest rising with his breathing. Time slows with the movement of his hand.

He finally brings my hand to his crotch. "Dammit, don't keep pretending, Gabriel. You know what we do to each other."

I inhale jaggedly from the physicality of touching him—feeling him hard. We haven't been in this type of compromising position since stopping in a parking lot in New Jersey in August, after we were nearly blown up in some old rich guy's house. He had comforted me, because of my shock that we almost...

...Died. And a few days later, he almost died again, with a gun to his head, seconds away from an evil man killing him. This brings to the surface how I feel about him. The last two years suddenly compress. I can feel the Earth falling away to just him and me. I had forgotten what us being together *really* was like. Even in August it wasn't fully realized—or I was trying to block it. Not the sex, the connection between us. It's like opium at its most potent and it's making my head swim now.

His expression is just as intense as what I'm feeling. I know from the shock of the car chase and danger, I've woken up. The façade has crashed.

And seeing that, Joel becomes relentless. "You know it. You feel it too. I don't imagine this."

He puts his hand down between my legs in turn, makes me feel my desire, makes it real; I catch my breath again. For the first time since he's been back, we're looking at each other truthfully.

"God, *you feel it too.* I knew I saw it in your eyes. You want me, and not just your dick."

Joel brings his head close to mine again, his voice soft. "You can't say it...but I know you care about me; you still love me."

I'm without words still, lost in the fire of what he's doing to me.

"You can't tell me this isn't powerful to you." He kisses my face, my neck.

"We can't stay here like this..." But I'm not moving. I don't want to. My words aren't true. I don't want to stop feeling him. Somehow, right here is magical.

His voice becomes a purr. "You said we were safe." He pulls my head down to his shoulder, pressing himself against my erection. The heat between us burns almost painfully in his closeness. His hands play over me. "*This* is how you feel, baby. You get us out of trouble like you always do, and then your body is calling me. Every part of you wants me like I want you, even when you try to tell yourself otherwise."

He stays against me, and I breathe him in. The layers of protective feelings I've built up are stripped. Truth. He's my truth.

And so close he's surreal, making me lightheaded. He brings his face to mine, brushing his lips against me...testing. And that spurs me to be the aggressor this time.

I back him against the car as I want to do, against the driver's side door, and cover his mouth with mine. I feel his body pulse.

My own body is commanding my actions, making me thrust against him. His leg curls around mine, pulling me even closer. Our bodies grind together so hard it lifts him off the ground. His arms go around my neck as I hold him up against the car. I want this. I *want* to lose control; I want to flood the trauma that's overtaken my mind in the last few weeks.

For a few moments we move in tandem, breathing hard, all barriers falling away. The urge has never been so strong, even stronger than when we almost hooked up again in August. This is the vortex of intimacy.

And when I'm so wrapped up in it, gripping his hair in one hand and the back of his jeans with the other, dry-humping against him...he pushes me away slightly. Snow is suddenly falling and hitting us. In my mind it's hitting our skin and sizzling. He pauses, meeting my eyes, and kisses me again, still holding me back.

And his kiss is not wild and fiery now, it's slow and romantic and delicate. He uses his tongue and lips to draw over mine so sensuously my blood is pounding in my ears from the feeling. He holds me away to keep his lips barely touching me, back and forth with the tip of his tongue.

Then he eases a little with his hands to allow me closer. Our lips together; pressing gently then moving away, coming back. And it has the effect he wants. This slight contact makes me want more, so much more...and the tiniest feeling is magnified.

Damn him, I taught him about drawing it out.

He finally allows our mouths to come together. I feel us conjoin this way with his tongue against mine, matching my force. The kiss feels longer than all space and time. And I feel as if we were inside each other, sharing each other's bodies.

We don't realize we're moving until he starts to fall backwards on the hood. He catches himself, but I don't let him get up. I'm beyond control; now I cover him again with my body, and his legs go up and around me. I'm half-climbing on the car to be with him, not caring if we make a dent in the car.

This feeling is as powerful and transcendent as the first time we were with each other four years ago, both overcome by what was between us.

I have a desperate need to go further...reaching down between his legs, while my mouth is still on his. I hear him grunting in response. And that drives me to yank his zipper down and shove my hand inside. Where he's impossibly hot, burning my hand.

Touching him makes us both inhale. He looks up at me, hyperventilating. I feel the staccato rhythm of his heartbeat through his shirt, against my chest.

"Gabriel..." His voice is helpless.

I get up on my knees, with his legs between mine. My phone rings again in my pocket. I take off my jacket and toss it, with the phone still in it, to the ground. Then I bring my own zipper down, and take his hands.

He stares at his hands in mine, then up to my eyes. A train passes overhead, making the ground tremble.

And as I start to move his hands to me, we hear the sound of a car coming down the path.

We break apart instantly; I'm off the car in a second to see if it is the man who was chasing us.

It's actually a State Parks and Forestry Department pick-up truck. A lone man inside, probably coming to work on the fence.

The state worker pulls up next to the Camry. I've zipped up, picked up my jacket and I'm taking out my keys as he rolls down the passenger window to look at me.

"You need some help?"

From the look on his face, I know he's being polite.

I open the driver's door. Joel is already inside.

"No, I thought I was having car trouble but it's fine." I get inside and start up before he can say anything else.

The man waits as I reverse and pull the car around the front of his truck and drive back up the path. I'm sure not it's not the first time he's seen something like that, and not the first time I've been chased away from such an area—though it's been a *long* time.

I glance over at Joel as I head back out to the highway. We both have to laugh over the spectacle of getting caught like teenagers.

He lights a cigarette for me. I take it while I call Michaela to see if she's at her office in Newark. I let her know we're coming over. While I'm talking, he keeps his hand on the back of my neck.

On the way, the phone rings again.

"Why don't you just answer; deal with him and get him off your back?"

Since a Dunkin Donuts is nearby, I pull into it. Joel goes inside while I get out and walk to the edge of the parking lot to call Alex back.

He gives me a hard time about not answering before, and I remind him that I was working. He wants to come over and I beg off until tomorrow.

As this back-and-forth continues, I watch Joel go back to the Camry and wait for me. He's watching me too. And with Alex on the phone and Joel in front of me in the car, the seriousness of this situation suddenly hits.

The implications overwhelm me. So much for my double-life with the façade.

And I know it can't go on. But for now, drowning in my mind, in my trauma, I feel helpless to do anything now. My emotions are too much to handle competently. At the moment, I need to engage in my own compartmentalization. I manage to convince Alex to come by my place tomorrow, and I'm off the hook there.

When I return to the car, Joel hands me coffee. He has my iPad out. "I'm looking for more stories about Charlotte Merical. That's the next serious lead, right?"

"Definitely."

He reads to me what he finds online. By the time we're in Michaela's Newark office, I've covered up reality again inside. But he hasn't. I can hear the subtle difference in his voice; feel the energy. And I don't know what to do. I want to hear him like that.

Luckily, a distraction arises in telling Michaela about what happened in Elizabeth.

She holds up her hands "Whoa. I just got out of court with a judge who wouldn't give my client bail because I got another decision of his overturned. And he *likes* me. But I still have a kid sitting in jail. Now someone trying to kill my investigator—investigators."

She gives me a look of compassion and sternness. "Gabriel, I should have known that giving you a strange case would only make it stranger. But go ahead, tell me everything."

Inadvertently, Joel and I glance at each other.

I tell her the rest of the car chase, anyway.

"And why did you not call the police when you knew he was after you?"

"No time. We were in a moving car with this guy trying to shoot us. We couldn't pull over. I did what I thought was best."

She turns that over in her mind. "Okay. Maybe I can buy that. You know the fact that someone tried to kill you *possibly* has a link to Sophie's case, meaning that it could be exculpatory evidence. You know what you need for that? A police report, with an arrest and information on the person trying to kill you. Not YouTube videos of you going the wrong way on 327."

"I was a little tense at the time, Mikki—because this guy was trying to freaking *shoot* us or run us off the road. However, we can still report it. Better with you here."

"Okay, I suppose so. Do you think you have some kind of mark on the car from the shot?"

"Absolutely. And it went wild —I bet they can find the bullet on that street."

"And your driving prowess?"

"I may edit that a bit. No cameras on any of those roads except the Turnpike and maybe the stoplight on 1-9. I doubt they'd appreciate the circumstances for me to tell them the truth."

"I'll back up what he says."

Michaela looks at Joel carefully. Then me. We're not sitting close together. But maybe that's obvious that we're not sitting close together.

"All right, gentlemen. Prepare to stay here while I call the authorities."

A couple hours later, the day is over. My tension rises as I drive back to the city. I feel his as well; waiting for me.

I want to take action; do the right thing. And at the same time, I want to run away. It's not his fault.

Even more so than with Alex, I don't want to come across harsh or abrupt to him. I make my voice as normal as possible.

"I need to take care of some things tonight," I tell him. "Do you mind if I drop you off?"

"Of course, whatever you need."

And I'm then able to let him out at his building. He kisses me briefly before he leaves. I feel that kiss stronger than the previous ones, because of my tornado of guilt and anger and passion storming inside. And because I don't know what to do next, just feeling the chasm ahead of me.

∞

Six ◆ 6 Conflict (Sòng)

Heaven over Water: Contention is approaching from bluntness and division inside the soul. The parties involved mix in turmoil like water and air. The second line (yang/nine) moves: If one of the parties is headstrong, the situation becomes more troublesome and the other may need to retreat.

The Heavens open. The realm where the spirits are, his family. They stand by and hold their hands out as if saying goodbye as he falls backward toward Earth.

He sees the cobalt blue of the sky...the dazzling white of the clouds as he goes head over heels.

The sun makes the air glimmer—he cannot even see the ground in the slow sinuous descent. The music of the spheres is in the tradition of the most transcendent classical...but as he falls in slow motion the music fades into what seems to be dance music from his youth.

Although enraptured by the vision of Heaven above him—fainter in the descent—he becomes more concerned about reaching Earth. He could almost be sure he had wings in Heaven, but as the music changes he's become mortal. Now he's without wings, like Icarus too close to the sun. Transformed...heading toward death.

Then a hand takes his, seemingly from midair. Suddenly he's right side up, standing on a cliff, a rock tableau. The Prophet has his hand. The Prophet smiles, and the ground flames around them—but they aren't burned. In this rich saffron fire, flowing like the robes Buddhist monks wear, the Prophet pulls him closer, holding both his hands. The fire evaporates, the clouds around the cliff fade away to reveal a gentle slope to a paradisiacal valley. Rich in green flora, isolated, sun-kissed, perfect.

The Prophet faces him. "You're mine."

The Angel realizes they have both become naked, and the Prophet has him in his arms. Somehow, they fall again, entwined. Even slower this time, the Prophet's body so warm against his. The Angel finds himself helpless in that sensuous embrace, enraptured by the Prophet's eyes. He seems to be carrying the Angel down to the floor of the valley, landing gently without impact.

The Prophet finally kisses him, making the Angel overcome by his own desire. Feeling the burning of the other against him. The Prophet's hands caress his face. "Say my name," he demands.

The Angel tries and can't speak. Even though he feels his ethereal self has become so rawly physical, almost embarrassingly so; he's not supposed to show this—voicing the Desired One's name is forbidden magic—Abracadabra, Open Sesame. The Buddhist precepts are clear about this.

"Say my name." The Prophet prods the Angel with his own sexuality, forcing him to speak, to erupt, to admit the truth.
"........."

∞

"...Joel..."

I wake up. Immediate feelings of shock, along with more physical reactions from the dream. I look over to the other side of the bed, but I'm alone tonight.

∞

Tuesday, December 7
Elizabeth, NJ 9:30 am

THIS MORNING I HAD CALLED the Women's Freedom Network, and made an appointment to speak to the legal director. I'm able to see him today.

I'm alone this time, because I'm afraid of what will happen if I bring Joel with me. He texted several times over last night and this morning to ask if I'm okay. That's hard to answer, although I tell him yes. My action, or inaction, is not fair to him, but the vortex is engulfing me. I just want time. Just some time to get ahold of myself. Especially as something's been opened inside. I've been flooded with thoughts about when he and I were together, what happened with us, what was right and what went wrong.

Working as usual helps. The WFN is on the third-floor office of a nondescript old building on the west side of town, with a large parking lot in back edged by trees. When I arrive upstairs, the receptionist tells me "Mr. Carlson, the deputy director, will speak with you today."

"Really? I thought I was speaking with your legal director."

"Mr. Carlson heard about your call and wanted to handle it personally."

She takes me back to meet Frank Carlson. We go down a hallway to a square open area with cubicles, and offices along three sides. Carlson's office is along the front side, facing the street. He's in his late forties, a white man with short, dark, wavy hair shot through with gray. Muscular, fairly tall. He has a plain blue dress shirt, striped tie and chinos. He's waiting at his doorway for us, and before inviting me in, talks to the receptionist a minute about her upcoming wedding.

Then he leads me inside with what seems like a genuine smile. His right hand is wrapped in a carpal tunnel neoprene glove. "I hate to be rude, but my hand is really giving me a problem this week. I can't shake hands."

"That's all right."

"Please have a seat. Can I get you anything? Water? Coffee?"

"No, I'm fine, thank you."

He sits back behind his desk and tents his fingers.

"So as I understand this has something to do with our former director?"

"It might. I'm looking into what I think was a slavery operation in the area some years ago, involving some Balkan and Central European women. I wanted to know if your organization might be aware of who might have been behind that slavery ring, or know the identity of any of the women in it."

"You're looking for names of these women?" He nods thoughtfully. "I'm not familiar with the cases from that time. I started here just about a year ago. May I ask why are you looking for this?"

"It's in connection with another criminal case. I have some indicia that the slavery operation may be connected to Ms. Merical's murder. No one was caught for her murder, at least not that I found."

"That's right." His expression turns grave. "I think many people here, and we have a good deal of staff who were here then, never got over that. I was shocked myself to find out about it. No one was caught, you know."

"Right. I didn't even see any stories about possible suspects."

He gets up to look outside, then returns to stand and look down at me. "None that we heard of. I asked our legal director and some other staff about what happened when I heard of your appointment. I'm not from New Jersey, so I hadn't even read about it in the news."

"Where are you from?"

"Michigan, originally. My family lives in Canada now. I've worked overseas for the last fifteen years in some NGOs—Asia and Africa. I was ready to come back to the states and an acquaintance let me know about this position."

"You've done similar work as the WFN, I take it."

"Yeah. Not trafficking exactly, but I was in areas where it was going on, and people were being smuggled to other countries. Thailand, India, Tanzania. My work was helping refugees, building infrastructure, getting medical and food supplies through military blockades."

"No doubt dangerous."

"Sometimes." He shrugs. "It's what you do if you want to be effective. "Blogging and writing letters to the editor don't do much in places with real repression and lawlessness."

"So you understand practicalities. I respect that. I hope in turn you can help me if possible. As I've read about the WFN, you do education, research, lobbying and some direct services —help with getting victims back to their original countries, help with INS, law enforcement. I read of the cases where the organization discovered the existence of trafficking operations and helped shut them down. I'm looking for any information you can share about what was going on in Elizabeth around 2000."

Carlson puts his hands on the desk, then flexes his gloved hand with a grimace. "Not on our server. I've looked for old information, and it seems to have disappeared. We may have hard copies in storage, case files."

Then he suddenly smiles. "Sorry if I seem edgy. I need a cigarette. It's a terrible vice, I know."

I take out my pack of gum and offer it to him. "I'm trying to quit."

"You sure? I'm helplessly addicted myself. We can step out, if you want to sneak one."

For the first time, he seems really relaxed, at the prospect of smoking. I follow him through the office. Some staff stop him to say hello, and he introduces me. Then we leave, heading around the corner of the building to the parking lot. I can tell from the scattering of butts on the ground this is a favored spot.

We light up. He has some trouble holding the cigarette with glove on.

"Any possibility I could see those records?"

He thinks about it. "I could send an intern to try to track them down, if that could help."

"It might help a great deal. Could I talk to other staff members here about Ms. Merical?"

"I'll see what I can do to help. I just ask that you not upset people. Don't make it personal that I said that. I know you're doing your job. But this was such a traumatizing thing."

"Of course, I understand."

I glance at his hand. He doesn't handle that orthopedic glove very well. He should try smoking with his other hand.

"Is that a recent injury to your hand?"

"No, a chronic condition. Carpal tunnel, gets painful at times."

"You planning surgery for that?"

"I *want* to. I'm allergic to general anesthesia. I've been looking into alternative treatments, but Workers Comp doesn't cover it."

"Insurance companies suck, don't they?"

We both laugh over that. Then he checks the watch, also on his right hand. He has to push the glove up. I don't wear a watch, not since the altercation on the subway I told Chiang about. The watch I had then was smashed, the crystal driven into my wrist, leaving a scar. I prefer to keep my hands free now.

"I have a staff meeting coming up. Let's see who's around or who we can make appointments for you with."

We go back upstairs with some more small talk about how the Jets are doing versus the Giants. Once inside, Frank introduces me to the director, Elaine Anthenon, who looks suitably grim about the topic and suspicious about my wanting to know about it.

"Gabriel would like to talk to the staff about Charlotte, those who knew her."

Elaine gives me a less than sincere smile. "Well, while I understand that, I think we should discuss this first. May we get back to you?"

"Yes, certainly."

Frank, looking a little irritated once the director has walked away to a conference room, takes me back to his office to retrieve my bag. His assistant comes over to tell him he has a phone call.

He puts his hand on my shoulder. "I'll talk to her and work on convincing her to let me get those records and for you to talk to the staff. I don't see any harm in it."

"Thank you."

"Can Dee here see you out? I need to take this."

"Sure."

The young lady leads me down the hall again. I notice one of the offices we pass is Seth Monroe's, the legal director. The door is open and he's tapping on his computer.

"Just a second," I tell the assistant. I knock on Monroe's open door.

He turns around. "Yeah?" He's a sixty-ish white man in a rumpled dress shirt, with thinning gray hair and darker mustache.

"Hi. I'm Gabriel Ross, an investigator. I was just talking with Mr. Carlson about when Ms. Merical ran the organization."

He raises his eyebrows. "Yeah, I know he took the appointment you made with me. Why are you investigating it?"

"It's tangentially related to another criminal case I'm working on. Can I talk to you a minute?"

Monroe's curiosity gets the better of him. "I have a meeting soon, but sure."

Dee backs away allowing me to go in. Monroe scrutinizes me. "What do you need to know?"

I sit across from him. "Depends upon how well you knew her and what she was working on right before she died."

"Well, we weren't *close*-close but we talked about things."

"Anything get her concerned that you remember? That maybe she heard about or was told about, like a new slavery ring in the area."

"Told about?" He bites on a pen absently. "I'll tell you, I was sure her murder had something to do with some operation—that she had gotten information about a gang."

"Do you remember maybe if she was contacted by a man named Leonard Mathers?"

"Why does that name sound familiar?" He Googles it before I can say anything.

"Yeah. The dead man found a few weeks ago. Is that your criminal case? I see your name mentioned."

"Yes."

"You think that woman, the one arrested, had something to do with Charlotte's murder?"

"No, but I think Leonard may have tried to tell Ms. Merical about a trafficking operation he discovered."

Monroe stares at me. "I looked you up online, when you made the appointment. You like unusual theories, don't you? Like with the lawyer's case and that foundation. But you were right it seems."

"I was. I'm good at my job. I might be right here, too."

"Hmm." He thinks hard. "Charlotte heard some information, sure. She didn't give me the source's name, but said he sounded a little mentally ill —paranoid or delusional. But she still thought it was worth following. And she said it was connected to a private college in the area."

"Keane?"

"No, Prentice-Cane. I *think* the source worked there. But that's all I can remember."

"Did you tell the police?"

"Yes. We gave them all the info we had. They seemed to think the staff were suspects and that pissed me off."

I laugh. "I know what you mean."

An Outlook reminder pops up about that staff meeting.

"I know you have to leave. Can I have your card?"

"Sure." He hands me one. "I'll see if I can remember anything else."

∞

Tuesday, December 7, Continued
Alphabet City, 7:20 pm

I feel a hand on my shoulder. I jump, unintentionally, from where I'm sitting on a chair next to the kitchen counter. I had been lost in thought, or trying not to think. I didn't hear Alex come in.

Alex steps away. "My God. Take it easy." He scrutinizes me. "What's going on with you? You have me worried. You didn't get back to me about tonight, so I just came over."

His concern strikes me, but also stirs my guilt. I have a hard time calming down inside but try to cover it. "I'm sorry, I'm just tired."

"Really? I wouldn't have guessed." Alex's voice is wry. He looks around the apartment carefully and I realize he's looking for Joel.

Then he moves closer and brings my head to his shoulder. "Maybe you need a change of scenery. Get out of town."

"Um. Can't. Cases are too much work." This is true. I have my other work piling up besides Sophie and Geneva's cases. Now that I'm "allowed" to start working again, I've spent the rest of the day catching up on my regular clients. Background checks, tracing some people who've skipped town, security recommendations for companies and individuals, some legal research for my friend Jim, and fielding emails from various potential clients and nutjobs.

"Come on." He takes my hand and leads me into the bedroom; he pulls me down on the bed and we lay there, his arms around me.

I start to feel like I could go back to sleep again. Daytime is safer for sleep. Less likely to die. Less likely to seem like death. Less inclination to dream and have to face what one dreams about.

Alex tries to make his touch comforting, but it eventually takes on the hint of being sexual, at least for him. We didn't do anything Sunday night; even that has its limits. Alex tends to keep to one way in sex, topping. Not that he isn't good at it, and he'll do more if I make a point about it, because I'm fluid. But I haven't bothered to make a point lately. So I had pretended I needed to sleep Sunday, avoided him Monday, and now I ignore the hint in his touch.

Alex picks up on that and adopts a gentle tone. "I'd like you to talk to me about what you're going through. You did that when we first met, but you're keeping to yourself these days."

"I don't know. I'm just Orpheus descending."

"And that tells me what?"

"That I have some issues."

"You don't have to handle them alone."

I just stay quiet, trying to will myself to sleep.

"I do wish you'd let me in. You have no idea what it feels like to be locked out."

Actually, I do. From being with Joel for two years, I know exactly how it feels. And now I understand what he's going through and also know I can't do anything about it, because I can't tell him. I'm still trying to freeze time.

Alex starts talking about going out of town. "...and my father has this place in France, a family place. You read Patricia Highsmith's books, right? Well, it's like Tom Ripley's villa. He would be happy if we stayed there. I often thought you would do so well in Europe, and my contacts..." He starts stroking me again, pressing against me, sliding his hand under my shirt while talking.

I let it go on, not really listening until I realize he's asked a question. Something about actually moving to this French villa.

"Alex, you haven't known me long enough to ask that. I'm not leaving New York."

"I'm just talking a few months. We can arrange..."

Now I want to scream from frustration, hoping he'll stop as he shifts from the magical villa talk into the school talk. I do care for him; I do appreciate him. But he just doesn't get it. My lack of response makes him tense up.

"I just can't understand why you wouldn't want the opportunity to get an education outside of CUNY. Somewhere very respectable, like NYU..." He takes my shirt off, caressing my back.

I don't resist, but anger rises. "Fuck NYU. Don't insult my intelligence, or my schooling."

"I'm not insulting you; get the damned chip off your shoulder. I don't talk down to you, I just want to see you take advantage of your intelligence."

"Okay, sure." I breathe deep. "You know I've told you enough about my background. You're talking about villas when I want to celebrate surviving childhood. I've told you about being homeless with my mom, when we had to go on welfare, or stay with strangers out of charity because my fucking father abandoned us again. I'm proud of what she did for us, and making something of myself that *she* was proud of."

He starts kissing my neck and my back. "I understand."

Does he really? It sounds like he's just mouthing the words. I lose heart in calling him out on it. Even worse, I know the opportunity is here to resolve this situation, and I can't do it. I'm not just in two realms, I'm in two lives. Feeling his affection, I can't hurt him right now. My own pain makes me not want to hurt another living soul. And feeling what I did for Joel yesterday conversely makes me want to placate Alex, to distance them, to buy me more time.

Sex as anesthesia. Sex as a means of *deferring* intimacy. My disconnection gets worse, thoughts getting in my head even as I let Alex do what he wants, hearing the drawer open and the condoms coming out. Then my body takes over, because that will happen. I give in to it, the vulnerability of being a sexual person, even if that part is not really satisfactory anymore either.

But still, it's a distraction. Or it's guilt, trying to make up something to him. Or it's frustration from what almost happened yesterday with Joel, still needing release. I try not to think about *that*. But I can't help it, because it's so vivid in my mind. And my physical response to my thoughts makes Alex more impassioned, forceful, in what he does. Maybe I feel *his* anger too, and take that as my burden. For a moment, in the physical part of it, I forget.

Afterwards, he lies curled next to me. Four months ago, I would be luxuriating in his embrace, after sex. Instead I feel cold with guilt. Disconnected again, now that it's over. Ashamed, wanting to run away. He can't see this, for which I'm glad.

∞

Wednesday, December 8

On Wednesday I meet with Geneva at her studio in Hicksville, to update her on the case. I could do it by phone, but she has a collection of posters she wants to show me since I'm a movie buff. I want to see her studio and how she does restoration and bookbinding. Joel comes with me this time, as she expects him too.

On the way over, I make a point of talking about anything other than what happened with us. His words get fewer and fewer as we drive, but his feelings get louder. I'd like to pretend it isn't happening, but I can pick up on his frustration. I'm almost afraid of him in the helplessness of my not-dealing-with-it-mode.

But we disengage from that while Geneva shows us her restoration work, the tools and paper, the finished projects, the movie posters.

She has several books in various states of repair. "Because I know you love books when you said you were coming, I set this up."

She starts demonstrating her book work. "See, first I unbind the old book, and take out the old binding threads with a scalpel, that separates everything..."

Geneva goes through the various stages of bookbinding, finally finishing with a piece of red leather. "I make a design in the leather with a bone folder, glue in cardboard for the front and back. I can stamp any kind of logo on the front of the book, put some decorative paper on the inside of the book, attach the pages of the book with leather hinges, and it's done...I'm giving you a hell of a lot of detail, but the work keeps me from thinking about life."

"I'm with you there." I'm fascinated by this, and almost get too distracted to talk about her case, but eventually I tell her what I've found out. Since she's gotten past the initial shock of the birth certificate being fake, she handles the information about the black-market baby issue as best as anyone could. Calmly, but with a sense of surrealness I can relate to.

"So...you think I was the child of someone important?"

"An influential family, yes, perhaps locally famous. It's a hunch. Tracking down who will be somewhat more difficult. We're going to go up to Rochester..." I look at Joel and he nods. "We'll go soon and follow up on it."

"God. I don't know what to think about all this. I guess...my life could be anything. You understand that for me, getting past other people thinking I'm a freak is an accomplishment. This just puts me further on the outside." She stops and puts down her tools.

I walk over to her side of the table and take her hands. "Geneva. Whatever we find out...your life is what you have made it. Not your birth. Look at me; you don't know my story, but trust me, my father thinks I'm a complete failure in life. But I'm not, because I do what I want and I'm good at it. Joel is even better at making his life what he wants it to be. So if you're happy with who you are, what you were and what people think of you mean *nothing*."

Joel backs me up. "He's right. I couldn't say it better."

She hugs us both. "I think I really need to move back to the city. I never was crazy about the Island. It has a way of telling you that you don't belong. I shouldn't have run away, because I don't fit in here." She shrugs and looks at Joel.

"We can help you find something."

"So expensive though...not that Long Island's cheap. I just feel alone sometimes. When I got out of the Army, I had a hard time. I didn't have much money, and my skills were in combat and weapons, and then intelligence and language. Hard to translate into civilian life...I lost connection with a lot of people while I was overseas. And then, coming back I wanted to be alone. I was trying out my new identity. I'd go to stores and buy women's clothes and test them out. People who knew me as this fairly well-built guy, kinda scruffy and tough...I had a hard time showing them my new self. I kept in touch online and came out very gradually."

She stops and goes into a drawer to show us photos of when she was in the Army as Cesare, or Chez, as she liked to be called then. "I found some military LGBT support groups, and that's where I found people who had some similar feelings and experiences. They helped up through the operation, and then I met this guy. And he was good for a while. But he didn't want to tell his family about me. They never clocked me, but he'd have to say something eventually. And he couldn't. He couldn't deal with it. I got tired of waiting for him to deal with it."

"I'm sorry about that. But he clearly doesn't deserve you. And you're brave to be taking care of your business, making these decisions, running your own business. Not to mention living as you want to, and your strength is showing in how you're facing this issue with your birth."

She smiles. "Something about your face makes me want to talk to you, your compassion. Joel said you do that with him too. How long have you known each other?"

I feel his eyes on me. I have no idea what she knows or doesn't know about us, but he usually doesn't share much from a deep-seated caution. "On and off we've known each other for four years."

"He said you're close. You seem so in sync. And do you work out together? You're both in great shape."

I smile at that. "Not really. I do some at home and some at a gym. I think Joel is just naturally the way he is."

"Watching out for Gabriel is a lot of exercise," Joel says.

She laughs at that. "Well, I'd like to get a new routine going. Maybe not an obstacle course like in the Army, but something. I have curves but I don't want spread."

I tell her, "Come into the city again. I'll take you around to the gym I go to. You can prepare to move back. We can even run, and I hate running."

"Where do you run?"

"On the track at CUNY Midtown. I have a student ID; I take a course once or twice a year to keep a student ID, so I can go where my uncle taught. Try to stay in touch with him spiritually."

"How long have you done that?"

"He died in 2004, since then."

"You must be a good way towards a masters.

"I'm not in a program. I just take what I like."

"Maybe it could count as interdisciplinary."

"Maybe, yeah."

She laughs. "Wow." She leans over her work table. "Did I hit a sore spot with you? Your aura just changed to red."

"It always shows on his face," Joel says not-helpfully.

I disregard that. "Nothing to do with you, Geneva. Just my own problems."

"No one should be angry about school, honey."

"Some people think he's not ambitious enough. Naturally, I think differently. Like what you were talking about, with being able to deal. I wish Gabriel would listen to me more often."

I give Joel a sharp look before I can stop myself. That ambition line is from a text Alex sent the day I locked myself in the bedroom.

In any case, we're still supposed to be professional, and his alluding to our personal life bothers me. His returning expression to me is absolute defiance.

Geneva sees something's going on. He makes it obvious. But I'm going to pretend it isn't happening.

"So when can you come into the city?"

"Friday. We'll get together. Joel, are you going to join us?"

He looks at me. "If it's okay with you." He has a slight undertone of sarcasm.

"Of course it is."

Geneva is being nice, acting as if she doesn't see our tension. "Good. I'd like to hang with you together, and not just talking about my strange case."

"Strangeness is how you know you're in Long Island. Did you live in Hicksville originally?"

"Coram. Even worse. You know about Long Island?"

"The crazy parts? Yeah. I've had friends out here. Amy Fisher and Joey Buttafuco. Joel Rifkin and Colin Ferguson."

Geneva nods smiling. "Plum Island. Brookhaven Nuclear."

"Pilgrim State and Montauk Air Force base."

"The Montauk monster and the various Satanic groups."

I'm appreciating this. "Then there's the guy who built a dungeon in his house for his student, the cannibal killer. And the guy who killed his wife and set it up to look like an abduction. Ted Ammon's murder—his wife and her lover. Long Island is bad for spouses."

"And lawyers. Sol Wachtler. And the "Homeroom Hit Man," the "Angel of Death" nurse, the Islip Garbage Barge." She shakes her head. "Now I *really* feel like running away."

"Don't forget the bodies turning up now, more missing people. It's so weird, when the island itself is so beautiful in parts."

We talk some more about her work, until finally we have to let her get back to her own business.

But I'm feeling a little wound up by Joel's testing me. And rather than drive back right away, I need to calm down. I ask Geneva about any good spots to look at the water nearby.

Geneva's recommendation is a now-deserted parking lot near the ocean. Once we arrive there, I get out to stand by a wooden railing separating the parking lot from the beach, which is a gentle slope to the water. It is beautiful; the ocean is turning stone-colored in the winter weather.

Although I'm intending this as a peaceful interlude, I'm fooling myself. The countdown to a confrontation is up. I can sense his thoughts from here, and when I hear the passenger door open and his footsteps on the asphalt, I know what's coming.

∞

Joel's head is buzzing now. Gabriel's pretense that nothing's going on is fueling Joel's frustration. Conflict is one thing; b`eing ignored is torture. The rest of Monday itself was torture for him. He went home and just lay down for the rest of the night. He couldn't concentrate on anything other than what happened between them. Eventually, that led him to do what he does so many times at home, getting himself off imagining them together. In his mind, taking what happened under the bridge all the way—while also trying to pretend he's not on his bed alone.

He's waited for the resolution, and it didn't happen. This morning he listened to Gabriel rambling on through the day about the Yankees, Tarot versus I Ching, whether another James Bond movie would be made—anything other than the giant unspoken issue between them...and he felt unreal. Sad, scared, angry, unreal. And what was before, the pretending, is no longer an option.

Joel leaves the car and follows him over to the fence. He knows he provoked Gabriel with what he said back in Geneva's place. But that was deliberate. Even an angry reaction is a reaction.

Ready or not, it's going to storm.

Gabriel suddenly speaks without looking at him. "One of the primary concepts in Daoism is *wu-wei*, not taking unnecessary action."

"Really? It sounds so *fucking* profound." Joel's voice is more sarcastic than he intends, but it just comes out.

Now they face each other. Gabriel finally lets his emotions show, his face getting red at the edges.

"Bringing our personal issues into a client conversation is unnecessary, to say the least."

"You could just say don't put our business on the block. But you overthink it, making it all *spiritual* and shit."

"Goddamn it, Joel, I'm trying to deal with you like an adult. You were doing it deliberately."

"*Of course* I was. I wanted your attention. What the fuck happened with you yesterday, with Monday night? What did you do? Did you do...*anything*?"

The look on Gabriel's face tells him. Joel thought from what went on between them on Monday, Gabriel would have to finally end it with Alex. What other possibility could exist after that? And he said he was going to "take care of things." He had to have meant that.

But apparently not. Because Joel sees by the deer-in-the-headlights expression that Gabriel realizes all this right now.

Joel takes a deep breath, surging with adrenaline inside. "You've shut down again, haven't you? Jesus Christ, you talk about unnecessary action. What about you living a lie right now? "Unnecessary" is you being with him. You're with him to *avoid* being with me. Living the lie."

Gabriel tries to keep control nonetheless, under the spotlight of Joel's fury. "We both have issues in deception. But I didn't want to talk about this now."

"Fuck that. I deserve to *know* what you're thinking."

Gabriel runs his hands over his face, taking a step back. "Please, Joel."

"No. This has gone on long enough. Do you want him or me? Say it."

"Fuck!" Gabriel stares at him. "It's not that fucking simple of who I want. It's whether things are different."

"You mean with me, don't you? If *I'm* different. You need to give me a chance to show you."

And now what they've gone over in the email drafts is really coming out. Without a filter, without a means of distance.

"Give you a chance...Well, welcome to my world. That's what it was like for me when we were together. Do you know what a failure I felt like? How frustrated I was that you'd never trust me, that you couldn't even tell me you loved me, because it didn't occur to you to give *me* a chance?"

Gabriel suddenly slams his hand against the wooden fence hard enough to make it rattle. That surprises them both. "I wasn't lying, Joel. I wasn't going to hurt you. And you kept running away."

"But I'm *here*, Gabriel. I'm here for you."

Gabriel closes his eyes, reacting to Joel's desperate tone. "I was so glad when you came back. I spent two fucking years wondering what happened to you. I missed you every Goddamned day for months. I couldn't get involved with anyone else. I wondered what was so wrong with me when we were together, that I couldn't convince you to be with me. Not fuck me, Joel. *Be* with me. There's a difference."

Gabriel tries to take out and keep hold of a cigarette. But the cigarette bounces away from his fingers and the entire pack spills from his hands. He gets down on the asphalt to try to pick them up.

Joel gets down as well to help him, seeing that Gabriel is losing control. Tiny snowflakes are falling and sticking on them. But a totally different tenor than the snowfall in New Jersey.

"I know the difference," Joel says quietly. "I was afraid. I admit that. I regretted it every moment." Joel's voice loses the anger he had before. "I didn't mean to make this worse, I want to make you better. You don't understand; I would do anything for you."

Gabriel sits back on his heels, taking the cigarette Joel hands to him. He stares at the sky for endless moments.

"I *know*. You think I wouldn't do anything for you too? That isn't the problem. I'm to blame for this. I put you in a bad position...you came back in my life, and I let you work with me...knowing what you feel. And I did that because I didn't want you to leave again. And I was so moved to hear about what you're doing with your art. I just wanted you to be happy. I just wanted to be part of that. I still love you."

Although Joel was so sure of this, he wasn't sure at the same time. Gabriel saying that is like a revelation from the Heavens. And it sets them on a different course, because it can't be taken back.

But the revelation is not making things any easier. If anything, Joel feels like the world suddenly became more difficult to navigate. Especially as the confession seems to put Gabriel in more pain.

They're starting to be covered in snow, but it doesn't matter. Joel struggles with what to say. "I was two people when we were together. One part of me was terrified you were...toying with me. I'd give anything to be able to live that again and tell you I loved you. So that you didn't have to wonder. I drove you away like a self-fulfilling prophecy."

He reaches over to touch Gabriel's arm. "How am I supposed to show you things are different if you don't give me that chance?"

Gabriel wipes the snow out of his hair, and digs for his lighter. "I'm afraid now, Joel. This is what happens with you and me. I feel too much for you. I couldn't live with you leaving me again."

He lights up as Joel stares at him. "You left *me*."

"Did I? I walked away, but you left me before that, by refusing what I gave you. You lied to me about what you were doing. I thought we were building something, but that wasn't the case at all. You held yourself back from me. You shut me out."

Joel gets up, defensive and frustrated. "No. No, that's not how it was. I didn't lie. I just didn't talk about it. You were always the most important person to me, ever. You don't *know*, do you?"

"You never told me. How could I know? Each time you left for days and didn't say where you were going, each friend you didn't introduce me to, each part of your life you didn't share with me, it killed me...and it still happens."

The two men look at each other from their respective positions. The snow falls harder, wind making it sting. The words make their ears throb, chests hurt, throats feel tight.

"I love you so much," Joel whispers, the words falling out.

Gabriel is still kneeling on the asphalt. The tears finally come to his eyes. He's not moving, just looking up at Joel, like he'd just stay there until he's buried in snow. Joel realizes Gabriel is shaking uncontrollably. He remembers seeing Gabriel passed out, remembers that Gabriel has been crashing mentally, and his protective part kicks in.

"You're freezing. I don't want you to get sick." He takes Gabriel's arm and leads him to the car. "I'll drive us back, okay? Just take it easy."

∞

Inside the car I feel how cold and wet I am. Joel starts up the Camry, then finds paper towels from somewhere. He wipes the snow from me and makes sure the heat is directed at me.

We don't say anything on the way back. He keeps the radio on loud.

When Joel parks in my neighborhood he says, "I'm going back to my place, okay?"

He reaches for his bag out the back seat.

"Don't do this," I tell him. "Maybe we've said too much. But don't leave. We can still talk."

He opens the door and looks at me before getting out. I see my own pain reflected back to me. "Sweetheart, I'm talked out."

He moves quickly before I can stop him. And the irony is when he walks away, I feel exactly what I was afraid I'd feel if he left me.

∞

SEVEN ◆ 23 STRIPPING AWAY (BŌ)

Mountain over Earth: Things are falling like a landslide from a mountain. Foundations are unsteady, strange forces may be at work dismantling empires. The third line moves (yin/six): In spite of the turmoil, the superior person seeks out wisdom in order to protect against the landslide and stay upright.

∞

Gabriel's in prison now, on death row. A man appears in front of him. Murray Head as Judas in *Jesus Christ Superstar.* His mother had the album from the early Seventies London production.

Judas/Murray speaks to him. *Why are you doing this?*

He grips the bars in front of him. *Sophie didn't deserve this. I can take on her sins. I can take on her punishment.*

Even to be executed?

It's the only right thing to do.

Judas nods. *If you think so.*

The cell door opens. He walks out and Judas begins reading the 23rd Psalm.

They end up in a small room. A window presumably allows an audience to see this execution, but he can't see anyone outside.

The prosecutor is waiting with a smirk for Gabriel to get on the cross-like table.

Then he's strapped down and his arms are punctured with tubes.

You ready to pay? The prosecutor is about to pull down the switch. The switch was for the electric chair, but it's working the drugs now. *Last words?*

Yeah. Innocent people have been executed before. Cameron Todd Willingham. David Spence. Larry Griffin. Ruben Cantu.

The prosecutor shakes his head. *Liberals.* With a sneer, the prosecutor pulls the switch.

On the table, he sees silver mercury flowing down the tubes toward his arms.

Then a voice from the audience. Kent's voice. *Gabriel. You can't be killed for this. You didn't do anything.*

He responds. *I can take it.*

No. You don't go this far. Get up and take those out.

Kent's voice is imperative. He sits up, tearing off the straps. He goes to the window and puts his hands on the window. He can't see Kent, but sees his hands against the window.

Take them out. Take them out. Take them out.

He stares at the tubes in his arms and reaches for them. Can he get them out in time before he dies?

∞

I WAKE UP SCREAMING...soaked in sweat. Another hour to get the shaking under control.

In the elevator, my downstairs neighbor gets in and asks me if I'm okay. "I hear things...like you're having night terrors..."

"Sorry." I look away. "It's a bad time."

"Let me know if I can help," he says in that way people do. Good intentions but they know they can't do anything.

I leave the building as fast as possible for my car.

∞

Thursday, December 9
Union County Jail, Elizabeth, New Jersey, 10:30 am

By the time I'm at the Elizabeth jail, I've recovered. I've been to this jail many times to speak to Michaela's clients, so the staff knows me and I don't need special arrangements from Michaela to get in.

Soon enough, I'm in an interview room with Sophie again. She smiles, happy to see me. "Mr. Ross."

"Call me Gabriel." I reach over the table to touch her hand, trying to be strong for her, not let her feel like she's in a bad way.

"Okay, Gabriel. What can I do for you?"

"Tell me how you are doing."

"Well...it's hard. I can't go out. I stay to myself. I'm not like the other people here, and that makes me nervous. I read when I can, to have something to do."

"I'm sorry about this. We're trying to find out anything helpful."

"I know. I know it takes time."

"I was wondering if you can tell me some more about Leonard."

She looks sad. "I can't believe he's gone. He was such a nice person. What did you need to know?"

"The other places he might have worked or hung out, besides Wildemore."

"We didn't often talk about work. He liked to tell me about things he could see in the universe, and about opera, of course. He could see so many beautiful things, especially if the music was playing. He said music could create things in the ether. I wished I could see what he did.

"I wish I could too."

"He would try to draw them. He didn't want to talk about unpleasant things with me. I don't need to be protected, but he was like that."

She then stares at the floor like she's thinking. Five minutes go by without her moving. Then her head comes down with a different look. Edward. He falls into a similar posture I saw the first time.

"Gabriel..." He nods at me.

"Edward. How are you holding up?"

"I can handle it. I take over f' her when I can. You're asking about Leonard. Did you find out anything so far?"

I tell him about what I found in Wildemore —the tribute to operas, the costume from Carmen, the names of the women.

"Does any of that mean anything to you?"

"It's reminding me of stuff. Yeah, Leonard liked women. He respected them, ya know? But, it's kinda ironic, he was always around or working for people who treated women bad."

I start to ask questions but he isn't finished.

"Leonard felt women have been slandered in history. That's how he put it. So for him any tragic or fallen woman is actually good; an angel."

I think about that. "Like Carmen for instance. I saw he favored that opera. A Gypsy woman who was free with her favors. Possibly assisting in criminal endeavors. With his love of opera, she'd be supreme in his pantheon."

"Ex-*actly*. He was a rescuer. And Carmen, I remember him talking about her. She was magic; he was sure she could help others."

I imagine Leonard invoking the power of Carmen to help him rescue the women in Elizabeth. Perhaps he thought the sexually-trafficked women were slandered. Certainly, in a way, that's true.

I read Edward the names that Joel translated.

"They don't sound familiar. If they aren't characters in an opera, if they're real people, they are women who had something bad happen to them, probably."

"He'd think Carmen could save them."

"Or bring them back to life, yeah."

"But Leonard wouldn't have hurt them."

"No, never. That wasn't him, ya know? He was sincere about that."

I write all this down quickly in shorthand. I realize I'm using some of the Gregg shorthand I've picked up in translating Kent's notes.

"Did he ever work at Prentice-Cane?"

"Yeah. Maybe not formally, but for some professor there. He had a girl there, too. I think she's left town. He didn't tell me everything, because he was...how d' I say, discreet. I couldn't always tell what was real, an' what was real just to him."

"He had a girlfriend. Okay, I need to follow on that. You know her name?"

"Sara. No last name. He said she liked art. That was about all he said. Never saw her."

"And this professor. Was this person one of those ones who didn't treat women right? See, I want to find anyone who Leonard might have known, would have had negative feelings towards, and who could have been involved in a criminal operation exploiting women."

"Well, the professor, I don't remember his name, but I think he was in psychology. But if you really want to know about someone who knew Leonard and hated women, that would be Don, his brother."

"His *brother*...I haven't seen anything about him even in the case file. Is he in this area?"

"Don was supposed to have killed himself back about ten years ago. But his body was never found."

"Excuse me?" I stare at him. "He killed himself in 2000? Tell me about that."

"It was a strange situation. Don was a fuckin' *bastard*. Leonard hung with me, as I told ya, and every once inna while Don would drop by. He didn't fuck with me, but Leonard would be a nervous wreck around him. Don taunted him and shit. Couldn't stand that guy. He was supposed to have hung himself in Black Mountain Park, don't know why. Believe me, we didn't care."

"Would you remember if Leonard talked about anything that happened that year, maybe about women in trouble...something he discovered?"

"Okay, yeah. He said some women in town might be in danger and he had to look into it. He said he was looking for a muse like this writer in one of the operas he liked, a German guy."

"E.T.A. Hoffmann."

"Yeah, *that's* the one. He said this Hoffmann guy wrote horror stories, right? Well he wanted to help these women. He may have. He didn't speak about it again after Don hung himself. But I'm remembering it now 'cuz Leonard's been saying lately he was haunted by Don. Some mechanical doll version of Don. Him and not him. Like in Hoffmann's stuff."

"I'd like to know more about Don."

"Talk to Bob. We felt the same way about that fucker."

I shake his hand. "Thank you, I'll do that."

Then I wait for him to leave, and Sophie to come back. And talk with her some, to help her feel more comfortable before I leave.

∞

 I call Bob, who's got time for me to visit him in Paterson. We could talk on the phone, but the drive is my version of meditating and winding down from the visit to the jail, which has me wired with this new aspect of the case. Being on the move gives me a better sense of purpose. Paterson isn't that far from Elizabeth in any case.

 The drive also reminds me of the car chase. And what happened after. I'm worried about Joel. I'm listening to his playlist of my iPod with songs like *Kissing a Fool, Another Sad Love Song.* I guess I know the theme.

 Last night and at various times today I called him and texted him. No response. Nothing. That's like him; but nonetheless, he has me worried. Not just about what's between us, but whether he's safe. Somewhere out there are people who tried to kill us. Before I go in Bob's apartment, I text him again. I don't push it yet. I just hope he'll relent and say something.

∞

 "Don-Fucking-Mathers." Bob sites back in the La-Z-boy in his apartment in Paterson. "I hadn't thought about him years, but of course I hadn't thought of Leonard either."

 "How did he get along with Leonard?"

 "He didn't. Very different persons. Leonard was crazy but decent. Whereas Don was a cold man, violent, probably a sociopath. See, Leonard and I would hang out at Edward's place, the garage in Sophie's house. Edward would work on our bikes. I was riding then; thought I was Peter Fonda or something. Edward could make those things hum. Other people in town would drop by. Edward didn't tolerate funny business, so it was like Rick's at Casablanca. Shady people like me, but no trouble.

"Leonard wasn't close to Don by any means, but Don would show up and listen to us. I think just because he scared Leonard sometimes. Brothers can be cruel, and Don was a cruel man. He was freaked out by Edward a little, being in Sophie's body. He didn't mess with Eddie much. But Don did like to talk about some of his...I don't know what to call it. Terrible things he claimed he did. Mostly violent, often involving women. He hinted he had killed people. We never knew if he was lying or not. Leonard was always bothered by what Don would say, and how he would speak about women."

"Leonard wasn't a criminal mastermind at any time, then. I need to be sure about that. He wouldn't do something like kidnap or pimp women."

"God, no. Never. Leonard was into some iffy things on occasion, like I was back then. Me, I needed the drugs. And Leonard couldn't hold a 9 to 5 job because of his mental condition. He wasn't the criminal type. He could never handle it well because he thought too much. Like you, really."

"Thanks."

"Not a bad trait, Gabriel. In any group you'd be the moral center. We need people like you. I sure as hell can't serve that purpose. In any case, Leonard was seriously delusional and you aren't."

"Ask Danny for a second opinion on that."

He smiles. "Danny's a good guy, but he doesn't run your life."

"That's why he isn't talking to me right now. Back to Don. Did he hang himself or not?"

"Seemed like it. I think the cops found DNA on the rope. It was broken off. The theory was he tried to, fell down, and wandered off in a daze. Got lost, had a heart attack, eaten by animals."

"The grizzly got him, huh? You believe that?"

"Who the fuck knows? It was creepy though. Don was the kind of guy you drive a stake through his heart and cut off his head to be sure, and then salt the earth. But no body ever turned up."

"What did *Leonard* think?"

"Well, this being Leonard, he thought Don had made a pact with the Devil, that the Devil inhabited Don's body, and the Devil took his body away at some point."

"Ah, *Faust.* The Devil. This makes Leonard's writing suddenly very clear. Edward said Leonard believed Don was haunting him recently."

"Don kind of haunted us all while he was alive. I couldn't say what's going on lately, though."

"I take it Don had little trouble hurting women?"

"He hurt several women that I know about. And some men. We saw him beat up a few people. Bar alley fights, that kind of thing. He bragged about what he did to women, but he never did it in front of me. I wanted to kick his ass so many times, but I wasn't in good shape. But if I'd seen him hit a woman, I would have done *something.*"

"How did Leonard feel about Don's violence to women?"

"Hated him for it, but he was also terrified of Don. Don carried this aura of coldness, of brutality. Hard to explain unless you met him. We always felt that going against him was deadly." Bob frowns, going back in time. Regrets in the past.

"What did Don do when he wasn't being a general son of a bitch?"

"If I remember right, Leonard told me after Don finished college, he worked for some crime victims compensation board in the county. Yeah, I know—the irony, or whatever. But apparently he was well-respected there. When I knew him, he worked at Wildemore. As a patient advocate."

"Seriously?"

"He didn't show them the same face he did to us. That I know. I'm telling you; he had a spotless rep in town with the 'good' people. That's one reason Leonard never said anything to anybody except Eddie and me."

"Jesus. Okay. Was Leonard at Prentice-Cane when you knew him?"

Bob lights a cigarette and offers me one. "He had just started. I moved from Elizabeth in 2003. This professor had also worked at Wildemore."

"You remember this guy's name?"

"What was it...something maybe Serbian. He's in prison now..."

"Serbian? No shit, that connects with what I think Leonard was looking into."

"Yeah. This guy, he was running some kind of weird scam on campus with some students, a cult type thing. Devanović. That's his name."

After leaving Bob, I call Michaela and update her on what I found. Then I do some research in Elizabeth again, looking for people who knew Don and Leonard.

∞

Notes: Faulkner, Sophie L. #UC 11795
Pretrial —Attorney Work Product
SUMMARY INTERVIEW
Ellen Richards 515 Forest Road, Elizabeth NJ
Neighbor of LM's parents
12 /09 /2010

ER cooperative. Has no opinion on case. Does not know SF. Knew LM and DM's parents for 20 years. DM was a "perfect son." Attentive to parents, excelled in school. Friendly, outgoing, a "good citizen." Parents leaned on him b/c of LM. LM always a problem b/c of mental issues. Parents didn't want to institutionalize him. ER appreciated that DM would "look out for" LM. Even tried to be LM's guardian, but LM fought that.

SUMMARY INTERVIEW
Daniel Osterberg 8432 Twohill Street, Elizabeth NJ
Coworker of DM at Union County Board of Crime Victim Advocacy
12/09/2010

DO cooperative. Had not heard of SF's case. DM excellent worker, dedicated. Peacemaker at work. Volunteered while getting BA in public policy at Rutgers. Always cooperative and committed to helping crime victims, especially women. DO said he wished he knew more people like DM. DM had sometimes spoken 'sadly' of LM. DM even suggested even that LM was 'dangerous' to others.

∞

Thursday, December 9, Continued
Newark, NJ 1:10 pm

"Are you still having a rough time, Gabriel?"

"Not in work, I think we're making progress in setting up a different narrative. If you mean personally, let's not go there."

Michaela's reviewing over my notes while we're having a late lunch in her office. Or at least she's eating lunch. I have some fruit juice and an uneaten sandwich, which she keeps looking at and frowning. I'm listening to another concerto grosso on her Bose device, where every note sounds like my soul being torn.

"You aren't taking care of yourself. Eat, for God's sake. You look absolutely miserable. Doing anything tonight?"

"No. You want to?"

"Yeah, but I'm not sure what. Put you to bed and watch over you, maybe. How are you feeling?"

"All right. I've been keeping busy. Sleep sometimes is hard. I'm staying up late…which doesn't mean I'm having problems in my work."

"Okay, don't get defensive. You're busy; we know it's good. So where's Joel today? He's supposed to help, right?"

"He's busy too."

"Taking care of other cases?"

"No…well, not for me. I'm not sure what he's doing.'"

"I'm not hearing that. I saw how you two were with each other in my office the other day. You tried hard, but he was practically at your feet. I knew something had happened."

"Yeah, something did. But I didn't handle it well." I tell her everything that's been going on with Joel and me, up to Wednesday.

She nods. "So that's what's bothering you. You're tired of Alex wanting to change you and you're still in love with Joel. I'm just damned surprised Alex didn't see it. Now I know why you never wanted them to be in the same room. I saw you and he had unfinished business. I was waiting for something to explode eventually."

"It's exploding. In my face."

"Try to be kind to Alex."

"Like I wouldn't?

"Look, I want you to work it out with Joel. He's my boy. But separating one's self means romanticizing the one you want, and demonizing the one you don't—I've *been* there."

I play with the straw in my juice. "Right now, I'm not romanticizing, I just want him to call so I know he's okay. Anyway, I'd rather talk about work. I can still do my work right, at least."

"Yes, you do, honey. You're right, we have a good lead with this brother. Although I don't look forward to how our prosecutor will treat this. It's Stan Cooper. You know what he's like."

"Yeah, Stan. He'll be glad to know I'm involved. We're lucky if he doesn't ask for the death penalty." Suddenly I remember my dream. Perhaps Stan was the prosecutor there. He'd pull a switch on me for sure, since I made him look bad in a trial not long ago.

I sweep the uneaten lunch into a bag to throw out. "I gotta go now. I want to see someone if I can. If you want to do something later tonight, I'll come back."

"Yeah, we can see a movie. Bring Veronica, maybe. And try to eat now and then. You can't live on feelings for nourishment."

"Sure. I'll take that into consideration."

She looks at me knowingly. "And keep calling him."

∞

On the way back to Elizabeth, I get a call from Bettina Carver. She's the attorney with whom I interned back in 1993, during college. I had talked her into the position even though I wasn't in law school. I stayed in touch with her on and off. A couple times when she had big cases, I went up to help. She's why I know Rochester pretty well. And I miss her. In the midst of my misery, I'm so glad to hear from an old friend. To bring some light in.

"How are you? I've seen some of the stuff you've done. Some good work."

I laugh. "Really? My press has been bad lately."

"Pish posh. Word gets around. What can I do for you?"

"Do you know anyone in the police records department? I need a file."

"They have FOIA form online."

"Yeah—if I have a month or two to wait. Come on, beautiful. I know you can talk someone into snatching a file."

"God, you're too much. Maybe. What are you looking for?"

"July 17, 1976. Arson case. A building belonging to Bernadette McCabe burned down."

I give her the address. "I need whatever's there, but the police reports at least. Interviews, witnesses, suspects."

"I'll see what I can do."

"You need to grease the wheels, that's fine. Let me know how to get it to you."

"I'll front it. I know you're good. If I get anything, I'll overnight it."

∞

What I want to do when I get back is see Bertrand Herrmann. I call him once I'm back in my neighborhood and ask if I can visit him in Brooklyn; he's up for it. I hit a couple stores before I catch the trains there, using the time to wind down.

Bertrand Herrmann is in his seventies; over six feet tall, a little overweight, a bushy beard, wears rumpled chinos and sweaters. He smokes heavily and has various dogs and cats running around his brownstone apartment. They are all my friends, particularly two bulldogs, Larry and Michael (Herrmann is a basketball fan), and Jonah the tiger striped kitten. They run up and greet me. I have indulgences for everybody, including for Bertrand a few Padron 1926 Serie No. 2 Belicosos, which run $18 each. Herrmann runs his hands over them with pleasure, taking in their scent, and then tucking them in his humidor while I play with the animals.

Herrmann has a faint German accent and occasional tendency to pepper his conversation with German or Yiddish. "So, you are still continuing your secret studies, is that right?"

Herrmann had once worked for the West German Central Office of the Land Judicial Authorities for the Investigation of National-Socialist Crimes (ZS) in the early 1960's, hunting Nazis. Herrmann knows the whole story with the Tertullians and I, as well he should. He had explained the origins of the group to me. The intricacy of their work, and the effort to which they embedded themselves in global financial culture. I think only Herrmann can appreciate my quest, at least now that Kent Varney is dead.

I haven't visited him since September, and I should have been, as a friend. He is the only person outside of Joel who knows the whole story of what happened. Somehow, visiting him, an older man with the weight of experience, comforts me. Like visiting Chiang. I don't feel like I have to pretend to be completely well.

I tell him about information I found two weeks ago in Kent's notes, about the bank.

"You're going to keep looking into this, Gabriel?"

"Yeah, but not right away. I'm having some difficulty with the cases I have now, because of personal issues. But I will, I'm not giving up."

Herrmann gets up to makes some tea, and comes back with a tray. Then he lights a pipe and considers me.

"What are you going to do with this information? You risked your life more than once to find out about the Tertullians. It did some good. But what are you planning to do that you could do safely?"

"I was told to stay away from anything to do with them. Zest made it clear I would be watched."

Bertrand picks up one of the cats. Jonah stretches in my lap and luxuriates in my scratching his chin. "They are not a large group. Just well-placed. They have too much to do to be following you. But if you were *obviously* investigating them, then you'd have them on your back."

"I don't like being warned off. I'm not foolish about it —I'm not going to publish anything; I doubt any newspaper would believe it in any case. I can't let it go, though. People have died over this —for decades. If they were exposed enough, maybe they could be broken up and disappear. But it's something to work on in the future..."

"You are continuing with your regular detective work, pretty well, I hope?"

"Business has been good. In fact, I've come up with another difficult situation, involving human trafficking. Slavery. I wanted to talk to you about it. Maybe you could give me some ideas on where to proceed."

"Really? How did this come about?"

"Criminal defense. We're not defending the traffickers, but these people may have committed a crime our client was accused of. I think some women were imported here from Baltic, Slavic or Central European areas. They were likely kidnapped, kept captive, maybe forced into sex work."

"The connections will be difficult to establish."

"Tell me about it. I might be able to uncover something in Jersey, but not necessarily where they came from."

"I know people who know people, as they say. Do you have any names?"

"Of some possible victims, yes. Also, a man who might have been involved. I'm going to look into that further. Nikola Devanović. I did some research today and found out he had involved some students in a fake psychological self-improvement program. All female victims, looks like he was a predator. He's in prison now, but not for fraud. No one could prove that. They found out his medical license wasn't good. He's in for four years, but due for parole soon."

I explain some of the background of Sophie's case. "Devanović is Serbian, like some of the women. Leonard's brother Don is known for being violent with women —maybe he was running the slavery operation. Devanović is a psychiatrist. He probably knows something about manipulating people."

"I'll ask my contacts if they've heard of Devanović. You connected him with Leonard Mathers. Now you need to connect him with Don Mathers."

"I have. He worked at this hospital Don worked at. And, Leonard worked there too. Don's sure a better suspect for killing Leonard than Sophie."

"This Don Mathers, he must have other family. Someone had to report him missing..."

I think about the case file I read. "The parents did, some time ago. They're deceased now." I pull my iPad out my bag, leaving room for Jonah the kitten to crawl in and make a nest. I call up my notes application. "I want to see about Don's death. I'm suspicious of that, because of my last case..."

"Use your instincts. Who would be Don's heirs? The parents?"

"Probably. I can look and see if by chance anything was filed in Union County Chancery Court."

"Perhaps, if Don and Devanović were working together, they might have had some sort of legal venture or agreements. That happens with criminals as well as legal businesses, and most likely with anything fraudulent."

"Like a business? If Don is dead, or pretending to be, he couldn't remain on the documents...I see what you mean." I think about it. "I have to search for any legal documents with Devanović's name."

While Herrmann smokes, I check the Union County database, and also Westlaw. Twenty minutes of reading gets me some interesting information. "Listen to this. Devanović had a court case while in prison; he had Don declared dead. Not easy, because he was incarcerated and not a relative, but apparently Don had a life insurance policy listing Devanović as beneficiary. Devanović and not his parents. How weird is that?"

"That gives you an idea of their connection—Don Mathers had to escape the notice of the police. Devanović...maybe he kept up the operation."

"Right. This connects Devanović with Don even more so. Now the question is can I find out what happened to Don? And would Devanović be willing to talk?"

"I'll see what I can find out from my contacts about him in particular. Maybe it will help with leverage."

"Thank you. I'm going to look at the case file for the declaration of death and see if anything else interesting turns up."

∞

Eight ♦ 36 Brilliance Injured (Míng Yí)

Earth over Fire: Someone is injured, a situation has become difficult. The key to overcoming the dark time descending and remaining true to what one believes. The fourth line moves in this reading (yin/six), which means somewhere internally one recognizes danger, and uses that information while biding time.

∞

From the Rochester, NY *Times Gazette* December 3, 2010

Rochester firefighters battled a blaze in a former retail store on south Dewey Avenue Thursday night. Three people in a neighboring two-family house were treated at Rochester Memorial for smoke inhalation. The store was completely destroyed, and the house sustained significant smoke damage. The store did not have a sprinkler system.

In controlling the fire, one firefighter was injured after falling through a second floor in the store building. Authorities say the cause of the fire was likely arson. Investigators were at the location today with a dog to sniff for traces of accelerants, but no word has been given regarding a particular cause. Rochester has had a record number of suspicious fires in 2010, including locations in Henrietta, East Rochester, Gates, and Irondequoit. A source told the *Times Gazette* that this fire was similar to others in the year in that the fire completely surrounded the building from the outside, as if an accelerant was poured around the entire perimeter of the building.

∞

Friday, December 10
CUNY Midtown 100th Street South Campus 9:38 am

GENEVA AND I are on the track at CUNY Midtown, pretty much alone. It's an outside track, just cold enough to keep moving.

I held out some faint hope that Joel would just show up, but no. Eventually she asks where he is.

"He couldn't make it." What I really want to do is ask her if *she's* heard from him, but that would be so awkward.

"Is he giving you a hard time?"

I smile, not genuinely. "No, of course not."

"Now, I know better. I've seen star-crossed lovers before. I've *been* there. You don't have to tell me."

I feel suddenly exposed. "Really?" Does the whole world see my personal turmoil?

"Gabriel. You two are so obvious. You may not be 'together,' but your feelings radiate around you both. Look, when Joel first described you to me, I knew he was in love with you. And you care about him so much. It's in your eyes. His not being here bothers you. Do you want to talk about it?"

"God, I wouldn't want to add to your stress by talking about the problems in my life."

"It's easier to be there for someone else than yourself, right?"

"Yeah, but you're a client. How bad is it for me to just break down when you're depending on me?"

"Joel told me that you never, ever fail a client. He admires and respects you so tremendously. I'm not going to see you being upset as a problem with my case."

I'm getting back to the feeling of running again. Dominic drilled the exercise into me in spite of my dislike of it. The familiarity allows the mind to wander. But now I stop, and lean against a nearby post. I'm trying to think of something to say. Talk about it, not talk about it. I look at her, now standing next to me.

She puts her arms around me, a simple gesture of compassion. I feel so lost. What am I doing? What have I done?

And then my chest hitches as I lose control for a moment. She stays with her arms around me. "It'll be okay. I know it will. We'll both be okay. Just hold on to me."

∞

Friday, December 10, Continued
Canal Street, 12:45 pm

"You remind me of an obscure philosopher in ancient Chinese history. Mo-Tzu. He was from the peasant class. But inside he was superior, his character. It's not what class you are, it's what you are inside. Mo-Tzu went against the mores of society at the time —he didn't believe in class structures. He believed in equality and the principle of universal love."

"Why isn't he better known?"

"His ideas clashed too much with the idea of social stratification. He was harshly criticized by the Confucianists. But he's not forgotten. He was a man of honor."

Gabriel is sitting cross-legged on a mat, sharing tea with his teacher. "I appreciate the comparison. Honor is a difficult concept. It's misused so often that one can argue it has lost meaning."

"Granted. But answer more directly. What is honor to you?"

Gabriel thinks carefully. "Understanding a personal code of ethics —and doing your best to live by that."

"Yes. Keep in mind that it means bearing a lot of weight at times. Having to be strong when others cannot. Having to act when others cannot. The fundamental part of the Dao is going with nature. Feeling the rhythm of the universe. Just as Hinduism is other-directedness. And Buddhism is compassion. All of that must override your anger. At yourself and at others. You have the ability to heal others with your words and actions. That means you can hurt them severely as well."

Gabriel burns in rushing mentally through every harsh word, every wrong action in his life. Chiang holds up his hand. "The past is a lesson, but not a punishment. Don't move to act from guilt, the action becomes meaningless. Act from compassion because this is right."

Chiang puts his hands on Gabriel's shoulders. "You have to heal yourself, coming through the fire. What I see about you is more and more positive. I see your strength. You are still living with one foot in the ghost world, and one in this world. The ghosts are not as hungry, but you're reluctant to leave. Consider that you're meant to visit that world now and then."

Gabriel stares at the ideograms painted on the walls of the studio. "All my work now seems to involve people, events, horrors...erupting from the past and demanding attention."

"That is what you do. Think of the past as being in bondage. You're freeing something that needs to be freed. The Brhadaranyka Upanishad says, "As a man acts, as he behaves, so does he become. Whoso does good, becomes good. Whoso does evil, becomes evil. By good works a man becomes holy, by evil works he becomes evil.""

Gabriel thinks about that, imagining one's work making one's character. Imagining things being released from bondage.

"You have learned to rely on yourself. Be strong for yourself. Trust yourself. Most certainly part of this is due to your mentors being taken from you, and others not being there the way they should. That has harmed your ability to trust."

Since this dovetails into what's on Gabriel's mind, he becomes even more attentive.

"I'm not talking trust in business, but in life. You are guarded. You trusted me to teach you the moves of Baguazhang, right?"

"Yes, sir."

"But not about your emotions. In the five years I've known you, you were reluctant to address this. Finally, you broke away because you could not trust me. Not about your internal forces."

Gabriel looks away again.

"No, you don't have to feel bad. You were right."

He builds upon the surprise in Gabriel's eyes. "Maybe I had to learn something too. What you needed wasn't advice but guidance to find the truth in you. It's there. I just want it to flower now, not spend years to tear down that Berlin wall you have inside."

Chiang moves closer to Gabriel, to make his words more important. "You're ready to hear this now. You want me to tell you, and you need it. I knew from your posture. You're defiant, but you want guidance. That is the same with trust. You take on too much, and close yourself. Let me give you a metaphor. You know of troubled children, adolescents?"

"Yes." Gabriel has volunteered with these children, been one, knows ones who are adults.

"In all but the most far gone, the child will always want to be loved by the parent, no matter how angry, defiant, or challenging the child is. That is why these children will run to parents who are horribly abusive. They hope for change; they desperately want that. The child never leaves inside."

"Humans don't stop hoping for the best."

"Humans want to be good, so they believe others want to as well. And with the child, when a betrayal occurs, that is the worst thing to happen. The trust slowly becomes locked away. Most people aren't bad. But the child as adult will see them all as bad."

"Self-fulfilling prophecy," Gabriel says, and remembers where he last heard those words. Why that now seems so important.

Chiang gives him a minute to collect himself. "Yes, expect the world to be a horrible place and it will not disappoint you...Your father betrayed you, Gabriel. He made it clear he was not there for you. Men betray you —this is in your mind. Manuel did when he died. Dominic did when he died. You wanted that eternal father's love, approval. You still do. You can let your father out of your mind. He may never give you the validation you need. You have enough here with me to make up for that. To give you a basis of love, of trust."

Chiang is not put off by the tears he sees. He expects that. Welcomes it as the message of transformation.

"I realized I need to be here for you. We do not have a typical teacher-student relationship, but in the Dao, you go with intuition. Mine has always told me to nurture you, and to help you find your truth. Oliver Wendell Holmes said, "Alas for those that never sing/But die with all their music in them." Most people do what someone tells them, what they feel they must do. And often for the wrong reasons."

"I feel like I know what I want to do, to be, who to be with. But I have a real trust problem."

"But something within you recognizes that life can be given another chance. You survived this summer because you needed another chance at life. You came back to me, because you wanted to give yourself another chance. Not me, *yourself*."

Gabriel feels a resolution. It's mixed with fear and uncertainty, but he can feel it getting stronger. "Second chances. It's a leap of faith."

After seeing Chiang, I drive over to Union County Civil Court to go through the case file for the official declaration of Don Mathers' death.

As I'd hoped, the file includes a police report of Don's missing person report. It also contains the police report of his supposed suicide and photos of the area in Black Mountain State Park. I make copies of all of these.

The work keeps my mind busy, and I'm helped by Bettina's efforts. She doesn't waste time and she goes the extra mile. She's found the reports on Bernadette McCabe's case, scanned them and emailed them to me in a zip file. I take the printed-out files with me to an area coffee shop for some consideration.

Fire and police reports. McCabe is listed as missing. Knox is noted as an employee sought for questioning. The detectives on the case spoke to Knox's mother a few times. She lives in Greece, a neighborhood of Rochester.

A quick search on my laptop turns up Terry Knox at the same address. Ms. Knox would be about 78 now. I go ahead and call her. I introduce myself and say I'm looking for McCabe.

Her voice is low, clear, and strong. A touch rough. Her tone is definitely unfriendly.

"Why are you calling me? I don't know who that is."

"Your son worked with her? Arthur never told you anything about her?"

"No. Arthur never talked about work. Why do *you* want to know?"

She says that in an offensive way—but she's not hanging up. She wants to know what's going on.

"A current investigation, ma'am. When was the last time you spoke to Arthur?"

"I don't remember. It's none of your business anyway. What kind of investigation is this? Are you a cop?"

"I'm an investigator. I'm not at liberty to discuss the case. Is Arthur still in the Rochester area?"

"I haven't seen Arthur in years."

That rings false to me; she says it too fast and her voice rises. If that was true, she'd either say it flatly or with bitterness. "You know Arthur was suspected of being involved in the fire that destroyed McCabe's house back in 1974."

"He didn't do anything! That woman was responsible for it all, McCabe. I told the cops that. I told his sister too when she..." suddenly Terry shuts up. She said too much, contradicting her previous assertion she didn't know who McCabe was.

I make my voice soft. "If he's innocent, wouldn't you like to prove it? I'd like to talk to Arthur about that."

She curses—very nasty for a senior citizen—and hangs up. No matter, I wasn't interested in her concern for his guilt or innocence.

She made another mistake, mentioning the sister. I go back to my notes, documents and databases. Knox's younger sister is Nicolette, now Nicolette Kellian. She lives upstate in Skaneateles, New York. I try her home, no answer. She may be working.

Around seven that evening I try again, and get her this time. I give her the same explanation.

Nicolette isn't hostile, but very cautious. "What *exactly* are you looking for?"

"I want to talk to Arthur. I can't find out where he is now."

She draws in breath sharply. "You don't want to find him. *Believe* me."

From my own experience I recognize the tone of a family member who is *done* with another.

"I do, I need to in order to help someone else. I know some of his history, if that's what you mean."

"Not *all* of it. Not when we were kids."

Her tone alludes to something dark. "I'm sorry about that. Sounds like it was very tough for you. I got the impression Arthur was unrepentant about his problems."

"He *liked* what he did."

"Setting fires?"

"That was the least of it."

"Something sexual?"

"Oh yeah. The less said the better. And he stole, all the time. I thought he'd be like one of those guys the FBI profiles."

"Your mother...didn't feel the same way. Maybe still doesn't."

"You talked to her? Good luck with that. She didn't believe me, the teachers, the cops, no one who tried to tell her about him."

"I take it you're not in contact with him."

"Hell no. If he shows up here, I'll shoot his ass."

"Any chance he might be in Rochester still? Maybe visited your mother?"

A pause. "Yeah. I know she's been in contact with him. He can do no wrong with her. I don't speak to her much either. But I called her on her birthday last month —and I heard his voice in the background. The angry whine he always had. She hushed him quick and when I asked, she said it was the TV."

"Thank you for telling me this."

"Are you trying to do something about him?"

"Indirectly. I'm not sure where this is leading, so I can't promise anything. But he's not someone I'd protect. Let me ask you one more imposition—do you have a picture?"

She hesitates. "Not recent, if I do. I don't have many happy memories of him."

"I understand that completely. But *any* kind of photo would help. I've never seen him."

"I think...in one of my storage boxes. You need this now?"

"Yes, as soon as you can. I'd pay you to send it to me, or a copy. If you could even scan it and email it to me..."

"You don't ask for much, do you?"

I am asking for a lot from her. But she has a lifetime of anger to drive her to do so.

"If you can't, I understand. It doesn't change history. I'm just trying to help another person, who was caught up in the schemes he had going on."

"He's probably still setting fires."

"I don't doubt it. That never stops."

She's thinking. "No one has really tried to stop him. I don't understand how he falls through the cracks. If you find anything that works against him, are you going to hide it? Let him go? Make deals with him?"

She has bitterness, understandable. It's colored her outlook. I know those cops would be happy to put Knox away. But I won't argue. I can't outright lie, but taking on an obligation is hard.

"No, anything that serves as evidence against him that I can turn over, I will."

"All right. You sound sincere, I guess. I said what I had to say. This is the last thing I wanted to do for the holidays, but since I have to dig around in those boxes for Christmas decorations, I'll take a look now, get it over with before I change my mind. If I find something with him, I'll take it to Kinkos. I'll have to take a Valium for this."

"I'll reimburse you for your efforts. I know this is horrible." I give her my contact information, thinking of personal hells people live in, that follow us around regardless of how we try to rebuild life.

Then I call Bettina to thank her for her efforts. "I have a request. Do you have, or know, any criminal informants who can give me the lowdown on Rochester happenings?"

"Anything specific?"

"Someone who might help me find an arsonist. I see fires have been increasing in the last couple months."

"You have a particular arsonist in mind?"

"Yes. This person may be the Rochester area, but keeping under the radar. If you know a good prospect who could possibly have an idea where he hangs out..."

"Yeah. Antonio. Let me call him and vet you. Probably cost you a hundred or so —and you'll probably need to come to Rochester, he doesn't do things in ways that can be recorded."

"I can do that; it'll be good to see you again."

∞

Notes: Faulkner, Sophie L. #UC 11795
Pretrial —Attorney Work Product
SUMMARY INTERVIEW
Wende Newkirk   978 Joslyn Street, Apartment 12, Elizabeth NJ
12/10/2010

Phone contact. Knew LM and DM in high school and later. Reluctant to talk. Does not know SF. No opinion on case. Said the sole person who might kill LM was DM. Would not elaborate for some time. After lengthy talk, WN said she has a history of drug use and did not want that to come out in court as she's trying to rebuild her life. Said DM was a "fraud." Was sure he had hurt animals and abused girlfriends. Had two girlfriends at once many times, one "good" girl he was public with, one less so —troubled or vulnerable, he'd be terrible with —physical mistreatment. WN said she and other "rejects" like LM knew about DM's real personality but the rest of the world "thought he was freaking Clark Kent." LM not dangerous. Mild-mannered, gentle, terrified of DM. DM often cruel to LM, but not when any "good people" could see.

SUMMARY INTERVIEW
William Church   P.O. Box 13821 Viscount, Michigan
12/10/2010

Phone contact. Knew DM and to a lesser extent LM, at Rutgers. In DM's classes. WC had problems in college w/anxiety and drug use. DM did not use drugs but hung out w/WC and others who did. "Seemed to like to watch us like lab animals." WC picked up that DM was abusing a girlfriend, Anne. WC told Anne she should leave DM. DM later ambushed WC outside a bar, "beat the shit out of me with a 2-x-4." DM called police anon. Police found cocaine on WC. DM had alibi for the time and was not arrested. DM claimed to police he was trying to protect Anne from drug user's influence. WC in hospital for a couple weeks, then had a 3-year prison term for drug possession.

∞

An apartment building on 17th Street off 9th Avenue, close to midnight. A window opens on the second floor and a fortyish man looks outside at the front stoop. A short in the buzzer is making a loud crackling noise every time someone presses the button for an apartment number. And the second-floor resident has heard this ten times in a row now, from the man on the stoop.

The resident says, "Will you just give up already on the buzzer? That's *Goddamned* annoying. He isn't home or just doesn't want to talk to you."

The man on the stoop, in a black leather jacket and jeans, ignores him. The resident recognizes him as the melancholic person who visits the artist on the third floor. Some drama must be up with them tonight, since the man presses the buzzer again. For twenty seconds straight. The crackling sounds like someone being electrocuted.

The second-floor resident angrily leans out the window. "Fucking maniac! I'm calling the cops."

The man below smiles. "Why don't you mind your own business, or come out here and *make* me stop?" His tone is polite, but his face is serious. It unsettles the other man enough to make him slam the window down.

The second-floor resident checks out the window every so often and sees the unwanted visitor sitting on the stoop, his head down on his knees, for the next forty minutes or so. He stays still, even with the snow starting to fall on him.

∞

Saturday, December 11
Alphabet City, 10:27 am

I'm in bed late in the morning. While I told Alex I was wasn't feeling well last night, we're supposed to have dinner with his prep school friends in from London tonight. I know I should just cancel, but I can't work up the nerve. I'm lying here with the window open, to cool off from the night sweat. Archie's watching out the screen for birds. He looks over at me. *Hasn't this gone on long enough, man?*

"Yeah," I tell him.

I get a text from Alex about the dinner tonight. I don't respond for now, staying in the darkened room with Archie. Feeling alone.

You're not alone. Archie comes up to lie beside me on the damp sheets. *You just gotta get a fucking move on things.*

Things are moving—outside the personal life. Late yesterday Frank Carlson called to say he had some case files for me to look over on Monday or Tuesday. Also, I had called around the Prentice-Caine campus looking for someone who would be willing to talk about Leonard, his girlfriend Sara, and/or Devanović. An art history teacher recognized the names and told me I could speak to her next Wednesday, after her finals were through.

But then there's today.

And while I'm debating getting up or just staying in bed. Giselle calls me. She's just saying hello, not really having any questions or concerns.

"I'm seeing Sophie today. Would you like to have lunch with me? Just to say hi."

I do, and take the PATH train to avoid rush hour traffic.

Visiting Giselle is a relief, an oasis of sorts, because she's so nice. When we meet at her shop, she takes my hand gently in hers and gives me her smile, like she's genuinely glad to see me.

We make small talk for a moment. She considering adding a tarot class to her repertoire and when she finds out I know tarot, she's delighted and wants me to help out. She also shows me new items in her store that came in.

"Do you have any women in your life who you'd like to buy a gift for? I can give you a nice discount."

I think of Veronica, who doesn't wear feminine clothes. And Chris, who I know sometimes does. That leads me to Joel and I block the thoughts. "I have several female friends. I should get them all something."

"Holidays are coming up. I'll take you around and help you out."

"Next Saturday maybe? I'm grateful for the help, actually. Thinking out gifts is troublesome this year."

Giselle gently pats my arm. "I can see you're a little stressed about something. Just relax while you're here. We can play with the cards."

And we do, at a cleared display table. At least until the store gets busy. It's Saturday, a shopping day, and she's up and helping her two staff people. Some customers ask me about the cards, and Giselle encourages me to read for them. It's such a spontaneous thing, and I enjoy it. I also like watching her cultivate and help the clients. I end up staying past lunchtime. A male couple come in to look over a selection of Buddhist and Hindu charms, and I explain their meaning, which gets more people interested.

Giselle's brother Jacob comes in and sets up mail orders. Giselle does a huge amount of business online, more than the foot traffic. Jacob is like her, just with dark hair. He's a little shy at first but warms to me eventually.

Somehow, I stay at Giselle's shop for hours. She has a way of making me feel I already know her, and she involves me in what's going on, and I've been introduced to tons of people as her friend.

Finally, around four she sneaks out back for a cigarette, and I join her.

"You have been so good to have around here, such good karma. I hope I see you more often."

I have to smile. "You don't know how revitalizing this was for me today."

"I do. Sophie says you're a strong compassionate person, and that Edward thinks you're smart, right on the case."

"I'm encouraged by their confidence. I hate to drag in the case, but did you ever meet or hear about Don Mathers? Leonard's brother?"

She drags on the cigarette. "I knew Leonard had a brother, but he died or committed suicide before I met them."

"That's what I heard. I suicide in Black Mountain Park. Did Leonard ever mention a man named Devanović?"

"That was his boss. He hasn't talked about him for a while. I think Leonard stopped working for him and went on disability. He seemed happier, but then..."

Giselle looks like she's thinking back. "Something was bothering him."

"Did he think he was haunted?"

"Yes! I didn't want to say it. I believe in ghosts. I don't know what Leonard saw, but he felt it was someone connected to his brother, or a messenger from his brother? He talked about operas that involved deception or doubles. He used a German word...I bet you know it."

"*Doppelgänger?*"

"Yes —I knew you'd know. Do you believe in ghosts? I thought so. Leonard wanted me to find charms to drive the doppel...whatever it was, away. I wish I knew you then, you'd probably know what to use. This shows you're meant to be on this case, Gabriel. I'm so happy you're here. You and Michaela. I couldn't even talk to that other awful attorney."

"I'm glad I'm on it too. I heard Leonard had a girlfriend. Did you meet her?"

"Oh our poor Leonard. He was careful when he talked about others. He mentioned his girl. She was special, you could see in his eyes. I encouraged him to bring her around the shop and he was thinking about it. I'm sorry that didn't happen. He needed someone. I want to find Sophie and Edward someone. What about you, Gabriel? Do you have a boyfriend?"

The question takes me by surprise. "I don't know how to answer that. No, that isn't true. I do." And I have the strange feeling I have no idea who I'm referring to. But that isn't true either.

She sees that. "Someone's on your mind. He is special, I hope."

"Yes." I think of my situation and what I need to do. "He is. He's here for me when I need him." Even though he isn't right now, ultimately that's true.

"You'll work it out, what's bothering you. With my boyfriend, we haven't been together *too* long but he listens so well. He works so much, but our time together is great. He's been a rock when I need to talk. A lot of men just would be nodding their heads, like "Yeah baby, you have some crazy friends. Let's go to bed." Tom isn't like that. He takes an interest in Sophie's case, going over things with me. He keeps me calm when I get angry about things, tells me I have to be strong for Sophie. Like about that idiot defense attorney. Tom tells me not to make it personal. You'll have to meet him."

"I'd like that. We should get together. God...I just realized I have to be somewhere tonight."

"With your boyfriend?"

If I answered yes or no, it would be true. For some reason, I can't lie to Giselle even to pretend. "Um. Not exactly. But I hope to see him soon."

She puts her hand on my face. "You do what you need to do. What's next for the investigation, if you don't mind telling me?"

"Monday, I think I'm going to Black Mountain Park. I want to follow up on Don Mathers' death. I hope we get some real information out of this."

"You will. I feel it." She hugs me before I walk away. And then as I head to my car she says, "What's his name?"

I stop and look back at her. I could just say I'll tell her about the situation another time.

"Joel."

Giselle smiles. "I want to meet him, too."

∞

Saturday, December 11, Continued
Canal Street, 10:37 pm

Joel is working on one of his pieces in stone and clear acrylic, in the loft studio he's rented. What he likes about this new place, besides the light from big windows and a skylight, is that no one cares about the frequent use of electrical tools for carving or the implements needed to shape glass. The area is noisy anyway, day or night, on Canal Street. And he likes taking a break to look out on the street eight floors below.

His work has moved into sculpture, for the very physicality of it. He's been doing this since his time spent with Jan in Amsterdam earlier this year.

The studio has the potential to be a showpiece. However, he doesn't have it set up for beauty or comfort but to have the tools where he needs them. For now. His idea of living here and of making it a *place* with his own furniture and style is on his mind.

Right now, the studio is white walls and ceiling, wood floors, minimal appliances other than large speakers for his iPod dock. There's also a couple of kitchen chairs, a few small wooden tables with more computers, a bicycle, and a mattress on the floor covered in one sheet.

Much of his previous work is also stored here: on shelves, under tarps, in cabinets. Some of his several dozen paintings hang on the walls, contrasting with the white and sparseness with depth, color, and most of all emotion.

He hasn't yet told Gabriel the details of the showing. He hasn't even introduced Gabriel to Isabella. As Gabriel had said, which is hard for him to acknowledge.

Isabella is here with him, preparing for his showing. She's a tall voluptuous dark-haired woman of Iranian descent, a couple years older than Joel. She makes notes, takes pictures, studies each sketch, painting and sculpture with an intensity of a person who loves her work. She has known Joel since they were both street people in the 1990s. She likes to give him a hard time, reflecting back his own kibitzing. Her confidence in him abates his fear of being out in the world.

But she's also his friend. She knows something of the situation between him and Gabriel, and she's interested in the works that represent Gabriel. Many, many sketches of this man Joel is hung up on, and several paintings that are slightly surreal, of Gabriel represented by mythological figures or other symbolism.

"So have you talked to him about your showing?"

"Yeah."

She's used to his taciturn responses. Joel doesn't tell everybody everything about his life. Different people hear different aspects, some of him is hidden from everyone. Even the persons closest to him can only get so far. With each he has certain vulnerabilities.

"And you say he's coming to the gallery when it opens?"

He doesn't answer. His hardheadedness is worse tonight.

"Maybe he better *see* them first."

Now he stops, in wiring the delicate system he's set up for his current work in progress, to see which one she's looking at. "He's not going to be bothered by nudity."

"I would hope not, from what I see." She then flips through some sketches. "What is this—a take-off of that drawing in *Titanic*?"

"I figured out an inside joke between him and a friend of ours and drew it for kicks."

"Hmmm. You went full frontal here, too. He won't lack for admirers...much like you."

He frowns. She's reminding him of the occasions they slept together. Nothing shameful about it. But he's having issues with everything now, she notices.

"Let's just keep that drawing private."

"I see. So, has he seen *any* of these?"

"A few things. Back when."

"Well, he's going to be knocked out." Her tone is dry. She's thinking that if Gabriel has any feelings at all he'll be deluged by the effect. And that Joel better show him first. She'll have to work on convincing him of that. It gives her ideas to make the showing even more dramatic than planned. Multimedia, breaking fourth walls, all kinds of ideas arise.

Joel doesn't comment further, and she lets him be for the moment and goes about her planning.

Then his phone, on a table between them, rings; he glances at the caller ID but doesn't answer. Three rings and it stops.

Five minutes later, three rings again.

Five minutes later, three rings again.

After the fourth time she's irritated, more at him than the noise. "Either answer or turn it off, for God's sake."

He ignores her. She pauses in her evaluations and considers him. When he acts childlike, he's impossible. She goes to his phone while his back is turned. The rings start again. The caller ID says *Gabriel.*

Aha. With a natural impudence Isabella answers his phone. "Hello?"

Joel drops his tools and jumps up.

On the other end, Gabriel sounds both surprised and concerned to hear her voice. "Hello. I'm looking for Joel."

She likes his voice. "Yeah, I can *tell.* He's here working in his studio. I'm Isabella, his gallery agent."

She hears him sighing, as if he's relieved. "*Isabella.* You're the one who convinced him to have a showing. I wanted to meet you, though he's been very circumspect about it."

"Circumspect, ain't that the truth." She smiles at Joel's scowl, which bothers her not at all. "I'm *dying* to meet you now. I feel like I know you. Not just from what he's told me, but from what I've seen of you in his work. I want to talk to you about it."

Joel's burning her with his eyes, while Gabriel is nonplussed on the other end of the phone. "Really? I didn't know he had much stuff with me."

"Oh, he does. We were just talking about it."

"Oh...um, his work is great though, isn't it?"

"Oh, yeah. He's going to be big if I have anything to say about it.

"Well...I hope to see it all someday...if he has me over there."

"You will. You'll be *my* guest at the opening if nothing else. In the meantime..."

Her voice trails off, helpless as Joel walks away from her to the other side of the loft. "Uh..."

"He's there, right? He doesn't want to talk to me."

Isabella feels terribly awkward now. "Well, um..."

"Goddamn it, I'm sorry to put you in the middle. If you know him, you know what he can be like when he's stubborn."

"Yes, I know." She's staring at Joel's back as he's looking outside.

"Please tell him this—and again, I apologize for asking you, but these are special circumstances—tell him I need to know he's all right. We had trouble in New Jersey on Monday. We were in danger. I've been worried about him, regardless of what's happened between us. Especially after some things that went on this summer."

"I'll tell him." Isabella mutes the phone, and walks over to Joel. "Talk to him. He said he needs to know you're okay." She tells him exactly what Gabriel said.

He turns his head towards her. "He told you that? He doesn't bring up our business with strangers."

"Well, he did with me. It sounds like he's more worried that you're *physically* safe than about whatever argument you had."

Joel goes back to staring out the window.

"Did you know he was worried about you?"

He shrugs. "He left messages. I just didn't want to talk. You told him I was here, so he knows."

"You're such a brat. If he wants to know you're okay, don't make him suffer. If he doesn't say things to strangers than he must really want to hear from you, to tell me that."

Joel suddenly feels a rush of guilt stronger than his anger, especially thinking of his ignoring Gabriel being outside his building last night. He takes the phone from her. She retreats to his kitchen area to give him privacy.

Joel unmutes the phone and sits on the floor. "I'm sorry."

Gabriel sighs deeply on the other end. "Jesus Christ, don't do that to me again. Please. I don't care if you yell at me, if you're angry, even if you hate me. You haven't been talking to anyone—not Veronica, not Geneva, and they're worried too. I don't *have* Chris's number. I've felt fucking helpless. I was going to call until doomsday if I had to...but please don't *make* me. Don't let me worry *if you're still alive.*"

Joel feels his face burning. "I forgot about that. I was feeling hurt and I didn't think..." He hears street noises. Gabriel's gone outside somewhere.

"Joel, you don't know what it did to me when Nelson took you. Because of *me*. And now someone else trying to kill us..."

"I do know, I'm sorry. I was upset..."

"I understand what you feel. You and I, we need to talk, to make things better between us."

"Better. Okay. Where are you now?"

"Daniel." An expensive Manhattan restaurant. "I'm having an evening I don't want to have. I'd rather be with you, even if you're angry with me."

Joel doesn't realize he's crying until a tear hits his hands. "I'm not. I was just being an idiot. Leave him. Come over here."

"We're not alone. I wish I could walk out. I did to make this call, and that already pissed him off."

Joel feels his heart pounding so hard he has trouble talking. "What can I do to help?"

"I just need you. I don't know what else to say right now. It's not the right time to really talk, not when I have to go back in and put up with his friends pretending I don't exist for another hour."

Joel hears the strain in Gabriel's voice. "You don't have to. Get out of there. Come over *here* and be with me."

Now Gabriel's breathing deeply. Thinking about it, maybe. Caught between ideas about what the right thing is.

Then Alex's voice, irritated, in the background. "Here you are. What exactly are you doing?"

A pause. "I'm on a business call. Do you mind?"

"When you keep getting up to make calls, yes. When you just walk out without a word, yes."

"I didn't just walk out; I wasn't part of the conversation inside."

"So you left to sulk. Charming. Who are you really talking to? Let me see..."

Alex must have tried to reach for Gabriel's phone. Now Gabriel sounds angry. "Are you kidding me? Don't ever try that. Just go back inside."

" *You* come back inside. You know what this looks like?"

"It *looks* like I took a phone call. Now it *looks* like I have to leave."

"Excuse me?"

Joel holds his breath, listening to this.

"I have something to take care of. Sorry."

"Are you joking? Wait, you're *seriously* going. Gabriel! What the fuck? What am I supposed to tell them?"

"Tell them I left, obviously."

Joel can tell Gabriel is walking away from Alex.

"You can't just do this," Alex says.

"It's an emergency, it happens. Go back to your friends, Alex. They won't even know I'm gone, trust me."

"Gabriel, *please.*" Now Alex suddenly sounds contrite. But it doesn't stop Gabriel.

"I'll talk to you later."

Joel waits another minute, hearing Gabriel get in a cab, and telling the driver to go to his address on Canal Street.

Joel closes his eyes. "Gabriel?"

"Yeah. I'm coming over. You're at your loft, right?"

"Yes. You've never been here; something else I should have done. It's on the 8th floor. It's the whole floor."

∞

Joel's suddenly a tornado of activity, putting away his tools and the paintings with Gabriel in them. He's not ready for that. Isabella watches him, amused. When Gabriel arrives, she buzzes him in, and greets him at the door.

She looks him over. "Damn, you're all he said and more."

He laughs, taking her hand. "He probably said too much. I'm so pleased to meet you, for what you're doing in getting him to move his ass on showing his stuff."

"I want to talk to you about all this, sometime soon. Tonight's probably not the right time, but we definitely will."

Joel comes up behind her. He has his arms folded from nervousness. "Uh, you want to look around?"

"I already see that it's better than the place in Chelsea."

Isabella steps aside, and Gabriel reaches out to touch Joel's head briefly.

Then his attention is caught by the line of paintings, and the sculptures in progress.

"You *are* serious about this."

Gabriel walks in further to the center of the loft, and crouches to look closer at what Joel's doing with an acrylic work on a pedestal. "It reminds me of Frederick Hart."

Joel goes over to stand beside him. "When we met, you told me my drawing reminded you of Doré. I had to look him up. I realized it was a compliment. I read about Hart from your books. It's what inspired me."

Gabriel looks up at him. "It's supernatural, the figures inside."

"Took me forever to figure out how to do that. See, when it's turned on..." Joel presses a hidden switch. Different hues of white light create more intricate patterns in the acrylic.

Gabriel spends several moments staring at them. "This reminds me of what I've read about art in Daoism. An effortless projection of the world that becomes real itself. The *Zuangzhi* speaks of artisans who use the Dao as they work, by losing themselves from the world and self-consciousness...the tools never get dull because they move in the spaces between the materials...Joel, whatever credit you get for this won't be enough."

"Does he talk like this all the time?" Isabella smiles.

"Yeah. You get used to it. Eventually. It just becomes more startling when he goes back to being street and starts saying 'motherfucker' every other word."

She laughs and walks up to Gabriel. "He will be appreciated. I'll make sure of it." She kisses his cheek. "I'm going. I hope to talk to you soon, Gabriel."

Joel accompanies her to the door, where they say their goodbyes.

Gabriel is now staring out one of the windows. "This isn't far from Chiang's place, actually."

He turns and surveys the room again. "I didn't realize how much work you must have created over the years."

Joel watches him walk slowly around the loft. He tries to cover his nervousness by straightening up tools that have already been straightened. "Uh, yeah. I should have showed you more than I did. Isabella, she's like, doing something different. You know how I told you the community is changing around here? The art galleries are being pushed out by the technorati?"

"Driving up the prices." Gabriel goes to study a couple of the paintings hanging on the wall. "You're sort of art deco/surrealism/romantic. I hate to keep saying that it reminds me of people, but it does. Yet, I see you in there. I see where your heart and soul is in the imagery."

"Yeah? You can say what you think about it—I mean, who it reminds you of. I'm not insulted or anything. So, like, Google's moved in, and other tech business...the prices of building space is going for $125 a square foot. And then, other stuff is going on. More artists are being encouraged to create for the benefit of the super-rich patrons. Sometimes being a gallery owner is as Quixotic as owning a bookstore."

Gabriel laughs. "Jason would agree. All right, I'll tell you. I see influences of Tamara de Lempika, Giorgio De Chirico, Joseph Stella, and Phillipp Runge."

"Damn. Yeah. I forget, your uncle must have known those styles."

"Are you kidding? He *tested* me on them when we went to MOMA. So what is Isabella doing different to show you off?"

Gabriel looks back at Joel.

Joel smiles hesitantly. "Do you want something? I mean, to drink."

"What do you have?"

"Same stuff you have. Wine. You could probably use it."

"I could."

Joel goes back to the kitchen, brings over a bottle of rosé and hands him a glass.

Gabriel sips it slowly, looking at the sculpture. Joel turns off the ceiling light with a remote control. It makes the piece even more surreal and beautiful.

"Isabella's going virtual and mobile. She's reserved a gallery in a cultural center on the East Side that still has reasonable room rates, rather than rent a street-level space anymore. No regular foot traffic but she's banking on a strong internet presence. With a revolving stable of artists and investing a lot in publicity. She focused on me because we're old friends."

"Or because of your talent. She can't afford to just be nice."

Joel shrugs, looking down. "Well, I don't do what's trending."

"Baby, I suspect you'll *make* the trends. It's so hard for you to hear something good said about you. I've always seen that, like you're feeling now. Is that why you don't tell me about this, what you're doing?"

Caught by surprise, Joel moves away to his iPod deck, messing around with the controls. "I don't know, maybe."

"You believe what I tell you, that I'm sincere?"

"Yeah.

"Foolish boy. That first night I met you, I just told you I liked that drawing of angels to get you into bed. The whole "painting a mandala for me" thing was all a ruse. I hate having that on my wall for four years. I've seen better stuff in a Motel 6."

Joel finally is provoked into smiling genuinely. "Okay. I get it."

He meets Gabriel's eyes. Gabriel walks over to him, and holds his arms open. Joel embraces him. They automatically hold each other tighter. He feels Gabriel stroke his head. Softly, but with emotion.

"This is crazy, baby," Gabriel says. "I'm crashing inside but still, I need you. I realized that over the last couple days. I need you with me."

Joel exhales, hearing that, and buries his head in Gabriel's shoulder.

"You're not as bad as you think, you're just...traumatized."

"It's more than that. Joel, you're about the only person who understands that right now I have to work. I haven't fucked up these cases yet and I'm not going to. Working will ultimately save me. Especially if you're here. You see why I need you? You understand me. I think I understand you, and how you've changed."

Gabriel kisses the side of Joel's head. "Neither of us want to 'talk' like this—like the line in *Seinfeld*, "nobody *needs* to talk." But we do. You and I have trust to build."

"We don't trust each other, you're saying."

"Um. Come on, let's just sit together a minute...well, you don't have a lot of furniture yet."

Joel lifts his head. "Uh, no. I haven't thought about that, but I need to get stuff. These chairs are just utilitarian. But you know, you can have the mattress."

"Sit here with me. Baby, I'm not here for sex, or revenge. I'm here for you. I'm here for us. And bring the wine over; I might have another glass."

The mattress is under a window cracked open for a slight breeze. Gabriel kicks off his boots and sits on the mattress next to the window, resting his arms on his knees, closing his eyes, leaning his head back. The cold air slightly ruffles his hair.

Joel gets down in front of him, with the bottle, filling his glass. "What does that mean, *here for us*," he says carefully.

Gabriel opens his eyes. "You know what it means. But I think I need to tell you because you're uncertain with me. I guess that's my fault. It means I realized we should be together. But I have to do it right."

Joel puts his arm across Gabriel's knees and rests his head there. "What do you have to do, then?"

While he talks, Gabriel reaches to take Joel's other hand. He holds it in both of his, massaging it. "I need to tell Alex. And I have to do that in person. It sucks, but I have to do it. I do care about him but it's not the same as with you. Nonetheless, you have to understand that. I can't just say *fuck you* and walk out.'"

"Is that so?"

Gabriel smiles wryly. "Yes. I don't always handle things well. I chose to be here with you, but what I did to him was bad. I should have canceled going out with him altogether but I was a coward about it. You know, living a lie, like you said."

Joel reaches for his cigarettes, takes one out and then gives Gabriel the pack, putting an ashtray next to the mattress.

"You walked out on *me* back when, although you say otherwise."

Gabriel takes a cigarette out slowly, lighting up. "Granted. And you lied to me back when, although you say otherwise. And you don't like talking like this. You want it to be romantic; you want it all to be like Monday. But to be together, we have to be able to live with each other outside of fucking.

"I walked away from you in the heat of anger. I shouldn't have done it. I'm sorry for that. You'll forgive me for that, I hope. You shouldn't have been doing what you were doing, either. But that's over. We were both acting out. With Alex, this is leaving cold and I have to do it better because I have to learn from mistakes. You too. When you disappeared over the last couple of days, I was out of my mind. It was like you were back in your old habits. And I was scared something had happened to you."

"I won't do that again." Joel blushes, seeing how upset Gabriel really is about that.

Gabriel inhales the smoke deeply, regaining his composure. "God, I hate these things. You only smoke them just to spite me, I know."

Joel smiles. "No worse than the incense. And fewer toxic chemicals than your brand."

"Yeah, I feel healthier already. To get back to the point...most people aren't doing what they should be doing, a very wise attorney and teacher once told me. That applies to work and personal life. We're doing what we should be doing in work. Now we need to in life. Can you do this *with me*, is what I'm asking."

"You didn't do anything then I have to forgive. It killed me, but it woke me up about what I was doing with my life. What bothered me was when I came back —you refusing to acknowledge what we felt. To not give me that chance."

"This isn't all about me. It's not me giving you a chance now. It's us giving us a chance. No more hedging, no more running away."

Joel takes Gabriel's hand again. "There's a part of me that *wants* to run away; I don't know how to do this. But I don't want to be without you. So whatever. We'll talk. I just hope fucking gets equal time."

"It did before, didn't it? But regardless of how much we want each other, baby, we don't trust each other. I'm afraid you're going to walk away from me. That you're going to disappear again, you won't let me know what's going on inside. And whatever it is that you're scared of with me you'll have to be honest about that."

Joel's discomfort comes up, hearing this. He traces symbols on Gabriel's hand while he talks.

"Your anger scares me. I hate anger, even though I have it myself. And sometimes you refuse to listen to me. You tune other people out when it suits you. I know you won't...reject me, I guess, for what I say or who I am or what's happened to me. But because I care about you so much, I'm afraid of that rejection."

"I'm afraid of you running away, and you're afraid of me turning away. Okay, we know what we're facing. Before...we depended on sex to get us through when we couldn't communicate, or to make up for it. That's not enough now, not to survive. There's going to be times when we're really uncomfortable with each other. Times when we misunderstand each other. Times when we have negotiate, to compromise, to let things go. It's every single day that happens."

"I can *do* that, Gabriel."

"I have faith in you. What we had before...we were doing it without a guidebook. The bodies were willing but the minds were in chaos. We can do this. I promise we'll figure it out."

Joel moves over to sit beside Gabriel, in his arms.

"I love you," Gabriel whispers.

Joel feels relief. "I love you too." Gabriel kisses him, and this is the first time Joel sees Gabriel looking at him like he used to, with the intimate affection they had when they were together before. He sinks into Gabriel's embrace, with his head on Gabriel's chest, listening to his heart beat for a long minute. Also something he liked to do before.

Then he says, "So what's next?"

"I will handle what needs to be done with him this week. This is the truth. For now, let me take some comfort in being here with you. Tell me what this virtual part of Isabella's venture is."

"Uh, virtual tours. People with big money like this kind of thing. They can have an image of one or more artworks temporarily in their homes, through an app in a projector smartphone. We send them the phone, see, like it's on loan, and they see different works they might buy. I like it 'cause it goes against the status quo. And the showing at the cultural center will be in February. Around your birthday, maybe."

Gabriel kisses his head. "And after the showing, we'll do something. I mean, go somewhere. We never did that together. You telling me about all this means a great deal to me. Sharing it. Isn't some of your stuff what you did in Amsterdam? You should tell me about Jan. I'd like to know about him."

Joel, still not used to this, begins describing Amsterdam, and the places he visited while he was there. And some about Jan.

"You know, he left me some things. Money. Some other stuff."

"He must have cared for you. I know you took care of him, right?"

"I didn't do it for money."

"Baby, I know you. I know how you roll. Don't get defensive. Jan leaving you something was a beautiful act. He'd be proud of you."

Joel hopes so. He isn't saying how much Jan left him for now. That's a more complicated conversation. Especially with how Gabriel feels about money and rich people.

Gabriel hasn't had more than the two glasses of wine. Joel can't recall ever seeing him drunk. They share that habit, or lack of habit. He seems very tired, nonetheless, almost falling asleep.

And his phone has buzzed with texts several time that he's ignored. But it rings now, and Gabriel picks it up when he sees who it is. Veronica.

Joel can hear she's on the verge of tears. "We're being evacuated; the police and fire department are here."

They both sit up. "What happened," Gabriel asks.

"The cops found a meth lab in one of the apartments. I have to get Bella and me out of here." Bella is her gray tiger-striped cat.

"Hold on. We'll be there in a few minutes." He gets up and takes Joel's hand. "Come on, we need to take her out of there."

∞

NINE ◆ 34 GREAT POWER (DÀ ZHUÀNG)

Thunder over Heaven: Yang energy fills Heaven after a retreat. The person is in motion like thunder, and the energy combined with Heaven's strength means righteousness in action —ethical strength is more important than physical strength. The fourth line (yang/nine) moves in this reading: the strength is focused, channeled by the necessary restraint.

∞

From the *New York Scene*, December 5, 2010

Humanity Unchained, the New York-based NGO that works to document human trafficking, is holding a retrospective on its twenty-year history exposing how slavery operations work across the world —from India to Haiti, Thailand to the Balkan states, Africa, South America and here in the US.

The retrospective being shown at the Spanish Harlem Cultural Center features photos, legal papers, as well as video and audio narratives from persons who were caught in slavery and some who fought to rescue those persons.

Many visitors expressed surprise that slavery is still happening across the world. It's commonly thought of as forced sex work but other forms exist, including economic situations of becoming indentured to work. However, news programs highlighting forced sex work have brought new attention to the problem overall.

An expert in the organization explained that women are often lured to another country during desperate economic times with promises of good jobs that will help support their families. Once arriving, the women's passports are taken away, they are beaten and raped into submission, and forced to work in strip clubs or as prostitutes. Their families might be threatened as well. The women's captors charge them for food and housing so they are always in debt, and they are intimidated by their lack of ability to speak the language of the country they are in. In addition, they are reluctant to attempt to contact authorities —perhaps fearing worse treatment.

Organized crime is often involved, but some rings are small operations. Since the worldwide economic collapses started in 2008, more persons have responded to bogus ads for lucrative international jobs, and have become trapped in a trafficking operation.

∞

Sunday, December 12
12:02 am

VERONICA'S APARTMENT BUILDING in the Hell's Kitchen area is indeed being evacuated right at this moment, because a superintendent/tenant dispute led to the discovery of a meth lab being run out one of the apartments. The fire department is telling everyone to leave so they can assess the biohazard, no mean feat at nearly two in the morning.

In the twenty minutes since her phone call, Joel and I have gotten a cab to my car, and then driven to meet her near where her street is being taped off. We store her and Bella in the back seat and move away from the growing chaos. She held it together during the initial emergency, trying to keep Bella calm. But she now starts crying. Joel leans over his seat to comfort her, as we go crosstown to my place.

Veronica is about my height and age, ash brown hair in a David Bowie androgynous stacked bob, and blueish eyes. She feels very fluid in gender psychically and otherwise, appreciating the male as I do the female. She's more compassionate and giving than I am, and I rely on that when I need someone to remind me to be human. I realize today she's a good deal like my mom.

She explains the situation to us, accepting a cigarette. "We've all been complaining about various health code violations anyway, after Storm Louise. Danny was helping me try to fix the situation."

Danny is director of a tenant's rights organization located in Harlem. Just before we had our fight at Thanksgiving a combination snow and tropical storm hit New York City, Westchester County, and parts of New Jersey, leaving many buildings in crap shape after flooding. Veronica's building still has problems with heat and water. I had asked her to stay with me then, but she was trying to muddle through stubbornly. Like I would. You don't want to give up your home.

"You can stay in my apartment," Joel says. "I'm kind of in the loft a lot now anyway."

I shake my head at that. "Um. You could, but if Joel's not too insulted by my suggestion I'd rather you stay with me. I know you don't need to be alone right now." While Veronica and Joel became close the moment they met, she and I have a special relationship. Being with Joel this past evening has galvanized me to try harder to repair my life. Despite lying about an emergency last night, now I need to step up to the actual emergency.

As I drive, she gets calls from a couple of her neighbors. The Department of Health is making an emergency inspection due to the meth, flooding, and various other problems. It doesn't look like she'll be able to go back for some time.

At my place we get her set up in the spare bedroom. Bella knows Archie and they get along, but right now Bella stays locked in the spare room until the vibes calm down.

Veronica continues confiding about her stress. "I was just starting to feel better about the apartment to try to counteract freaking out about work."

Her part-time job is with a professional investigations firm. She's very good in her work like I am. We've worked together several times. She supported me in my bad time during the summer, and she and Joel helped me rescue an elderly lady that Ethan Nelson attempted to institutionalize. They also were with me in the horrible situation in October with the man who wanted to kill me. The two of them saved me from being shot in the head in the abandoned Chrystie Street station.

We all finally rest on the sofa. "This is such bad timing," she says. "I can't afford to find any other place right now. The agency has new management. I have a contract about to expire at the end of the year, and the new director doesn't like part-timers who aren't independent contractors. He's coming up with all sorts of bullshit. You know how the workplace is. No appreciation, no loyalty, just bottom line. I have great references and I've brought in business, but he doesn't care."

I move closer to her. "Let's take care of the home situation first. I know a couple people who can move cheap and I'll pay for it. When they let you back in, we'll get your stuff out and put it in storage. And you and Bella stay here for now until you can go back. It's the most important thing to feel stable."

Joel takes off a little later, and then she and I catch some sleep. Later the next morning we go online to Manhattan Mini Storage and reserve a space. I take her out for brunch as well. I have some ideas to talk over that can help both of our situations. While we're eating, she calls Danny to tell him what happened with the apartment. I want to tell her to say hi for me but that reminds me I'm too stubborn to pick up the phone and call him myself.

"In the meantime," I tell her after the call, "I have a lot of work I need to make progress on, while handling these cases for Michaela and Joel's friend Geneva. If you want to take the chance, I'd like to work with you; we could even combine our business somehow to benefit both of us."

She agrees to this. We start discussing our various caseloads.

And then Alex calls. He had texted a few times last night after I left and I didn't respond. I don't want to now. But I answer. And when he starts in on me about the dinner, I cut him off and briefly tell him what happened to Veronica.

"You're using her as your go-to excuse now?"

I wince inside, thinking of Joel's text to him two weeks ago when I was passed out.

Our conversation becomes a little heated when I refuse to come over to his place and talk, and tell him I need to work. He doesn't hang up on me but comes close. I'm just delaying the inevitable.

Not long after we get back Joel comes over, wanting to help in whatever we're doing. Veronica and I both feel better; I'm less stressed over focusing on Sophie and Geneva; for her, moving on things alleviates some of the stress of being evicted and suspended.

Joel asks me, "So are we still going to Black Mountain tomorrow?"

"Yeah, so long as Veronica's situation doesn't change. If they don't let her in the apartment then we'll go. But if the building's open, I'd like to be there."

Veronica snorts. "Go anyway. If they do let me in Danny's coming with me. And because you and Danny are sulking little babies, neither of you should be together right now."

Both Joel and I roll our eyes. But she's right, this has to stop — at some point.

Joel gets up. "I need to finish something in my studio. I'll be here in the morning regardless."

He hugs Veronica. Then he meets me by the door. "See you tomorrow," he says, casually. But he's hanging back, his fingers play with my shirt.

"Okay." I feel the physical tension between us as he moves his hands to touch my hair, getting close to me. For a moment, what flows between us is without words, but incredibly powerful.

∞

Monday morning, I wake up with Veronica, or rather she wakes me from my nightmares. We fell asleep together the previous evening and then I started having dreams about being a demon Joel's forced to paint.

When we get up, I find an email from Alex. Holding my breath, I have her read it with me. Not as bad as I expected. He's disappointed in my rudeness and lack of remorse. Which he's right about. He says he'll be out of the country a couple days to see his father and hopes I'll spend some time considering my actions.

"You're lucky," Veronica says. "He could have just said, *"Fucking asshole.""*

"*That* would have been easier. But true, he just bought me some time. And I am an asshole for being glad I have that time."

Veronica laughs at that, and puts on music to try to inspire me to get dressed. Today she's going to meet Danny and record everything about the building and start packing her stuff.

Mariah's *Heartbreaker* plays, putting me in a better mood, as Joel arrives at the apartment, with Chris. Chris hugs both of us, and Joel looks critically at me.

He walks over to me, keeping up his scrutiny. "You're not dressed. Can you like, wake up already?"

"Sorry. I don't have a closet full of the entire Patagonia catalogue like you do—obviously." I look him over.

"I should have brought something over for you. Right now, you have two styles of clothes. Good stuff you don't wear, and shit a thrift store would laugh at."

"I'm so glad you're here to help," I say sarcastically. And he smiles because he knows I am glad he's here.

Chris adds, "And I'm here for Xena, Warrior Princess. I'm going to help her pack."

Joel says, "That makes me feel better about it, since Gabriel and I must play Von Trapp family in the New Jersey woods." He tilts his head to the bedroom. "Let's see if we can find a lovely t-shirt and jeans combo for you today, to change from your usual t-shirt and jeans combo."

In the bedroom I start pulling out clothes and he stops me. "I'll handle it. I have something for you, anyway. To begin again." He reaches in his messenger bag and takes out several objects, setting them on the unmade bed. A book, something metal, and what sounds like coins.

Change? I come over and look. I recognize the book—Ken Wu's *I Ching*. The metal objects are eight coins. A little smaller than quarters. Each has different designs and ideograms, but I can tell head from tails. One has a black and white yin yang symbol, so tiny. For the moving line. The coins have a rough beauty; they're made from hand. He's created them. The metallic object, also hand-crafted, is a rough copper-colored grid, to put the coins on.

Overwhelmed, I pick the coins up and feel the carving. That he spent time to do this...hours to get them to look right. And so casual about giving them over. He's picking stuff out of my dresser, not looking at me.

I'm speechless. He has a little leather bag as well; Archie and Bella jump up on the bed to investigate. I'm holding the coins like psychometry, picking up the vibrations. He's had the coins close; the heat is in them. I rescue the bag from the cats and slip the coins inside. "Thank you...I have to put these in a special place."

Is that good enough? No. He's laying out clothes on the bed. I move closer and say in his ear, "You never fail to amaze me."

His eyes light up at that. I lean over and kiss him; he draws himself into my space and puts his hands on my hips. He wants to do more, but this isn't the time to play grab-ass. I put all of the objects on a shelf Archie can't get to, and get dressed. He doesn't leave while I change into the clothes, watching me. We can hear Chris talking incessantly to Veronica about some ancient aliens show. It's a comfortable counterpoint to the quiet intimacy here.

When we go back to the living room, Chris is going through one of Veronica's bags, checking out her cosmetics, while still talking aliens. They're barely able to acknowledge we're leaving.

In the car, Joel is quiet for some time, through the Holland Tunnel and the New Jersey interstate. The music on the stereo is one of the Brandenburg concertos, quiet as well. Reflective.

I finally say, "What you gave me will help me take my Daoism more seriously. Chiang will like that."

"What happened with you and Chiang that you left?"

I think about it. "I got lost. Last Christmas, I felt my mother's absence profoundly. Even though I gave her such a hard time as a teenager, she always grounded me in my soul. She never gave up and she helped me find the good in myself. I lost confidence in my ability to find that in myself for some reason. Maybe because I was approaching the other side of 35. Before 35, you're still a young man; after 35, you're heading for 40 and have to consider the rest of your life. Mom was 51 when she died. Dominic was almost 50. I thought I had them to watch for how to handle that time of life, and then I didn't. They were gone and I had no one to guide me through the milestones.

"Chiang said it was time for me to build my own legacy. I felt like he did not understand the loneliness and despair. I do have depression every so often. You can't think right in depression. I started getting angry and sad. The financial situation was getting bad as well. I stopped caring about spirituality on a daily basis."

"And that was it —why you were upset with him?"

"No...Chiang always had the freedom to be blunt with me. But he started saying I needed to handle life better. Wrong thing, wrong time. He said I could learn from past mistakes, and forget what others had done. And I just felt like...are you kidding? My life's falling apart..."

"You were in a bad time. I'm sorry."

"It happens, like it is now with me destructing internally."

He frowns. "I understand how you feel from Raymond's case, but you didn't seem that bad when I saw you again in July."

"No, but I was angry. Hitting the preacher actually did me good, as awful as it is to say that. He stood in for my father, the bill collectors, for anyone who had ever done something wrong...In any case, I was paid back when I was jumped. And what happened in the subway."

Joel doesn't like that. "That isn't karma."

"It is to an extent. I'm violent profession, because my life has been permeated with violence. From the first time my father slapped me through every fight I had in school. All through my teens, when Danny and I got used to seeing violence and getting in fights because there just was no other way to survive. Dom stopped me from the worse of it, but it's a path. I've been in it and now it's attracted to me. The vibes seek me out. The discipline of Buddhism and Daoism keeps me tuned to how to act properly. And a love of, I don't know...beauty in life or something. The concept of *rasa* in Hinduism, to develop a consciousness of sensitivity and appreciation of life in all its facets, in the physical and otherworldly dimension all at once. Something I seek out and sometimes sets me apart."

I sigh. I feel heavy, like crying but without tears. It helps that Joel is listening seriously. "But the violence is there, like the anti-Kundalini, waiting to strike in brutality rather than wisdom. No matter the violence around me, I can enjoy the blameless beauty, like your art. But see, *Carmen's* playing again, and it is beauty, but in an opera that ends in violence."

I take out my cigarettes and he reaches over and takes them from my hand. "I think you're taking on blame that you shouldn't. I *saw* the videos, remember. You were being reasonable to the preacher, asking him to leave. He stuck his face in yours and spit on you. Literally. He was screaming right at you. I know what those words are like, what they're meant to do. He knew that as well. I'd argue that was provocation."

"Doesn't matter. I still shouldn't have done it. For me, those words were the precursor to a physical fight, the bell rung. I did it too many times when I was young. Times when Danny and I were minding our own business, and some jackasses would say something to us. Even if we didn't want to get into it, we had to. The bell was rung. I saw on the YouTube page all kinds of comments; they didn't understand what was going on. Some were saying this is why LGBT persons shouldn't have rights, that there were probably roving bands of homosexuals going around beating up good Christian straight people...I felt like I single-handedly set back human rights."

"Seriously? Because of comments on fucking *YouTube*? I saw those. I added some, too."

"Oh, did you?" I smile wryly. "Were you the one calling me a cocksucking Nazi? That was probably one of the nicest."

Joel laughs. "No, I invited some of the cowards to visit me in Amsterdam if they wanted to back up what they said."

I look over at him.

"True story."

"Well, after I was jacked up, they said I deserved it. I kind of felt myself it was payback."

"Now I know you're high. Someone swinging a baton against your face is punishment for defending your friend?"

"Didn't do any good, did it? Did Bunton stop protesting funerals? He's down where the blizzard hit in Texas right now, starting shit. It just stirred more violence —like what happened at the Chrystie Street with that follower of Bunton's."

"Turn it around. They aren't your karma. You're their karma. Don't give me that look. Chiang said you were a protector, right? You can't do that without getting your hands dirty."

"How do you know what Chiang said?"

"You talk in your sleep." He lights up. "Whole Goddamned monologues sometimes."

I feel caught short. When did he hear that? Maybe while I fell asleep the day he had Chris over. The revelation is very unnerving.

∞

We come to the entrance of the park, with a large lot surrounded by a wooden gate. The park itself is mostly uncultivated wilderness about a thousand acres situated north of Elizabeth. Don's 'suicide' site should be not too far in from the main entrance. I open the trunk to take out the rope I keep in for emergencies along with copies of the police report on his disappearance. As we walk, I think about Don making the same walk, with his own rope. Leaving his car, coming to the clearing. Putting the rope over the branch.

The large rectangular parking lot abuts the beginning of the park. The park is open but no one is in the guardhouse. No other car is in the lot; it's off-season, and no hunting allowed here.

A large brass plaque is situated right behind the gate of the plain wooden fence surrounding the lot. Next up is a clearing between parallel sets of woods. The clearing is about fifty yards long. It's natural, so it widens and narrows and ends up to a point where some wood trails begin. At the beginning of the clearing just beyond the fence are large rock outcroppings—a few boulders piled up on either side of the clearing, some higher than our heads.

We walk past the rocks and hike up the clearing a couple hundred yards to the tree in question. It's one of the few trees that dot the clearing. We can match it to the photos. While I don't expect to see anything from ten years ago, I'm startled to see a ring around the branch of a tree where the bark was worn away. I check the photo of the scene. It matches the photo of the torn rope.

"Yeah. It was here, if it happened. But this is strange."

"Why?"

"Just hanging himself wouldn't have stripped the bark like this. The tree is permanently scarred."

"It's not recent?"

"No." I reach up and can just barely touch it. "Scarring trees takes a lot of effort. The Australian Aborigines scar trees when they remove bark to make shelters or watercraft. I've seen pictures. The tree is still alive in the branch, but the bark won't grow over this."

He shakes his head. "You always been like this?"

"Yes."

"No wonder you got into a lot of fights at school."

"Yeah, the teachers used to hold me down so the other kids could whale on me. Now getting back to this, the rope Don supposedly used was manila, looks like quarter-inch in the picture. Mine is static block-keel kermantle, rescue rope."

He raises his eyebrows.

"My father taught me about this when I was supposed to be his soldier-in-training. The manila would have something like a 500-pound break, so the fact it's broken in the photo bothers me. It wouldn't necessarily scar the tree. This is like someone rubbed it away to make it look like a person was hanging. And then, see how high this branch is. You can throw the rope over it..."

I throw an end of my rope over and bring it down, reflexively making a basic bowline. I pull on both ends against the tree branch, just to feel it. "But, see where the rope is tied in the photo? Very close to the branch. He couldn't do this without a chair or something to step up, or someone helping him."

Joel comes up next to me and reviews the photo and the tree. "I see. So could it have been murder? Nothing in the photo is near the tree to step on."

"Exactly. But this isn't murder, to me. It's faking suicide. Reminds me of some insurance cases."

"Or what happened with Raymond...where Nelson faked Raymond's accidental suicide."

I undo the rope and look around the quiet clearing. Snow is on the ground, a few inches deep. Although many trees have shed leaves, enough red spruce and white pine are around to have a peaceful green cover. Don's naked tree stands out in the natural clearing.

"Yes, that occurred to me. Michaela said it's my go-to theory. But I feel this is wrong. And the body disappeared."

"I believe you."

I meet his eyes. "An animal could have taken him down. Black bear perhaps. I don't know, anything's possible. Bears can do that. But I'm still not feeling it."

I fall silent considering my own words, reaffirming my conclusions. I'm surprised when Joel takes out a hunting knife from his boot and tosses it in the air, catching it and twirling it in his fingers like an expert. He smiles briefly, seeing me watch him.

"Where did you learn to do that?"

"From a crazy kid who used to hang in Times Square. He liked knives a little too much. He scared people. He scared me, so I had him show me how to do it. Took the fear away."

"Did you carry?"

"I liked the protection. I stopped carrying one years ago. I didn't want to be tempted to use it, and I tried to keep myself out of situations where I needed to."

"But you feel the need to have it again. I guess I can't blame you, since I wear both guns now. You ever use the knife?"

"Those records are sealed." He smiles again, carving something on a tree at the edge of the clearing. One of the *gua,* Heaven.

I undo the rope as a falcon flies overhead, and I watch its grace and beauty and follow its path to the woods on our right. "I wish I could be like that sometimes. *Rasa.*"

We end up staring at each other. He looks back at his carving, slipping the knife back in his boot.

The woods fall silent, seemingly contemplating us.

And then the hairs on the back of my neck stand up.

It's as if a radio signal breaks through. Something makes me look over my shoulder and movement catches my eye. The smallest sort of movement beyond us in the other side of the woods.

Everything emotional drains away. Like that. And my training kicks in. The trouble sense. I turn into the other part of me, the yang. This is different from the car chase, an evolution in mode. Feeling the threat from the predator. I know that movement was a human. And no human is hiding here for benevolent purposes.

Possibilities go through my mind at the speed of light. Something will happen imminently. My skin feels the danger. I'm already pulling Joel closer to me, shielding him.

As the branches around us split from bullets I shove Joel to the ground under my body. More bullets go over our heads. Most miss but a couple get close. I have his head covered with my chest, feeling him straining against me. The bullets stop. The shooter can't see us anymore. I pull out my Glock from my ankle holster and give it to Joel, rolling off him.

"Go. *Now.* Go near the parking lot and wait for me."

He shakes his head. "I'm not leaving you."

I feel very different all of a sudden. Feeling the extreme isolation of where we are and the danger of being alone. Like in the warehouse. And the responsibility for that. I have fear, but it's a fear that can be used.

I don't argue with him but get up and grab his hand, pulling him up and along with me. I move through the woods around to the arc of the clearing. We're enough inside to be out of sight and I can move quietly. But we're close enough to watch the edge of the woods on the other side. It recalls the war games my father made me practice with him. How to flush out the prey. I keep Joel right behind me. He's picked up on my change and the abruptness subdues him. He responds to my signals, moving carefully.

The old and thick evergreen trees, winding their way up 90 feet or more, provide good cover to get around.

The shooter across the way is not as quiet as us. In the stillness of the day I can hear him stepping on branches. I have my Sig Sauer ready while I'm keeping low and circling. He has to move and see where we are —he has no choice. He's probably going toward the lot, thinking we'll try to escape. He gets there first, shoots out the tires, then we'd be trapped.

We're coming up behind him. And the irony of my father's insistence on teaching me to hunt, although we never killed anything, becomes clear as I re-enact the drills he put me through.

We go around the arch, and now we're on the shooter's side. I can see the dark form moving in the woods. Not going fast, stopping to look around. Heading in the direction of the lot. I put my hand on Joel to stop him, and signal to him what I want him to do. He watches me as hard as he was listening to me before. I tell him he has to stay behind this man while I'm going to get ahead of him. We have to be very careful and keep him in sight, but also know where each other is. I indicate where he should go and where I'll be, and what he should do.

He starts to put his hand on mine, and I stop him. Emotion can't get in my way or his. "You have to do exactly as I told you," I whisper, and leave.

Seconds later I've gotten to my position and I get a better look at the shooter through the trees. Tall, thick, white, in his thirties, wearing dark green clothes. He's staring at the clearing, not looking at his back. Good. I aim near his feet and fire. It sounds impossibly loud in the still day.

He whirls around and raises his rifle. Before he can do anything, Joel shoots from his location. In the air, so he doesn't hit me by accident.

The man ducks, realizing he's in a crossfire. He's not expecting this and changes his plans. He fires in both directions, but moves toward the edge of the clearing.

I shoot again. Close. Joel does too, immediately afterward.

The man breaks for the clearing, running serpentine. I'm right after him, shoving the gun back in my back holster. Dominic's training, making me run to be a like a boxer. I have to be faster than this man, not give him a chance.

He looks over his shoulder.

I catch up and slam into his back, a football tackle. He struggles trying to swing the gun back at me. I get my arm around his neck and a leg around his leg. We roll on the ground, matching equal desperate strength. He drops the rifle and is now just trying to get away. He tries to scratch at my face and I hold on to his arms. His elbow catches me in the ribs hard enough to loosen my hold and he forces himself up on his feet again. I'm right there with him, not letting go, and he starts swinging at my face.

I have my hands ready to block. His punches come, quick and ugly. I meet them with my own. I'm too fast for him to hurt that much, but he's brutal. We circle each other. I know Joel has the gun on us, but he can't shoot without risking hitting me.

The man lands a couple blows that hurt. This guy is big, bigger than me, very thick and muscular. Maybe army training somewhere. His style is serious—most street fights are bullshit. Doesn't mean people don't get hurt, but the fighting is not like in the movies or TV. It's rough, ragged, and quick. This man is moderately disciplined and he's not just fighting to leave, he's fighting to kill. But I've had experience fighting people bigger than me.

We go at it for a minute, a fight club in the snow moving with the punches. He's a challenge in his brutality, trying to overwhelm me.

And then as I duck back from his fist, Joel smashes the stock of the rifle against the side of his head, having come up behind him.

The man pitches forward stumbling, and still grabs at me. I use my foot to yank his from under him as Chiang did to me, and he goes down. But in his mad rage he pulls me down with him. But I have the leverage, and I hold him down. Nonetheless, he reaches for my throat and tries to dig in.

Then his head is yanked back. Joel has gotten down with us, behind him, and has the man's hair in one hand and his knife in the other. He puts the knife is right up against the man's jugular.

"I wouldn't move. I'm not nice like him; I'll cut your fucking face off."

The man freezes, breathing hard under me. Joel moves the knife up to the man's mouth. The man stares down at it the best he can. Knives are sometimes more intimidating than guns, and this is the case with the would-be assassin. He lets go of my throat. I'm able to take my Sig Sauer out and aim it at him. His hands fall to his sides.

"Who the fuck are you," I ask him. He doesn't answer, of course.

"Blow his dick off. That might make him say something."

The man rolls his eyes up at Joel. He mutters an invective in a foreign language, one Joel has apparently heard before. This gets Joel to move the knife closer to his eyes. "You really want to say that? Two of them kicked *your* ass."

The man shuts up, in fear of his eyes.

Joel is trying to follow my mode but I feel his anxiety. Despite his words, I'm colder. "Who are you working for?"

He glances down at me, furious and desperate. "I won't tell you shit."

His tone is scared and defiant. He thinks we're going to kill him anyway. Which makes him a problem. If he thinks we'll kill him, he won't say anything. If he thinks we won't, he won't say anything. I'm not going to torture him. Although he doesn't need to know that, which might help to contain him for now.

I grab the front of the man's shirt and rip it, tearing off a strip of material. He starts cursing me.

"You should shut up," I tell him. "My partner is a little crazy with his knife. I can let him *be* crazy with the knife, if you know what I mean."

Hearing that, Joel gets around to stare at the man straight in the eyes, with the knife pressed against his throat, right under his jaw.

"You can lose a tongue that way," I assure the man, who's trying to watch the knife.

He's subdued enough from the fear that I can flip him over and bind his wrists thoroughly with the strip of cloth. I tear off another strip of his shirt and tie his ankles, loosely, so he can walk.

Joel catches my eye. "What are we going to do," he asks silently.

"Back to the lot." I'm not sure after that. I go through the man's pockets. No ID or keys. Just money, cigarettes, a pocket knife, a spare magazine for the rifle. Scraps of paper folded small. Scribbles and what looks like a map. I put these papers and the magazine inside my jacket.

I grab the back of the man's jacket and pull him up.

"Come on, asshole. Move." I hold the Sig Sauer to his head to encourage him. I look at Joel. "Can you get my rope back, and that rifle and stuff?"

He collects the gun, my rope and the messenger bag with the case information I had dropped when this dickhead starting shooting. Meanwhile, I keep my gun trained on the man. He stares at me, and glances over his shoulder.

That makes me realize he's not alone. Maybe he works with the Elantra driver who tried to kill us. Maybe that man is nearby, keeping lookout near the lot. I put my gun to the man's face to discourage him from yelling out. And after Joel returns, I rip off another part of the man's shirt to stuff in his mouth.

"Walk," I tell him.

Joel keeps the rifle pointed at the man. Someone once taught Joel to shoot, but I taught him to shoot well. We're working in tandem again. I have Joel stay behind me with the rifle. We walk on the edge of the woods on our right. I keep hold of the man's collar, using him in part for cover while I'm scanning ahead.

They must have a car. Probably they followed us, pulled in after, and separated. The other man maybe thinks the gunshots were all from our captive. Eventually he'll check. As we get closer to the rock outcropping, I slow us down.

We've come up to the first set of large rocks, some chest high and some sloping up over our heads, about ten feet in length all together. We can see part of the lot from here. I stop Joel, and take the rifle from him then have him bring the Glock back out. The man twitches in front of us.

I prod him in his back with the rifle. "Get going."

He looks back at me, his face swollen and bleeding and angry.

"Move! To the parking lot. We'll catch up."

He staggers forward hesitantly. I rest the rifle on one of the rocks and check it quickly. A Barrett REC7, a serious weapon he's not good enough to use. Thirty-round magazine, and most of the rounds still there. I scan the area. The man passes the similar rock on the other side of the clearing about 20 yards to his and our left, and a little closer to the entrance than where we are. He suddenly snaps his head to look toward those rocks, which is stupid. I lift the rifle, get closer to the shield of the slope of the rocks we're behind, and pull Joel further in to cover him.

Shots come from the vicinity of the rocks opposite us, way over our heads. I can see a little of the second man around the other rock. He has a handgun. I fire back, at the top of those rock and the sides; three careful shots to let him know we have the rifle and also that I'm not a wild shooter.

Our idiot tries to stumble over to the other person. I shoot near his feet, which makes him trip and fall on his face. Now he can't get up, with his hands behind his back and feet hampered.

A moment of silence. Then the prone man spits the cloth out of his mouth and yells something to his partner.

We hear a low reply. It sounds negative. The other man is not going to come out and rescue him.

"What do you want to do?" Joel is breathing hard against me.

"I want him gone."

I address the man behind the rocks. "You need to leave. If you try anything, I'll blow both your heads off."

And in that moment, I mean it, because I have to make them believe it. I'm talking loud enough for both of them to hear. "I'm a better shot than either of you. Let me prove my point." I aim near the idiot's head and shoot. Risky, considering I'm not used to the weapon. But, as I wanted, it just hits close by, making him jerk away.

He says something to his friend, panicking.

The answer sounds quiet, hesitant.

I say louder, "If I want to kill you, you'll be dead. Same with him. Walk away. Leave him here."

The other man looks cautiously around the rock, holding his gun out. I track him with the barrel of the rifle.

I feel the hesitation from him. Should he try to go out and get his partner, or attempt something else.

He starts shooting towards us. From what I could see and the sound of it, he has a fully automatic pistol. I stay calm. My main concern is if these two have any other help around. But I think they would show by now. Even a closed park gets patrolled—so they need to kill and leave as soon as possible.

The man on the ground is saying something, but I'm not worried about him. He's not going anywhere.

I need to disarm the other man. The rocks are good cover and concealment for both the other man and me. Neither of us is going to make a difference until we take a chance. His gun likely is a 33-round magazine. Mine is about the same. I have another magazine, he probably does too.

When at a stalemate like this, time to change the setup. I have to resolve this so we survive.

"Wait here," I say to Joel. "Keep an eye on him." I gesture to a crack in the rocks. If he starts to shoot again, cover me. When I tell you, go out with the gun."

He nods, holding the Glock out. I back up in the woods a few feet to the first good tree. The trunk is wider than I, with several thick branches rising out of its massive base. I sling the rifle over my shoulder and begin climbing. This isn't just my father's reconnaissance training—as a kid I used to like to get vantage points to search for trouble to get into, or out of. But it helps that climbing feels natural, especially having to do it fast, in seconds.

Once up twenty feet or so, resting on a branch, I can see the other man clearly behind the rock. And I can aim at him. Or near him, since I don't want to kill him.

Still. Breathe. Focus. Shoot.

I watch his reaction, see where he ducks, then shoot again nearby. I watch again, shoot. Until he gets the idea he's under sniper fire from the trees.

When he tries to go in the woods, I shoot ahead of him. When he tries to move in other directions, I shoot in front of him. Now he understands. All he can do is hunch down to be less of a target.

"Give it up," I call out. "Throw away the gun, and get on the ground. I *will* shoot you. You aren't walking out."

Hesitantly, he throws the pistol to one side.

"Come out to the clearing. Get down with your hands behind your head."

He walks out slowly, looking up. A few feet from the rocks he gets on his knees then lies down.

"Cover them," I tell Joel. I wait until he's out in the clearing and pointing the Glock towards the two men.

Then I go back down the tree. I don't like the second man being free so I keep the rifle on him while Joel goes to the Camry for plastic binders, which I keep in the trunk. I use those to restrain the second man.

"What are you doing with us," that one asks.

I don't answer. I feel anger rising now both because he tried to kill us and because of what comes next. Calling the police and dealing with that again. I don't want to, but this *has* to be related to Sophie's case and the evidentiary potential can't be denied. And so I call Michaela first and then the state police. I put the papers we found and the Glock in my trunk, which has a special compartment not visible to a routine search.

I see their car parked on the far end. The Elantra, worse for wear. Good. It gives credibility to the report to connect it with the previous attack.

Over the next few hours we talk to the state police and Elizabeth police. But neither of our two would-be assassins are talking. Not a word. Their lack of ID and foreign accents have the authorities' interest. They're taken to the Elizabeth jail, the nearest one to the park.

We've told the authorities that we were investigating Sophie's case, trying to trace the brother of the victim. These men stalked and tried to kill us much like the car chase in Elizabeth a few days ago. Nine of the police we talk to like *that.* Law enforcement is naturally suspicious when a person is involved in too many such incidents. But since they have nothing to hold us on and since we reported the Elantra driver previously, we can go.

After finishing with the Elizabeth police department at One Police Plaza, state police take us to the Troop Road Station to talk. Then it's done. One of the state troopers drops us off at our car, still in the parking lot. The Elantra has been confiscated as evidence.

I drive us out to a strip mall and pull over so we can recover. Out of protector mode, back to myself.

"Are you okay," Joel asks, while I'm staring into space.

I'm still hyper-aware of the innocuous surroundings. I had become someone else, a different persona, when these men showed up. After the routine of dealing with law enforcement I'm having a chance to return to myself. I start feeling where I was hit—places on my arm, chest, just barely on my jaw, and also feeling the fingerprints on my neck. "I don't think I've been without a bruise since I was eight."

"Fighting since that time? I know."

I have been. New, poor kid in class. Suspect kid in middle and high school. Then in regular life shit just happens, especially this year. In learning how to fight, I learned to lose too. The point isn't always to win, it's to show you can't be intimidated.

I look over at him. He's only seen this other persona when I defended us on the subway a few years ago and at the warehouse last summer. The time on the subway was very fast, and at the warehouse he was drugged. Seeing this mode clearly is disturbing to him.

He leans over to look at my face, putting his hand on my chest, where I wince slightly. Then he checks my hand, which is scraped and cut some.

"Maybe I need a tetanus shot."

He ignores that. "You never have anything in this car for first aid, like Veronica does." He gets out and walks to the 7-11 nearby, making me nervous at him being exposed.

Calm down, it's over. Over. You're safe.

He comes back with coffee. And other stuff he uses on my hand, making me flinch again. He's amused by that. He glances up at me while disinfecting my hand. "What are you thinking?"

"We survived. There must be a reason for this, Joel. For you and me to be able to do this."

"The case? Or us?"

"Both. Sorry to sound motherfucking intellectual again, but in Huayan Buddhism there's a concept of interpenetration—don't even say what you're going to say —it means in the cosmos one thing contains everything in the universe, and all in the cosmos contains that one thing."

"I think *my* definition of interpenetration is much more—"

"And anyway, I believe metaphors can be real. We're in a metaphor of working together to overcome danger."

I lean over and kiss him on the side of his head. He puts his head on my shoulder and I caress it, locking the car doors by instinct.

His hand slides along my side. Even where I'm bruised it still feels good.

"Do you want to go back home?"

"Oh, we're going back. I don't know if I can concentrate on work but...I don't want to have to worry about you somewhere else because I'll do enough worrying about you right here. I don't have to tell you be careful, correct? Who knows who else is out there?"

"*Why* were they there? How did they know?"

"God knows. They were following us somehow. This has to be connected to Don since both times this was here in New Jersey, when we were looking at these sites connected with Leonard and Don. Don faked his death—let's assume that. Just as I'm assuming Don was the Devil in Leonard's writings. Don was trafficking these women. Leonard found out what his brother was doing with the women and decided to stop him."

"The incident Annie Mallerman was talking about. Where they just hauled ass before the cops showed up."

"Right. They wouldn't have known necessarily how much Leonard had talked about. Don fakes his death to disappear, to avoid the police. And he could be back. Leonard said he was being haunted again. Ten years later Don returns—that explains why Leonard was murdered. Revenge. Whatever he's doing now, he has help. He knows about me, maybe because Michaela was in the news about being Sophie's attorney, and I was mentioned in the same article where the reporter basically asked if I'd fuck up the case by my very presence. Maybe they were watching Sophie's house, too. In any case, Don clearly doesn't want us investigating this. Now all we have to do is prove he's alive, and his involvement."

"So what next?"

"Tomorrow I'm going to go over some case files at the WFN. And Wednesday, we see the professor at Prentice-Caine who knew Leonard. We have the drag the Devil out in the open."

∞

TEN ◆ 5 WAITING (XŪ)

Cloud over Heaven: Part of the journey of righteousness is searching. While the power of Heaven is strong with the person, the appearance of water, clouds, means danger ahead. The sixth line (yin/six) moves in this reading: certain persons will have opportunity to advance, even with difficulty around.

∞

He's feeling his need to protect, to search someone out —the person who's hurting women. He relives the car chase and the gunfight in the park. But in remembering what else happened, the guilt rises as well. He travels through Elizabeth, through Wildemore, looking for Alex to tell him the truth. But only finds a card, a funeral card. Alex is dead.

But I didn't know, he says out loud. *I should have told you.* He then finds himself in the jail. *I have to help Veronica...* And Sophie gives him another funeral card for Veronica. His panic rises; he needs to tell Danny he's sorry *now.* But in going outside, he finds Danny's funeral card on his car, and those for Jim and Michaela inside the car. He goes back to his apartment. And finds Kent in his apartment. Kent watches sadly as he searches for Joel, to tell him he loves him before it's too late. But Joel's card is on his pillow in the bedroom. He falls down on his knees, screaming.

"*This can't be happening...*"

"*Gabriel, you have to be careful.*"

"*How could they all die and I don't know about it, I can't stop it?*"

"*It isn't them.*" Kent takes his hand and suddenly they're in another place, where Raymond's funeral was held. A coffin is ahead, draped with Buddhist prayer beads and flags. Chiang stands there with his hand on the coffin. Joel is on the floor leaning up against the coffin.

He can't see Joel's face but he feels his grief; watching Joel's artist's hands trace the initials GR on the casket. He senses the other persons in his life; he can see hazy versions of them walking by, not seeing him. The idea his body is in that casket is horrifying. He wants to scream, to take it away.

"No, I'm not dead. I haven't crossed over. I don't have the coins to pay for it. They promised they'd chant for me."

"The Bardo Thodol...You went too fast. But you can go back, Gabriel. It isn't set yet for you to cross over. You just need to be in the realm of the dead to be a protector. The Bodhisattva who went to the hells to rescue others. They will understand, but you must go to be reborn. "

∞

Tuesday, December 14
Elizabeth, NJ 10:43 am

AT THE WFN Frank's assistant takes me to an empty cubicle to look through a stack of fifty or so case files. These are women the WFN had direct contact with and helped find legal assistance for or helped with passage back to their original countries. I want to see if any of the names match those in Leonard's notebook.

Monroe sees me in the cubicle and stops by. "Anything interesting?"

"Not yet. But it makes me think. In what you turned over to the police were there any notes Ms. Merical had made —concerning what we talked about?"

"I'll check it out."

Then Frank comes up, greeting us both. "Seth, I see you've met Gabriel. Do you know he's looking into a case that might possibly be connected to Charlotte Merical's death?"

"Is that so? We could talk about it."

"Let's be careful about anything said. I would love for that murder to be solved. But nothing should get out. We don't need sensationalism."

"Of course not. If Mr. Ross here finds anything, we can have a meeting about it." Monroe goes back to his office.

Frank takes a seat beside me and picks up a file at random. "Find anything?"

"I'm looking for names against a list I have. If nothing matches, I'll check details of where the women were—and who was holding them."

Frank watches while I go through files. I'm used to people watching me. You have to learn to tune it out.

I open a file and recognize a name. Stephania Ivanisevic. I can't help but smile, thinking about Leonard's symbols. I have a copy of his notes, and I briefly glance at them. The swan and the ship.

"What's that," Frank asks.

"My source for the women's names. Someone who may have met them."

"Very strange. How do you...you can't even read that."

"It's a code."

"Where did you get it from?"

"A source... I have to keep it confidential."

"Oh yeah. Of course. I appreciate that, since you're doing the same for us."

I'm reading the summary of the file. It says she was given WFN's contact information anonymously. She had been in the rented house on Virginia.

Frank leans over my shoulder. "Wait a minute. I thought these were redacted. Our intern should have....I'm sorry, Gabriel. There might be confidential information here." He closes the case file I'm reading.

I look up at him. "Did you represent them in a legal capacity?"

"No, but the files may have HIPAA info."

Frank is standing in front of the files now.

I try not to be annoyed. "Always a possibility that if these files are evidence, they'll be subpoenaed."

"Understood. And we'd cooperate. But I have to ensure the women's information is protected."

"In that case, why don't you have Monroe go over them and take out the confidential information?"

"I'll ask him. It might take some time. You know nonprofits. We're overbooked time-wise."

"Granted. But again, this might apply to Ms. Merical's death."

"Yeah. I haven't forgotten that. Hold on."

He leaves quickly. I'm tempted to examine another file but I don't want to piss him off if I'm caught.

Frank comes back with Monroe. "I need you to help Gabriel so I need these files redacted, including the names."

"The names are the information I'm going on."

"We can do initials," Monroe says. "If anything matches take it case by case."

"One did match." I tap the file of Stephania Ivanisevic. Monroe picks it up.

Frank nods. "Good. Seth, review that one right away. Gabriel, honestly I'm not trying to frustrate you. Anything else we can do to help you?"

"I realize that. And yes. I had told Seth here that if Ms. Merical had any notes—if she had spoken personally to any of these women or anyone else—maybe she had a description of the persons holding the women."

"Her office files are in the same storage. If anything's there, I'll get it out."

Monroe says, "I'll do it. Also, the notes might be archived on our server."

"Good thinking, Seth. I appreciate you stepping up for this. We need to do what we can."

"You're both a lot of help. I guess I'll leave now." I turn to Monroe. "I'll be in touch."

He shakes my hand. Frank leads me to the entrance. "Sorry to make this more work and time."

"I understand. When I work for an attorney, I do the same."

"You're a good man for not making it personal. Your professionalism is admirable."

Frank shakes my hand too, carefully with his glove. On that note, I take off.

∞

Wednesday, December 15
Eastern New Jersey, 9:04 am

The day feels like it is going to be promising, if at least because I am alive. But I feel like I have to double-check that. Archie, indifferent to my existential crisis, demands his Fancy Feast. I try finding out more information about Don aside from the interviews. I really want a picture of Don and I'm surprised that none of my interview subjects nor the court or police record has any photos. Only a vague general description. Since Don and Leonard's parents died some time ago their belongings are gone. No photos were in Leonard's space in Wildemore.

Then I need a process of clearing some things out my mind to reboot my soul. I start some tai ch'i exercises. It's very simple, disciplined and graceful, which I like.

Still being simple and to an extent distracted by my dreams, I throw on a t-shirt under a top coat and jeans and I'm ready to go when Joel shows up with Chris again. Chris claims he's cat-watching while Veronica takes care of our more mundane cases.

On the way to Prentice-Cane in North Jersey, we come to a sign for a town called Waterford and he turns from the passenger seat where he's watching. "Stop in town for a moment."

I turn off the exit. He points out where to go in the small village, which is a cobblestone, touristy sort of place. "Up ahead, park on the right."

I do so. "Something you need to get?"

"I want to get something before we go to the campus. C'mon." He gets out, waits for me to lock up, and heads up the block to a men's clothing store. The items in the window tell me it has nice stuff.

"So what are we doing?"

He just takes my hand and pulls me in the store.

The proprietor, a fiftyish small white man, nicely dressed, closely cropped graying hair and sharply arched eyebrows. He comes around the counter. I see he recognizes Joel, and they shake hands and speak quietly to each other for a moment. Then the man walks over introduces himself to me as Curt.

It turns out Joel had a suit made. He knows my measurements.

He's amused by my reaction. "I could see you haven't quite gotten to yourself yet. I was going to give this to you later, but since you're supposed to be talking to a professional person, I think you need to look the part. You would have argued with me at the apartment."

I can't argue now; we have to get going. Joel's brought shoes and everything. He's right, I just have not been in a right mind to face the world. The suit, appropriately black, is very well-done. Curt is an artist. That does not surprise me that Joel knows someone like this.

In the car, He's pleased with the result. "And to think, probably back at your place, Veronica and Chris are exchanging their clothes right now. Or trying on the few things you have that are still good—which would also be what I bought you."

"She wears my stuff all the time. It wouldn't fit Chris though. And I don't have anything feminine."

"That's true." He looks out the window. "I did that for a couple clients. Cross-dressed."

"I'll bet you looked good."

"I did, actually."

∞

The Prentice-Cane campus is on three acres surrounded by woods. We go to a spacious building with a gallery on the first floor. On the third floor is Sabrina Wheatley's office. She's a professor of art history, and Sara, Leonard's girlfriend, is her student.

Wheatley is polite but cautious. "Why are you investigating Leonard's death?"

"A likely innocent person has been accused of being responsible. We're trying to find out the truth. So, we wanted to learn what he was doing on campus. He wasn't a student as far as I know."

"No, he wasn't. He was assisting another professor. This is a difficult situation; you have to understand."

"I would like to know as much as you're willing to tell me. I need the information to help others. You could really make a difference and people don't often get that chance."

Wheatley considers me, tapping a pen on a book. "You seem sincere. You have a very open manner. That probably works for you."

"I studied psychology in college."

She smiles. "Where did you go?"

"CUNY Midtown. My uncle taught art history there, in fact. Dominic Sheehan."

"Dominic! Oh, my God. I knew him. We used to go out for drinks after art history faculty conferences. He helped me with more than a few journal articles." Her face gets mournful. "I'm sorry about what happened to him."

She fiddles with something on her desk feeling awkward. I'm a little taken aback as well; I had no idea she knew Dom.

"Thank you for saying that."

Her expression changes. "I see it now. Where you look like him. Your uncle was very respected."

Her voice hints—why do I have this profession instead of Dom's respectable one? And dare I trade on his good name? I feel I can. "Then you know he had ethics; he taught me ethics. And I live by that. I'd never do anything to make him ashamed of me."

Her expression wavers. She glances at my suit. A private detective doing poorly is a sleaze. A private detective with an expensive suit is on the take. "You dress like he did, too."

"When I'm feeling right." I smile and nod towards Joel. "He bought the suit for me so I'd look good. I've been dressing down these days."

That takes Joel by surprise but Wheatley laughs with me. "You sound just like Dom. Blunt and never took himself too seriously. The way you looked just now saying that, exactly how he would. Wow. Strange I never met you. And the suit does look good." She turns to Joel; "You bought it for him? That's pretty nice of you, considering the suit."

Joel is speechless at the moment, so I fill in. "We're close."

Her eyebrows go up and she nods. I'm like Dominic; if she knew Dominic, she knew that about him. He was very open. She's not going to judge. But more pressure on the reciprocity. I'm in a euphoria that she said I was like Dom, even in such a small way.

"I didn't meet as many of his colleagues as he wanted. I was pretty stubborn about doing my own thing. You can imagine how he took that but ultimately he supported me."

"Why did you choose this line of work?"

"Dom asked the same thing when I told him I wanted to do it at 17. Because it helps people. Because I like finding things out. Because I have the drive to do it. People need help, and this is one way."

She nods. "I remember now I read about you, Mr. Ross. The incident a few months ago down in Buckston."

The video that never disappears. "Not my best moment, I'll admit that. I'll have to carry that with me."

She shakes her head. "Dom would have done the same. Absolutely. When I read about you, I didn't know you were his nephew, but that doesn't surprise me. He was a man to step up. I get the sense you have principles. And you were beat up over something a little while ago, weren't you?"

"Yes, a client of mine was set up and murdered." I touch the scar on the side of my jaw reminding myself of what happened. "Three men were hired to beat me into leaving the investigation. They hit me in the face with a baton or something. Nonetheless, we found out what was behind the murder."

She winces when I mention being hit.

"He's like that," Joel says to her. "He'll face anything if he feels it's right."

Wheatley puts a hand over her mouth. "I hope that's true; I hope that's true." She thinks a minute. I keep her eyes the whole time. She locks on me. Somehow, I feel we understand each other. That like Dom she has a much more vibrant personal life outside staid academia, that she knows when boundaries have to be pushed.

"You know about Leonard's girlfriend, Sara. She was my student. A protégé, even. I hope to continue that at some point."

"Continue...She's not in school now?"

"She's on leave. I met Leonard a few times. He had issues but I couldn't figure them out, and not my place. Apparently, he was a good enough person that his occasional oddness wasn't a problem for her. I didn't care for the other professor—you know he's in prison now? Yes. Well, I didn't hold that against Leonard. Sara was very close with him. I thought about trying to find a job for him here. And then..."

I wait, on edge. She's talking herself into giving this up. I will her to do it.

She looks from Joel to me and back. "I don't want her to be hurt again. I'm still in touch with her. She wants to find out what happened to Leonard. She knows he's dead and that is devastating to her along with what else happened, which was very traumatic. I can see if she'll talk to you."

She's searching for whatever cues I have to make her feel she's making the right decision. I lean forward, resting my arms on my legs and keep my voice low and steady.

"I'll protect her. This is background material. I don't want her hurt, either. That is my personal responsibility."

She breathes deep. "Could you excuse me for a moment?"

"Sure." I get up, and catch a glimpse of a book on her shelf I recognize. "Oh, I know that book. Dominic is in it."

"Take it with you if you like. I'll be a few minutes. You can wait in the faculty lounge down the hall."

I thank her and pull out the large, Rizzoli-published book on Florentine art. We go to the hallway and close the door behind us.

He smiles as we walk down the hall. "I can't get over how people just tell you shit out of nowhere."

"Yeah? If they didn't, my job would be so much harder. In any case, it's because she knew Dominic, not my pretty face."

"Don't sell yourself short. She's smart enough to know Dominic is no guarantee of your *bona fides. You* sold her on you."

"I'm honest." I shrug.

"You're good. They can see that, in your aura. You seduce them too. You have a *very* pretty face, those dark Irish bedroom eyes."

"The suit helps."

"The suit? You blew its cover. But I have to admit, that "Aw shucks, my boyfriend bought the suit" bit made you hotter in her estimation."

"Either way, it still made a difference."

We go into the lounge. No one else is around. "That and you being beat down, having to prove things the hard way." He glances at the scar on my jaw. It stirs his anger to be reminded of violence, the same way mine gets stirred being reminded of cruelty.

But he also slips his fingers in the collar of my shirt, gently touching the back of my neck. For a moment we're acutely aware of being together. Somehow the empty room makes that more obvious than being in the car. He moves closer to me and I feel his lips against my ear. Not teasing, but just connecting.

When he steps back, he says, "Show me the book."

I put the book on a table. "Okay, check this out." I turn the book to page 214 and point down on the page. "This part on Botticelli. That's my uncle."

He kneels on a chair, bends over the page and reads. It's a half-page analysis of the artist's motivations in the context of Italian politics and spirituality. "This is good. You can understand it, but it's still deep. You don't have this book at home."

He's looked at most or all of my books, especially on art. "You're right. I think he gave it to his boyfriend."

"We'll get Jason to find a copy. I like the picture of him. You don't have this picture either. He looks like he's ready to kick someone's ass. Like you do so often. This professor was right on about that."

I have a bit of a hard time looking at Dom's photo, but I have to smile as well. "He usually was kicking somebody's ass. I was first on his list."

We look through the book some more. I find myself keeping my hand on his back while he turns pages. Until Wheatley suddenly appears in the room. "Gentlemen."

We follow back to her office. She sits on the edge of her desk. "She's willing to come over tomorrow. She's driving in from somewhere else; I can't tell you where or her last name for now. As I said, she was severely traumatized by what happened to her."

Her eyes flicker over us. "You can speak to her in my office, but..."

I do my damnedest to look trustworthy. "What is the concern?"

"Talking to strange men...it's hard for her. I sort of vouched for you, Mr. Ross. Knowing your uncle, what kind of man he was. But that wasn't enough, although I have a good feeling with you. I called someone who knew Dominic and knows you. This person gave you a reference—that you do what's right. I hope I'm not making a bad mistake."

I don't know who she might have called; maybe one of Dom's colleagues who was also one of my teachers. Doesn't matter, although I'm gratified for the reference.

"I wouldn't want to disappoint Dom. I would not do anything to make Sara's life worse, not hurt her, not put her in danger. Not intentionally. I know a risk is involved with everything."

"You seem to understand." Then she looks at Joel. He returns her gaze, sincerely.

"Everything Gabriel says applies to me. He doesn't want to disappoint his uncle. I don't want to disappoint him. I'd back him up to protect her as far as it goes."

She exhales heavily and gets up to look out her window. "You two are unusual. I can tell. For what you do...investigations." She glances at Joel.

"He partners with me sometimes. He's an artist as well."

"Really? What kind?"

I've made Joel uncomfortable, but he rises to the occasion. "Different mediums. I have a gallery showing coming up."

"Send me something about it, would you? I'd like to see what you do. What would help is having a female presence, comforting...I could be there, although that might make it difficult for you, but...even good men are hard for her to connect with."

I'm struck by what must have happened to Sara. "I understand that, knowing women who have been abused or attacked. Could I make it easier by having a woman there, a colleague of mine who is like me? Sara could focus on her."

"What is this colleague like?"

"She has the same principles we do. And she's helped women who've been subjected to violence and stalking. She identifies s genderqueer, but she is biologically female and empathetic to women."

"Could she be here tomorrow? I don't think Sara will change her mind about the date—it's hard for her to even come tomorrow."

"Let me see."

I step out the office and call Veronica. "Everything okay at the homestead?"

"Yeah, it's great. I thought about cleaning but didn't. I was afraid it would become my own personal war."

"You don't have to clean my place, it's not that bad."

"Sure, keep telling yourself that."

"You and Joel are too picky. I hate to ask a last-minute favor, but I will. I need you to help me interview a woman tomorrow, who's been traumatized and has difficulty talking to men."

"I was supposed to be at an office meeting concerning my status there, but I'll call in."

"Are you sure? This is a terrible imposition but I need you."

"I'll do it. I'm already *persona non grata*. Is it Michaela's case?"

"Yeah. This could be a real break for us. I'll call you later."

After goodbyes, I go back to where Joel is talking art with Wheatley. She's now looking at Isabella's website and talking with him about the art scene in Chelsea.

"It's set. Her name is Veronica Gianni." I have Veronica's cards with me as she carries mine. I give both to Professor Wheatley.

"Good. This will be early afternoon. Let me talk to her and give you an estimation."

"Thank you."

Joel and I leave. In the car, the topic changes to Geneva's case.

"This Rochester thing. You're going there to talk to a source?"

"Bettina's informant. Then we try to find Knox. I've found a history of fires over the years. I think he's behind some of them."

He's thinking about it. "I've never been there."

"It's a good town. You'll like it."

"When do we go? "

"Depending on what we find tomorrow, probably Friday. You okay with that?"

"Yeah. You know, Geneva left me a message not to give you a hard time."

"Which you clearly took seriously."

"I take everything seriously. I just don't always do what I'm told. I'll have to let her know everything is copacetic. What do you know about arsonists?"

"Serials arsonists are usually male, angry, don't have good jobs. Broken families. Mental issues. Not otherwise violent but may have had some related crimes. Arson has one of the lowest clearance rates in law enforcement so a lot of misconceptions abound about them. Actual pyromaniacs are few. This guy might be doing it for revenge. He might stay around to watch. His methods aren't likely to be very fancy, but in this case, he seems to have a signature.

He reaches over and takes the cigarette from my hand for a draw. "You mind?"

I try not to show amusement. "And if I did?"

"This is the way to cut down. Share it." He hands it back. "You were saying?"

"A signature is actually rare. John Orr who was an arson investigator and instructor in California, killed several people across the state with his fires and had a signature method to start the fire, but he was an exception. However, I saw an article about a fire recently I think is Arthur's method. He pours accelerant all around a building like a circle. A Rochester cop told me Arthur had done that before. It's overkill for setting a fire. He must like that."

"I don't need Wikipedia anymore, being with you."

"Well, I am the traveling automaton."

∞

Before we can leave New Jersey, Seth Monroe calls me. "I have something for you. Can we meet at a place, a diner on Worthington? The Starlight."

"Sure. I'll go there now."

When we get to Elizabeth and Worthington Street, Monroe's at a booth in the back. I introduce him to Joel. We sit across from him. He leans over and smiles grimly.

"I'm tempted to hire you, although I know that's a conflict of interest."

"Yeah? What's going on?"

"Some weird shit. I *know* Charlotte had notes. I read them. Yet, now there's nothing in hard copy for that month and nothing on our server. As if..." he spreads his hands on the table. "Someone removed them. And deleted."

"Not a coincidence, is it?"

"I have to wonder. Everyone in the damned office knows about your investigation. We all want to see something done about Charlotte's murder."

"And anyone could have removed the files?"

"I haven't looked at them in ten years. The storage room just needs an access code. The server is open to staff. Someone wanted to eliminate those notes."

I wait, because Monroe still has his tight smile. He takes a folder out his bag and places it on the table. "But that someone forgot or didn't know I had to make copies of her notes for the police. And since it was a legal matter, I had a separate file to record those notes I turned over."

I open the file. On top is a paper clipped copy of the notes, with a signed affidavit by Monroe."

"You're sure as hell efficient."

"If I can't hire you, I can try to help. Look at the fourteenth page. I think that's the relevant one."

—A man called and asked to speak with me. He was very insistent that a trafficking problem is going on in Eliz. He said his name was Leonard. He didn't give a last name. He told me he knew a place where women were being held. He couldn't say much now b/c he would be killed. Wouldn't talk to police. Said he was outside the office.

Went across the street from the office. Leonard clearly mentally ill but spoke clearly and sincerely. Said his brother was keeping women hostage in Eliz. Asked him where. He said he'd get back to me. Wanted to make sure women were safe. Asked if I listened to Carmen, the opera. Would not give contact info.

I have to smile at the mention of Carmen, even as I feel a surge of adrenaline.

"Then on page twenty."

—Leonard called. Said he would show me the house tonight.

"She was killed that night," Monroe says. "April 15th."

Just before the incident on Flora Street, with the men suddenly leaving the big house.

"Leonard Mathers' brother. Do you know who this is?"

"Yes. Leonard was right. He was killed about being right, probably."

"Ten years later?"

"He was beaten like Charlotte was."

Monroe studies both of us. "I hope this leads to him."

"Me too. You're an attorney. You know. If we go to trial on this, we likely don't prove my client innocent. We present an alternative theory for reasonable doubt. The police might or might now look into it."

"I'll call in the press if I have to."

"Let's hope something breaks."

"I can't trust anyone, Gabriel. As I said, this is all over the office. Destroying the notes has to be connected, although I don't know when it happened. At least half the staff was here when Charlotte was in charge."

"And the ones who weren't? I saw you've gone through a couple of directors. And Carlson started a year ago."

"I don't trust anyone now. Would you?"

"No. Not even you, to be honest."

"Good. That's the best way. Keep in touch."

Joel and I get up to leave.

"The police have the notes, but they haven't made the connection," Joel says on the way out.

"Charlotte's murder is a closed case by now, after ten years. Those notes are probably buried in the case file."

Inside the car, I call and update Michaela. Joel takes note of the detectives who worked Charlotte's murder. Then I call the Elizabeth police to see if we can speak to those detectives. One's retired and one is still around, Trina Murphy, and she's willing to see me tomorrow. That will have to be after we visit Professor Wheatley again.

"She'll listen, detectives are haunted by cold cases. But if I'll ask Michaela if she thinks she should contact the detectives on that case. But if they don't make the connection, we will."

∞

ELEVEN ◆ 8 UNION (B1)

Water over Earth: The situation requires people to care for one another, attention to how relationships between different forces flow. A person with a restless mind is going to have significant effect due to his inquiries, due to an expedition. The fifth line (yang/nine) moves here: the yang element is strong and steadfast, approaching a goal, a hunt, with yin elements showing support.

∞

Wednesday, December 15
Eastern New Jersey, 12:22 pm

WE'RE ON OUR WAY BACK to Prentice-Cane with Veronica. She's up to date on Sophie's case after we discussed it with Michaela last night.

In fact, Michaela had met us at our friend Jason's bookstore in the West Village, after hours. This was a chance to pick up the replacement Daoism books, music books, and the Rizzoli art history textbook Joel had asked Jason to find.

Jason also had a Yamaha Motif XF8 prominently displayed for sale, which he and Joel made sure to point out to me. I start playing around on it and he gets out an acoustic guitar and we play some Billy Joel songs. Giselle had been playing Billy in the store the last time I was there, and it renewed my interest in him.

Jason said to me, "You know, I'm in this little combo that plays small venues. Cover songs, more for fun than fame. Our keyboardist just left; and you have bar-band experience. Why don't you sit in with us?"

I'm not feeling too serious about that but Joel encourages me to give it a try, and attempts to buy the keyboards for me. I stop him, and purchase it myself, agreeing to meet with Jason's band in the near future.

I'm concerned that Wheatley's student might decide to bail but when I call the professor, she reassures me Sara is on her way there.

An hour later we've arrived and Wheatley meets us all outside the office. I introduce her to Veronica, and she gives us a very brief smile. "I'm not going to be in there other than to introduce you all. She knows why you're here. I'll be in the faculty lounge. You promised not to make it worse for her and I really expect you to live up to that."

"We will," I tell her. "It's on my word of honor."

Wheatley takes us in. Sara sits in one of the chairs in front of Wheatley's desk. She's black, in her late twenties, with a bob haircut. She wears dark glasses; we can barely see her eyes. I can feel she does this as a matter of protection, to gain distance.

Wheatley speaks up. "This is Sara."

We introduce ourselves without offering a hand in case she's uncomfortable with physical contact.

Wheatley reminds us where she'll be and leaves. Veronica takes the chair nearest her. Joel and I sit further back behind the desk. We've all gotten into professional mode.

Veronica begins. "Thank you for speaking with us. If it gets to be too much, let me know."

Sara nods. "It is difficult, but...I felt this is important for Leonard. I heard his body was found. Professor Wheatley said you don't believe the woman arrested killed him."

Veronica keeps her voice calm, low, direct. "No, we don't. More likely, from evidence uncovered, is that his brother had some responsibility for this. We know about Don Mathers, but we'd like more details about his relationship with Leonard."

Sara's hands dig into purse on her lap at the mention of Don's name. We can hear the crunch.

She reaches into herself for the fortitude to continue. "I met Leonard on campus three years ago. He was different; I suppose you heard about that. He functioned fairly well. And he was kind. He had a way of speaking that would enrapture me. He told me I was like Leontyne Price. He loved opera. I would go along with his conversations the best I could until he got too esoteric. At some point I would get lost because his ideas were too much in his own head, if you know what I mean."

Veronica nods, and Sara shifts around, looking briefly at Joel and me before focusing back on Veronica.

"What kind of work did he do? Something on campus?"

"Sometimes. I saw him sit in on a big lecture, and at first I thought he was a student. But he just liked to do that. He was an assistant to Professor Devanović."

I put in the next question. I want Joel and I to say something so she sees our sincerity, but for Veronica to mainly handle this to keep Sara calm. "What did Devanović teach, Sara?"

"Abnormal Psychology and Interpersonal Conflict. Leonard said he first met him at the old hospital."

"Wildemore."

"Yes, before it closed. Then he came to teach here. The professor was a little off when I met him. He couldn't keep his eyes off my body, although he didn't say anything improper to me."

Veronica asks, "How did Leonard help him? What he did?"

"Professor Devanović had some kind of experimental self-help group going on. Leonard worked with him on that and some financial or business thing. I'm not really sure but I know the professor got in trouble for it."

Joel follows up. "Did this group, the self-help thing, did it focus on women?"

"It did." Her head comes up. "Young female students seemed to be his target audience. He made a point of that. Kind of vulnerable. The professor invited me to it but Leonard told me not to go. It was like he realized something was wrong. That the professor wasn't trying to help the women at all."

She turns back to Veronica. Moves her chair closer. Veronica gives off vibes that let people take comfort from her. She waits until Sara settles before speaking again.

"Did Leonard mention any other women he was concerned about?"

"He talked about women a lot. He liked women, particularly in the opera, of course. Sometimes I couldn't tell if he was talking about real people."

"Ever about women from another country?"

"Yes, I remember...he talked about —he didn't seem to know them personally, but knew them a long time ago. Women who might have been from Devanović's country of origin —I think Romania or Serbia—but Leonard wasn't clear about it. And then Don..." She looks down.

"Don also knew Devanović."

"Yes. Leonard told me they all knew each other. And I thought that was strange. Because while Devanović claimed to help women, Leonard said Don hated women. Absolutely. Horribly."

Her hands shake a little. "And then I saw him. Don. It was in his eyes, his voice. He vibrated with it."

"Can I get you something?"

She turns her head to me. "Water?"

"I'll get it." Joel gets up and leaves the room. Sara reaches over and takes Veronica's hand. Joel comes back with a bottle of water. Sara takes a moment to regain composure.

"I can tell *you*." She says this to Veronica, focusing only on her. "Because this is so hard. So...what happened...Don was supposed to be dead. Long dead. But Leonard said he was seeing him again. Don was showing up. Telling him things on the street. Where Leonard stayed —in the old hospital. Leonard was terrified. Then...Don broke in my place. He was waiting for me when I came back after a night class. This was right before the end of the spring semester this year. He waited in my apartment, hiding. And then he jumped out of my closet. He grabbed my throat...he said he wanted to see how Leonard would like this."

She begins trembling again, but keeps her voice up. "He said...horrible things to me. I can't repeat. About...me, about what I did with Leonard, about my body. He hit me over and over again. I tried to fight but when he punched me, he made me dizzy. He said he wanted me to know what was going to happen. He wanted me to be scared. He said he was going to cut me open while I watched. He'd cut my breasts off, he'd cut...my private parts. That he'd rape me with the knife. He said..."

She leans forward. Inside, I hurt so much for her, having gone through that. I can see her eyes wide behind the glasses. She grips the arms of the chair. "He knew where Leonard "worshipped" women, and he had a hell to corrupt Leonard's heaven, and he would put me in his hell with the rest of them. The other *bitches*, he called them. I would be like them. I would be like them, and Leonard would never know."

Her breathing is labored. Veronica holds a hand out, and Sara grips it hard.

"He said he knew *where* Leonard worshipped women?"

"He said..." She suddenly snaps her head up to where Joel and I are sitting. "Do you hate women?"

"No." I lean forward now, making my voice plain and sincere. "My mother was the strongest influence I had, my conscience, my soul. I'd give anything to have her back. This woman here, Veronica, is not only my colleague but my best friend. I'd protect her with my life."

Veronica has a small smile with that. I keep my eyes on Sara. She seems to look at me, perhaps judging my veracity, then to Joel. He holds her gaze with honesty.

"I feel the same Gabriel does about Veronica. I don't hate anyone except cruel people, and never women." He glances down at his hands then looks up and smiles. "One of the persons who rescued me when I was thrown out as a teenager was a young woman, who showed me compassion and love. We took care of each other until she passed."

Sara contemplates him. "How did that happen? I mean, what happened to her?"

He answers, looking only at her. "She was pregnant when she met me and took me in with her. We stayed together for a while; I was in love with her. We were living in a squatter building and she was afraid the baby would be taken away, so she didn't go to the hospital. Jennah was 18 and I was 16, when she gave birth. The baby was fine, but Jennah got an aneurysm of some kind and died in my arms."

He stops for a moment. "I made sure she was...found. I wanted her sent to her family for a proper burial, which is what happened, at least. But I knew she didn't want her little girl sent to the foster system in New York or back to her parents. So I took care of her baby until I could figure out who was best to hand her over to, because I wasn't going to let Jennah's baby be hurt. My friend Chris and I figured out the best place to take her. I think I was able to go on with my life—which wasn't good at that point —because I was able to help her."

I did not know this story, and I can tell Veronica didn't either. I keep my surprise to myself. Sara seems affected by the emotion in his voice.

Veronica adds, "And me too. Not because I am a woman, but my mom taught me right, and I've loved women, some very deeply."

Sara's grip is so tight on Veronica's wrist I can feel it.

"It's okay...can you tell us what Don said? You have the ability to defeat him now, to help other women he hurt."

Sara is shaking, but she speaks. "He said *altar*. Leonard's altar. I don't know what he meant, but I knew, I *knew*, he killed people. He was going to torture me, kill me. He had stuff with him. He showed me the knives. He had tied me up, and was taking out the knives when Leonard broke in and stopped him. They fought with each other; Leonard fought him off for me. Don ran out, finally. Then Leonard told me I needed to leave town. I did report this to the police, but I didn't mention Leonard being there. I didn't say anything about Leonard at all. I just said I escaped. I was really afraid the police would think he did it, because of his condition. And how do you explain a dead man attacking you? Leonard gave me money and told me to hide out. I asked Professor Wheatley to help me with a leave of absence. I'm not sure when I'm coming back, because I know Don's out there, and Leonard's dead."

She starts crying. "I still can't feel safe."

The interview is done. She's exhausted, having shared her pain. But my mind is ringing from that word. *Altar*. It hits me cold—I know what it means. I had a hard time not reacting when she said it.

Veronica has moved closer to Sara, comforting her. "Nothing's going to happen to you. I promise. I'll go back with you if you want. I'll give you my number and if you see anything that disturbs you, you call me and I'll come there and protect you."

Sara nods. "Professor Wheatley is going to go with me, but..."

"Just call me. I want you to call me to let me know you got home safe."

"We'll all protect you, Sara." I get up. "I'm going to get Professor Wheatley."

Sara is calmer, but shaking. Veronica holds her hand until the Professor returns.

∞

I pull the car up to more or less where I parked when I was at Wildemore before with Bob.

The building—large, looming, decaying, silent, seems like a stone monolith. A malevolent Stonehenge. A temple to something evil underground, whereas before it was just mildly scary. We're all subdued, in a different frame of mind. Sober. Grave.

Keeping myself calm, sort of, I point to the west wing. "That's the side Leonard's special room was on. Toward the back, near us."

Joel nods. "So there might be a corresponding place on the other side?"

"There is. It's in the building plans. A mirror-image basement." Talking is hard. I take out my cigarettes. They both accept one. I get out and face the building. Although Leonard's altar had struck me as a warm, beating heart, a place of spiritual love, this side does not give me that feeling. It makes me cold to think of what was under our feet when Bob and I made our way through it before.

I can't fight that sensation so I try to work with it, letting it accompany me. I get out of the car and finish the cigarette. Veronica and Joel get out too, taking the lantern from the trunk.

I look up as a few random snowflakes drift down. Proof of nature's delicacy against humankind's horror.

We had considered calling the police to see if they'd go in. The building is not exactly public property and not exactly private. I called around and found out that if no emergency was known, city officials might get some sort of approval to go inside after a couple weeks' red tape. And I can't call in an emergency I don't know about.

Joel is gripping my arm, reminding me why I'm here.

"Yeah. Bob and I went through there." I point ahead to the gap in the fence.

"You okay?"

"God, no. You can feel something is there, right?" I stare at them. "Ghosts. They've been called. No one heard them before, but in Sara telling us this they're awakened now."

Veronica and I exchange glances. "Exactly. Crying out. Hungry ghosts."

Joel is unnerved. "Do you want to do this, then? We could find another way."

"Not if the truth is there. Then it's dharma. They brought me here. You mentioned before ghosts talking to me. I know being in contact with death, the underworld, led me here. The other spirits...sent me on this journey."

They're both staring at me.

"I don't make sense to myself."

But they aren't judgmental. Joel nods, seeing it in my eyes. He's with me. And I know Veronica is like me, understanding more to life exists than what can be observed, even if unspoken.

I get out of the car and move ahead, through the fence with them following. Three people crossing the chilled grounds of an abandoned hospital. Rising from this, one would see the scene blend with the woods, the county, the state, the Earth, the ether. Far enough up and this disappears, like Plotinus's idea of evil being a fading of the light from The One.

The ether is not at the back door. It's relocked. "Someone's been here." I lift the new padlock up with a knuckle. "This wasn't here before."

"Maybe the state did this?"

"I can't see that they suddenly start caring." I dig my picks out of my pocket. "This was someone else."

The Devil. Leonard's Devil.

Concentrating, I have them open in 30 seconds.

The daylight penetrates a few feet. The dust and molding slime on the floor. The corresponding rotting building smell.

"I'm so glad you two are with me."

I feel their touch. Mutual. Comforting. Veronica takes my hand and Joel takes her hand in turn. I turn on the lantern. The sodium light gives a false illumination to the corridor as we walk.

Remembering the layout of the west wing, Leonard's side, I look for a niche to our left. And there it is, set aside. The mirror image, the evil twin. An older lock on this door with smeared dust. It's been used lately.

Veronica holds the light while I work on it. Longer this time because I'm sweating in the cold. It's running down my back. Fearing the hungry ghosts. I have this image in my head of stone faces with open mouths, waiting.

The tumblers click. I take the lock off and hang it on the door. We push it open.

The staircase going down is a darkness that takes light, eats it, hides it. The light that struggles through shows the plain cement stairs.

As cold as it is, the scent from below is patent. I hear a roar in my head. Blood calling out.

"Stay here." I hold a hand up. "Let me go there. You don't have to see this."

"We're going with you." Veronica's hands are still shaking, making the light flutter.

Joel's hands are on my shoulders. "You're not going alone."

I put my hand out to the railing. Step down. The light shows a few steps ahead. Down slowly, in the dark. It swirls around us.

I'm breathing heavily and it echoes. Or maybe it's all of three of us.

The room is anticlimactic—an assortment of junk and tools like the twin room on the other side of the hospital. But then, Leonard's altar was in a subchamber, behind a door.

In unison, we look at the matching door here. It seems dark red. It's peeling paint, dull metal underneath. The door is unlocked, not even fully shut. "In there."

The scent is stronger. It's sad and horrifying to be right. I briefly flash on finding Raymond in the heat of summer; now here with death again in the depth of winter.

My heart pounds harder. My dreams have led me here, dead people calling me. Like my mom said in the dreams. Find them. Rescue them.

Go now or you won't go at all.

I push it open and the blackness waits, like a vertical sea, like the inside of a mouth.

Veronica shines the light on the floor, where we step inside. Some feet ahead is a dark line of what was liquid. As she raises the light, what was gray in shadows becomes clear.

I inhale, wanting to scream. I lose all sensation of anyone around me. I can see them all, and all individually.

Seven, eight...maybe more. Women thrown around the room. They were dumped here. Some have been here for years, losing their vestiges of humanity. Some are more recent.

One woman is closest to us. Her eyes still open, her mouth open. Crying out. Lines of blood from her body on a table, to the floor. Frozen. This had to have been done within the last week. While we were working the case, someone was trapping and killing this woman.

With my eyes on her I fall to my knees; blood draining from my head. In my stupor I stare at her from eye level. Twenty feet away, hands clutching at nothing. Cuts, gaping cuts, more. What was promised to Sara was done to her. It's not even comprehensible to see the mutilations. Someone put his hands in her and ripped her apart.

The rest of the women are equally in agony, death agony. Hands, feet, limbs thrown out, bodies open, as if their souls were literally torn from them. They all scream at me. I feel their spirits awaken and claw at me. Hungry ghosts. They've waited for someone to find them. That's what I'm here for.

My hands hit the concrete floor.

I feel them on me, clawing on me to take them out of the ghost world. Then I realize it's not the women. Live human hands draw me up from the floor. Veronica sits the lantern on the floor and gets down with me, Joel following. And we're all kneeling in the center of the horror, bonded together.

I don't feel human anymore.

We've all seen dead persons before, close. From disease, violence, hate. This is hate. Someone hated these women ferociously. Tore them apart. Left them here to hide them —a last contemptuous act. No one knows they're here, wandering in the darkness. The Devil must be laughing at this secret.

I'm hollow inside, except where Veronica and Joel are holding on to me. Buried underground in a room of Hell. The polar opposite of Leonard's altar. This is the hunting ground of demons.

Someone is saying he or she is sorry. It might be me or Veronica or both. Underneath I hear Joel's voice. "...*go*. We have to go. We have to go."

He's keeping his face turned away, in between us, which is the only way to not be frozen in place here. His hands are reality, drawing us away. I know why the three of us are together. None of us can stand and move on our own. I still have to look at the women, to hear them. These women are missing, and no one knew what happened to them. They needed to be brought out of the darkness for transition to the other side, for the families to mourn, to be released.

And to take care of this we have to leave. I feel Joel's hands pulling on me, taking my arm and Veronica's, leading us through the awful metal door to the deceitful anteroom. The door remains cracked open but the gulf between us and the screaming darkness inside is now a million miles.

Delayed reaction hits. I'm afraid I'm going to lose consciousness. Not here. Not underground.

My head starts to ache from tension, nausea. We pick ourselves up and move quickly for the stairs. In the corridor, even in the dark, the atmosphere is completely different. But we can't get to the back door fast enough. We're suddenly out in the schizophrenic sky. To the east, the sun is blinding, unreal. On the west, snow is falling lightly, delicately.

As soon as we're in the parking lot, Veronica and I both feel the need to throw up, going different directions to the woods.

In the beauty of nature, I fall again to my hands and knees. Venting my insides for what seems like endless minutes. I try to collect myself, waiting until my body stops compulsively heaving.

When I make my way back out, I feel strangely alone —I don't see them anywhere. I think I'm imagining things. Then Veronica emerges from the woods, her face pale. She comes to my arms, shaking.

Maybe Joel was sick as well. But when we go back to the car, he's sitting on the ground in front of it. His arms around his knees, his head down between them. We sit on either side of him.

Veronica and I stroke his head. He looks at her, then me. "I know what you're going to say, you're sorry about us being here. But you needed us here."

"I did." I find my phone. "I did need you."

I call Michaela, give her the story slowly, because it's hard to put in the words. She carefully, calmly draws it out to help me prepare. I have to call the police, and this is going to be a nightmare. As a defense attorney, Michaela has heard everything, and she's still stunned. But she leaves her office immediately to come to our aid.

I hang up. "I'll tell them I went in. You all stay out of it."

"No way. You need the back-up."

"Veronica, you don't need any more. With what you're going through with the agency..."

"Fuck them. I can't let you be alone."

"You know I feel the same way." Joel raises his head. We get up, find cigarettes, wait.

The police arrive. The stories begin. I take them as far as the stair door. The process begins; the questions and the suspicion. I had also called Detective Trina Murphy, the one who investigated Charlotte's murder, to get her in on this. Michaela gets there shortly after the cops, and works on steering them to connect the bodies to Sophie's case. Detective Murphy is very interested in making that connection, at least.

After being questioned separately we're given a reprieve. We watch the forensics team arrive and begin processing. A couple of trucks and ambulances, persons in uniforms, equipment. Some techs take samples from us in case we contaminated anything. It's a factory process—banal and excruciating.

Meanwhile, Michaela has caught up on the details. While she hasn't seen any of it, she feels our shock, and tries to distract with practicalities.

"I hope we can get Sophie out on now. Maybe we can prove Don Mathers is still alive and did this."

I reach in myself the best I can to be practical as well. "We need to set that scenario, then, any way we can. Starting with the media."

I know Alex has returned to the city and as awkward as this is, he's my best national media contact. Michaela knows what I mean and nods. I look at Joel, who's in the back seat, with Veronica's arms around him, leaning on his back. He's listening to the conversation. He glances at Michaela and then me.

"Do it for her, Sophie, and Michaela." He brings out his cigarettes.

I step away and call Alex's cell; he doesn't answer. This pisses me off even though I can't expect more from him under the circumstances. This is my own doing.

But I have to try further. I call the *Herald-Standard's* editorial number and his extension.

He answers now which angers me more, both at him and myself.

"It's me."

Pause. "Hello. It's not a good time, right now."

"This isn't personal; it's about a news story."

"What do you mean?"

"We found bodies in Elizabeth. Several. In the hospital here I told you about, Wildemore."

"What the hell...Are you there now?"

"Yeah, with the police. I know it's New Jersey, not New York, but it's a big story. You remember I told you about the murder of Leonard Mathers, Michaela's case in Elizabeth. I think Leonard's brother Don Mathers is behind this. These women have been down in the basement...some for years."

"A serial murder thing? You didn't see them before, when you went with Bob."

"No, of course not. They were in the opposite wing."

"I'll send someone out. Are you with Bob again?"

"No." I want to hang up. Send someone out. Fuck it. But I have to help Michaela. "I'm with Veronica and Joel, we were following up on a lead. It's important that we get this information published because the prosecutor here is going to protest our theory. But I'm telling you this proves Sophie is innocent, if we can tie it to Leonard's brother. A story supporting our perspective in The Standard would help."

"I'll see what I can do."

I hang up at that. I'm still shaking from the women's agony. This personal shit is too much. I walk back to sit in the car with Joel and Veronica. She looks at my face.

"What was that about?"

"My problem with him." I try to get a cigarette out of my jacket. "It's my fault."

"Forget about it." Joel reaches over and takes my hand. "Don't worry over him if he wants to be that way."

An hour passes, and the forensics are just beginning. The bodies probably won't be taken out for a while. I think of the women inside, screaming for release.

We wait in the car. I'm giving prayers to the dead in my head, like I did for Raymond Booth. But the living need care too. I wake from a reverie and check on them. "If we get out of this, we go back to my place and crash, okay? Get drunk. Let's be together. This isn't the time to be alone."

They agree.

Michaela is back. "Hey. You all okay? This was really so horrific...I don't know what to say."

"We're glad you're here."

"To help you out, of course I am. I don't think the police believe you all had anything to do with this. And you did call Alex, then?"

"Yeah. He didn't seem very enthused."

"Really? Because he's here." She gestures over her shoulder.

We all look in that direction. And damned if he isn't getting out of a car with some other man.

"Well, fuck me."

Alex looks across the parking lot at me. It's hard—in spite of or because of everything —to meet his eyes.

The police aren't going to let him over to where we are so Michaela and I walk over to him. His companion is an Asian-American man around 30.

Alex nods at me. "This is Clark Ahn. He's doing the beat I used to. Crime. I wanted to ensure he would get a good story out of it."

I take Clark's hand, as friendly as I can be under the circumstances. Alex says hello to Michaela.

Michaela handles the interview with the input of details I have. Clark gets some background information—he been told my history already. I let him go with that. Alex watches me on and off as we talk. We're not feeling the warmth, but that's okay. Clark wants to speak to Veronica and Joel too. Michaela needs to keep control of the situation, and she and I talk, before I go back to bring them over.

When we return to Clark, I introduce him to Joel and Veronica. Alex also greets Veronica. Joel is pointedly not looking at Alex, and Alex is returning the favor. I don't care. I share Michaela's hope we can get something done, so personal feelings don't matter.

Michaela watches over their brief interviews. Meanwhile, Alex pulls me aside. "We'll work on this, call in some questions to the prosecutor."

"Thanks. Did you need anything else?"

"No, we'll see if the police have anything to say and then we have to get back."

"Thank you again for helping her out."

He nods. "Are you okay?"

"No."

His eyes flicker over me. "Can I do anything?"

"You did, bringing Clark here."

"Right." The snow begins to light on us again. The inches between us seem like a chasm. "I'm sorry you went through this." Out of sight from everyone else he takes my hand briefly in his. "You need me to be with you tonight? You know I will."

My face flushes. I didn't expect his offer and it causes an eruption of guilt inside. A hideous feeling. In spite of my issues with him and pretty much having ended the relationship in my mind, the fact is I still have feelings for him. And he's doing the decent thing here for me. He doesn't know what's going on with me. It's easier to be angry —then those feelings can be ignored. Mikki was right.

"I'm okay. We can talk later. This isn't..."

He frowns. "If you need me, Gabriel, call me. Aside from what else is going on. I'd never leave you alone."

I nod; I can't say any more. When I don't tell him what he wants to hear, he turns away. It makes me hate myself for a minute.

Clark is talking to Joel. When Alex comes up to him to lead him away, he glances at Joel, and nods once, coldly. Joel gives him the exact nod back.

And I feel twice as bad; the living, the dead. But when the women are brought out on stretchers, covered, I feel relief. They're out now. We watch the terrible process. My mind is reeling. At this point, I think I'm like the atomic scientist who said he'd seen death so much, he was almost inured.

"You're so white." Veronica hand goes to my face. "Michaela, any chance we can leave?"

"Let me talk to the detectives in charge. They know me."

And our triad is left alone. I'm thinking about what's been discovered. "The Devil. Don. He must have done this when he was here before, and since he's come back."

"Something set him off to start killing again."

I turn to Joel. "Remember Leonard indicated some of the ones in the notebook were dead. They may be there."

"They might be, but you need to let it go tonight. Let's just crash."

I think again about the dream I had with my mother. Find them. Set them free.

∞

Twelve ♦ 25 Not Untruthful (Wú Wàng)

Heaven over Thunder: *This* gua calls up the concept of a turning point that leads to truths. It invokes strength, betterment. The third line (yin/six) moves in this reading: some misfortune may occur, but the superior person is being true to the way of nature.

∞

Saturday, December 18
Chinatown, Canal Street, 10:12 am

"Do you understand what's around you," Chiang asks.

"Death," Gabriel says.

"I know, but can you understand why? You say you realized your purpose."

"I think so. I just didn't realize...so much pain would be involved."

"You were called to work on this. This is why life has become difficult for you lately."

"I don't want to stay in death."

"Then you need to *live*. And the Qi knows who you are and what you do. Now you're involved in something new, and you'll see even more you're a protector. In knowing yourself, and being yourself, you'll find extraordinary strength.

Gabriel takes in the idea. "Am I always going to be haunted?"

"You'll have to fight ghosts on occasion. But I think you will also want to speak to ghosts. The benign ones. If I didn't think you could do this, I would not have encouraged you to take the responsibility."

∞

Saturday, December 18, Continued

Michaela has arranged for me to talk to Devanović on New Year's Eve, no less. I've pushed back the trip to Rochester to next week, as it's not something I can handle now. However, Michaela and I like the fact that the New Jersey and New York papers are playing the story of the women right. Unfortunately, the prosecutor, Stan Cooper, is not giving Michaela any break —he refuses to actually lock into the connection between Don and the women. He's leaving it to the police on the case, a mix of local and state police that's becoming a task force. Detective Murphy is sharing her case file with that group of law enforcement personnel, believing in the connection.

In the meantime, someone has finally leaked Sophie's condition to the press. We have no idea who —but it doesn't matter. Reporters call Michaela demanding to know how this fits into the murdered women. It doesn't, but in the reporters' initial rush to the story, some confusion gets into the stories —even assumptions that Sophie might have killed the women herself, through Edward or using Edward as an excuse to kill. That is clearly wrong, as the most recent victim was killed while Sophie was in jail. I'm not surprised this is going to be an uphill battle as we try to connect the women to Leonard's case.

We've stayed together over the last couple days, Veronica and Joel and I, almost afraid to leave one another for very long. We feel isolated in a phantom world by virtue of this contact with death.

Veronica's agency swiftly terminated her, claiming cause from the 'controversy' over what happened at Wildemore. While not unexpected, I feel my own responsibility is to ensure she does not suffer since she enabled me to find those women, and that furthers our intention of combining businesses.

Something positive is needed after Wildemore. For a recognition that the holidays are ever nearer, I take Joel with me to meet Giselle at her shop to move on buying gifts.

Giselle is both sad for what we found but elated to meet Joel. Once I tell her I want to find something for some of my friends, she offers to help with the shopping.

"You're having a difficult time, still."

"He is," Joel answers. "He needs the help, and he was right about how fine this store is."

Giselle's very pleased to hear this. They talk some more while I'm listening to the Erasure song playing on her sound system. *Solsbury Hill.*

"You like them? They are so my favorite."

"That's his favorite song, actually," Joel says. "I remember."

"Let me set up more." She changes her music playlist, which is synced with a video monitor showing nature scene slideshows, and then walks us around the store.

Eventually we get around to talking about the case. She tells me, "I saw the story in the New York papers. The one that suggested the person who killed these women likely killed Leonard."

"We think that's what happened."

"I know you're right, Gabriel. How do you prove it from here?"

"Trying to find as many connections as possible. The police are on this now, so they might find out more—they have the resources."

"What's really awful," she tells us, "is this speculation now that since Leonard lived in that hospital, *Leonard* killed the women."

"We saw that. The police naturally consider that theory, but they've at least listened to ours. Hopefully we convince them ours is the right one. It may take time for evidence to turn up, unless they find DNA that can be matched."

"These stories, the ones in Jersey, are even saying Sophie might have killed Leonard in revenge for him killing the women."

"I know, it's terrible. But all kinds of speculation is going to happen before the truth comes out. We need to be prepared for that."

Giselle shudders, and changes the subject to finish our shopping excursion. We end up staying until closing again. Joel has made an even better impression with everyone even better than I did. It's kind of an oasis experience, and a first in the sense of him and I being around others as together. He feels it too, the pleasure of interacting with Giselle and her staff as part of a couple.

Once the shop is closed, he offers to draw Giselle right there. I watch him enjoying that. Jacob is watching as well, and then Joel draws him and Giselle together. He can draw fast and has both done within an hour.

"This is so wonderful," Giselle says. "I'm going to put them up in the office now...Gabriel, can I ask you something really quick?"

I follow her into her office. Jacob has shown an interest in sketching so Joel starts to show him some drawing tricks.

In her office she stares at the sketches. "He's wonderful. I knew it was going to work out. I want to see you both again, I'll take you out somewhere. But...I had a request. God, it seems weird."

"No, tell me."

"You have your own practice, right? Outside of what you do with Michaela?"

"Yes. Did you need something?"

"I might...I don't know. I might need you to look into someone. I don't mean like a credit check. I mean like if someone's lying about who they are."

"Not one of the staff?"

She turns pink. "I don't want to say right now. But I think I want to do this. I just don't want to be paranoid." She reaches for my hand.

I can tell she needs comfort. "I understand. Look, I'm here for you. If something is bothering you, go with your instincts if it strikes you wrong. I can investigate it, without the person being aware, up to a pretty good point. You can move from there. But if it's bothering you, let's talk about it."

"Okay." She takes a deep breath and smiles. "But not today. You need to process what you went through, or just enjoy your time with Joel. I'll be all right for now. I have to psych myself up. But we will talk. I feel you're going to help me."

∞

Sunday, December 19
West 86th Street 11:00 am

I still have my personal battles. The time has come to resolve one. In the three days since we were at Wildemore, Alex has checked in on me periodically by phone. The conversations have gotten increasingly tense.

I'm well aware from seeing the last moments of others of the benefit in living like life is short. People too often put things off they need to do; delay how they want to live.

The women took my attention as they deserved to. And I needed some time to process having found them. But now, with wheels in motion to bring them over from darkness I need to resolve this thing with me and Alex as I promised to Joel. The beginning can't really come until the end has arrived.

I've begun to do things I usually do when a relationship goes to hell, like getting tested again—an RNA test, because I'm impatient. And thinking about what I need to say.

I ask to meet Alex at his apartment tonight and he's willing. I'm terrified and anxious all at once. I'd rather pound nails in my hand than have this kind of talk. Still, I'm hoping it goes forward in an adult way.

He lets me in his apartment. We embrace for a few moments and briefly talk like nothing has happened, almost relax with each other on his sofa.

He's scrutinizing me. "Are you okay? After what happened? You look lost."

"I am. I feel awful, but I hope these women are moving on spiritually."

"The families can move on at least. You helped with that."

I have to do this before the conversation goes much further. Yet as I'm preparing to say something to start, I'm surprised when he suddenly sighs. "Knowing how hard this was to go through, I don't want to make it more difficult. I don't know where to begin."

"With what?"

"You, of course. With us."

I think back to the night I walked away from the restaurant. I remember that he doesn't know why I'm here. He thinks I've come over just to talk. God, I feel like I lived a lifetime in the days we've been apart. Surreal, because in my mind I've already moved on from him.

He frowns, as if he's about to launch into a speech.

"I don't want this to go wrong. I'm trying to put us back together. This means I need to really tell you some things, and I need you to listen."

My heart sinks in a pit of adrenaline even as my hackles rise at his lecturing tone. "Alex, I want the same thing for this not to go wrong, but I guess for a different purpose."

"What do you mean?"

"What I'm saying is I can't go on with us." Getting the words out is difficult enough that at first, I'm concentrating on just doing it. It takes me a moment to register the utter shock on his face.

"*What?*"

He stares at me, and when I meet his eyes, I see something totally alien. In that moment he becomes a stranger and the chasm opens between us. I feel a psychic ring of fire in the room surrounding us.

"So it's like this?" Even his voice becomes different, darker.

"No good way to say it. I'm sorry."

"You're not even going to try to talk about this?"

I have to look away, and continue talking while taking out a cigarette. "We can talk."

"Really? You'll allow that?" His tone becomes sharper. "I didn't want to end what we have, you know. I just wanted time."

I have to look down at the floor. "I know. But I can't go on."

"You came here to tell me *that.*"

"Yeah. And apologize. I didn't want to put you through this—"

He interrupts me. "I don't know what that means, Gabriel. You don't want to put me through this. That matters if you were trying to work with me. *This* is fucked up. I know we haven't been together long, but it hurts terribly."

I'm caught short by his words. "I'm sorry; I truly did not want to hurt you."

He shakes his head. "And I was trying to spend this time thinking on how we could mend the relationship. What were you thinking about? I suppose I know that already. You forget everything important. No wonder you're hampered from progressing."

Adrenaline courses through me. I suppose I could let it go and just get up and leave. Nothing stopping me. I said what I needed to. But...his words land in me like a fishhook. "*Progressing...*what the hell are you talking about?"

"I truly don't want to say what I'll say, but I want you to know how I feel...you have a tendency to be wrapped up in your mind, to the extent you lose touch with a healthy way of life. This job is so dangerous; I know you're good at it, but it takes you over. You've lost perspective because you hide things."

His voice has turned authoritative. I feel my anger rise slightly. "Oh, for fuck's sake, Alex."

His look turns vaguely contemptuous. "I already know, Gabriel. Don't tell me Joel is a *friend*. I can see your feelings for him. And yet I spent the last few days missing you. I don't think I ever felt that way, and that's dangerous for me."

"I know it was bad; I'm sorry I didn't resolve this sooner."

He covers his eyes. "Big of you to say. Fuck, I don't want to be this way. I'm trying one last time to get through to you. Not to change your mind but out of concern for you. Of course *he's* seductive, and element of chaos that must seem so much more enticing than stability. But it's not what you need."

I'm compelled to get up and put some distance between us, by walking over to his windows. I feel on the defensive now. "Why is that? Because you want to be able to tell me how to change my career? When and where I'm supposed to go back to school? Where I'm supposed to live?"

"Yes, anything said to help you is really against you, isn't it? Your attitude is incredible."

I turn back around. "You still don't get it. I never wanted my life changed for me."

He walks over to get in front of me. "I was trying to make *our* life better. I wanted *you* to grow the fuck up."

I'm momentarily unable to speak from hearing that verbal slap. I try to regain my composure. "*Excuse* me?"

"You're lost in your world of the past and because of that you hurt others. I didn't say it was deliberate, but you don't realize what you do. I can see you don't believe that."

"How could you *ever* say such a thing?"

He snorts derisively. "You're not as impenetrable as you think; you *wear* your emotions, your attractions, your hatreds. You eat and sleep and smoke them. Your perspective is fucked-up. You're trying to get something out of life to make up for the past."

I shake my head. I try to put on the internal brakes, but he's just gone somewhere that's like stirring a killer bees' nest. And I hear buzzing getting louder in my head. "What kind of bullshit is this about my past?"

"It's an explanation. You see, over the last week I've actually *thought* about us; I doubt you have—you were busy being seduced. He tries to make you think we're *so* different and he understands you better, right? I know you haven't had an easy life. But it *did* leave you with a martyr complex, or maybe a messiah complex. You get too involved with people and you don't see the harm it does to you, much less anyone else. You think what you went through as a child —and I know it was really, really bad for you—gives you entitlement to act as you want."

My face is hot, feeling the anger between us.

"What the fuck are you saying?" I want to put my hands over my ears and hide. I feel the walls of the room fall away to let in burning demons—cackling, laughing, at the turn of events.

He doesn't see these demons; he's becoming one. "Instead of taking in stray animals, you take in stray people. Clients who get you to do illegal acts. Lost causes to put your life in danger. So-called *friends* who play you into an emotional affair. You need to get out of your tragic kingdom, Gabriel. What you do to others has consequences. You're selfish in that way, figuring you can get away with it because you say you want to be a good person. But you're not examining your motives. And you're making others pay for your childhood."

My heart pounds louder than his words. I can hear demons' screeching underneath. And I feel another mode coming on. Similar to the protector mode, tough and cold. To battle. To become something I don't want to be, out of anger. Like when I used to argue with my father—going to war.

"Do you even understand how unbelievably wrong you are? I've never taken advantage of anyone or hurt someone because of what my childhood was like. What the hell did you want me to be, anyway? Did I shame you, is that it? Embarrass you because I'm too low-class for your prep school buddies? Did they tell you they don't understand what you saw in me?"

I get to him with that. He doesn't want to be honest about his class issues. I realize, though, he's internalized them.

His authoritative voice gets colder. "Maybe you keep yourself down on that level because then you don't have to challenge yourself to be better."

The anger in me rises again like a geyser. The demons feed on it, become more frenzied.

"*Fuck* you. You have no idea about me or my life. You think you can come from a position of privilege and judge *me* and what I went through? You and your asshole Social Darwinist friends have no Goddamned idea what hard times are like."

Now we're in each other's faces, invading each other's space. When I said *fuck you*, he looked like I had struck him.

"I know enough about you—because you never, *never* stop resenting what fucked-up deal the world has given you. But self-pity isn't attractive, Gabriel. Part of being a man is to stop sulking and facing life."

"Who the fuck do you think you are to tell me that? Easy to do what you want when you got your father's money backing you up."

His breathing gets harsher. I keep thinking, *I don't want to do this, I don't want to do this,* but the other part of me in control is not backing down.

His words become louder and more vicious. "You need to face reality. You somehow think you have more character because you lived on the dole. Time to get out of your fantasy life if you don't want to stay damaged goods."

Somewhere in the anger the true me feels seriously wounded. The many times I told him about my family, my life—did he just think my bearing my soul was just a character flaw?

"Goddamn it. You think you're *better* than me, don't you? *Fuck* your reality."

He pokes his finger towards my face. "Piss off!"

My father used to stick his hand in my face like that, and it triggers my defenses. I want to slap his hand away from me, but I back up instead while he keeps talking.

"You're being a fucking idiot. You know what's so sad? You'd rather be a gutter-level messiah to people who will fuck up your life, then be with me."

"Jesus, I can't believe you..." My voice no longer sounds like my own. The demons sing a chorus behind me, willing me to do and say more, but I stay still. I have to extract myself even as he continues talking.

"Me? You don't know about me, because you're stuck on him. God, you love that seduction, don't you? He tells you what you *want* to hear not what you need to. And *he* betrayed you. I know what happened because I was trying to understand why you have him around. You left him because he fucked around on you—sold himself, yet. And knowing what he is, you prefer him over me. I *know* that was your "emergency," don't bloody well tell me otherwise. And you want to know *why* I want you to get out of your "profession?" Because *this* is what your ethics have become—you slagging me off in favor of your rent boy."

The buzzing in my head gets impossibly loud from shock. I have the ugly urge to get physical for what he said. To slap his face now, and if he wants to get into it, knock him senseless. But if I did, I'd become the monster he seems to think I am. I'm not that person and I won't let him provoke me into being that person. I don't give a damn what he thinks anymore. I back away, not feeling the floor under my feet.

"You have no right to say that about him. You think I'm so awful—well, you don't have to suffer with it anymore. You are I are *done.*"

I grab my jacket and leave. I slam his door, which I know he'll hate because it makes a scene for the neighbors. Very childish.

In the elevator I'm overwhelmed by the poison of my anger and smash my fist against the wall, making the car shake. It doesn't get better when I'm leaving the building.

"Fuck this shit," I mutter to myself. On the sidewalk I can barely get my cigarettes out without ripping the pack in half. Bits of paper and tobacco go flying. People move out of the way.

I want to get to my car back in Alphabet City, get out of here, out of town. Right now, I'm connected with the demons. I shouldn't be around people. Even out on the street. I force myself to stop and try to calm down, a volcano in winter. I lean against a Chase Bank window, hoping for self-control, willing the demons to leave.

And then I realize someone is beside me.

Joel. I should be glad to see him, but the fury stoked in me is too much, too deep. It's the wrong time for him to be here; right now I'm a minotaur, something unearthly from rage. He looks concerned—then disturbed—upon seeing me.

I have difficulty in moderating my voice. "What are you doing here, Joel?"

He's so taken aback he actually moves a step away from me, eyes widening. "Jesus. You *told* me yesterday what you were going to do, remember? I knew it wouldn't be good. I got the impression you wanted me to be here and I wanted to make sure you were okay."

I have to turn away. I take out a cigarette from the pack, light it. Buy time, and defuse the rage that's overtaken me. I want to say something completely different, but I can't. Part of me is fucking pissed off at everything and that part's in control.

"You were waiting out here for me to have the fight with him."

I've completely flustered him. He didn't expect this just as I didn't expect to be so in this depth. I can see that, and yet right now I'm so in this other self that I can't say anything to help him, because my anger will lash out like a cobra. I focus on the bank window, breathing in the smoke.

Next to me he struggles to come up with an answer. "You...you don't remember what you said yesterday, do you? That you hoped I'd be around. Maybe I didn't understand what you meant. I don't know what you...look, I knew it wouldn't be easy for you to talk to him...but what did he do to you? To make you look at *me* that way?"

I can't remember exactly what I told him yesterday. I had been talking too much out of nervousness. Of course, I wanted comfort from him, but God, I had no idea this would go so badly. In seeing Joel's hurt, I hate Alex for what he said.

I don't know how I'm looking at Joel so I cast my eyes down, staring at my hands, at the cigarette burning like my insides. Remembering Alex grabbing my hand and becoming infuriated again. No. Stop. It can't continue like this.

I throw the cigarette in the street. Stare up at the sky. The rage is a strong, all-encompassing feeling. It comes so naturally that getting rid of it is not unlike Sophie transitioning from Edward. It takes enormous effort.

"It's not you. It's not you, Joel."

When I look at him again, he's trying to cope like I am. He takes my hand and smiles. Knowing how he feels about anger, it's brave.

"Hey, it's okay, right? If you need me to leave, I'll go. But I just want to help you."

He's not a child anymore but the child is there, scared of anger. I take a deep breath and pull him in to hold him. I can't calm down; I'm just trying to seem calm now for his sake.

"I'm leaving for Rochester now. You coming with me?"

"Now? *Really?*"

"I need to go."

"Um, sure. I'm ready."

"I know Veronica will take care of Archie, so I just want to throw some stuff into a bag. I want to be on the road as soon as possible."

"Okay." He steps in the street to hail a cab. I can't talk on the way home. I'm not myself by any means; I can still hear the buzzing in my head.

I go back to my place and he returns to Chelsea for his stuff.

Veronica has seen me at my worst; we've seen *each other* at our worst, so she can listen to me vent for several minutes without being affected. I try to pack a suitcase, and she stops me.

"For God's sake. I know you want to leave right now but do this properly." She empties everything on the floor to the cats' amusement. They jump in and out of the vacant suitcase and play hide and seek among the clothes.

I'm still in my rage. I realize in looking at my front door I need to change the lock, since I'm not asking Alex for the key back. I go into the hall closets to my containers of locksmithing equipment and find a spare cylinder. I start taking the old one out the door. Joel shows up while I'm putting in the new cylinder. He comes in without saying anything. My fury must still be evident.

Veronica has repacked my suitcase. "Think about what equipment you want to take with you."

"In a minute." I change the keys for the apartment on mine, hers, and Joel's set of keys, then go in my bedroom and start tearing through my closet and drawers.

"What are you doing," Veronica says from the doorway.

Alex has kept some clothes here for when he's stayed over and gone to work the next day. I want it all out of my place, now.

They wait for me to finish throwing the clothes on the living room floor. Once I'm done and hyperventilating, she puts her hand on arm.

"Okay, take it easy. Finish getting your stuff. I'll take care of this."

"I want to send it—"

"I know. I'll do it."

I start gathering my phone and other equipment together, barely noticing that Joel is silently watching all this.

Veronica is folding Alex's clothes. "Are you all right to drive?"

"Yes, no problem."

"Maybe Joel should drive."

Joel lights a cigarette. "Are you *sure* you want me along?"

I frown at him. "Of course, I want you along. Just...fuck, I'm mad, I know. He said some shit...look, I'm not talking about this now. And I'm driving."

I walk around the apartment several times, making sure everything is safe. I can't be still now. I go over to Veronica and put my hands on her face. "Thanks for helping."

She hugs me. "Of course. Try to center yourself. Joel, you have to watch out for him."

Then Joel's picking up the bags, looking doubtful. "Let's go then, so I can get busy watching out for you."

It is, despite my mood, a good night for driving. Clear, lots of stars, not too cold. I head for the Holland Tunnel then into Jersey for the New York Thruway. The drive helps me power down, and from that comes regret that Joel got caught in the storm.

We're getting to the exit for I-80 and Pennsylvania, which turns north toward Rochester. By this time I'm much calmer. Joel has been staring out the window. The music playing emphasizes the silence between us.

"I'm sorry," I tell him.

"It's okay." His voice is soft, but he resists any further conversation.

By the time we hit Rochester I'm exhausted and my muscles are tight; I'm welcoming the Best Western. Joel had called ahead to reserve while we were on the road. I've also sent Bettina a message to let her know I'm in town. She offers to meet us late in the afternoon the next day and to get in touch with Antonio.

It's one room, two beds. After I undress to my boxers, I collapse on one of the beds; I realize he's taken the other.

He sees me staring at him and fiddles with the TV remote. "You're still angry."

"No...and I wasn't angry at you anyway. I was caught off guard." I feel my throat close, the regret rising strong. "You know that, right?"

"I saw how you were in the park in Jersey, and you got over that. This was different. For a moment, it felt like when you were mad at me before. I can't deal with you like that. Anyone else, not you. Not to look at me you did."

I sigh, and it comes out almost like a sob. I bury my face in the pillow, for a moment feeling hopeless. That everything has gone wrong that could.

"I was never mad at you like that, never. I shouldn't have let you think what happened today had anything to do with you. I'm sorry. He tried really hard to hurt me and it worked. He pushed my buttons so bad..."

I listen to the television in the background, underscoring the silence.

Then I feel him sitting on my bed. I feel his hand on my back.

I turn my head to look at him. After some time of just lying there feeling his hand on me, my mind revolves around what he's been through.

"Will you tell me about Jennah?"

Joel's surprised. He had already put her away in his compartmentalized memories. Unsettled, he runs his hand down my back, glancing around the room. "Well...you heard the fundamental part of the story."

"I'd still like to know more, because she was special to you. I was struck by that. Where did you take her baby?"

His eyes change, and I see the most hidden side of him for an instant. "We took her to a fire station in Connecticut. It was known for being a place where babies could be left anonymously. I'll tell you more at some point. I can't now. It's kind of like I have to take it out and prepare it before I do. I don't know how to explain."

"I understand. That impresses me more that you were willing to share that with Sara."

Then he's quiet again.

But I can't be. Compulsively, all our conversations play in my head, him and me. How many times has he sat by me when I'm feeling bad? I remember the Friday when I knocked myself out. What he told me shortly before. "What about the other time you had a gun to your head...will you tell me about that?"

He frowns at me. "I should never have said anything about it. You're looking for more to feel guilty about."

"No, I want to know. You never told me much of your life, although you're trying."

"Does it matter right now? Just let it go for the time being. If I told you, you'd get emotional about it. Or angry. I don't want to see that now."

I sigh. "I'm so sorry, Joel."

"This was just bad timing." He caresses my head and makes me lie down again. He's still feeling my rage, though pretending not to. I don't want it to be this way.

"I won't ever do anything to hurt you, Joel. I'm trying to change too."

He nods. "Okay. This is more dangerous than those two men being after us."

It is. We can get over people trying to kill us. We can't get over each other.

As I'm lying there looking at him, I'm suddenly overwhelmed. I don't want a chasm between us. Our new being together seems so tenuous. I don't want this to go wrong.

He doesn't realize at first. Then as my mind crashes, his expression changes watching me.

The tears spill out from me like a waterfall.

It's so much, Joel is alarmed. He grips my hand harder. It doesn't stop the flood. I feel myself breaking down. Everything that happened flies up in my mind and beats me senseless.

Joel gets up, panicked, and finds a box of tissues from somewhere, rushes back. "No, no, it's okay."

He tries to blot away the tears, but they keep coming, like I'm bleeding tears. I'm almost physically sick.

I feel his desperation yet I can't stop anymore. He climbs on the bed, pulling my head to his chest. Holding tight. "Okay. Okay. Cry against me, baby. I won't let you go. You're not alone. I'm here, right? Tomorrow I'll piss you off cracking wise, and you'll go on for a half-hour about some obscure shit even Wikipedia don't print, and things'll be normal again. Promise."

And helpless, it continues as if my soul has been opened. All the dead are there, all the hurt and regret is there. My mind, fighting me, finds more despair...finally going back to my mother. Feeling the loss.

True to his word he holds me through the whole thing. When I cry myself sick enough to throw up, he waits and then holds me again until I pass out.

∞

"Alchemy. It's important to heal." Chiang is there by the bed. Transformation. *Nei-Tan.*" He has Joel's coins. He feeds Gabriel the coins one at a time.

"Precious metal will help the alchemy. The Immortals are in the coins. They will transform you. It's time for the *Chai.*" The *Chai,* a liturgy specific for exorcism.

"The *Kuei* (demons) must leave now." Suddenly the bed is outside, in the spring, when such a rite must take place. Chiang and his student are surrounded by orchids and cherry blossoms. Chiang closes his eyes, meditating.

Then thunder, lightning. Chiang turns toward the storm. Gabriel's mother approaches from the horizon. She holds out her hands and small globes of effervescent white light hover over the 12 joints in her hands.

Chiang begins breathing deeply. He calls out the esoteric name of the 12 earthly powers, and holds his hands up in mudras — hand signals of the sacred. As he does, smoke from each globe travels to him. He breathes it in, until after the 12th he is translucent. Gabriel can see the lightning within him, showing through his skin.

Chiang takes a paper scroll and reads from it over Gabriel's body. "In the name of the Jade Emperor, the evil forces must leave this man immediately." He sets this paper on fire with his fingers. The smoke from it rises to the sky.

His mother takes his hands, sitting on his bed. Chiang stands behind the bed, and breathes on Gabriel's head. He says the names of the deities again, in 12 long exhalations.

The smoke from his mouth surrounds Gabriel, giving off sparks.

"It is finished. The demons are vanquished. They cannot hold you."

"You're safe, baby," his mother says. "You have me with you." The globes disappear into her body. She turns into thousands of tiny glowing crystals that fly into one of Joel's sculptures.

He jumps up to see her in the glass. Her hand shows on the edge of the glass, waiting for his. He places his hand on the glass, and starts crying.

∞

I wake up with a start. The witching hour, 3am. Joel is still with me, his arms around me from behind. When I move from waking —I must have cried out —he tightens his hold. "I have you; it's okay."

I let the adrenaline die down, feeling my body racked with exhaustion and sweat. "She was there, my mom. God, I miss her."

"I know."

I feel the reality now.

"I love you," I say softly. "I'm so thankful I have you with me."

His head rests against mine. "I love you too. You have no idea."

∞

In the morning, I want to start the day differently. Remembering the dream, I try to make myself stronger as my mother would have wanted. I take Joel around downtown Rochester pointing out what I remember, like the high falls, and noting what's changed. We don't have tension but everything feels tentative.

Late in the afternoon we walk to the café on Genessee where Bettina is going to meet us. It has a mix of people, avant garde art, and pop music. Mostly younger people in attendance, a few tables of older persons. Bettina, who's in her fifties now, a tall plump white woman with black hair and strong brown eyes, waves us over to a curved booth.

She gets up to hug me. "Well, don't you look good. A *mature* young man."

"You look good too, beautiful."

"God, he's such a charmer." She turns to Joel and holds her hand out. "And this fine-looking person?"

"Bettina, this is Joel, Joel McFadden." I look at Joel. "He's my significant other. No, more than that. He's my life."

Joel's eyes go wide. Bettina raises her eyebrows. "Well, then, do sit down. I'm so pleased to meet you, Joel." She shakes his hand. We sit on the bench facing the inside of the room. She slips around the bench to sit closer to us. "Gabriel, he's a picky, picky man. So I know you must be special."

"Beyond that." I say it emphatically. I feel his eyes on me and just smile.

Bettina says to Joel, "You can't imagine how much trouble he was."

Joel's expression indicates he may have some idea. But I have to protest. "My work was killer. And I almost took off a semester to stay here longer."

She laughs. "I remember. Dom would have had both our heads. Gabriel, I would have hired you on the spot if you wanted to stay in Rochester. That wasn't the trouble."

Bettina leans forward, clasping her hands together. She's having fun giving the story to Joel. "See, I hired him as an intern in 1995 because he convinced me to over the phone. He had set up a place to stay and saved money to do the move. I wasn't sure about a New York City boy coming up to the Roc to work..."

"I had to get out for a while. Dom was driving me crazy."

"And then Dom drove *me* crazy. Called me every week, sometimes twice."

The expression on my face gets another smile from her. "You didn't know, did you? Dom called to introduce himself. He 'explained' about you."

She turns to Joel. "I didn't understand until after the first week. Gabriel's work was pristine. Never had to tell him twice. He was creative, punctual, professional. Dedicated and caring. Then I took him out after work, and he tried to drink me under the table. And I could see he was looking for trouble, or someone to get in trouble with."

"Joel, I forgot to tell you Bettina's a compulsive liar."

"Yeah, right. Joel, you look surprised. I know how much he's changed. But he had a wild streak. He liked to trespass. A closed door or off-limits sign was a personal challenge. He always talked himself out of trouble with an innocent naive look he carefully crafted."

"That I *do* believe. He still does it."

"Right? Here's what was amazing. Dominic went out of his way to cultivate a friendship with me, to convince me to watch over Gabriel. Dominic made it sound as if it was life and death to keep you in line. He told me of your problems with your family, dropping out, what it took to get you to go to college. How much he hated your career choice."

"He promised to shut up about that."

"To you, maybe. He said you had an attitude problem. Which I didn't see...Joel, Gabriel was always respectful to me, so I used that to my advantage. I paid him to work nights, too. I caught up a lot that summer. I took him to places during the day and the weekend to keep him busy. He even went with me to take care of my mom. She loved him."

"I told Joel I was magic with the older ladies."

"To an extent. My girlfriend hated you. She was sure we were having an affair. Projected guilt...I ended up leaning on Gabriel some as we were breaking up. He was willing to listen. And it kept him from going out and getting in trouble. Some."

She pats Joel's hand across the table. "Dom was worried that he'd fall under the influence of a bad boy. But Gabriel *was* the bad boy."

"You're exaggerating for cruelty, because I didn't move to Rochester."

But Joel's giving me an 'is this true' look. I shrug. "My personality characteristics were as sublime as my work."

Her laugh is loud enough to turn heads. "Gabriel. Re-writing history. I see he still talks like that literary detective he likes. Oh, you were sweet and charming and kind. But get you riled...the defiant streak. I had to hide him once after he gave the finger to a notorious Rochester cop who told him to move along and pushed him, when we were passing an arrest. I had to grab him and haul him away. We hid in the back room of a dim sum place while the cop went up and down the block looking for him."

While she's talking, I take note of the younger persons behind the bakery counter, the couples up front of the cafe behind us. And two older men, in their fifties, sitting a table a few feet away, dressed in truckers' clothes. Plaid and vests, one in a Bills cap. They look a little weathered, rough, quiet. They glance at us while I change the subject to tell her about Joel's work.

She keeps beaming. "You two are so cute together. Dom would be so happy to see you."

"He would." George Michael's *Father Figure* starts playing. I start to tune into it, leaning back in the booth. Joel and I keep looking at each other. The lyrics, each verse, seem to apply to us. Such a beautiful song anyway, and now it's like it was written for us. When he rests his hands on the table, I take hold of the one next to me.

I see in my peripheral vision that the two older men at the table have noticed this. That isn't going to bother me now. I'm prepared to end whatever they start, if they choose to start something. I don't tense up, but Bettina sees the subtle change, and glances around.

Joel doesn't appear to notice; he's focused on our hands. And as the song ends, I lift his hand to my lips. This is what he means to me, and I spend the moment enjoying his reaction.

I sense movement from the other table and look over, drawing myself up.

The two older men are now holding hands on top of their table as well. One is smiling at us, and the other is gently adjusting his companion's jacket.

I smile back.

Bettina snickers. "Gabriel, you didn't realize I invited you to a queer cafe, did you?"

"I guess not."

She laughs more. "See? You're so ready for action. You were going to teach them something."

I turn red. "I think I got taught."

Joel moves even closer to me. "It's okay. You're the valiant defender. Someday, we'll be those two guys."

"I could cry, watching you two. But I'm getting a message from Antonio. We should go meet him."

I get up to pay at the counter, and Bettina runs over to argue about paying.

"I will." Joel has shown up behind us, handing the cashier his credit card. He leans over to speak softly. "And put that table on it as well." He subtly nods toward the older men, and leaves a very generous tip.

I follow Bettina's car to a hotel downtown. We park and meet up outside to go in. Bettina leads us to a well-built light-skinned black man in his thirties, reading a paper on a sofa in the lobby. He is a sharp dresser and his short hair is style to razor's edge perfection, as is his goatee. He espies Bettina and greets her with a bright smile. She in turn gets us acquainted.

"Thanks for meeting me." I shake his hand.

We have some small talk for a while.

"I really appreciate your trying to help."

"Sure, no problem." Antonio smiles.

I take out the photo of Knox his sister emailed to me. "This is the guy I'm looking for. Granted, it's thirty-five years later, but he has a scar on his neck like someone tried to take him out. He's also a firebug."

"Hmmm. He'd be like, fifty something?"

"Fifty-four to be exact. I hope his scar and his penchant for fire may make him unique enough that you may get an idea where he hangs. I need to talk with him ASAP, and not scare him off."

"You think he's doing something these days?"

"You got more fires here, right? I read about the pattern of fires back in the Seventies, same thing going on now."

"Damn." He looks at the photo. "Can I have this?"

"Sure."

"Give me a day or so. Let me check around."

"I'd tell you be careful, but I suppose you know that."

"More than most, man."

I take out my wallet and palm the cash, sliding it under a newspaper. He puts the newspaper under his arm and shakes our hands. Then he gives Bettina a hug and casually walks out.

We decide to go into the hotel bar for a couple drinks. We spend a little more time catching up on each other's life. Bettina then excuses herself, early morning, etc.

I turn to Joel. "You ready to leave?"

"This is nice, too."

"Um, okay then." I relax and sit back at the bar with him, the first time in so long.

"I like this," Joel says.

"Just being together, you mean?"

"Yeah. In places like this. Quiet."

"We'll make a point of doing it." Sitting next to him, watching him at ease, I'm acutely aware of how we have not yet returned to our sexual intimacy.

After some time, he says, "You're better now, I can tell. That whole shit with him is over."

I reach over to take his hand. Reading my mind—which is easier for him than me, he slides his fingers against mine.

"I realize how nice this is, because it's back to what I liked before. But now, it's in a whole new perspective."

He looks up at the ceiling, thinking, then eventually comes back. "So, when you said what you said to Bettina, I was surprised. You don't admit things easily. But you did that for me. And it was to someone who doesn't know our history. So, she looked at it like it was normal. Not like some great thing like Veronica would say—not that she's wrong—and not like some terrible tragedy, like Danny would say. But just at face value. And she was positive. She said we were cute."

"Those guys thought we were cute."

"You're too funny. Going to go pit bull on some old gay couple."

"It was funny, keeping in mind I wasn't wrong for doing so. If it wasn't a quote unquote queer cafe, they would have been men ready to give us trouble."

"We could take care of it, like in the woods."

"We did well, but luck plays into that. All the self-defense training in the world doesn't protect against someone in the city walking up and shooting you in the head. Sad to say we can't forget that. But I'll protect you with my life, wherever possible."

"I know. That you would do so means everything to me. I'd protect you the same way. But what I wanted to say was, Bettina thought I was normal because I was reflected in you, your companionship."

I don't like terms like normal. I want to launch into some lecturing —God, like Dom would, I realize. But he's not finished.

"I know what you're going to say. Just let that lie for now. This is something new for me again, that shows I did something right. I want to enjoy that. And...I feel something different. I can't put it into words but I could draw it, maybe, with one of Leonard's symbols. That something new was created. That feels strange, but good. Like a shot of something. It's making me feel kind of pins and needles-ish."

Then he looks at me a certain way. Remembering how he used to do that, and what would happen afterward, makes me flush with adrenaline.

He leans forward, holding my eyes. "So, do you want to go back to the hotel now?"

I want to be cool about it, give him a smartass remark.

He waits for my response.

"Yes," I say.

∞

He stops at the front desk, telling me to go on ahead. In in room, I put on my iPod in the little dock by the bed and then go in the bathroom to take a shower.

In this more expensive suite, the shower is in its own little alcove. After a few minutes, I hear him come in the room, then he's here in the bathroom, standing at the opening to the shower.

"About time you got naked for me," he says.

I reach out to put my hands around his head and kiss him. "Get in here with me."

He strips while I watch and steps in. We stand under the water, feeling the whole of our bodies together. I run my fingers over his head in the water, getting him to smile with me, from the sheer enjoyment of it. The fun part of being together.

And that transforms into the erotic part. What we're anticipating. I use this time as a prelude, to know his body again by washing it. Slowly, using a sponge over his arms, his chest. Going down his legs and between his legs. I get on my knees and take his feet, one at a time, massaging them. And then kiss my way up his body.

He's breathless now. "Come on, I have champagne."

"Really?"

"Fuck yeah."

He takes my hand and leads me out of the shower, out to the bedroom, still wet; I grab a towel on the way. He has a bottle of Moet in a bucket on the dresser. He opens and pours this while I start to dry him off. We drink one glass right there. And after he refills the glasses, I take mine to the bed, and hold my hand out to him.

He walks over and takes my hand; his eyes become more intense. I gently pull him over to me so we're facing each other kneeling on the bed. I run my hands down his sides slowly. He breathes in; his body rising with expectation.

When he touches me in turn, it makes all the hair on my body rise, the electricity crackles. My hands go down his back, slow. He matches the rhythm. I gently run my mouth over his neck, his chest, tasting. His fingers entwine in my hair. He's shuddering against me.

I kiss him again, feel his beard press on my mouth, taste the champagne on his tongue. He exhales and I'm breathing him in — soap, alcohol, and his own scent—whatever is the foundation of the chemistry between us. For a moment I can see thousands of glints from him reflecting on me.

His hands go on my back, on my hips. Pressing against me where I'm hard. The anticipation is fire in my veins.

I take a moment to feel him completely against me. His skin, his muscles, the hair on his chest, his legs and arms. I talk in his ear. "You're mine again..."

His breathing accelerates. "Yes..."

And we lay down on the bed. This time, every emotion I've had for the last few months since he's been back fills me, making me envelope him with my body.

And part of the feeling with him is tenderness, underlying the passion. I stop moving just to look at him under me, sensing time freezing as well. We're entwined tightly, flowing with each other, reminding me the sensuous carvings of Khajuraho in India. Both erotic and the union of the divine.

Retaking his body becomes important. I touch him, kiss him, everywhere in this new discovery. It's important for me in rectification, in building the new thing between us. He lets me do this for what seems like hours; I play him like my instrument as the heat builds.

My exploration on him leaves him sweating and on edge. Finally, he rolls over on me, brings his mouth to my cock; takes me in.

My pulse is pounding in every part of my body, feeling this. He goes slow, finding the rhythm. Then gradually gets faster. He stays with me while I luxuriate in the feel of his mouth. I get up on my elbows to watch him; then I entangle my fingers in his hair to further savor his head going up and down...until I'm convulsing so hard I almost black out.

The sweat is running down over both of us by now. I remember when he first did this with me, and what it felt like. It's better now, sublime in the eruption. In knowing how we're together.

I bring him back up to me and kiss him, while letting my hands keep his cock hard. He watches me while I move down on his body. He lets himself fall into it. I see a look on his face I missed for two years, when his wall goes down and he frees himself with me. Then I do the same to him, take him in my mouth. His hands move over my head. I hear him breathing hard. I feel his thighs straining against my hands as I push him down, then pull him harder against me, showing him the passion. Hearing, feeling, tasting him coming...losing himself, sharing it with me.

After, when we're in each other's arms again, I'm unbounded; my words no longer have to be locked up. And so I touch his face, gently, and then hold him closer. "What is that song by Dave Matthews and Carlos Santana? *You are the love of my life...*"

That does it; the tears come with him—not easy as with me. Surrendering to the bond between us. I run my fingers down his face to catch the tears.

Love is an endless series of pools with diving boards, either getting deeper or shallower. And now, in this consummation, I fall in love with him a second time, in the deeper pool. It brings on my own tears. You don't know tears can be a good thing until they come in love.

And we share those tears in this embrace; lying together without words, wrapped in each other...until we both feel the desire for more.

∞

THIRTEEN ♦ 29 DARK GORGE (KĂN)

Water over Water: Danger is ahead, a chasm. One must maintain confidence and trust to get safely out of a dangerous situation. Water doubled with water is a strong force, dark, and overwhelming. The fifth line (yang/nine) moves in this reading: the pit is filling with water; one's mind is necessary to rise above the danger.

∞

Tuesday, December 21

The next morning. Rochester in the middle of a winter rainstorm, everything seems new. I realize this when I wake up. I have my head on his chest, hearing the rain and wind outside. I almost have a sensation of having gone back in time. But it's real. I feel everything of the last month, the last six months, the last few years.

In this sense of being reborn I raise my head and look at him sleeping. And he opens his eyes. I have that strange sensation I did when we were first together, that we are in our own world separate from the rest of the universe. Now that I've opened myself to this, I'd sacrifice everything I have to keep it.

We didn't get much sleep. After recovering from the first time, we both wanted each other again. I run my hands down his legs, which a few hours ago were tight around my back.

I don't realize I'm smiling until he's doing so, responding to me. And then I see the rest of my life.

He takes my hand. "What are you thinking..."

"I love you." I can't say it enough. I owe him that.

He moves closer to kiss me, and he's savoring the words and the feelings. "I love you too."

∞

The rain has turned to snow falling lightly at 9am. We're on Rae Drive in Greece, in North Rochester. We're at Terry Knox's house; it's a beige stucco affair. Well-kept, if undistinguished.

I have the Camry double-parked a half-block away. We're watching the house. I note that Terry, or somebody, has two cars in the driveway by a side door of the house facing us. An Outback and a cargo van.

What does a retiree need with a cargo van? That serial killer-special vehicle bugs me.

"What are you thinking? I love to see you thinking."

I unwrap a stick of gum. Cigarette substitute. "Fill me with flattery, baby. I'm thinking I want to look at that ugly-ass van."

"Maybe it's his?"

"A hunch."

"Want me to stay here?"

"Yeah. Keep watch for anything that's trouble."

I get out and carefully look around. Some people down the block are leaving for
work and don't pay any attention.

Terry's shades are down, which I hope gives me cover as I approach the dark blue van. I'm guessing it's 10-15 years old. Nothing personalizes it, no stickers other than New York State inspection.

I move to stare into the windshield. The back of the van has some boxes. I wonder if the interior would test for accelerant. I can see that one box has the name "GenWorks."

The Camry's horn sounds lightly. I move back and check the side door of the house. No one there.

Because she's behind me. "What the hell are you doing?"

I turn around. "I was wondering if it was for sale."

This impresses her not at all. She's standing on the edge of the sidewalk, wearing a dark blue coat that matches the color of the van, and is barelegged in sneakers. Her tight gray hair and heavy face reminds me of Madalyn Murray O'Hair. She must have seen me, left from a back entrance, and come up behind me. Sneaky.

"Get off my property!"

I move down to the sidewalk. She stays put.

Joel has already left the Camry and comes up to about 20 feet behind her.

I smile at her. "So not for sale then?"

"What the fuck do you want?"

I'm guessing asking her about Arthur will not be helpful. But I have to try.

"I wanted to see if Arthur was selling his van."

The change in her face is dramatic. Already scowling, she actually gets mottled purple with rage. "Get the fuck out of here!"

I back away a bit. For the first time, I see she's holding something—a broom. It almost seems funny. "So he's not home, huh?"

She takes a step towards me. Joel moves a little closer. She doesn't see him. I hold my hands up in a placating gesture, which does nothing for her.

"*Leave*, asshole!"

"I'd like to talk to him if you don't mind."

"I told you to leave, motherfucker!" And with that, she swings the broom at my head.

She's so fast she catches me off guard. The straws smack against my face hard. "Hey!"

Apparently she thinks she's Ruth Buzzi on *Laugh-In*. I have to raise my arms in protection as she begins whaling the broom on my head and back.

Joel has come up beside me. "Back off, lady!" He grabs the broom and yanks it out of her hands, allowing me to regain my balance. Joel tosses the broom across the street then we back away from her.

I try one last time. "Ma'am, I just would like to talk to Arthur. If you could give him a message..."

She spits in the snow on the sidewalk, and then unleashes a string of invectives that would make the Mafiosos in *Goodfellas* blush. The CS word is used generously.

I take Joel's arm and head back for the car. Since she's now going for her broom, we walk fast.

As I start up the car, she keeps up her litany, at the top of her voice. Somewhere in the snow, she finds a rock and throws it at the car. It bounces off the hood. Now some neighbors are coming out to gawk.

Another rock hits the driver's side door. "Jesus!"

"You might consider getting in gear, Fast-and-Furious."

"You're a real help, thanks..." I have to drive backwards, as she's rage-stomping towards the car, until I can turn around and get out the neighborhood.

Joel has gotten on his knees to look out the back. Then he starts laughing. "What the fuck was that?"

"That hell-beast needs to jump on her broom and fly back to whatever cave she came from."

He sits down and pulls straw from my jacket. "So, your *magic* with old ladies—how's it working out for you?"

"Fuck you, man. I'm bleeding."

This is true. I have blood running down where my scalp is cut. He finds some tissues and tries to take care of it, but he's still laughing.

"What do you think she does to census takers or the Witnesses? Probably throws hot coffee on them. I wonder how Zest would handle *her.*"

"Other way around. Even Zest would think twice before going there. Even that dude in *No Country for Old Men* would call it a day."

"You need to go on tour with Wayne Dyer on how you inspire people."

"The 'fuck you' still stands, sweetheart."

We return to the hotel. I do some research and find out GenWorks, the name on the boxes in the van, is a chemical company. The website lists various industrial solvents that I know work as accelerants. Now the harridan back in Greece, or her reprobate son, may just be using an empty box they picked up on the side of the street for any purpose at all. But. Fires have been happening in Rochester over the last year. More than usual. Most have been abandoned buildings, buildings in foreclosure—or about to be, failed businesses. More than usual in these times. The phrase "arson is suspected" repeats itself like a Zen mantra.

I'm still reading about that when Antonio calls. "I found a couple places where this boy is hanging out. I got the impression he does things for hire, but people don't like him."

"I can't imagine why." No doubt Arthur learned his personality skills from Mommie Dearest.

"One place is a bar on Dewey Ave. I'm pretty sure he's going to be there tonight. Y'all can go with me."

∞

The bar is large but not fancy. Most patrons are low-key; several are probably ex-cons. I apparently have enough of a criminal aura to fit in, and Joel was on the street too long to ever feel uncomfortable anywhere.

Antonio greets various people across the room or passing by. At the bar, we both have Crown Royal in honor of Bettina. We actually drink ours. Joel has the same but leaves it. He hates whiskey.

Scanning the room, some action to our right catches my eye. Pick-up poker game. Antonio notices. "You want to get in on that? Good cover." He takes me over to the table.

He knows most of the group of men around the table and introduces me. They deal me in, and we talk about the Bills. When I watch football, I'm a Giants fan, but upstate it's Bills or nothing

I keep an eye on the bar, and see Joel deep in conversation with Antonio about something. Damned if some passing patron doesn't try to subtly cruise him. Very subtly—it isn't the place for that—but I catch it nonetheless. I'm shocked by my urge to jump up and have words with the man. Joel notices my look and smiles to himself.

Despite my friends' insistence that I don't have a good poker face, I can actually play well. I'm into the game until I realize that Antonio is now talking to Knox. It's him. In his fifties, tall with a thick build. Short graying hair. Hard angular face, and the scar around the neck. I drop out of the next hand and after saying goodbye I join them.

Antonio tells Knox I'm someone with needs, whom he could help. Knox nods at me, carefully.

Having established contact, Antonio takes off. Knox engages in some small talk, then stubs out his cigarette. The bar isn't obeying state smoking regulations. "So...am I to understand you have a job you needed done?"

"Something like that. What we're really looking for is information."

"Well now. What kind of information could I have for you?"

I order another drink, and indicate I'm buying Knox's as well. He's drinking straight scotch.

"Something that happened a long time ago. You understand, I'm only interested in finding out names?" I meet his eyes.

He nods. "Sure. Don't know if I can help, but I get you."

"I just want to make that clear. I don't care about anything else. Not my issue."

He sips his scotch. "Sounds very intriguing." His eyes move from me to Joel, like he's evaluating us.

"Like I said, this was a long time ago. You remember a couple of people, McCabe and Corey?"

He doesn't show reaction to the names. "You looking for them?"

"No. They aren't around as far as I know. But I need to find out who gave up a baby to them."

"Really." Knox surveys the bar casually. "That *was* a long time back. You would have been just a lad yourself."

"I suppose."

"Well, they handled a lot of babies, people say. You think I'd know them all?"

He seems to be out of cigarettes. I offer him one of mine. "No. But this one was special. The last one McCabe handled, maybe. Corey kind of took over the baby from her. Maybe planned to screw her out of her fee."

For the first time his expression changes. He turns to face me directly. His voice is no longer casual. "You seem to know a lot about it. A real smart guy, huh?"

"I know that much. Now I need to know whose baby this was."

"Why?"

"Why doesn't matter. All I want is the name and we leave. It's worth some change."

"Money? What else?"

I put my drink down and fold my arms. "What do you mean?"

"What are you trying to do about it?"

"Nothing. Get a name, that's it."

"And him?" He indicates Joel.

"He's with me."

"Oh, your bodyguard?"

"For all intents and purposes. I'm just here to find the name, that's what I'm paid for. I don't care beyond that. I don't work more than what I'm paid for."

Joel is good at keeping a straight face, and doesn't laugh at that.

"And how much is this worth to you?" He stubs out the cigarette.

"A grand."

He turns it over in his mind. "Well."

Now he finishes his scotch. Then he scans the room again. "It's a *real* private matter, you know? I don't want to talk about it here."

"Where then?"

"Place nearby. Friend of mine is trying to renovate a building. It's empty now."

I smile at him like, what the fuck? "Why not in the parking lot? Right now?"

"I don't want to be seen with you." He smiles back. "No offense."

I shrug. "You're being seen now."

"This is casual. I need to tell you the story behind the baby. Too many chances someone can overhear."

I look skeptical. I can tell Joel is tensing up behind me.

"Hey." Knox spreads his hands. "You just want the name, I just want to get the money. But I have to do it this way, I don't want people to know."

"All right." I finish my own drink. "Where is it?"

"Up the road some. You have a car? Good. I have a van outside. I'll leave first. You follow me there."

He nods at the bartender then walks away. Joel and I don't say anything until we're in the lot. Knox's van—the dark blue one that was outside the banshee's house—is waiting by the exit. We walk back to our car.

"I don't like this." Joel stares at the van.

"Nothing to like about it."

"You believe him?"

"We'll see."

"Could be a set-up."

We get in the Camry. "Arsonists work alone. We can handle this, if it's a trap. Not like I trust him."

"He's bad. I can fucking feel it."

"Yeah." I smile grimly to myself. "That's the problem with this profession, right? We have to deal with people like Knox."

But as we turn down Dewey Avenue a bit behind van, I think about it. "There's a 7-11 up ahead. I'll drop you off there and you call a cab back to the hotel."

He looks over at me. "Are you kidding?"

"Don't take the chance."

"The hell you're going there without me." He slides back in the seat, with his knees up on the dash. "And we *could* be going to Niagara Falls instead of this shit, but no..."

The place turns out to be practically out of town. A one-story ugly building in a dirt parking lot. Woods around the back, not much else. No other cars. A few industrial buildings surrounding this one.

Knox stops his van. I survey the building. It's old, solid. Windows boarded up.

Knox is out and unlocking a padlock on the door. He waves us over.

The snow from this morning has turned into rain, accentuating the isolation of the area. We walk up to Knox at the door he's opening and follow him in. Surprisingly, the lights are on.

"My friend tried it out as a bar, didn't work." Knox's tone is conversational. The room is not large, and does have a bar. Also a few broken chairs and tables and cardboard cartons. "He wants the place renovated. I'm handling that. Fixing it up."

He turns to us. "He used the storeroom as an office. I have some stuff back there. Since we left the bar earlier than intended, I'd like a drink. I have a bottle back there. You're welcome to join me."

He heads down a disgustingly dank hallway to a wooden door at the very end.

Knox opens the door and steps in, switching on the light. The room is a storeroom, with various stacked boxes of liquor and spare parts for the bar. One bar bulb in the ceiling, no windows. A large heating vent high up on the wall is sputtering some tepidly warm air. A desk is shoved against one wall, with some papers stacked on it.

Knox then takes a bottle of Johnnie Walker Red off a shelf and pours into a paper cup. He offers the bottle to us, but we decline.

"Okay." He runs his hand over his brush cut, sipping from the cup. "Let's see how this goes. You're the smart guy, you'll understand. Corey was a real bad man. He thought he was onto something."

"Okay, I got you."

He looks at me standing by the desk, and at Joel standing in the doorway. Knox pats a large cardboard crate. "Still some liquor here. My friend should have moved it out. Oh well. Corey. He was trying to help some big shot politician. His daughter got knocked up."

"Politician? Like a mayor or something?"

Knox shakes his head. He looks again at Joel, who's got my cigarettes. "You mind? I could use one."

Joel comes in and gives him one. He borrows Joel's lighter as well. Then he gets up and lights the cigarette, running his hands through his short hair and pacing the room.

"Yeah. Big important guy in the area. Corey wanted more from Bernadette. She's not dead, you know. You can't find her, but she's not dead. Doesn't matter, does it?"

"I don't care. I told you why we're here."

"Well. In any case, Corey was planning some shit. Get more from Bernadette, and then maybe arm-twist the guy."

He stops near the open door to the hallway and frowns, looking outside. "I didn't want to be part of that."

"Okay."

"Corey thought he knew it all. A real jerkoff. This man could have had him whacked."

He turns back to us, leaning against the door frame, as if he's tired. "He was a state senator. Rich guy. Nice house in Pittsford. Still has it, probably."

"I see." I exchange glances with Joel.

"Daughter got herself in trouble. No way could he have let that be news. Not back then."

"Naturally. And this senator's name?"

Knox sighs and looks at the floor. He stares for a moment, turning Joel's lighter over in his hands. Then he lifts his head and looks at me. His eyes are black. "You should have stayed away from my mother, Mr. Smart Guy."

And he quickly backs out, shutting the door.

I go to the door and grab the knob, but I hear a bolt on the other side being drawn. Yanking on the door does not help.

"What the fuck is that about?" Joel is now beside me.

My mind is racing. "Best case scenario, he wants a head start to leave."

"And the worst case?"

I don't answer that. Because I realize what he meant by renovating the place. And those cartons in the bar were the same size and shape as the GenWorks in his van. I go cold.

"Can we take the door off?"

I back up. "The hinges are on the outside..." A carton of spare parts is next to the desk. I dump it on the floor. A few rusty tools are mixed in the nozzles and pipes. I find a crowbar lying in an old wine box with some washers. "Maybe the door can be pried open."

I take the crowbar over to the door and consider where the weakest point may be. I start jamming it in the lower half of the jamb.

From inside the bar, a noise—*whooomph.*

I pull Joel back from the door.

"What was that?"

I can't tell him. My panicked imagination doesn't let me speak. I'm reminded vividly of one of my deep fears. Because of a trailer fire my mom and I went through. Fire. You couldn't pay me to be around a bonfire, or Burning Man, or even an old gas stove. I'm sweating under my clothes, trying not to show it. Time—life—is going to be measured in seconds.

"See if your phone will work." I'm already looking around the room; I wonder if I could bust through the wall. The room is at the very end of the building, sweet outside just beyond. "Call 911." I try to keep my voice calm, but his eyes go wide.

"We're on *fire*..."

"Stay calm, Joel." The heating vent catches my eye. It's fairly big and still sputtering. Probably Knox had the heat on to get the accelerant to the flash point. In a matter of minutes, it will suck up smoke to pour inside and kill us. But then, the fire might flash over and take the entire building before that happens. As terrified as I am imagining I can hear the fire screaming at me, I can't let this happen to us.

The vent might open to the outside. I trust vents. They've worked for me before.

The rustling outside turns to crackling. Block out the sound. You can't panic. You have someone who's depending on you. And he's staring at me. No time to waste.

"Help me." I start pushing heavy cartons up under the vent and he follows. In seconds we have a platform of sorts. I can sense that the oxygen is being eaten up. The air seems slightly grainy. Maybe it's the vapors. Doesn't matter. I get on top of the boxes and with the curved end of the crowbar I pop out the grate. Easy enough. The hole itself is big enough for us to get through. In the black space I can feel heat inside the wall vents and smell smoke. Tiny wisps curl up out of the space and drift into the room.

"Fuck. Okay." I reach over and feel the back area of the outer wall, about a foot away from the inner wall, with the air duct in between. Thin metal. It's also a vent. Reversing the bar, I begin prying. It's screwed into the drywall, no doubt to prevent intruders.

"Gabriel?"

I realize I'm talking out loud, and not to him. To my mother. *Help me. I don't want to be scared.* Joel starts coughing behind me. I speak to him over my shoulder. "Get down on the floor."

"You need help."

"Just do it!" I can't maneuver to kick the grate, so I take the curved end of the bar, and jab as hard as I can against the metal, prying. It groans and bends. It's screwed into the wall from the outside, so this takes brute strength.

I feel dizzy and fight it. "Not going to happen." My mom and my uncle. I'm not going to join them yet. Joel and I are not going to die in the Godforsaken storeroom. I hold my breath and swing again at the grate.

The grate scrapes against the crumbling brick and pops out an inch. The screws must be loose now.

The roar in the hallway is louder. The door crackles. Flashover in the main part of the building...a little smoke drifts in, along with some ash. "Don't worry." I say out loud—to Joel? Myself? My mom again? "Don't worry."

I'm ten. I stick my head out my room. The whole wall covered in black smoke and flames. My mom grabs me and pulls me down the hallway as the flames shot up overhead. *Help, Mommy. I've got you baby. Hold on.* Seeing and feeling the flames. She covers me and runs through, holding me tight against her body. She had scars on her feet from that, where the flames touched.

The metal gives a little more. I swing harder against it. I dimly hear Joel moving around. "Stay down!"

I can hear the door bending, which isn't really happening but I imagine I feel it, and picture the fire roaring in to consume us. *Harder*, Gabriel. I pry at the grate, have my whole body leaning against the gaping hole and pushing down on the crowbar, sweat pouring off me.

The grate pops out so suddenly the crowbar falls out with it. I've used enough oxygen to want to fall down again, but I manage to lean over and take a deep breath and look around. I can see outside, the dirt parking lot.

I move back down unsteady but determined. "Okay, you need to get out." I pull Joel up.

His eyes are red. Ash is falling on our heads. The antithesis of snow. I point up and shake him. "*Out.* Move it." I push on his shoulders to get him going. He climbs up and puts his hands on the edge of the hole.

And looks back. "Can you get up here too?"

"Yeah, *just get the fuck out,* will you?"

He doesn't want to leave. "You go first. I'm lighter, in case you can pull—"

"*Get out of the fucking hole, Goddamn it!*" And I shove him out, hear him hit the ground.

I start coughing from the smoke and start to go behind him and almost fall, suddenly dizzy. Ash sticks to my face. I'll pretend the fire isn't coming in. Never mind the smoke at the bottom of the door is snaking upwards hypnotically. My most basic fear beyond that door. I realize now that I got Joel out, I can't move.

"Gabriel?"

"Yeah." Come on, what are you doing? The door is burning. Fire has a sound, a voice. It's calling to me. *Missed you earlier, now I'm back to get you. Just wait for me.*

I hear Joel's voice louder, panicky, like he's coming back. "*Gabriel?* I'm coming in to get you."

"I said get out!" I snap out of my terror and get up angrily to rebuke him, and feel like I've been dosed with hallucinogens. I see him on the other side of the wall, at least his face. He's hanging on the edge of the hole with his arms.

"C'mon, I'll pull you." He heaves himself up enough to hold one hand out.

I stick my arms in the hole. The fire is about to go through the walls. I can feel the waves of heat. The door cracks open behind me and I can hear and feel the fire coming in. Joel's hand pulls on mine, then he lets go of the wall and pulls with both hands. I feel stuck for a moment, then Joel, bracing his legs on the outside wall, yanks on my hands, and my torso is roughly jerked outside. Then I kick myself out the rest of the way; we land on the gravel together.

Coughing follows with hitting fresh air. Up above us, the building is glowing orange with flames out the front doors and windows and the vent hole, and crawling along the roof. More ash is flying through the air with cinders.

I jump up and pull him with me to the parking lot, moving as fast as I can. Bits and pieces of the bar are falling around us in the rain.

I'm reaching for my phone, when something in the building explodes, God knows from what. I cover him with my body on the ground. We're near the Camry, and I get him inside and manage to peel out down the street to call for help.

The fire engines come first. The first responders take us aside and make us breathe oxygen. By the time the police arrive, I've called Bettina. She's horrified to hear what happened, but then she serves the same purpose as Michaela—to take suspicion off of us. I tell the police part of the story—that we were looking into Bernadette McCabe's operation, and spoke to Knox as a source. We make it clear that Knox is probably at Mother Harridan's house. With Bettina's help, the detectives finish with a report and don't arrest us. Knox's name is not unknown to them.

After being separated for interviews at the scene, the EMTs want to take us to an ER for evaluation. We could just refuse Against Medical Advice, but as much as I hate the idea, I don't want to skip medical attention. Or rather, I don't want Joel to. Smoke inhalation injuries may not show up for hours, or even days. I just move the Camry to a safer area before we go in the ambulance.

By late afternoon of next day, we've been more or less vetted to leave the hospital. We're okay. Half the time was waiting for tests to prove that. On no sleep, Joel and I take a cab back to the car.

I start to take out my cigarettes and catch myself. The burnt hulk of the bar is a few dozen yards away. Looking at the blackened structure fills me with horror. In the sunlight, it's worse. The smell of fire. I can see the side we crawled out of was the last to burn.

"Hey, let's go." Joel puts his hand on my arm.

I turn to look at him. What we went through this summer, and again. The breeze is blowing bits of ash, which sticks to us. I think of the women we found. They were not that lucky. That's what I should remember. We have a chance. A chance to live. That means *everything.*

∞

FOURTEEN ♦ 14 GREAT MEASURES (DÀ YǑU)

Fire over Heaven: Following a rise in harmony, people are drawn to help harvest. The fifth line (six /yin) moves in this reading: a person is able to take on leadership and fire the will of others.

∞

Wednesday, December 22
Downtown Rochester, 9:30 am

THEY'RE BACK AT THE HOTEL, finally. Joel feels every part of his body hurts. He lies on the freshly-made bed, closes his eyes and wills sleep to come.

Yet he senses Gabriel's restlessness. When he looks up, Gabriel is examining the fire escape plan by the door to the room. Then he walks over to the windows and stares down at the street below for a few minutes.

Finally, Gabriel turns away and grabs the key card off the dresser. "I'm going out for a few minutes. Put the bolt on and don't let anyone in but me."

"Gabriel..."

But he's already out the door, saying again, "Put the bolt on now."

Joel gets up to do so, both annoyed and concerned. Through the peephole, he sees Gabriel stalking the corridor, and then going to the stairway door.

Vexed, Joel calls Veronica to tell her what happened, and to psych out Gabriel's behavior.

"He needs to go on reconnaissance, it's what he does. You never noticed?"

Joel remembers how Gabriel first changed the locks in Joel's apartment after they escaped from the warehouse in Westchester, and then walked through the entire building to scope it out. Gabriel also checked the floors in his own apartment building after they returned from Black Mountain Park. And, of course, his restlessness after breaking up with Alex.

"I guess I didn't realize it, but I see how that works with him now."

"Some years ago, he and I were in Maryland on a case together. I went back to our hotel room by myself, and this guy followed me. Just hung outside the door—but wouldn't leave. I called Gabriel when I couldn't get the hotel people to come up. He came running back and had it out with the guy. Finally, some security person showed up and made the guy leave. Then Gabriel patrolled the entire hotel and parking lot. Something gets stirred in him. Just let him work it through."

Feeling better, Joel then calls Geneva, to let her know what happened. An hour later Gabriel returns. He doesn't seem any calmer.

Joel lies back on the bed, watching Gabriel stare out the windows again.

"Can you come over here, baby, just for a minute?"

Gabriel sits next to him on the bed. He can't keep still though.

"Tell me what's going through your mind."

"When I was 10, our trailer caught on fire. My mom literally ran through fire with me."

"Of course she did. She knew I needed you."

Gabriel smiles distantly. "And he's still out there, Knox. I called Bettina. The cops haven't found him yet. She's heard that the fire investigators found accelerant all around the building. His thing, his signature, remember? But it didn't work to trap us, because of the rain."

Now Gabriel reaches over to Joel, runs his fingers over different parts of his body —as if checking to see that he's real.

"You should sleep," he says. "You're tired."

Joel sits up and slides his arms around Gabriel. "I can't sleep while you can't sleep. And you can't while you're thinking of your mom, and Knox. Let's just go back."

"It's late..."

"I'll drive first. Or you can, and in a couple hours I'll take over."

They get their stuff together and leave. Gabriel drives at first which allows Joel to doze, if not sleep. Somewhere around Binghamton they switch for the rest of the way to New York. He's relieved by Gabriel immediately passing out in the passenger seat.

They get back after Midnight, and briefly speak to Veronica and play with the cats. The cats know, as cats usually do, that something's been up with them. The felines race around the apartment, crackling with shared energy.

Then Gabriel and Joel can finally crawl into bed at home. Undressed and reassured, far enough away from the fire. They can look at each other in this new context, together. What it means to be together now.

Without words they hold each other, to truly be able to fall asleep.

∞

Thursday, December 23
Alphabet City, Avenue A, 10:12 am

I answer the phone, not entirely awake.

"Are you up? I'm in town—Midtown right now, and I wanted to drop by and say hello."

"Who's that?" Joel asks me.

"Luz," I tell him, sitting up in bed. Luz is Danny's sister. I see it's late morning. Veronica must have fed Archie since I'm not covered in scratch marks.

"Yes, come on over."

I get out of bed to find Veronica. She's in the kitchen going over files. I tell her about Luz, then Joel and I dress.

Luz arrives now. She's six years younger than Danny and I. She's been attached to me since I first met Danny and started hanging out with him. She's just come back from Seattle, where she had been living. I know she recently broke up with her husband. The details of that are vague.

Luz shares Danny's coloring and black wavy hair. Otherwise she's short like their mom Carlotta, whom we call La Doña, where Danny's tall, a soprano to his bass, bright and optimistic where Danny's cynical.

I let her in and she squeals with happiness to see Joel. Another difference between her and Danny, I guess. She's brought her 8-year-old daughter, Anya. I last saw Anya during the summer, and she's delighted to be back now. Anya throws her arms around me and I pick her up to hold her. A small thing, kind of a family thing that is very comforting after what happened in Rochester.

"So what's going on?" Luz turns to me after the general greetings are over.

"All kinds of stuff."

"Knowing you, I can only imagine. More coffee?"

"Do you have to ask?" I lead her over to the kitchen. Anya remains playing with Veronica and Joel.

Luz and I speak in Spanish in the kitchen. Veronica and Joel know *some* Spanish, but not enough to get our conversation. I explain a little about what happened in Rochester, which has Luz concerned.

"Does Danny know? Why isn't he here?"

I shake my head. "Long story. What happened with you out in Seattle?"

"Jay turned into a jerk. It happens. I decided I had to leave. It's not easy; he's going to be a prick about visitation and we haven't even filed yet. I'll have to deal with La Doña, Danny, Antonio and Ruben." Hers and Danny's older brothers. They have never, over twenty-plus years, been comfortable with Danny and I being gay. Even after La Doña told them to chill out many years ago.

"I see things are different with you, too." She glances significantly at Joel. "Why didn't you tell me?"

"It kind of just happened. Remember, I told you Joel came back, started working with me. Meantime, I got involved with...someone else. But it imploded. Or exploded. And Joel and I needed to get back together."

"That's wonderful, isn't it?"

"*I* think so. But Danny, he and I had problems."

"Is that why we haven't seen you yet? Danny wouldn't talk to me about it. And La Doña wants you to come over."

I'm embarrassed now. "I've been in a bad way. Danny and I aren't talking to each other, if you don't know...I'd like to come over and see her. Antonio and Ruben would throw me out."

"They don't live there. Come with me and Anya. She wants to see you. La Doña isn't feeling well, and it will make her day. Joel too, she likes him."

I nod. "Okay."

"And Danny, what happened with him?"

I roll my eyes and check the living room. Joel has gotten out a box of Christmas decorations from a closet, and Anya is directing them on what to put up.

"This was before I broke up with, um, the man I was dating." I'm careful because I know Joel is listening and trying to interpret, even though he's pretending not to.

"He was out of town on Thanksgiving. And Joel was with Veronica that day. They both came over here after Danny and I got back from seeing your mom, because I don't like to leave them alone on holidays. We were just hanging out. But I guess Danny thought Joel and I were, I don't know. Flirting, I suppose. To be fair, we were. Danny started this slow burn all night, and finally he corners me."

I remember how *that* conversation started tensely in Spanish.

"Danny said something to me about how Dominic would have been really disappointed in me for how I was acting. So I asked him if his being at my place was interfering with finding a hookup on Grindr. I suppose we both said bad things, but it stung me. To say that about Dom. I didn't talk to him for the rest of the evening, and he left early."

Joel glances up every time I mention his name. Knowing him, he already has deduced what we're talking about.

"You both need to get over thi —you're seriously not talking? After you almost get killed?"

"I don't like it this way. You'd think we'd be used to each other. But now I'm telling you, he's not going to come over here and treat Joel like a second-class citizen. That's over."

Luz shakes her head. "You're right, but seriously. You need to talk to him. Before it gets worse."

"He knows my number."

She switches to English. "Men. I swear to Jesus y'all crazy. It's almost Christmas Eve, at least let's go over to the Bronx and have lunch. All of you, we're your family."

∞

December 23, Cont.

A strange thing, love. All of the sudden songs one might laugh at for being saccharine or cheesy take on great meaning, and seem as profound as U2. With those songs in his head, Joel has things to do back in Manhattan after the visit with La Doña. Gabriel has gone back to the apartment to do some work before sitting in with Jason and the band later in the evening.

One task Joel has is to call his attorney to make an appointment about some practical matters. Years ago, the woman who ran the escort agency he worked for taught him to be efficient in business affairs—how that made life a lot easier in the long run. While his emotions can get the best of him, he excels in taking care of business.

But love also involves different actions, different thinking. Joel also realizes Christmas is imminent. He rarely buys cards for any occasion unless he'll look like a dirtbag if he doesn't. But he needs to for Gabriel. Now he's in CVS awkwardly trying to figure out what kind of card to get that reflects his feelings. He watches some women look over the card selection. He follows their choices, tries to picture the words and images as his.

Ultimately this task is not successful—he'll just have to draw a card himself and think of something profound to say —but the act of searching felt wonderfully adult in its responsibility, and invokes the thousand little things that will change. And reminds him of one big thing he feels he should take care of now.

He goes to Danny's apartment on the Lower East Side and gets in without buzzing, as he knows he's not likely to gain admittance otherwise.

He knocks on Danny's door. It's opened a minute later by a teenager. The kid is a couple inches shorter than Joel, medium build, wearing jeans with chains, black t-shirt, short black hair upswept with red tinges, and an overly-large black suede vest decorated with various insignias and buttons of alternative bands.

The kid smiles at him. "Hey, Joel! Remember me?"

Joel has to think about it, but recognizes the eyes. The kid's father is Danny's cousin Carlo.

"Marianne."

"Right. But I'm *Halo* now."

"Got it."

"My dad hates that. Doesn't believe I'm not a girl anymore. He threw me out."

Danny comes up behind Halo. He frowns at Joel. "What do you want," he says quietly.

Halo steps back. "Why don't you come in? How's Gabriel?"

"He's good. Do you mind, Danny? I want to talk to you."

Halo is pulling at Joel's shirt to get him to come in. "Danny hasn't taken me to see Gabriel in *forever*. I want to show him." He stands up straight to show his look fully to Joel.

"He'll like it," Joel says. Halo then hugs Joel enthusiastically.

Danny's still disconcerted. Joel's being there is so unexpected, he's thrown off his game. "All right," he says finally.

Danny waves in the general direction of his couch and Joel takes a seat. Danny Martinez is six-foot, well-built, longish dark hair, very dark eyes, and olive skin.

He says to Halo, "Can you leave us alone for a few minutes? You can go in my room. Don't buy anything online or I'll kick your ass."

Halo now looks unhappy. "I want to talk to Joel. About drawing. You didn't *tell* me he was back."

"Sorry I didn't copy you on the memo. Inside. Now."

Halo drags his feet, but smiles brilliantly over his shoulder at Joel before shutting the door.

Danny turns back to Joel. He sits on a nearby chair. "I'm watching over him since his parents threw him out. So..."

He stops. He seems to be a little lost.

"That's good of you to take care of him, since I've been there. So, you know Gabriel and I just got back from Rochester."

"Veronica told me." Danny's voice has an undercurrent of hurt.

"He's okay. Really. You should know that. But why I'm here is, we have to get past each other for his sake."

"Is that so?"

"He needs you. He's been going through a bad time. You know that. You've been friends too long for this. And you seem to have your hands full as well."

"I haven't heard anything from him. What am I supposed to think?"

"Think about cutting out the bullshit. I told him to let it go about what you said."

"Oh, you *told* him?"

"Yeah. I don't care what you think, but he does, and I care about him. You didn't insult me, you insulted him—and you hurt him."

Danny bends a little. "I tried to say I'm sorry."

"So, you don't want to ruin your friendship with him because you hate me. Jesus, Dan, we were almost burned alive in Rochester. If he died, you wouldn't want to carry around with you that your last conversation with him was angry. That his last thought of *you* was an angry one."

The two men contemplate each other. Joel sees Danny feels what he said. Regret and fear. Sadness and frustration.

Danny finally speaks. "I don't hate you."

Joel shrugs. "Regardless. You want to fix this. I know he does too. And because I know what you fought about, you and I need to come to some kind of détente so he doesn't feel caught between us."

Danny doesn't immediately disagree. He's listening, rubbing his chin where he recently shaved his thick beard. "You never tried to cultivate me when you and he were together before."

"Come on, Dan. You didn't like me from the start, for whatever reason. You used to ignore me—the same thing Gabriel got pissed about with Alex's friends. You never tried with *me*. You say you don't hate me, but you sure as hell dislike me. Why?"

Danny doesn't expect that direct question. He doesn't really smoke, but the awkwardness leads him to find a pack of Marlboros in a drawer and light up. "What you did to him."

Joel nods. "You mean when he left me? Fair enough. I got the sense you think I'll do it again."

"Do I have reason not to?"

"Time tells. I can't make you read my mind. I always cared about him, that's what you don't realize. I never wanted to end it. I think you're confusing what I used to do with who I am. I suppose that's the way it goes, but it's not what I do now. You were uncomfortable about my having been an escort in the first place. I always picked up on that. I suppose you told Alex, but whatever. That part of my life is over."

"I never said anything to Gabriel about that. When you were together." But Danny looks away. His voice gets lower. "I know you had a hard life."

Joel shrugs again. "You know and you don't know. The choices you make at 15 aren't the same at 30."

"He never told me details. But I got the idea. I have no reason or right to criticize your childhood or whatever."

"I was in a desperate situation when I started that. I'm not going to apologize or hate myself for it. But since it's also part of what bothers you, just tell me, what do you want to know?"

Danny frowns. "About what, exactly?"

"Me. I'll answer you this one time."

He's succeeded in making Danny uncomfortable again. "I never said you had to do that."

"It's not for you, it's for him. What we say today is between us."

"You sure about that?"

"Yes. He'd be angry that I'm doing this, but it's the only way I can think of for you to get some kind of catharsis about me. Maybe, just maybe, if you talk to me it will help you talk to him."

Danny runs his hands through his hair. "I don't know what to ask you, Joel. You didn't have to keep doing that while you were with him, did you?"

Joel leans back and takes a pack of cigarettes out his pocket. Not his Djarum, but one of Gabriel's hidden packs of Camels that Gabriel thinks Joel doesn't know about.

Joel lights up and contemplates the question. "Change is hard. Even if something isn't a good thing to do if you are familiar with it, if you're *good* at it, it becomes the basis for self-esteem, being in control."

"But you did other work, right?"

"Yeah. I did and I still do. Remember when I helped your nonprofit with the computer system? Gabriel did help me see beyond myself to another identity, a truer face, so to speak."

Danny starts to speak, but Joel holds up a hand. "Let me finish. With him and me, I was scared he'd turn out like others I'd been with. Or that he'd get tired of me. Do you understand that when you fall in love with someone you become emotionally helpless? Maybe not, you don't believe in LTRs. But I didn't think I could live with that happening—his leaving me. So I tried to do what I could to keep some control—some distance. It was wrong. Anything else you want to ask?"

Danny's quiet while Halo comes out to get a soda from the kitchen and then goes back to Danny's bedroom. "You had some bad experiences, I guess."

"In escort work? Of course. When I was on the street, and less so afterwards, but still. I was beat up more than once. *Severely.* I have scars if you want to see them."

Danny shakes his head. "I shouldn't have asked. Anyone who hurt you...it was wrong. You aren't into drugs, right?"

"No. I saw people overdose. I woke up next to someone dead from that. My experiences don't keep me from being able to feel, to love, to be a decent person."

Danny contemplates the floor for a moment. "You've loved other people?"

"Yes."

"Men and women?"

Joel sighs and sits back. "Yeah, men and women. I knew that was the other thing you didn't like."

"He's okay with that. He says he understands it...but I just heard of these bi men who've used gay men for sex and then..."

"Gone back to their wives? That old urban legend. Did I do that? No. Look, Gabriel doesn't subscribe to the idea that bisexuality is either fake or perverse."

"I can't believe I'm talking about this with you." Danny gets up and walks around nervously.

"Because we don't have to be tactful with each other. Let it out, then."

"It's not a problem for him?"

"Why the fuck *should* it be? But when we were first together, some of his acquaintances used to say shit around me like "bisexual equals bipolar," or "straight, gay or lying." It was one reason he doesn't hang with those people anymore."

Danny frowns at him. "Who were they?"

"Doesn't matter. They probably wanted to fuck him and were jealous. The only important thing is that Gabriel doesn't find it a problem."

They're quiet for a moment.

"So...what do you want? We pretend we're friends?"

Joel smiles. "I don't think he'd buy that. Why can't we just be courteous to each other, if you can deal with that. If you have an issue with me, you talk to me rather than give him a hard time."

Joel then hands him a business card. "This is my number.'"

Danny reads the card. "Artist. You're selling your stuff?"

"I've *been* selling it. He's told you. That's why the card doesn't say *whore*, because I do this now."

Danny exhales. "All right, all right, I wasn't implying anything. Gabriel and I don't talk much about you, okay?...I have a hard time getting past what happened with you and him. But you're right that I don't want things to be this way. You're here, and I have to give you some credit for guts. But if you do fuck him over again, I *might* actually kill you."

"That isn't going to happen."

"Okay, we'll see. In the meantime, he's not talking to me."

"Just come over now. Bring the kid to say hello. Then I'll take him out, and you talk to Gabriel."

Danny gets up. "Jesus. I can't believe I'm doing this."

Joel smiles. "Neither can I. We must love him a lot, then."

∞

When they all walk into Gabriel's apartment, he is talking about cases with Veronica. His expression upon seeing Danny with Joel is priceless.

"Well, I sure want to hear the story behind this," Veronica says.

Halo runs over to bear hug Gabriel. Over the kid's shoulder Gabriel looks from Danny to Joel, as if perhaps he's hallucinating.

Joel goes over to kiss him. "I'm taking the kid to the Met to talk about art. And I'm inviting Veronica with us. So you two are going to stay here, and get over yourselves. Veronica, nothing urgent to take care of there, is it?"

"Nope." She gets up. "Sounds like a plan to me."

"Gabriel can't go with us?" Halo says, pouting.

"He and your cousin need to rekindle their bromance. We'll do all right without them."

Joel herds them out the door, leaving Gabriel and Danny alone.

They haven't spoken yet, standing awkwardly in the living room.

"Fuck it," Gabriel says. "I'm glad you're here." He comes over to where Danny is, but Danny's already going to meet him.

They hug for some time. Each trying to tell the other how sorry he is. It doesn't take long for them to be comfortable with each other again, although little flare-ups occur as Danny finds out about how close Gabriel and Joel have come to being killed over the last few weeks. But they deal with that, as Danny does his damnedest to deal with hearing about the great love affair of Ignatz and Krazy Kat (as he used to call them) starting over again.

∞

Fifteen ◆ 13 Concordance (Tóng Rén)

Heaven over Fire: People need to work together in harmony and form alliances. This is necessary to handle a difficult situation. The fifth line (nine/yang) moves in this reading. People must come together to fight against evil when the truth is known.

∞

Friday, December 24
Alphabet City 10:07 am

Joel's in a purposeful mood the next morning. While I'm consulting *Connexions* magazine about various LGBT-friendly vacation spots, he brings over his iPad to show me what he's found on Geneva's matter.

"This has to be the man Knox was talking about." He shows me an online biography. "Derek Baker, he's 81 now. His daughter would have been in her teens then. From what Knox said, it had to be a daughter. The other possible senators only had sons."

We look at the old photos for a moment. "Is he still alive?"

"Yeah, retired and doing whatever rich politicians do when they retire—use bricks of hundred-dollar bills for skeet shooting, maybe."

I have to laugh. "Okay, you're sounding like me, and one of me is enough. What about his daughter?"

"Brenda. She was married and divorced, and as far as I can tell is living alone. No other children." He shows me the lone picture available of her with her father at a benefit many years ago.

"She's pretty white. Geneva's father must have been of color. Seriously, 1975, upstate New York, conservative senator's daughter unmarried and pregnant, and mixed-race-hiding the whole thing would make a stupid sort of sense."

"Not anymore."

"Yeah, once again, digging up stuff that someone else wanted buried. Let's hope this works out better."

He picks up his coffee cup, looking at me. "I'm going in a minute, to take care of some legal things."

"Okay." I think about us having coffee together, like hundreds of times before. But it's new. It's new and familiar, domestic.

"Don't you want to know what?"

"I don't need to know. It's your business."

He toys with his cup. "You give me a lot of space, more than you have to."

"I suppose we have to learn the boundaries. I'm less concerned with what you do than what you think. But you seem to want me to ask. So tell me where you're going, then."

"I have a lawyer on 52nd Street. Her name is Voss. She does various things like estates. I asked her to make a will."

I close my eyes.

"Don't freak out on me. Have to be practical. You're my heir."

"Oh, God." I put the coffee cup down and pick up Archie for comfort. "You're sensible and I can't be sensible. It's hard for me to hear just for the implications."

"It *is* sensible. You can't prevent death by avoiding what's important to make survivors' lives easier. It's what needs to be done. I know from Jan's situation. *You* need a will, and a health care proxy."

"I have that, a health care proxy." I put Archie on the counter and find some treats for him —and Bella, who knows by the psychic cat network what's going on. "I had one done in 2008, and I never got around to changing it. I put you as my proxy, so you still are. Danny's the back-up. Since you and he are besties now, I guess that's not a problem. I don't have a will. Dom did, but I couldn't do it. I just had Veronica promise to take Archie and my books. Everything else, the hell with it."

"Good attitude. Very legal too —I can't wait to see Veronica trying to enforce that without breaking ten laws. You know your father inherits if you don't have a will."

"Fuck." I look at Archie purring over his snacks. "Yeah, that's true. I hate this-dealing. with death—but all right. Ask your attorney to set up an appointment and I'll deal."

"Good." He sets his cup down and holds me. The idea of a will, of his death, gives me a black feeling inside. But so does the idea of my father having any say over my life. Although I'll call him tomorrow on Christmas, to be human.

My phone rings. Herrmann. I disengage myself from Joel and answer, moving away. I know he's not liking that, despite our boundaries conversation.

"Gabriel. I have some information that may be helpful to you."

"Fantastic. I'll come over when you're free."

"I am free all the time, these days. Come over as soon as *you* are free."

Joel looks expectant after I hang up, but I disappoint him. Herrmann is off-limits for now. Joel finishes his coffee, and I reach for gum rather than smoke. I look him in the eyes so he knows I'm not hiding anything that involves him.

Joel asks nonchalantly, "What are you going to do today?"

"Following up on some information."

His irritation is so clear in his posture and expression. He leans on his elbows on the counter across from me with his cup, and goes through mental perambulations while looking at me. Then seems to come to some kind of internal compromise. "Okay. I'll talk to you later."

Not good enough. I come around to his side and make him hold me again. It's a good way to leave. I give him some time to get going to his appointment, then head for Brooklyn.

∞

"I can't give you names of my sources, but this was a chain of information that came back to me. I think it will help you."

"Excellent." I'm on Herrmann's study floor with the bulldogs, trying to play tug of war with them both at the same time. I've told him everything that's happened in the last two weeks and he's now telling me what he found out about Devanović.

"So. It comes down to what Devanović was up to in the Balkans. Before he arrived in the US in the late nineties, he was connected with some shady people in Yugoslavia. I suppose that doesn't surprise you."

"I can't say it does."

"And luckily for us, some of those people were in a Russian crime organization. If he had been involved with war criminals, my contacts wouldn't be helpful in this. But it seems Devanović had an operation going with the Russian contacts, in addition to whatever he was doing with area women. Probably drugs. In any case he used a different name with them. Andelko Predojević."

He spells it for me. "And even better, he double-crossed them for a good portion of money, which he probably used to finance his way here, and also turned some of his contacts in to the authorities. Yes, some time has gone by, but the men who were double-crossed would still like to find Predojević especially as they went through some prison time."

"Interesting. I could possibly suggest that he would have a welcoming committee if he's deported, and he likely will be. So he would have to choose between worrying about Don and worrying about the Russian mob."

"This Mathers can't compare to the mob." Herrmann gives me a few more details.

Then I tell him about my provisional plan for the Tertullian Society, which I've been thinking about. "I take this information I'm decoding from Kent's notes, and I'll set up a video identity and upload it to YouTube. It won't be connected to me."

He gets up to walk over to his window. "It's an interesting idea. But I'm worried—what if they trace it to you? You aren't just putting yourself in jeopardy, as I recall. You're putting the people you know at risk too."

I look at Jonah. "If I find out they catch on, and they make a move towards the people I love, I'll take myself out. No one will get hurt on my behalf."

Now Herrmann really is distressed. "Is this worth your life? These people? You know the world goes on in spite of them."

"I'll always fight Nazis, whoever they are."

"All right." He puffs on his cigar. "I hope I have some more life in me, because now I feel I need to be there for you."

After a moment he turns to look at me, and then back out the window. "Is there a reason why a young man is watching my house so intently, as if he perhaps expects aliens to land here?"

"Someone's watching you?" I stand up, concerned.

"Around your age, short blond hair and a beard, dressed casual."

"Oh." I have to smile. "Damn. That's Joel. I should have known he gave in too easily this morning."

"Joel. The one with whom you reunited?"

"Yeah. He used to follow me on occasion. I know it sounds weird, but it's how he vets people. He doesn't do it anymore, but today...I guess he was worried about what I was getting into."

"Really? From what you told me, he is trustworthy."

"Only with my life. But I haven't told him about you. He was the only one who knew what I was doing this summer. And he got a gun to his head for his troubles, courtesy of Ethan Nelson."

"And the one calling himself Zest took care of Nelson."

"No doubt about that."

Herrmann nods. "So your Joel. He's been through the fire. Then we should let him come in. I take it you haven't informed him of your plans?"

"No. I didn't want to get him involved...I don't want him in danger."

"And yet he involved himself. He is with you, right? So why leave him to wait outside? That will only confuse things." Herrmann opens the window, leans out and waves. "Young man! Come on over here."

I have to go over beside him just for the chance to look out and see Joel's reaction. He's halfway down a garden level entrance across the street and frowning up at Herrmann. Joel doesn't like to be found out when he's following anyone, and honestly it never happens. Which means Herrmann is good about picking up on this sort of thing. Very, very good.

I'm impressed and amused. "He likes to be in the shadows."

"He should pick a better hiding place, then." Herrmann leans out further. "Joel, is it? Come on inside. I invited you here, don't be discourteous to an invitation."

Joel pauses a second, totally taken aback, then comes up to the sidewalk and crosses the street to the stoop of Herrmann's building. Herrmann moves back into the living room. "You can buzz him in."

I go to Herrmann's door and press the buzzer. A minute later I hear Joel climbing the stairs and open the door. He has the same nonplussed look, which makes me smile. I kiss him. "Come in. You're among friends."

I forget to warn Joel about the menagerie, and when I lead him into the living room, they are already on the move. He's suddenly swarmed by dogs and cats demanding to check out the new guy. While he's on the floor with them, I briefly explain how I know Herrmann. The bulldogs are so happy to have a new friend they're struggling to climb on his chest and lick his face.

"*In deckung*! Let the man breathe."

"Oh my God. Now I know why Gabriel likes it here." He finds Jonah, my kitten, and picks him up, making the others jealous.

Herrmann holds a hand out to him. "Joel, welcome. I'm Bertrand Herrmann."

Joel takes his hand, giving him a look that is both reverent and analytical.

Herrmann smiles. "So. You are suspicious of me, young man? You think I would put your *engel* in danger?"

"I wouldn't suggest it." Joel smiles too, but not completely.

They regard each other. Herrmann nods. "I wouldn't either. Not with you as his *Beschützer.* Relax. You are both safe here. No one's going to break in, and if they did, they would regret it."

He goes into the kitchen and Joel follows him with his eyes as he pets the animals. I watch him watching. Herrmann brings back another cup for the tea. "As for me, I am not the kind you are concerned about. I'm not evil, *böse.*" He holds out the cup.

Joel takes it. "I know."

Herrmann takes his chair. "You don't, you're being polite. What it is, you've seen it. *Böse Taten.* Up close. Terror, *Schrecken.* You are familiar with the *unheimlich.* Beings who are almost human, but are not. I am as well. Your *engel* is not. He may think he has met them, but not really."

Now I frown. "Are you kidding? After this summer?"

They both ignore me. Joel nods again. "That's right."

"I think I've seen enough."

Herrmann reaches for his pipe, and then pours tea. "You have. You do not need to see more, though you might need too. This is not a bad thing, Gabriel. Do not be insulted. Neither I nor your *ehemann, frischgebackener ehemann,* feels this is bad. You are a source of light. That is why I'm concerned about this plan you have."

Now Joel finally looks at me. My *frischgebackener ehemann,* whatever that is. "Plan?" He says it in a tone of *Excuse me?*

I shrug. "Weren't you supposed to be at an attorney's office right now?"

"I wanted to make sure you weren't getting in trouble. I've seen you here before, so I felt okay."

"Seen me here—" I shake my head. "I give up."

"You tried real hard, baby. But I'm better, and I wasn't going to let you get in the wrong hands. The only reason he saw me today is that I was going to leave anyway."

Herrmann chuckles. "If you want to think so. But I have a long history of being followed and stalked. I know when it's happening."

Joel turns serious. "So what is this plan?"

"I'm working out a way to get what these people do out in the open."

"The Tertullians?"

"Those are the ones, yes."

"We just got back together." Joel takes out a pack of cigarettes and holds them up to Herrmann, who nods assent. "And you want to get killed already?"

"The whole idea is that I do it so it doesn't trace back to me. We'll use the Tor Project." I explain to Herrmann, "It's an open-source software that protects you in sending information on public networks, so you can't be traced. Political dissidents use it, like Anonymous."

"I'm not familiar with the technology." Herrmann sips his tea reflectively. "Are you sure about that?"

"I know it. I can add things to it. There's always a digital footprint somewhere, though." Joel is still hesitant.

"You are worried, yes? My question is, even if you can hide who you are in this video, don't you think this might be considered too much a coincidence that after you have trouble with them, suddenly there is this amateur news program exposing them?"

"I can't be the only person who knows about them..." I think about it. "I wouldn't mention the group by name, conspiracy debunkers wouldn't buy it anyway. I'd just be trying to get attention to the individual stories, let someone else connect it."

Joel is giving me a look much like what my mom used to do when I mouthed off to her, or when I was trying to pull a stunt like faking illness to get out of school. I match him with defiance. Herrmann remains in the background watching us.

Joel takes my hand. "Okay. Before you do anything, let me research it. Maybe it can appear to be from another country."

"Fine. Now, let me tell you what Bertrand found out about Don's friend Devanović..."

∞

I didn't think I'd have a party. Seriously, it is Christmas Eve and all. I'm just grateful to get through a holiday. But Joel seems to be having none of 'just getting through.' He was apparently busy while following me to Herrmann's, because after coming back and finishing Christmas decorations, he insists we go out.

I'm not thrilled with that, but he's a force of nature. He makes me dress better, fusses, corrects, admonishes, checks his phone constantly. Finally, after I nuclear-option attempt to change his mind by feeling him up, he actually steps away and says we have people waiting for us.

Well, then. Giving in, I find myself being led down the block to the neighborhood bar I most often go to. We used to go to it together. The greeting he gets from the owner tells me he put out some money, and it turns out he's reserved the back of the joint. It's set off almost like a separate room. And we do have people waiting for us.

Veronica is at the bar, and gets up to greet us, but waits until we're in further; I realize Joel has us in effect making an entrance. When I see my friends —Michaela is here, Bob, Luz, Jim and his wife Ella and his sister Evelyn, Jason, Geneva, Danny, even Isabella and Chris. And Giselle and Jacob are here as well. I recognize this our coming out party. It's Christmas Eve, but also a new beginning.

I'm not sure who's transformed more, him or me. But he doesn't leave my side while saying hello to everyone. I'm overwhelmed for the moment by so much affection.

Since the bar's music system is also under our control, there's a weird mix of Eighties music and contemporary. I become a little hyper inside from dealing with everyone at once, but to see him with me and feeling that sense of being together is priceless.

After enough champagne has gone to my head, I'm gratified to hear a song I haven't been able to listen to in a long time, INXS *Never Tear Us Apart.* There is so much both familiar and new here. I've slow danced with him before, many times. But I feel the newness in every nuance of touch.

The bass of the song pulses through us. It becomes our world. Michael Hutchence's voice winds around us. I put my head to his, my hands under his face.

We could live for a thousand years...

And without thought, we're moving in some kind of circle, our eyes only on each other, inspired to a hundred tiny touches and silent words between us.

As the music winds down like a slow dream, Chris says, "God, I guess you two mean it."

∞

Sixteen ◆ 11 Progressing (Tài)

Earth over Heaven: A person is now, more than ever, fulfilling his duty and moving forward with what needs to be. The second line (nine/yang) is moving. The person is brave and of the fortitude to fight a tiger with bare hands—which may be necessary.

∞

He's in the room he had in his mother's apartment in the Bronx when he was 15-16, but he's his current age. His mother is in his room, trying to wake him and he's not moving. He tells himself he's awake and he needs to get out of bed and talk to her.

Come on, Gabriel. See what the trigger is.

I'm trying. He tries to tell her. He thinks he's talking but he's not sure. He attempts to move and can't. He realizes he's dreaming and tells himself to wake up.

Gabriel, you need to get up.

I'm trying! I can't move.

Come on. She puts her hands on him, shakes him. He feels paralyzed.

I can't, I can't I can't.

You need to get up, see what the trigger is.

I don't know!

Her hands shake him again. Now his uncle is there. He can't really see Dom, but hears him talking. *Gabriel, time to get up. You need to look for the trigger.*

I'm trying, I'm scared, I can't move. Help me. Help me. Help me!

He struggles to move, but is still frozen. Now he feels like the women he found. They're dead, they can't move. He can't move. He knows what this is, sleep paralysis. Snap out of it. Wake up. They're both telling you to wake up. He feels their hands, feel them leaning over him. Inside he forces the thought wake up wake up WAKE UP.

∞

Tuesday, December 28

AND I'M AWAKE. I feel hands on me. Someone saying *It's okay It's okay It's okay.* I have to spend some time letting my adrenaline go down. When I look up and see him holding me, for the first time I feel...not alone.

∞

Canal Street, Chinatown, 11:34 am

"You've heard of the cold and hot hells. The Narakas in Buddhism. The *Diyu* in Chinese thought. You visited these places. Tell me."

"You're right," Gabriel says. "Wildemore was the Mahpadma Naraka, bodies frozen and cracked open. And being in the fire, that was the Avici Naraka —being in a furnace. I understand what happened to me, but these women can't be the ones who are supposed to be punished."

"No. Their punishment is over. But you are thinking you're being punished. That's not right. You're visiting these places; you're feeling the metaphor. Not to be punished but to continue helping others. This is why you're still having dreams calling out to you."

"What am I supposed to do?"

"Listen to the dreams. If the message is 'trigger,' then you've deduced that these men are continuing their evil acts. You want to follow up on it. That must be what you need to do, but do not any longer think of yourself needing to be in hell. Rather, consider yourself to be an avatar of a protective force who must go to these cold and hot places to rescue others."

∞

I know something bad has happened. Even as I get in touch with Bob about an idea I have regarding Don, I feel it. For one thing, during the Christmas Eve night out Giselle had said she wanted to talk to me for sure very soon and would call on Sunday. But I don't hear from her on Sunday. I call her and leave a message.

Monday morning, I find a voicemail from her. I missed her call while I was in the shower.

"Gabriel, I really want your help. Sorry about this being during the holidays, but I know you would understand with your intuition. See, it's my boyfriend, Tom. That's who I'm worried about. He's acting funny, and it strikes me wrong, like you said. He seems like he's turning into another person. He's asked me a lot of questions about Sophie, and even about the women you found. I don't know why—but he's so different! Can you get back to me?"

I call back several times and just get her voicemail. This bothers me enough that I finally drive to her shop, and she isn't there. Jacob is, and tells me not to worry. "I think she had to look into something. She'll be back. She has to be, because I can't run this place like her."

I don't like it. Boyfriend things make me nervous, for the possibility of violence. I talk with Jacob for a bit. I don't want to panic him.

"Did she say if she was going to see her boyfriend—what's his name, Tom?"

Jacob stops pricing things and thinks. "Uh...not that she said, no."

I consider her message. This Tom has been sympathetic towards her, supportive. Now is sounds like he's interrogating her about events she wouldn't know anything about, such as Wildemore. A murder groupie? Some people are obsessed about crime and murder. But turning back to what she said before Christmas. She wanted an investigation because maybe he isn't what he said he was. I've seen a lot of that lately. People who aren't who they say they are.

Jacob gives me Tom's cell phone number. I'm not ready to use it, because it might cause more problems. Eventually I have to leave; I have regular work to do for other clients. Everyday matters. But I drive by Giselle's house just to see if she's there. She's not. I'm concerned that she may try to investigate him herself, and what might happen if he finds out she's doing so.

I've left her six messages during the day, none returned. That is not like her; my intuition tells me that much. I don't have Jacob's number, but I'm able to track it down through my database later in the evening.

"I haven't heard from her either," he tells me. "Now I'm starting to be worried. What should I do?"

"Have you gone by her place?"

"Yeah. I have a key. She isn't there."

"Could she have gone somewhere with Tom?"

"I don't know, she hasn't before."

"What do you know about him? Where does he live?"

"Somewhere in Elizabeth. Never been there. I guess I didn't pay attention. He does some kind of nonprofit thing. He seems nice enough."

"Yeah. Know his last name?"

"Smith, I think."

How distinctive. Tom Smith. A man who may not be who he says he is, who's asking questions about her business. A con man, maybe. The lonelyhearts type who romances and steals. I hope that maybe Giselle, if she's in trouble, went into hiding. I tell Jacob to call the police and report her missing. Authorities don't wait around for 48 or 72 hours anymore; they start investigating. I then call Tom's number. No answer, and no voicemail.

I also call Michaela that evening, and ask her to report Giselle missing as well. I have a hard time sleeping, thinking about what she told me, her message, and my dreams. Why was Tom interested in Wildemore? Maybe he knew one of the women. Maybe he knew a woman who had disappeared.

In the morning, Michaela gets back to me, while I'm getting dressed. My thinking has not cleared.

"Gabriel, I need you to come over. And bring Joel."

"What's going on?" I look over at Joel, who meets my eyes and frowns. He's setting up Archie with food while playing some kind of video game on his phone, like an ordinary morning.

"Some things I need to talk about, but not on the phone."

"Mikki, I don't like the tone of your voice."

She speaks softer. "Gabriel, please come over to the office. Make sure Joel is with you."

My mind is in turmoil about why she wants me there. I grab my phone and keys, and Joel leaves with me. I can't talk on the way, only smoke. He doesn't get after me about it. I barely register he's in the car, wondering what's going on. What if Tom killed the women? Was I wrong about Don?

We park near the building. Mikki's office is a large one with a private bathroom in a suite of sublet offices in a large law firm. When we come in, she leaves her desk and waves me over to sit on a sofa with her. She takes my hand, and I know nothing good is coming.

"I didn't want to make you anxious, but I wasn't going to tell you over the phone." Michaela glances at Joel. He pulls a chair over next to me. I feel surrounded all of a sudden.

Michaela looks down for a moment then back at me. "The police called me back about Giselle..."

"No." I start to get up, and then Joel's hand is on my arm. Him and Michaela pulling me down. And then inside my mind, which has maybe blocked the realization up to now, I suddenly see truth.

"Gabriel, I know how you feel. You couldn't do anything about this."

"She's dead."

"Yes."

"The boyfriend?"

"They don't know. You'll need to tell them about that voicemail."

"How did it happen?"

"The police didn't tell me much but...I did speak to the detective, because this might be connected." Michaela takes a deep breath. "She was..." She can't say it.

"Was she *beaten*? Tell me."

Michaela frowns staring down at the floor. "Her body was found out back of her shop, like she was...thrown there. Yes. She was. Gabriel, I'm sorry. No, don't—"

I'm already up, ripping out of their hands, feeling the truth overwhelm me. "This was Don. This was *fucking Don Mathers*. He was her *Goddamned boyfriend!*"

She stares at me—either from what I say or what's overcome me.

"How do you figure that...?"

I've moved to the middle of the office, and for a moment, I can't see in front of me.

"I fucking *know*. She told me; I just was too stupid to realize it. He was *interested in the case*. He was just using her for the information. He harassed her about it. Who else would care? She thought he was *supportive*."

Neither of them say anything, and maybe at this point I'm only talking to myself. The kaleidoscope of events suddenly becomes a clear picture of everything that's happened since I began this case.

"We wondered how Don knew where I was for those attacks to happen. Giselle told him; I kept her up to date on where I was going. She didn't know he was using her. And I set him off. He kills when he's triggered. We found those bodies, and he didn't expect that, see. So he questioned her. And when she showed suspicion of him, enough that she called me, so he came back and killed her. I triggered Don to kill her."

"Gabriel, no. You can't say that."

Can you get back to me? Her last words to me.

Can you get back to me?

I'm not aware of how I got to stand in front of the wall of Michaela's office, and I don't feel it when I start slamming my fists against the wall. The fury takes me over. I've lost myself in it. I could pound this wall until I fall inside and disappear.

An arm goes around my neck, dragging me away. My hands in front of me have bits of plaster falling from them, flecked with blood.

I hit the floor, pulled off balance. Then Joel is on top of me. "Stop it!"

Michaela is standing next to me, wide-eyed. Like I've become something else.

Someone's knocking rapidly at her door. She walks to it almost mechanically. "It's okay," she tells whoever's there. "We've had some bad news."

Joel backs off me and I sit up, breathing hard.

Michaela shuts the door and comes back. Joel glances at the wall. "I'll take care of that. Don't be mad at him."

Michaela gets on her knees next to me. She's more horrified than anything. "My God, Gabriel, what did you do to your hands?"

I can't answer. I'm still in a rage, but frozen inside. She takes one of my hands. "You're bleeding. Joel, my bathroom. I have peroxide and bandages."

He goes away and comes back with whatever's in there, and tries to take care of the blood on my hands, dripping on my jeans. His hands are shaking so much he can't do it, and she takes over.

I try to talk, and the anger fills me so much I can't get the words out. Every time I picture Giselle, every time I'm replaying her message in my head, the rage overwhelms me. I want to jump up, run out.

Tears come, but it's part of the anger.

"Gabriel, nothing you could do."

"I triggered it. I could have stopped him if I paid attention. She didn't have to die."

Joel is pacing the office behind her. I've scared the fuck out of both of them. It's only been minutes, but I feel soaked in sweat already.

She puts her hands on me. "You can't blame yourself, don't let it be personal. We need to find Don Mathers. We need to find who he is. Because he sure isn't going by his real name."

Thoughts race through my head. Her words. *Don't let it be personal.* And then I hear in my head...*Make things personal. Make it personal.* Where I heard that phrase before. Who said it. And when I think about that, it gives me even more dread. "We have to leave."

"Hold on, now. Where are you going?"

"To see Bob. I was going to anyway. But I know. *That fucking son of a bitch*, I know!"

"Take a minute to center yourself. I don't want you to leave this way."

Joel is at the wall again, wiping it with a paper towel. He's so anxious he can't participate in the conversation other than to keep saying, "...I'll fix this. I'll have someone come here..."

She shakes her head at him. "It's no worse than what happens in a divorce attorney's office. Gabriel. Focus on me. What are you going to do?"

"Get a sketch of Don. See if it matches...what I'm thinking."

"All right. Let Joel drive, get the sketch, but tell me what you're thinking now, about him."

I breathe raggedly. "Frank Carlson. The fucking deputy director of the WFN. You reminded me by saying that, "don't let it be personal." *Frank* said it in a different way, "Don't make it personal." Giselle said Tom told her the same thing. "Don't make it personal." It's a funny way to say something."

"Still, it's pretty strange to think..."

I get up. "It is strange, but it's true. I'm going to get that fucker."

"Okay. Go. Get the ID. But don't do anything *else* without checking with me. Come back here later."

"All right." I finally feel the stinging in my hands. "I'm sorry I lost control."

"I know. We're good. *Let Joel drive.*"

I keep her gaze. Joel is frightened beside me, trying to clean up the wall and the floor. But she is calming me by her own calmness. Her own compassion.

I think of prayers for the dead, and start saying them. Trying to get the words out. Michaela holds my hands while I do this until I feel control coming back.

We're able to leave and for once I do what I'm told, letting Joel drive. But I'm sinking into something else. The hot anger is becoming cold, and drawing me away. Joel reaches for my arm while I'm searching on my iPad. Searching for Carlson, to find any photos. "He's on fucking LinkedIn. Frank *Thomas* Carlson. You *fuck.*"

"Gabriel. Stay with me. Don't get lost inside yourself."

I'm not with anyone right now. The coldness is like the protector mode, but worse. For the first time I can remember since I was young, I have the urge for revenge.

"What about Jacob?"

I hear this like I'm in a dream. "What?"

Joel's trying to look at me while driving. "Jacob. Where is he, do you think?"

It snaps me out of the darkness of my mind. I call Jacob's number but he's not there. I call Giselle's shop and talk to one of the assistants, Yasmine. She's in shock, trying to just keep the shop going just to be doing something. She tells me Jacob is at his apartment with a couple friends.

"We'll go by later," I say to Joel. He nods, lighting up.

I call Bob and tell him we have an emergency. He says to meet him at his office. He works in a rehab and reentry division of a nonprofit, in downtown Paterson. I've been there many times, sometimes with Joel, although he doesn't like Paterson for unexplained reasons.

Bob's happy to see us, although he raises his eyebrows at my hands. "What the hell you got into?"

"My own problems. I hate to be kind of blunt, but I need you to work with Joel on a sketch of Don, right now."

"No small talk first? You're all *serious* now that you're whipped. No, don't get mad, Gabriel. I see something's up. What do you need?"

"Your memory. Joel will draw it."

Joel always has a sketch pad in his bag. He takes it out and Bob turns to him.

"He's five ten or so, around 175 when I knew him. Muscular, not wiry. Brown hair on the wavy side, medium length. Brown eyes. Let's see, how much more can I go?"

"Let's try for some more detail. High or low forehead?"

"Hmm. High. Eyebrows pretty heavy, and the kind that start to go across. Not quite a unibrow, but hinting at it. Um. Nice-looking in kind of a generic way. Slightly sharp nose. Strong chin. Lips on the thin side."

"The eyes in particular will be important," I say. "I would guess he's had cosmetic surgery. Maybe not, but if he faked his death, it's a real possibility."

"He couldn't change his bone structure of his body, his height."

"But he can change a lot."

Joel starts working on it. Bob watches him and has him make adjustments. I don't watch because I want to see the finished product. After a half-hour or so, Bob is satisfied. "He's good, this boy."

"Don't I know it." I remember him sketching Giselle, and I want to cry again.

Joel gives me the sketch. It takes me a moment to confirm it to myself. I show Bob again. "The eyes are accurate, right?"

"Yeah, he could make people nervous with his stare."

I want to see it. I see it. I think. It doesn't eliminate him, anyway. "I need you to look at someone in person."

"No shit?"

"Yeah. In Elizabeth. He's had surgery, and not that much."

"What is he doing?"

"He's deputy director of the Women's Freedom Network."

However my voice is coming out, it must be bad. They both stare at me.

I put the sketch on Bob's desk. I trace the face without touching the paper. "His hair is shorter and darker, with some gray. He trims his eyebrows now, or had electrolysis. His chin is narrower. His nose has been shortened and flattened some. He's thinner in the face, maybe the body."

I take out my iPad and show Bob the photos of Carlson I found online.

"I can see it, but it's fuzzy. I can't say 100%. Don is my height and build. I sometimes wondered if I could take him. It was like that. But I remember his voice well. If you can get me close to him so I could hear him..."

I have to stop for a moment, realizing the implications of this. "Jesus. Those people don't even *know* what's in their organization...and I went to see Frank Carlson at the WFN to ask about Charlotte, and it *triggered* him. It made him angry enough to kill."

This has been in my dreams, the trigger.

Joel's voice is sharp. "Stop, Gabriel. You're not at fault. Something else would have set him off. You had to find out. He could gone on with whatever he's doing. Now it's just a matter of time."

I don't believe him but I have to listen to him. He has that effect.

I immediately call Michaela.

"Will Bob sign an affidavit?"

"Yes, of course he will, but I want a voice ID too."

"Good. If we can show Don is still alive—it will break this."

I then try the WFN main line to make an appointment with Frank Carlson on a pretext and fake name, but he's on vacation. Vacation. Human traffickers and killers go on *vacation?* I guess they do. The admin assistant tells me Frank is supposed to be back the first week of January.

Of course, he might be doing something else. I call the direct line of Seth Monroe, the legal director.

"I hear your Carlson is on vacation."

"Yes, again." He sighs in such a way that I get the idea this is a common occurrence.

"Does that happen a lot?"

"Why do you ask?" His voice is sharper, no dummy. "Does this have to do with the case?"

"I was curious about some timing. I'm not making any accusations. I just wondered if you'd tell me if Carlson is out of town a lot."

Another gamble, but I know he wants me to see this through. I hear him weighing the options.

"He's also in a conference for a few days in California." Monroe's tone is careful.

"Nothing wrong with that."

"No. How is the investigation coming along?"

"Evidence is gathering." I think of Giselle, and close my eyes. *That fucking bastard. I'll find him.*

"Good. You think this ties in to Charlotte?"

"I know it does. I know it."

"Were you going to talk about that to Frank?"

"Maybe. But he's out of town, so I have to wait."

"Yeah. As I understand, he has some other board work. In Canada. And his parents are ill. He often takes off for that. A few times a year. They're in Canada too, so I hear. In fact, that's where he's supposed to go for vacation now."

"Yeah, he told me his family is there. Let me ask you this. Do you happen to know his parents' names? Like, are they emergency contacts?"

"Is there a reason, a good reason, why you're asking me this?"

"Everything we've talked about up to now. And now it's more important than ever."

I hear Monroe tapping his computer. "Ellen and Michael Carlson in Ontario."

"Let me check that out, if you don't mind holding on a minute."

While I'm talking, we've gone outside to smoke, and Bob to watch us smoke, since he doesn't. Joel tells Bob about what happened with Giselle while I use my online databases. I find out that no one named Ellen or Michael Carlson live in Ontario. I fill in Monroe on this.

"All right, now I'm concerned. I'm going to look at this from here."

"I need to know when he's back. Please. This is vitally important. Tell me when he's back."

A pause on the other end. "Are you all right, Gabriel?"

I try to moderate my voice in my head. "Yes. Just that I need to...find him."

He doesn't believe it. But he'll read the story which will come out on the news and he'll know. I'm surprised it wasn't out this morning. Michaela wanted to save me from that.

"I want to keep track of him. That's all."

∞

Friday, December 31
Mid-Orange Correctional Facility, 10:05 am

Devanović is incarcerated upstate. When I check in, the authorities do not allow us to have a separate interview room. Even though I've been able to do that before at other prisons plenty of times without problems, a prison can make its own rules based on any security measure it sees fit.

So we're meeting in a general visitors' area. Square tables with welded seats on each side. Dark green paint, like the inmates' clothing. The correctional officers sit up front. The inmates have to sit facing the front of the room.

Not many visitors today. One of the officers points to the table where I should wait.

Ten minutes later Devanović is led out. He's aged significantly since the news photos I saw. He's over six feet, somewhat reedy. Swept back gray hair, rectangular face with square black eyebrows. Pale prison pallor. Thick glasses soften his Stokowski-like countenance.

I introduce myself. He accepts my handshake.

"I'm working on the Leonard Mathers case. You remember Leonard?"

He smiles. "I'm not going to answer that." His accent rolls around his gravelly voice.

"You're not going to answer an established fact? Okay. So you don't recall working at Wildemore hospital?"

"I'm not answering that."

"Teaching at Prentice-Cane?"

He just smiles.

"I suppose I could set up a top ten list of things you won't answer. You're about to be released on parole. You don't have to answer that either. It's on the DOC's website. So if you don't mind, Mr. Devanović, as you don't want to answer anything, maybe you'll listen."

He turns his hands up in a placating gesture. "Say what you wish."

"Thank you. Here's my theory. You emigrated here from Serbia—maybe with some help. You didn't quite have a legitimate psychiatry doctorate. But you talked your way into Wildemore. Their background checks were only one of their problems. You had some fun there torturing female patients. But maybe it wasn't enough of a challenge? No? Whatever. The place was shut down. Then you decided to get fresh prospects by 'teaching' college.

"But wait—we have another part to this story. You met two brothers, Leonard and Don Mathers. One was a sweet-natured man who was dissociative. You were able to exploit that. No doubt you learned some charm techniques in your psych studies. Leonard believed you were trying to help women because he loved women. But you don't. And you found a common soul in Don, because he despises women. And you and he got together to exploit women from your own part of the world so they could be tortured and enslaved here."

Devanović's expression hasn't changed. I can guess he's practiced in that. I keep my tone mild, not threatening.

"Everyone has weaknesses. I think Don was a lot more vicious than you —did you admire him? You developed a cult on the Prentice-Caine campus, and got caught in a fraudulent scheme. That's a weakness. But back in 2000, Leonard finally found out what his brother was doing. Then Don faked his own death. He even arranged for you to be the beneficiary of his life insurance. Don disappeared, but he's here in the area again. I guess he had to take over the slavery operation when you were imprisoned."

I sit back. "And I see you're due to be deported as soon as you're released. You'll be taken by INS right out of here to be shipped overseas."

Devanović sits back as well. "Perhaps it's time to go home."

"For you? You still have family there? At least they know where you are, unlike the families of the dead women for the last God knows how many years. You know who doesn't know you're here? The Russians."

Now I get a reaction. Subtly, his face falls and his eyes darken. His overall aura changes to fear.

I lean back in to speak softer, but still pointedly. "Maybe they're still mad about that drug deal, huh? People get killed over that. I *know* they're still looking for Andelko Predojević."

His breathing gets heavier. His face becomes clotted with blood. "What do you want?" Any trace of geniality gone. I've become a threat.

"I want what *you* want—to figure out a solution. How's this? You're more concerned about the Russians than Don. The system will ship you out like cargo. Don won't even get close. But once you get back, who'll be waiting for you? Nobody—if you help us."

"Help you with what?"

"An affidavit explaining Don's career in enslaving and killing women. How Don faked his death. What happened after that. And what you know about Leonard's murder. We don't care what you say about yourself."

He's thinking over the possibilities. "They could prosecute me again."

"Granted. No guarantee. But I think to convict a multiple murderer they'd work a deal. They want you out, anyway. Even if they tacked on a couple years, better than the Russians looking for you."

Devanović turns thoughtful. "Would your attorney represent me?"

"That would be unethical. She could recommend people."

He stares at me for a while. "Do you know who you're dealing with?"

"With you?"

"With him."

"Yes. Why do you ask?"

"Does he know about you?"

"Yeah." I smile.

He does too. "You've run into him."

"Indirectly, you might say."

"So you know."

I guess he means about Don's brutality. "Yeah, I'm acquainted. Since he knows about me, telling him isn't going to change anything."

"I don't have to tell him anything."

"I'm not worried about or scared of him. And you know what to be worried about."

"All right. So. What am I supposed to do?"

"Tell me what you're going to say. I'll type it up and come back with an affidavit for you to sign."

"Don't you want paper?" He indicates the correctional officers. Visitors can only bring money with them, no pens or paper unless they are attorneys. I don't want to bother with asking. "I'll remember."

∞

Friday, December 31, Continued

I didn't want to go out tonight. I handled Devanović well because I can't let this case down. I can't let Don escape. But it's only been two days since Giselle died, and I still feel it.

Joel and I have checked on Giselle's shop. It's still running with her staff, although they have no idea what to do. Jacob is trying to fill in at the same time he's stunned with grief. When we talk to him, he cries. Whatever he's gone through leaves him vulnerable. Everyone in the shop turns to me because they don't know what to do. I realize Giselle didn't have a network of friends, just acquaintances. She had to take care of her brother and that took up most of her social energy. Sophie was her one good friend. Michaela has told Sophie what happened, because I couldn't.

I have no idea what to do with Jacob, but I can't walk away and leave them. I spent all day there yesterday, leaving Veronica to handle the investigations. Joel tries to help Veronica and I both. I want him to be setting up his show rather than doing this. But he's here for me, like Veronica is here for me.

Jacob doesn't know how to arrange a funeral. I do. I've done it twice. I figured Giselle had to have an attorney to set things right for Jacob. She'd be practical, like Joel. Jacob searched in her desk until he found a business card for an area attorney. The attorney has Giselle's will, and was able to get the process moving at least. Giselle didn't want her parents involved in her life or her brother's. So I become more involved.

And by the time I left Devanović today I'm exhausted. Jason's band is playing at that bar he told me about, and he wants me there. I have no sense of celebration. On top of the guilt I feel for Giselle, I feel it for Joel. To be drowned in my feelings instead of being with him. But when I'm collapsed again on the bed, he talks to me. Saying to go out because we have friends there, to give them a chance to surround me.

As hard as it is, I go with him to the bar. Veronica and Geneva and Michaela are there waiting for us. Danny eventually comes by. We have a table next to the band. A part of me isn't here, it's somewhere else planning how to find Don. Although I keep having to go out and smoke when I can't take the cheeriness, at some point Jason plays a song dedicated to a "friend," someone lost to us. Billy Joel's *While the Night is Still Young.* One of Giselle's favorite songs.

∞

Monday, January 3

Michaela and I are in her office. The wall's been repaired. Joel even gave her a painting to hang there, but she isn't upset with me. We're comparing the sketch Joel made with the various photos of "Frank."

"I don't know. I kind of see it, but it won't convince Stan Cooper."

"As soon as he's back, I'm taking Bob to see him in person and get the voice ID."

"He works in a trafficking nonprofit. I can't get over this."

"Yeah. Great cover isn't it? Ted Bundy was a suicide hotline crisis center counselor. People don't want to believe the worst about another person. You know sociopaths have three defining traits: no conscience, so nothing holding him back from his actions; control of everything possible; and, a need to ramp up the risk. That fits in with Don's grandiose schemes, and probably why his cover lasts. He's been a fucking do-gooder in other countries, according to him. I bet he has. I bet other women have died in those countries, too."

"It makes sense, in a way. He kills Charlotte Merical because Leonard tells her about him. Leaves for nearly ten years, comes back and gets hired in her nonprofit...for some sadistic thrill..."

"He probably likes reading about how women are abused. He's always been a 'woman's advocate.' He still has fucking references for that. I'm sure his selfless work gave him insight on how to better run his own operation. The risk must have been a trip for him."

"And he didn't come across that way, when you met him."

"Fuck no. He was pleasant. Helpful. "What can we do to help, Gabriel?" Bundy was able to come across as likeable —totally hiding his brutality, like this piece of shit."

She shakes her head. "I know this is true, but Stan Cooper will never believe it. That's why when I gave them Giselle's voicemail on your phone, I didn't bring up what we've been looking into."

"He'll have to believe it, if we can prove Don is Leonard's brother."

"Exactly. I have the results of the DNA test on the weapon supposed have been used to kill Leonard. The DNA tied to Sophie has issues —it's older and degraded. The lab said an unknown one is on the weapon as well. Maybe it'll turn out to be Don's. But now with Devanović's statement and what happened with Giselle...I'm concerned that this Frank isn't in the WFN's office to talk to. I think we should see what happens with giving this to Stan. I hope he'll look into the connection with the bodies at Wildemore to Don. It's a risk, but maybe he'll listen to reason."

She faxes a copy of the affidavit and notice of witness to the Union County prosecutor's office. Cooper calls back a few minutes later and Mikki puts him on speaker. She goes into the story of Devanović. If he's deported, he won't be around when the trial comes, and so the affidavit can be used in place of in-person testimony, although it likely won't. But it is enough for the police to have probable cause to investigate Frank Carlson.

Cooper is not pleased over any of this, and we can hear his impatience even as Michaela explains about the women in Wildemore and Leonard's connection. "What the hell is this, Michaela? Do you think you're going to get a better plea deal this way?

Michaela shakes her head at me in exasperation. "Stan, this shouldn't go to a plea or trial. I'm going to ask for an evidentiary hearing and to have the case dismissed. I think you can see that this is a much bigger situation than Leonard Mathers. And that the exculpatory evidence for Faulkner is pretty —"

"*What* evidence? Her DNA is still on the weapon. Your affidavit doesn't say shit to exonerate her. *If* we even believe Devanović, who's going to be kicked out of the country anyway."

Michaela's irate at his obstinacy. "Stan, we believe Don Mathers killed Giselle Greenspan. And the women who were found at Wildemore. These tie into the case."

"This whole thing has your so-called investigator's prints all over it. You let him sucker you into his bullshit."

"Leave him out of it, at least he does his job. You might consider the possibility you're keeping an innocent person in jail."

"Go file a bail hearing then. Until you have real evidence, don't call me —I'll call you."

And on that clever note, he hangs up.

She looks at me. "Seems we'll have to go to court on this one."

"We tried. If he wants to be on the record looking foolish, fuck him. We'll keep going."

She gets up to look out her window. "Gabriel, Giselle's retainer has run out. I don't know if Sophie has any money. I'm not leaving the case, but I'll have to apply to the state for funds. I can't afford to keep you on until I get approval from the state."

"Don't worry, I'm donating my time."

"Why? You can't afford that either."

"Do you really believe I'd stop?"

She turns back to look at me. "No."

∞

SEVENTEEN ♦ 12 OBSTRUCTION (PĪ)

Heaven over Earth: A challenging situation is ahead. Good fortune and misfortune interconnect with each other. As progress has been made, so some cost must come because of that advance. The fifth line (nine/yang) moves here. A task has arisen for a person who knows not to forget—knows how to forge ahead.

∞

He is awakened by a woman in blue with red hair—Palden Lha-mo, the only female *Dharmapala,* defender of the faith in Tibetan Buddhism. He hears the liturgy around him and lies back, becoming passive and receptive. He becomes the oracle, as Lha-mo enters him and uses his human support to become a god (*lha bskyed*). She is transformative, sometimes seen as or linked to Avolokiteśvara. She is a protector.

He feels himself turning blue with her skin, riding on her white mule, drinking blood from the skull she carries in his hand. Flame erupts around him as an aura, twisting into mandala shapes. It should burn him, consume him, but because she's in him, he is not hurt. But he feels the heat, and feels her wrath against evil. His two arms become eight, and he hears her tell him of the weapons she has that she's giving him.

> *You will determine the lives of men...*
> *These are the weapons with which to hunt evil men...*
> *When you feel wrath, this is the only wrath to feel. The wrath must come from compassion, not violence...*

∞

Affidavit of Nikola Devanović
Mid-Orange Correctional Facility, DIN # L23487
DOB 07/27/1952 Home Country: Serbia

January 3, 2011

Having been duly sworn, the affiant, Nikola Devanović states the following...

....(page two)....

I met Donald Mathers in 1997. I had recently immigrated to the United States. I had found work as a clinical psychiatrist at Wildemore Hospital in Elizabeth, NJ. Don Mathers was working at the hospital as a patient advocate.

In my country of Serbia, I had known persons involved in human trafficking. Specifically, these persons were recruiting women looking for domestic or office jobs in other countries, and then forcing the women into prostitution. Shortly after I meant Don Mathers, I told him about this, and he expressed interest in setting up an operation in New Jersey similar to that I had told him about. He asked me to see if I could contact the people I knew in Serbia and other countries, and arrange for women to be transported here.

I agreed to this. I agreed under duress, because Don Mathers was a very threatening person. I had seen him become violent on several occasions, including beating people on the street. These people were often drug users or other "street-people" and therefore they did not call the police. I was afraid to call the police myself because Don Mathers threatened my life if I did not cooperate with him.

In 1998, Don Mathers told me he had arranged to rent houses in Elizabeth under assumed identities. He showed me the houses. The addresses are in Appendix A. He also found helpers. These were men sent to me from contacts I had in Central Europe, and others I found in New Jersey. The men were hired to guard and control the women. These names and identifying characteristics of these men are in Appendix A.

I had met Don Mathers' younger brother Leonard while I worked in Wildemore. Leonard was clearly schizophrenic, but sometimes functional. Don Mathers did not get along with Leonard Mathers and often intimidated him. Don Mathers asked that I find a job for Leonard Mathers because Leonard needed to be "distracted" or he would interfere with Don Mathers' trafficking operation. I helped Leonard obtain a handyman maintenance position at Wildemore in 1998, until the facility closed in 2000.

The trafficking operation lasted until April 2000. Between 1998 and 2000, I estimate over 50 women were in these houses and forced into prostitution. Some women were later "sold" to other persons. Some were sent back to their home countries. Some women disappeared completely. I did not know the details, but a couple of Don Mathers' helpers said Don would beat the women severely, and some he had taken out with him and not returned them. They suspected Don had killed these women.

Leonard Mathers somehow found out about the operation. He approached me about his discovery in spring 2000. I told him to leave it alone. Don Mathers also knew Leonard was aware what was going on with the women, and said he'd have to do something about Leonard in case he'd tell anyone.

In mid-April 2000, Don told me Leonard had contacted a woman in a nonprofit for help, and that he, Don, had killed this woman to stop her from any further investigation. He said he had beat and stabbed her to send a message, and that Leonard "was next." However, Leonard went into hiding and Don could not locate him. In fear that the operation would be exposed, Don Mathers told the helpers to shut it down. He then said he was leaving the country. I do not know where the helpers went to, or what happened to the women who were in the houses at the time.

I do not know what Don Mathers did once he was outside the US. He occasionally contacted me and said he was working in non-governmental organizations under another name. He also said he was changing his appearance. I did not pay attention, as I had a new position at Prentice-Caine College. Leonard had gotten back in touch with me shortly after Don left. He believed me that I didn't have anything to do with Don's trafficking operation. I had Leonard work with me as an assistant at Prentice-Caine.

In 2008, I was incarcerated. While I was incarcerated, I received a letter from Don Mathers saying he was returning to New Jersey, and wanted to revive his operation. I did not respond to the letter. I destroyed the letter. Later, in 2009, Don Mathers visited me under a false identity on a few occasions, saying he was now "Frank Carlson," which is not the identity he visited me under at the facility. He said he was working in the nonprofit that his victim, the one Leonard had contacted in 2000, had worked for. Don Mathers told me he had found new helpers for another trafficking operation, and that he was planning to stalk and kill Leonard. I said I wanted nothing to do with him and asked him not visit me. Don Mathers continued to threaten my life and so I did not contact authorities with this information at the time.

Don Mathers visited me one last time in September 2010, to say he had killed Leonard, beaten him to death, and hoped that a "nutcase" friend of Leonard's would be arrested as the killer, and he would do what he could to ensure that this friend, name unknown to me but believed to be Sophia Faulkner, would be seen as the guilty one and locked up.

As I have been granted parole by the State of New Jersey and am due to be deported thereafter, I am making this statement in hopes of clearing the record about Don Mathers and Leonard Mathers, in the best interests of Don Mathers' victims and their families.

∞

Wednesday, January 5
Alphabet City, 11:22 am

IN THE MORNING, Veronica is out with Danny checking the situation with her apartment building.

Joel and I are on my living room floor, because he wants to draw henna tattoos on my feet in different colored soy inks. He creates symbols in his mind and draws them in intricate patterns. I'm lying on my front, trying not to give in to ticklishness. He says he's doing this to help protect and heal me.

And as I do in most of my spare time lately, I'm thinking about Sophie's case, and if I've missed anything. I consider going to talk to Bob again. Joel's not thrilled with that, but not because of Bob. "Maybe we could meet him somewhere else?"

I look over my shoulder at him. "You're *from* Paterson, aren't you? That's why you don't like the place."

Joel doesn't look at me. "Almost. From Wayne. But I was in Paterson enough times." Wayne is a small town just north of Paterson.

"I should have told you long ago."

"It's okay. We don't have to go there."

"Don't worry about me. I guess I can handle it if we go." He continues working on my leg. "Hold still, I told you. If you're going to keep getting tattoos, you should get a phoenix on the back of your leg, here." He touches just above the tendon. "Not large. Flying toward your calf." He starts drawing there. "I need blue for this, but you'll see."

I look over my shoulder again to see what he's doing. This gets a growl out of him and his grip on my leg tightens. I try not to twitch against the fine-tipped stylus he's using. But lying prone, feeling the tiny point dot against my feet somehow helps me think. "Something else is bothering me..."

"What is it? And didn't Chiang teach you to talk without moving your body?"

"You're thinking of belly dancing, which I never learned."

"You'll learn something from me."

"Yeah? What's that?"

He stops his work. "To appreciate not being in control all the time. Makes you nervous to let me do this, doesn't it?"

"No."

"Living the lie, *still*. Control freak. But I know you better." He leans over me, on his hands and knees now, bringing his head close to mine. "You think you're such a badass."

"You challenging me, son? You've seen me in action."

"I've seen you in all kinds of ways. You've let yourself be true with me. And I've seen the side of you that's the bookish schoolboy, the good little boy." He traces a finger gently against my face. "The good little boy wants to be seduced, wants to give it up to me, let me be in control sometimes. Because we both know I'm the *real* bad boy, regardless of what Bettina said."

As so often when he looks at me that way, I'm at a loss for words. I haven't felt very amorous this past week because of the grief, and feeling like the grief would send me down the rabbit hole again. To absolute depression. He's been considerate of my feelings. And also starting to lead me back.

Knowing that he's getting to me, he continues. "And you'll let me because you know I'm not trying to control you to get my rocks off. But to be there for your needs. For the good boy who wants to show off what he knows, and be seduced." He now runs his stylus down my side, making me shiver.

"Yeah. I think I'll start schooling you now on that..."

He slides his arms around me; his hands work my clothes; he starts speaking in my ear, touching me with the stylus, which makes me focus on him. Everything else is forgotten in listening and responding to him. Feeling alive.

Until we're lying entwined together, sweat drying, and the ink has gotten smeared on both of us.

"So, you were telling me something was bothering you, baby..." he says with his eyes closed.

"God. I have to think now? Okay. I hadn't had the chance to follow up on those papers we got off the men in the park."

I have the copies of these papers in the case file, now resting on the coffee table. One has a couple words, the other has a small rough map. We've looked at them before, but my mind is recharged. I sit up. "It seems like this is a map, right? I'm pretty sure the hospital is on it. Something this helper guy didn't go to often. Maybe he needed reminders. Maybe he needed reminders how to put on his pants before his shoes for all we know. We should figure out where it is, and see if it turns up something with Don."

"Why do you think Wildemore is on it?"

"Well, in spite of the fact this guy's handwriting sucks —I thought lawyers had terrible handwriting, but really —I think it's Albanian. This word is *çmendínë*, mental hospital or madhouse, according to Google translate."

Joel takes the papers. "One of the X's has a 'c' with a cedilla, so that could be *çmendínë,* meaning Wildmore. What's the other word?"

"What we need to know. And if this first one is Wildemore, the line goes up north, northeast. With an 'f,' you think?"

"And an 'e' with a dieresis. The middle could be an 'a' or 'u,' then two 'n's,' or two 'r's.'" He stops long enough to test the combinations in an Albanian to English dictionary online. "The only word that works out is *furrë*, meaning furnace."

He gets back down on the floor. Now he's thinking.

"Remind you of something, Jersey boy?"

"Call me that again, and I'll be forced to hurt you. Not in a good way. It does remind me of something I knew when I was a kid. There's this kind of legendary place northeast of Black Mountain, Caraway Road. It's known for being haunted. It's a county road almost nobody uses because the highway is so much easier. And no one lives there. It's really a road to nowhere."

"Did you ever go there?"

"Yeah, with my best friend, Tim, when we needed to get away. The reason why I thought about it is the stone structures there. No one would go near them; they're real *Blair Witch Project* kind of things. Furnaces of some kind. From the 1700s. Tim and I really thought these things were haunted, but we didn't care, because we wanted to get away."

"Well, damn. Good thing I have you with me."

He picks up his stylus and bites on it, looking at me. "You have no idea how good it is to know me."

∞

Before we leave, I check in with Veronica. The situation with the apartment looks dire; she and Geneva have decided to find a place in New York City together. Joel has suggested taking over his two-bedroom sublet, as he's planning to stay in his loft.

I haven't heard from Monroe about "Frank" coming back, but that isn't good enough. I want this bastard, and I want to make sure he doesn't kill anyone else. Since we want to check out Caraway immediately, I ask Veronica to scope out "Frank's" apartment. She sets out immediately, with Geneva as back-up. Geneva's military training makes her an effective helper, and we can use that right now.

That leaves me in a better mind to drive Joel and me to Caraway Road, north of Elizabeth.

At first the road doesn't look that bad. It's supposed to be desolate, but houses dot the area. Then we see a clearly abandoned, rotting, boarded house, which gives the first bad vibes. As the trees get thicker, the road seems to get narrower.

We pass a historical marker. I stop the car and Joel checks the sign. "Used to be a foundry a couple hundred years ago. That explains the furnaces."

The road descends into darkness as we go further. The trees seem to be trying to meet overhead in a skeletal canopy. "Stephen King territory."

Joel has already taken out my cigarettes from where I thought I had them hidden under the driver's seat. "Don't make this worse than it needs to be, sweetheart. You can pull over just past this bridge."

We are going over a very old stone bridge that crosses a small stream. After parking on the side of the road, we walk back to the bridge. About a hundred yards long. A forty-foot drop to the sludgy water.

The surrounding woods arc over the road, leaving little of the gray sky. The leaves are coming off and falling around us. I lock over the edge of the bridge to the water.

Joel is already climbing down the embankment. I follow him to a circular gap in the surrounding trees. An overgrown path leads a half mile into the stone furnaces. As we walk in, the trees seem to close above us, like closing off the rest of the world. Really in the middle of nowhere, so not a good hangout. The darkness of the woods does make it like a horror movie.

"And you went here willingly?"

"That tells you how bad my home life was, doesn't it?"

"I don't see how you even found it, or got a bike down here."

"I was quite resourceful. At the time it was a good place to go. It's so remote, no one wanted to make the trek."

The quiet of these woods seems unnatural; direction is hard to tell in the late afternoon light. No path is visible on the ground —we're going by Joel's memory.

We eventually see the furnaces ahead, looming like obelisks. They seem black, Medieval. I have the sense of approaching something supernatural, something out of a King Arthur story.

Snow has fallen recently, making the scene surreal in the white plainness contrasted with the furnaces.

We're almost at the structures. There's three at different spaces, are very large. They get larger as we approach. At least 20 feet high, 10 feet deep and 15 feet wide. Arched openings not big enough to walk through upright—about four feet high. At one time they all must have had iron doors, but all that's left now are hinges.

I'm thinking about what might be here; anything is possible. I just want to find something that will nail this fucker to the wall, evidence-wise. But I'm stopped by the undeniable scent of death, just like in Wildemore.

"Oh my God."

"What..." Joel stops next to me. A breeze is kicking up snow around our feet. I feel like I'm frozen here, and the snow will cover us.

I know he's staring at me; his hands are on my arms. Finally I drag my gaze to his eyes.

"It's another body dump. More women. More women here."

Joel shakes his head.

I take his hands, squeeze them, and move past him to the closest furnace. I get on my hands and knees and look in. It's so dark, but something's there. Nothing moving, just oblique shapes. I can almost hear a roar from the blackness. A roar from the other world.

You have to do this.

And we've been drawn here, because the full nightmare of Don's evil needs to be exposed. I could barely handle being down in the bowels of Wildemore. But all I've gone through has changed me. I don't want to run and hide. I want the world to know who he is. I want to drag him out screaming into the sunlight.

Although I know this smell, decomposing flesh, I need to confirm bodies are here before calling authorities. In case I'm hallucinating this horror.

The furnace we're in front of has an opening at the top with some sort of grate, but it's too clogged with debris to be helpful in illuminating the small area.

I put on rubber medical gloves I had with me in case we found anything. Doing this helps me remain calm. I feel the hard dirt and scattered leaves under my hands as I crawl in. Once inside, I stand up. I can feel more strongly the shapes in front of me.

Then light. Joel is kneeling in the arched entranceway, with the lantern.

The cramped interior is, if possible, a worse misery than Wildemore. Adrenaline pushes my heart to my throat —or so it seems.

In the enclosed space are seven containers. Two against the back wall, three on the right side, two on the left. Some are cheap trunks. A couple look like packing crates.

We're in a crypt. Another crypt, with dirt and leaves trickling down from the top grate because we've disturbed the forces. Wildemore was evil by its means of hiding women in depth. This is another hell. Exposure. Animals have been here and dug into the containers. Insects have followed. Even in the little drift of snow inside, I can see tiny footprints of some rodent that has investigated the furnace.

I can't even guess if this area is a more recent body dump than Wildemore; the exposure has rendered the victims equal in destruction.

"You should get out now," Joel says. He hasn't moved. The light from the lantern he holds is vibrating from the tremor in his hands.

"I have to check."

"Are you sure you need to see any more than this?"

"Yes. It could be animals. We need to know before we call anyone."

I look at the two trunks on the left. The top one is newer. Little dirt or rust. But it's stained on the bottom as if fluids have seeped through from the inside.

"These aren't animals." Joel points at the walls behind the trunks. Dark streaks of blood have run down the wall. "Animals are treated with more respect."

The blood is sign from Don/Frank. I've seen that blood in my dreams.

I reach out to flip up the catches on the trunk.

Now I understand what Bertrand Herrmann said about having seen the darkness.

The trunk is not big enough for her, and her body's been mutilated it to fit. For some time, she must have been covered in her own blood; it's pooled around her. A few dead beetles are mired in the congealed, nearly frozen fluid. As terrible as this is, I'm rooted here, staring.

"I'm sorry." I'm saying it to her.

The light is moving crazily. I take it from him.

The woman in the trunk is more intact than the others. With the lantern, I can see clearer the way the other containers have been burrowed or broken into. Parts missing. The same hatred and contempt, expressed differently. To be hidden food for scavengers.

"Gabriel, please get out of there."

I think of the other women who must be here. Maybe more in the other furnaces. They seem like my property, my responsibility.

"Come on, we've done what we need to do." His tone is pleading.

Almost. We have to start back to call anyone. On the way, I'm saying the prayers to myself.

Outside, on the road, the forest looks even more dismal, like it's in mourning for what was kept inside.

∞

Hours later. Joel is outside the Elizabeth police station, walking back to Gabriel's Camry. He calls Michaela. She's at her apartment in Newark.

"Something's wrong. They kicked me out of the police station but not Gabriel. They wouldn't let me see him, and they wouldn't tell me anything."

"Okay. Let me call around."

Michaela calls back an hour later. Joel hasn't moved from the car, just waiting. When he answers his phone, he hears her draw a deep breath.

"What is it?"

"I want you to stay calm, honey. The prosecutor in Sophie's case—Stan Cooper—Gabriel has probably told you about him, right?"

"Yeah, you and he had some kind of conflict."

"Conflict is one way to put it. I'm not saying he's acting out of personal spite, but..."

" *What?*"

"Joel—need you to keep it together. Cooper doesn't like that you and Gabriel found two sets of bodies. In addition to the men who tried to kill you. He says he's going to hold Gabriel as material witness."

Back in Newark, Michaela has to hold the phone away from her ear due to the explosion on the other end.

"*Are you fucking kidding me?* We need to do something right *now*—"

"Joel! Stop and listen! I'm going to—no, *stop*. Listen to me. I know you're upset. I should have had Veronica come over to tie you down before I told you. It's not going to hold, what Cooper's doing. You hear me? It's a bullshit tactic and it won't work. He should know better."

"Why? Why is he doing this? Why didn't they hold me as well?"

"See, that's what I mean. Cooper has a thing about Gabriel. He also has a legitimate concern about all these events. As do the police. It's a hell of a lot to happen to two people—Joel, stay cool, don't say it. I'm telling you what *they* are thinking, not me."

"Is Gabriel arrested? Is he a *suspect?*"

"He's in custody. In essence, he's arrested. For the police, remember, everyone's a suspect. They have to be that way. Stan Cooper is different. He's not listening to us, and he's letting petty feelings cloud his judgment. This will be over tomorrow. Gabriel has to be given a hearing right away to be held as a material witness. But court is closed, and the emergent judge, the one who takes over after court hours, isn't available for some reason, unfortunately. So, first thing tomorrow I'll be at the hearing to get him out."

"Have you talked to him? Is he okay?"

"Very briefly. I'm leaving to go to the station now. They won't let you talk to him, so you might as well go home. I know what you feel, and believe me, he knows. Right now, he's afraid you'll lose it. He won't want you to freak out—right?"

Joel doesn't answer. He's texting Veronica.

"Joel?"

"Yeah. Don't freak out, you said. Is he going to jail?"

"Cooper didn't insist on it, so I'm going to ask the officers to keep him in the station. They'll do it. Transferring a person in custody is a pain in the ass. He's not going to make trouble and the cops probably know this isn't a solid charge. He'll be okay."

"What'll help in this? More evidence about Don?"

"Don't need it for the hearing. Cooper has to prove Gabriel likely knows information he's not giving, and will disappear. We've been trying to *give* them the information. Now, to close the case, help Sophie out, and clear any suspicion, yes. The affidavit may or may not be used in court —it has issues. We need other evidence to tie Don to the bodies or to Leonard's murder or both."

"We were going to take Bob to ID Don. His voice and whatever else. And Veronica just told me now that she's seen Don—Frank—at his apartment. He's not out of town like he said he was. I'll get Bob to see him tomorrow at the nonprofit somehow."

"That will help," Michaela says carefully. "Eyewitnesses are good, but some question always exist—"

"DNA," Joel interrupts. "He smokes. We'll get a cigarette he throws out. Hey, can I see Sophie? I can show her the sketch of Don. Maybe Edward would have some more information."

"The DNA is best. The police won't use it on their own as evidence because we obtained it. But if the results go our way, they might use it as probable cause to get their own subpoena for a DNA sample. When I go to One Plaza, I'll get you set to see Sophie. You still there in Elizabeth? Good. Wait for me, I'll bring you a letter of authorization, since the corrections officers won't know you like they do Gabriel. Whatever happens, try to get that sample. Be sure it's his. Do not—Joel, do not—do anything to raise suspicion or call into question the legitimacy of that sample."

"Did you forget he trained me? How many lectures I heard? I know the drill." He sighs. "I'm glad I can do something. I feel so fucking frustrated right now. And him being in *jail*..."

"He isn't yet, don't panic. Right now, you're doing good, and he'll be comforted to know you're taking action rather than freaking. Keep that in mind."

∞

Thursday, January 6

Joel is at the Elizabeth jail as early as possible the next morning, 7am. He has the letter from Michaela and is escorted to a visiting room, the same Gabriel and Michaela had used with Sophie.

Joel introduces himself to Sophie, telling her he works closely with Gabriel and Michaela.

Sophie seems to find his visit encouraging. She reaches over the table to take his hand. "I saw on the news about the women you found. That was a monstrous thing."

"It was. I want you to know, I met Giselle. Gabriel really liked her. I did too. I'm so sorry about that."

"Thank you. I'm so helpless here. I can't do anything for Jacob..."

"Her attorney is taking care of the situation. We'll look in from time to time. Gabriel's like that, and I'm with him. But this morning, I'm here because I need to talk to you about the person who killed those women. Maybe Leonard too, we think."

"Ms. Connor said something about that. She was going to come back and explain."

"She said I could. Leonard's brother Don is the one we believe killed her. I'm not clear if you met him or not, but we think he faked his suicide, and he's here in Elizabeth again."

Sophie stares at Joel for a couple minutes. Then Joel sees the change in Sophie's eyes. Edward is here. Joel draws his hands back, watching Edward's body language come into play as he settles in. Then he introduces himself, as Gabriel had told Joel he had done when meeting Edward.

Edward gets right to the point. "Don. Don did this, you're sayin'. Gabriel asked about him, ya know."

"Right. Bob Jarvey has tentatively identified him. Don has a fake identity, we're pretty sure, but we're working on confirming this."

"Damn, that man was bad news. He and Leonard —it was like some kind of Shakespearean thing, ya know? They couldn't stand each other, but Don would try to control him, get him to do things. Leonard...he was pretty brave in standing up to him. We'd see th' anger...it would just burn off him, when Leonard talked back to him."

"I really feel for Leonard. He tried, we think, to save some women Don was abusing. And that he did. That made Don set things up to look like he committed suicide. But when he had a chance to come back, he probably wanted revenge."

"Yeah. What Leonard did—to fuck up Don's business —that would have gotten him killed. You couldn't question Don's authority. We always knew something was *way* off with Don. He's a nasty fucker."

Joel shows Edward his sketch and the photos Gabriel found of "Frank."

"The sketch is him, sure. The photo *could* be."

"Anything that you remember identifiable about him, outside of his face?"

"His hand." Edward taps the sketch. "I don't think he could hide that. He has a scar on his hand. He said it was an acid scar. Now I don't even want to think of what he could have been doin' with acid—although Bob and I used to make jokes about it. It goes all down the side past his wrist..." He points it out along his own. "What's the matter? Did you see the scar on this guy?"

"I think Gabriel said this man in the photo claims he has carpal tunnel and wears a glove."

"So what will you do now?"

"Try to see that scar."

∞

"Your honor, I think that any normal person would find what happened to Ross stretches the definition of coincidence. Since he's refused to explain how he continuously runs up against would-be killers and stacks of bodies, then he's clearly withholding evidence."

The judge regards Stan Cooper and Michaela both for a moment. "Ms. Connor, you seem highly agitated, not usual for you."

"Judge Wilkinson, Mr. Cooper is exaggerating beyond sensibility. My investigator has not held anything back from the prosecutor's office. In fact, we have gone out of our way to get him interested in the connections with Ms. Faulker's case. We *want* him to investigate."

The judge looks back at Cooper. "This has become a very high-profile matter in the media, due to the number of bodies found, and the manner of their death. To say someone is withholding information about a serial killer is a very harsh accusation. What makes you think Mr. Ross is doing so?"

"Judge, I've dealt with him before. I have good reason to believe he violates professional ethics and possibly state laws in his work for Ms. Connor."

"And what evidence do you have of *that?*"

Cooper turns to Michaela, bristling at her sharp tone. "A confidential informant."

"I doubt that, very much."

"Counsel, please hold on. Mr. Cooper, you're not being very professional yourself in suggesting Ms. Connor's work is unethical, via Mr. Ross. Where exactly is the connection between Mr. Ross's ethics or lack thereof, and the information you think he holds? What specifically do you think he hasn't told you?"

Cooper is caught short, slightly. "That's what I want to find out, your honor. He's liable to know all sorts of things. He found evidence when Dejan Garasanin and Sava Peric allegedly attacked him and McFadden, the man he claims was helping him. But he did not turn in that evidence."

"Your honor, he turned it in to *me*. And I promptly sent it to Mr. Cooper. My investigator was shaken up by having to deal with two people trying to assassinate him and Mr. McFadden, who is in fact helping on this case under my authority."

"Not so shaken up that he couldn't go trespassing again to find those bodies."

"He's a professional, Counsel. He was doing his job in investigating this case. Judge Wilkinson, Mr. Cooper has no evidence whatsoever to justify holding Mr. Ross on a material witness warrant. While Mr. Cooper is understandably disturbed by these women's deaths, the fact that Mr. Ross was able to discover the women in both places is due to his skill, not to anything illegal or unethical. Mr. Cooper is wasting the court's time with this motion."

The judge scans the motion papers in front of him. "As I understand, Mr. Ross is licensed in New Jersey as well as New York, and his license is in good standing."

"Technically, your honor, he's not even supposed to *be* in New Jersey."

"That's irrelevant."

"The judge in Buckston thought Ross was enough of a menace to say—"

"Your honor? Please? Can we stick to actual law here?"

"He lives in New York. Once he's out of state jurisdiction, there's no guarantee he will return for questioning..."

"He will return any time he's needed. And he's been questioned, for eight straight hours yesterday. He didn't even ask for me to be present, because he was cooperating. I had no idea that Mr. Cooper would somehow mistake cooperation for indicia of guilt."

"Ms. Connor's faith in Ross is touching, but I'm afraid I don't share her trust of a man known to be violent."

"Irrelevant! Your honor, I can bring in dozens of people who will attest to Mr. Ross's ethics and professionalism, not to mention demonstrate he is not going to skip town in either state to avoid assisting law enforcement in this case."

The judge sighs. "Mr. Ross, please come up here to the witness stand. I'd like to ask you a few questions."

∞

Fifteen minutes later the judge, with no small irritation, dismisses the motion. I'm free to go although I have to go next door to the police station and pick up my phones and wallet.

Mikki and I both relieved, and I desperately want to go shower and get coffee. She walks with me to the station to retrieve my things.

I'm just about to ask her if she's heard from Joel when her phone rings. Looking over her shoulder, I can see it's Joel calling.

Michaela listens for a moment, then hangs up.

"Oh, my God. We have to leave. Now."

∞

EIGHTEEN ♦ 39 BURDEN (JIĂN)

Water over Mountain: Hardship follows the difficult situation, the obstruction. Be conscious of danger, and act accordingly. Part of life is not avoiding hardship, but knowing how to handle hardship. The second line moves (yin/six). The person, knowing of the danger, must go ahead to help others.

∞

Thursday, January 6, Continued

JOEL SEES MICHAELA'S PRIUS pull up to the building where the Women's Freedom Network is located. Joel is relieved to see them, but turns his attention back to the cop standing by the squad car Joel is now in.

"Officer, I *guarantee you* he isn't going to call his wife and son. He doesn't have *either one*. It's a ruse."

The cop doesn't like what Joel tells her, and starts jogging toward the building, telling two other officers waiting there she needs to check it out.

Joel then watches Michaela walking up to the squad car with Gabriel following. Joel sees her taking in the cops near the entrance of the WFN's building, the squad car where Joel's in the backseat, and the second squad car where Bob's in the backseat.

Since the window of the car where Joel is happens to be cracked open, she stops to speak to him. "What happened?"

"Don's DNA is in the trunk. Bob ID'd him."

∞

Earlier

Joel and Bob are waiting for Frank to come out for his smoke break.

"When do people smoke," Bob asks.

"They start jonesing before lunch, after lunch, midmorning, midafternoon, right before leaving for the day."

Forty minutes go by, and then a figure approaches the side of the building they're watching, and takes out a pack. "It's him."

Joel gives the binoculars to Bob.

He focuses on Frank. "He's not looking up. The general size is right, he's a little thicker now...Hold on. He can't stare at the ground all day. God, it's hard to tell, Joel. Nothing about his height and general appearance says no, if we take into account cosmetic surgery."

"Do you remember the scar Edward told me about?"

"Yes, but I can't get a look at it without him seeing me."

"I'll get a picture, but we'll have to do the voice test too. I'll go talk to him and record him. You stand around the side of the building and listen."

They get out of the car. Bob takes a roundabout way to the other side of the building, as Joel approaches from the other side. Frank does not see him, but Joel observes Frank flick away a cigarette and start another one. Frank is not wearing the carpal tunnel glove. But then, he's alone and perhaps not expecting company.

Joel comes up quietly and stands next to the discarded butt.

Now Frank notices him. Joel is sure he sees recognition in Frank's eyes. Frank knows who Joel is. Maybe one of the helpers took pictures of him and Gabriel before.

But other than in his eyes, Frank doesn't change expression. Neither does Joel.

"Hello. Are you Frank Carlson?"

"Yes." Frank smiles as if perhaps hoping Joel will be a new friend. He keeps his right hand down, although Joel sees a reddish streak on the hand.

Joel extends his own hand. "I'm sorry to bother you. My name is Joel McFadden. I'm working Gabriel Ross on Sophie Faulkner's case. He's spoken to you about this."

"Yes, he has. How is Gabriel?" After a hesitation, Frank reluctantly lifts his right hand. Joel does not look directly at it, but the scar is obvious. A deep red indentation that's puckered at the edges, and runs from the base of his thumb halfway down his arm.

"Very good. He couldn't stop by to see you today, so I have to impose, if you have a moment."

Joel hands Frank—no, Don, that hand clinches it for Joel—some photos of women. Bertrand Herrmann had sent Gabriel dozens of photos of women in Central Europe who went missing after they said they were visiting the US, and Joel has those photos in a folder he's carrying. "We were wondering if these women looked familiar."

Don shuffles the photos. He tries to only look concerned, as one would expect from someone involved in anti-trafficking humanitarian work. But his other interest manifests itself—the serpent inside. He lights another cigarette while going through the photos again, staring at each one carefully. The photos were meant to get Don to display his hand if he had the glove off. He's already done this in shaking hands with Joel. But his distraction with the photos allows Joel get a better look at the scar. The thought of what he was doing with acid—as Edward said—is horrifying. Joel has his phone out. He's pretending to check messages, but he's taking a picture of Don.

"Do you remember maybe seeing any of these women in your files or anything?"

Don suddenly glances up at Joel. "I'm afraid I don't—I'm pretty sure I've never seen them."

"I appreciate you going to the trouble of looking at them, anyway."

"Well, certainly. I hate to think what may have happened to these women. You're really dedicated to keep coming out here from New York."

"Coming out?" Joel keep his tone flat. "I've never mentioned where I'm from."

"I read about you and Gabriel, now that I think of it." He finishes his second cigarette. "What's next?"

"We're trying to identify the women that were found in the old hospital."

"Yes, that's where I read about you. The women found up north too?"

"Yes." Joel smiles faintly. Don also smiles, politely. Rather than flicking away his cigarette, he pauses a moment, then grinds it against the wall and slips it in his pocket. He's cunning, Joel thinks, not stupid. Only his henchmen were stupid.

Joel sees a subtle change in his face, like a hint of rain clouds in the distance. Don's disturbed, as if trying to analyze exactly why Joel is here. Joel in turn starts to feel anxious, knowing what Don does when he's disturbed.

"Well, good luck with the identification. Please let me know what happens, and if there's anything, *anything*, that I can do to help please let me know." Don walks away, glancing once at the Camry.

∞

Currently

"Bob...lost his temper a little. I think Don's trying to get away right now —I told one of the cops. But something else happened."

Gabriel has come up to the police car now. He doesn't touch the police car, but he and Joel lock eyes for a moment. Gabriel looks exhausted and wired at the same time.

Bob yells out, "*Listen* to him, Michaela."

"Joel, what the hell went wrong with this?"

"It didn't go wrong. But Don threatened you."

Her eyes go wide. "What are you talking about?"

Joel tells her what Don said. "Bob went after him. That was unfortunate. But we need to take the threat seriously."

Gabriel, hearing this, immediately blocks Michaela from the building, scanning the area. "Mikki, you know what we're dealing with in Don. If he's gone, you need to right now start taking precautions."

"Where is he?"

Joel says, "He claimed he had to make a phone call. Dollars to donuts he's gone."

∞

Earlier

Joel waits until Don's out of sight, then takes out a plastic bag and picks up the cigarette Don had first thrown away.

Joel goes back to the car and opens the trunk. Bob comes back from wherever he was hiding. "Everything okay?"

"So far, yeah. What did you think?"

"It was him. Like hearing a motherfucking ghost, I couldn't believe it. Better that I wasn't looking at him as he is now. We used to be haunted by that voice."

Bob gets in the passenger side, and Joel puts the cigarette in an evidence collection container inside.

When Joel closes the trunk, he senses something behind him.

Don is there, watching him.

Don meets Joel's eyes without speaking. Then he walks around the car casually, looking in at Bob. His expression doesn't change seeing Bob, although Bob is wide-eyed.

Then he's on the sidewalk by the car, looking back at Joel, smiling. The coldest, most false smile Joel's ever seen.

"I just wanted to say, Mr. McFadden...you're working for this attorney, this *woman*, right? Michaela Connor. Like I said, I read about you. I'm very interested in her. *Very* interested. You tell Gabriel that."

How he says 'woman' and Michaela's name makes Joel cold with the implications.

Don starts walking away.

Bob gets out of the car. Don stops, and they stare at each other.

"What did you say?" Bob's voice has gotten low and raspier than usual.

Don considers him. "I don't know you." But while not scared, he shows some caution.

Bob has his own angry streak, which he mostly never shows now. But the same part of his personality that led to his addiction also unleashes his anger. Joel remembers Gabriel telling him about a couple of instances in years past that he had to back Bob up in sticky situations made stickier by Bob turning from amiable to stone cold dangerous. Joel sees that coldness coming now, and Don must have seen it some time when they knew each other.

"You fucking son of a bitch. We hoped you *were* dead." He steps toward Don, and Joel has to follow to stop something before it gets out of hand. Don starts backing in a circle, with Bob tracking his steps.

Don's watching him closely. "Get the fuck away from me."

"I'll take *you down*, motherfucker." And while Joel is following Bob, trying to grab him, Bob swings at Don, catching him at the edge of his jaw. Bob slams Joel in the chest by accident in his fury, knocking Joel over.

Bob and Don circle each other and grapple more, although neither gets a hold on the other. Then a voice comes out of the windows above them all.

"Leave him alone! We've called the police on you! Are you okay, Frank?"

Don looks up, and Joel sees he's not happy the police were called. But he has to pretend. He lifts his hands in a defensive posture, and makes his voice fearful. "They're trying to attack me...thanks for calling."

Joel's up again and has hold of Bob's arm. Don turns back to them. His face is not visible to the people in the building. Don smiles a furious smile, and his real self becomes apparent. The Devil shows. He speaks softly so only Joel and Bob can hear.

"I want you to know—I'll rip her up, I promise. Gabriel's seen what it looks like. You'll get to see it too. I'll make it worse than *anything* you've seen before."

Bob lunges for Don again. Joel has to drag him back to the Camry. He'd like to get them out of there, but in the distance are police cars coming up. Too damn fast for the city; they must have been patrolling the area.

"Let me do the talking." Joel is straining to hold Bob back. He's locked in on Don, and if Joel lets him go, something truly bad will happen.

"What the fuck, man?" Bob's trying to get out of his grasp. "You heard what he said he would do."

Joel digs his fingers in Bob's arm to get his attention. "We'll take care of it. Bob, listen to me. Don't do anything. We can't go to jail now. We'll take care of her."

Bob stares at Joel now, but nods once. Joel quickly calls Michaela, who is apparently just getting out of court. Joel doesn't have time to be happy about the material witness hearing as the police cars are pulling up now, two cars in tandem.

Joel hangs up and locks his phone, and the Camry. The cops can't get in either without a warrant.

Don proceeds to tell the four officers approaching them that Joel and Bob threatened him and assaulted him. Joel guesses Don doesn't want police involved, but since they're here, he's going to make the best of it to get rid of them.

This could go badly, as Bob has a record for assault. Not to mention how many times Joel has *already* spoken to the Elizabeth police, who must be sick of him by now. Bob is doing a slow burn listening to Don, but containing himself the best he can. "You going to tell them about him?"

"No, they won't listen right now. They just want to control the situation. Ride it out and stay calm. That's the primary directive."

∞

Currently

Two cops come out of the building alone, the female officer Joel spoke to and one who had already been inside. They're both agitated. When these cops meet the two officers who had remained outside, Gabriel and Michaela can hear them say Carlson went into the WFN offices and then disappeared, apparently from a side door. Seth Monroe saw Carlson sneak out.

∞

Earlier

Two officers come to question Joel and Bob, and another goes up to speak to the WFN staff, one returning to a squad car. Joel and Bob decline to answer questions. When the other officer finishes running the Camry's plate in his squad car computer, he comes back to demand their ID. That leads to more computer checking, and Joel's not surprised when the officer and his partner escort them to sit in the back of the patrol cars. They're not in custody, but due to "Frank" being a fine upstanding citizen and director of an organization helping exploited women, and Joel and Bob not on record as being fine upstanding citizens, the cops want to sort everything out.

Joel is put in one police car, Bob in the second. Joel hears Don saying he'll be willing to go to the precinct and swear a complaint against them.

Fucker. He's trying to use this to keep us out of action so he can leave. He knows now the game is up.

And Michaela...

"He'll try for her," Joel says to himself. "He's angry now."

And then Joel hears Bob's voice from the other car, yelling. "Joel has nothing to with it. He tried to stop me. Let him go."

Joel turns around to look at Bob.

The two cops and Don are also staring at Bob, who's still yelling. "I wanted it out with Don. His name isn't Frank Carlson, it's Don Mathers. I *knew* him from years ago. He's a killer. He killed his brother! He's killed all those women in Wildemore and upstate!"

"Oh, Jesus, Bob..." Joel mutters. But he knows Bob is trying to help.

The officers try to process this information, as Don says he has *no* idea what Bob's talking about.

At the same time, Bob keeps up a counter-litany regarding Don's past. The officers look thoroughly confused for a few minutes, but then look like they're wondering. The dead women are all over the news, and the police have to consider the possibility. Everyone's a suspect, like Michaela said.

Don knows the situation is suddenly not going so well. He glares up at the windows then at Joel, losing control momentarily.

Then he politely asks the cops if he can go inside and call his wife and son to tell them he's okay. Since he's still nominally a victim, he's allowed to go into the building, with one of the police as escort.

It's such a blatant lie, Joel knows what he's doing. *Goddamn it, once he's out of that cop's sight, he'll disappear.*

Joel knocks on the window and another officer comes up. "Carlson's going to run away. You have to stop him."

She shakes her head. "No, he's going inside. You don't have to worry about that, sir."

"He's going to leave. Your colleague might even be in danger."

"Why is that?"

∞

Currently

Now three of the cops start to walk the perimeter of the building, while one stays near the cars. Michaela goes to talk to him. Gabriel follows, scanning the area.

Then Michaela turns from the officer and walks over to Bob. Gabriel now comes over to Joel.

"Are you okay?"

"Are you?"

Gabriel crouches next to the car. "I've been better. You did good here."

"I couldn't stop Bob freaking out."

"Nobody can. You got Don's DNA, though, baby. You did it right."

"So do I get a raise?"

Gabriel smiles. "I'll look into it. You'll at least get a check-plus on your performance review. How did it go with Sophie?"

"She's okay. Edward gave me some more info. A scar on Don's hand. I saw it. I got a picture of it. That should also be an identifying factor."

"Fuck me." Gabriel keeps smiling. "I'm proud of you."

Joel looks down for a moment. Hearing that, above all, makes him proud of himself. "What are we going to do now, about that threat?"

"We'll protect her. Let's see how this turns out."

Eventually, the cops find out that Don is nowhere in the building and doesn't answer his phone, and he's not home.

They have nothing to hold Joel and Bob on, not without Frank-slash-Don to file a complaint. What they're going to do with the information about Don's true identity is uncertain, but apparently the information will be turned over to the task force.

After police drive away, Joel embraces Gabriel. "Are you okay from whatever they did?"

"Nothing bad. I slept on a bench. Not the first time. It's okay. I had my Super-Lawyer get me out, and my boyfriend watching my back."

They hold each other while Bob is apologizing to Michaela.

She waves it away. "Just a typical day with this case. I'm only glad I don't have to bail out any more of my investigators or witnesses today."

But Gabriel is also watching her. "I'm staying with Michaela," he says now, including the rest of them in this statement. "She's going home. Not back to court. Cancel it. I'm checking out her building. Joel, I need you to take Bob home."

"I'm not going home, not while she's in danger."

"Guess you have company then tonight, Mikki."

"Oh, my God. No good deed goes unpunished."

∞

Saturday, January 8
Newark, NJ, 8:27 pm

I leave Mikki in her apartment in Newark after examining it thoroughly, extra thoroughly. I had been tired from practically being up all night, but no longer. While I'm outside in the building's parking lot, checking that out too, my phone rings.

"Gabriel..."

"Don." No sense bothering with his cover. He seems to hiss on the other end of the line. Separated from his pleasantly banal face, the evil is cogent. I turn on the recording app in my phone. I want to crawl through the phone and choke him.

"You understand why you're so repellent to me? You're a do-gooder. Like that means anything to the world. Like anyone cares."

"Is that why you called, Don? To tell me I'm not like you? Thank God. You're not even human."

"But we're the ones in the news, right? You're fascinated by me because you can't be me. That terrifies you—what I can do, and the power in what I can do—you can't because of your 'conscience.'"

With his facade stripped, it's talking to pure evil. I'd say like an animal, but that's insulting animals.

"You don't scare me."

The hiss again—if it's there and not in my imagination. "You have fear. I believe you, that you personally don't fear me. But you fear on behalf of others—that fucking conscience again. The man you work with. You *love* him, don't you? You'd be afraid of what I'd do to *him*. But he doesn't interest me. Now your lawyer friend Connor— *she's* the one. Another do-gooder. Tries to be tough, but a woman can never be that tough. That would scare you even more, since you seem to care about women. Like that other bitch I took care of. She *liked* you. Kept talking about how you were going to be a good friend. But you couldn't save her, could you. Feel bad about that?"

I have to stop and back up against the building. For a moment, the anger overcomes me and I can't see again. Just gray in front of me. *But it's what he wants. You to be out of control, so he can get to her.*

"I told her that, too. Sorry your queer boyfriend couldn't save you. I told her I'd kill you next, and it was her fault. She begged me not to, and I punched her in the mouth until she puked blood. That's what your do-gooding gets, Gabriel."

I feel the shaking coming on. I have to remember that I'm recording this.

"You're over, Don." I can barely speak, but try to put force in my voice. "You've been found out. You're on the run again. They'll find you, and you'll just be another pathetic loser in the system."

"Nice try to be brave. You know what I can do. I haven't finished. You've seen what I've done to women, Gabriel. Now you know that's what's going to happen to her. And I'll tell her the entire time it's because of you. I'll make sure it takes long for her to die. You'll know, because you'll see the results. I'll make sure of that too. You know what I made these women say before they died? They say anything they think will save them. They'll tell me they love me. They'll say they're worthless cunts. She'll say it too. She'll die hating you. And since you like to find bodies, you'll be the one who finds the body. I'll leave it outside your door."

I can't talk anymore. I'm afraid of what I'll say. He just laughs again and hangs up.

∞

Michaela opens the door to her apartment. "Come on in. Joel just got here. Bob is somewhere outside."

I've managed, after three cigarettes, to calm down enough not to alarm her. "I saw Bob. He's watching the lobby checking things out. Your doorman isn't the most attentive in the world."

She stands beside me. "He's mostly on the case."

"Not really. Joel got past him while I was talking to him a few minutes ago. Listen, Don called me. I have the recording. It's going to be very ugly."

"I've been threatened before."

We all sit in her kitchen and I start the recording. I have to get up and walk out when he talks about Giselle.

Afterwards, Michaela comes over to take my hand. "I know you're worried, but he could just be posturing."

"He'll try to do it, Michaela. You didn't see it all, but I know. I'm not going to let him. But the cops could help in this case by watching you."

"I doubt that will happen."

"I have the recording for you. It has a time and a date stamp. It's a viable threat; they have to do something."

"What exactly?"

"Look for him harder than they are now. And protect you."

I can tell she doesn't relish the prospect of approaching the police or prosecutor. But she turns it away from herself. "Maybe this is more leverage for Sophie."

"Of course. It's a matter of time now. But let's make sure you're taken care of."

"Are you seriously going to stay here?"

I meet her eyes. "You can kick me out. We'll stay outside your door. If you get Rumplestiltskin downstairs to escort us from the building, we'll watch it from the outside."

"You would."

We stare at each other. I didn't have an instant friendship with Michaela as I did with Jim. She hired me on his recommendation some years ago and we developed a professional respect that became a friendship, as she is careful who she lets into her life. She is often my conscience, which is yet another reason Don strikes home in trying to hurt her and me. I hold her hand. Joel takes her other hand.

"I'm not going to let it happen," I tell her.

"And what are you two planning, exactly?"

"I don't know past tonight. My thought is just to stay here, sleep in your living room, and make sure no one breaks in."

She goes over to the couch. "It folds out, but it's terrible to sleep on. Cuts down on houseguests. You really think he'll try something tonight?"

"I don't know, but we're not taking chances."

∞

In the middle of the night, my phone rings. "I know you're there, Gabriel. I know the police aren't. I keep her place under watch. You think you can protect her?"

It's the witching hour again. "Come over and find out."

"You'll just have to wonder when."

"No, I don't. You can't stay long. Devanović's turned on you. You can't stay here. If you're going to do anything you have to do it now."

"You think you can control when I will act?"

"I'm inviting you. You want to torture me, I'm here. If you kill her, how much worse is it that I invited you? If you think you can beat me."

I hear him snorting in derision. "I'm not stupid enough to be where you'll kill me."

"I'm not you. I don't kill people. This is just you and me. I'm not Leonard. I'm not someone you can easily beat to death."

A hiss. "I'll do worse than that. I'll break you so you have to watch what I do to her."

I stay up the rest of the night, periodically checking the door, and Michaela's bedroom, until Joel wakes up and tries to take over for me.

∞

NINETEEN ♦ 44 CONFRONTATION (GÒU)

Heaven over Wind: The time has come for necessary conflict. With the right reasons and mindset, the individual grows stronger in order to face that conflict —whether with action, preventative measures, or both. The fifth line moves here (nine/yang). One who lives by the rule of Heaven, of natural law, can stop evil with radiance.

∞

Monday, January 10
Elizabeth, NJ 1:27 pm

Michaela and I are meeting Stan Cooper in a mostly-deserted bar in Elizabeth. We all sit around a table. Better to meet here than in his office, where events can take on a bad tone if words get heated.

Cooper folds his arms and raises his eyebrows. "More on your conspiracy theory?"

"It's about the case, yes. We have good evidence Leonard Mathers' brother Donald faked his death shortly ten years ago. He's now directing the Women's Freedom Network."

Cooper turns his hand up. "What is your evidence?"

"IDs from witnesses who knew him. Confirmation of an immutable characteristic. An affidavit from an accomplice. We have a DNA test pending to compare to Leonard's DNA. And he's on the run now."

"And what does this have to do with the Faulker homicide case?"

"Don Mathers is a more viable suspect. He had motive for killing Leonard. Leonard knew that Don was involved with some kind of human trafficking operation. Nikola Devanović —you probably remember him —he's been working with Don, and he'll confirm this. Don has a history of brutality Sophie doesn't have."

Cooper looks away. "If that's your defense theory, fine, Michaela. But I don't know what you expect me to do."

"Look *into* it. Consider you were wrong about Sophie Faulkner and find the real perpetrator. Don is most likely behind the murders of the women."

At that, even though I haven't said anything yet, he glares at me again. "Find any more bodies today, Ross?"

I get more irritated than I should, because the deaths affected me so much. And I know he's angry over not keeping me in jail. "I realize solving the murders of sex workers and undocumented persons is low on your list of priorities, but what Michaela hasn't mentioned to you is that Don Mathers made a direct threat against her life. To me."

Cooper frowns. "When was this?"

"Yesterday."

"And you think this is Don Mathers."

"Yeah, who's been working as Frank Carlson in the Women's Freedom Network."

"Yeah, I heard about that incident, with your junkie friend. You think New Jersey is your personal playground to come in and act the hero. You go through a day without committing crimes somewhere, Ross?"

"Did what happened in court demonstrate anything to you? You want to back up what you say with proof, before getting a slander suit?"

"You'd have as much chance of winning as Oscar Wilde. I should have the judge down in Buckston revoke your ACD."

Michaela's hand touches my arm, but I'm already off. "*Do* something about it. I'd love the ACLU to take you down."

"I'm not going out of my way to make you more of a media darling. But if I *ever* get proof of what you do to break the law to help her cases, I'll go all the way with you."

"No thanks, you're not my type." When he starts to sputter, I talk over him. "When you're not busy worrying about me, consider your job. You are now aware of a direct threat against an attorney. Her life is in danger from a suspect in a series of murders."

He laughs now. "Please. I'm sure Michaela has been threatened before by the lowlifes she represents. How often has it panned out?"

He's taken Michaela by surprise. "Stan, I know you're not friendly to defense counsel, but this is unreasonable. Because you have a problem with my investigator, you're going to ignore evidence?"

"Anything based on *his* word..." He points at me, rudely. "I'm not buying it. He's a criminal, Michaela. You bail him out, but he hurts your credibility."

"Excuse me, counselor. We can discuss my 'criminality' any time. But if someone tries to hurt her because you refuse to take action, I will make sure your name is all over the news."

"We don't give a fuck what New York papers say. And be careful levying a threat against me."

"Criticizing public officials is protected by the Constitution. Miss that day in law school? In any case, *Stan,* I recorded this threat."

I put the digital recorder on the table and play it. We hear Don's voice hissing again, going through his litany of hate.

Michaela says, "This situation is different, Stan. I'm not concerned about the threat as much as Don Mathers is definitely a suspect you need to bring in."

Too much evidence is really there to ignore. But Cooper doesn't like admitting it. "I'm not surprised, considering how much trouble Ross gets you into. Give this to Zach Rossarian. He's the point person on the task force handling those murders."

"Are you going to do anything to protect her?"

"What, not enough of a superman to do it yourself? Have to actually let law enforcement do its work? Okay then, I'll ask Newark to have a patrol car come around her building periodically. What is it, downtown?"

"Yes." She gives him the address. He writes it down and walks out without a goodbye. But at least we got something out of him.

∞

Tuesday, January 11
Newark, NJ, 7:02 pm

Zach Rossarian is actually a decent guy, a former investigator from the Union County prosecutor's office in fact. He listens to us and takes the evidence. We find out they've searched Don's apartment, although he's mum about anything found. I ensure he will contact the Newark police as well.

But a patrol car circling her building every couple of hours or so doesn't make me feel that confident. I consider the worst-case scenario, and decide what should be done to end this. I recruit our friends to help.

If Don is going to really hit Michaela, he's got a limited time window. When the DNA comes back, he knows we're going to make it a shitstorm in the news. He's already on the run, this will make his face public. Any day could be the day it hits. And while he could be gone now, I doubt it. He'll want the revenge before he disappears. He thinks he can do it—again, always needing to up the risk, keep the control. Since his threat is specific, I'm not worrying over shooting her, at least from a distance. I'm worried over his breaking into her building. Michaela won't leave, but she's willing to have me protect her. I get the sense that she's not believing he'll really do it. Most criminals would just take off. But I know he's not leaving until he tries. I convince Michaela to cancel appointments for the next couple days.

While we don't know where he is, he must be watching her. Looking for the opportunity. Get in, kill her. He may not be able to take her body out, but he'd call me to tell me what happened. We can use that against him.

I have Danny, Jim, Bob and Veronica come in the building, on the edge of the downtown area, to meet up, with Bob in disguise so Don won't know about the reinforcements.

I explain my reasoning to them in the apartment. It's about 7 pm. "I can draw him out now, I think."

Jim frowns at me. Jim is a nice-looking dark haired, dark-eyed Jewish boy a couple of years older than me, with a perpetually stressed expression. "How do you know?"

"He's either watching the apartment, or watching me. He knows I'm here, I'm sure. Michaela's going to throw us out."

"You think he'll really be fooled by that?"

"He has to do this now. Doesn't matter if he believes it. He has no choice but to try. He thinks he can beat me. And he doesn't know who all you are, and that you're here."

Michaela raises her eyebrows. She still argued with me before everyone arrived, saying Don took his go-bag and left town for parts unknown and without extradition treaties. I'm not risking her life betting he's left.

"You all don't have to believe me, but it's not going to do any harm for you to be here a day to see. All of you. Okay, Mikki, you and I are going outside to pretend to have a fight."

Jim shrugs. "All right. What do we do here while you're doing that?'

"First line of defense if he gets up here. I'll be able to get anywhere in this building in a matter of seconds."

"And where will you be," Jim asks.

"Everywhere. Joel and I can get back in here without him seeing. We've already checked out the place and done a little work here. Keep your cell phones on."

"What are you trying to do?"

"We have the basement under watch; Joel's installed some cameras. These will alert us when the back door to the basement opens, the one leading to the parking lot. We'll start when area is closed off to residents, at 9. It's his best bet. When he breaks in, we'll see it on the monitor here, on my laptop, and lock him in then call the police. They're looking for him; they should hold him if he breaks in. I just want Michaela protected up here."

I walk towards the door and gesture to Joel. "Come on. Time for the show. After we leave, Bob's going to the lobby, Danny outside to watch the back door until it's locked. Jim, you and Veronica up here with Mikki. We'll just be around where necessary."

The three of us go downstairs, and pause for a moment to get in the mood. Michaela shakes her head at me. "All right."

Then she goes to the door of the building and holds it open. I'm right behind her. She shoves me out, speaking angrily. "I told you, I'm sick of this. I really mean it, Gabriel. If you come around here again, I'll call the cops on *you.*"

"You're out of your fucking mind," I respond viciously. "You can't talk to me like that when I'm trying to help you."

"You're ruining my practice, now you want to take over my life. Get out!" She throws my backpack on the ground in front of me. Now Joel follows and gets between us. "Stop it, just stop it. You're not right. Make some sense here..."

Michaela gives him a cold look. "Mind your own damned business. The two of you have put me at the end of my rope. I can't deal with your craziness anymore."

She steps back.

I sound desperate. "Whatever happens to you is going to be your own fault, you want to be this stupid!"

"Fuck off, both of you." She slams the door shut.

"Crazy bitch," I mutter, and try not to smile when she looks back.

I snatch up my bag stalk back to the Camry in a huff, with Joel following.

We drive to another lot a mile away, and pick up Danny's Jetta to go back to Michaela's building and park in the back lot. From having patrolled the area before, I know the lot is open and exposed. Don can't be near here. He's most likely watching the front, until he has opportunity to get to the back door. We're in disguise nonetheless. I have a cap and maintenance-type clothes, Joel has a hooded sweatshirt.

The two of us get in the basement with Michaela's key. Then we head back up to her apartment. After talking to her and Veronica and Jim for a moment, hearing the requisite jokes regarding our performance, I strip to t-shirt, sneakers and jeans, and Joel checks the laptop.

The lights are off in the basement at night. The camera is set to detect when the door opens and send a signal up to the laptop. It's almost nine now, so I tell him to go ahead and activate it. Then Danny goes outside to watch the parking lot area.

But I'm restless. I need to ensure that everything is okay. I check Mikki's apartment. I call Danny to make sure he's outside and nothing has happened. I go down to see how Bob is. The night door person knows me and is mellow about us being there. He lets me check out his little area to see no one is there. By this time, Joel has come down to join me.

"Veronica's watching the camera. I wanted to see what you're doing."

"Making sure all is well. Let's go over the basement again. Tell Veronica so she knows we're there, in case we set anything off."

He calls her as we walk to a door to the right of the lobby. It leads to the service elevator and the laundry room. The door to the basement and storage lockers for residents is there.

Downstairs is an alcove. Ahead is a locked area with the building utilities. Across the hall from that is the locker room. Beyond that is the trash compactor room and the door leading outside. I call Danny again while I think of it. Nothing happening outside.

Then we pace the area. It's dark down here and dark outside now, and I don't want Don seeing any light coming through the shaded, barred basement windows, so I leave most of the lights off.

I go to the back door of the basement, with Joel following. This is the one that leads to the parking lot. I check that it's shut and locked.

Heading back down the corridor towards the basement door, I think to myself how much I want a cigarette, as I'm trying to quit. And I realize why I'm thinking this. Because I smell cigarettes. Or rather, the smell of cigarettes that sticks to a person like cologne. Not Joel's — he's not smoking around me —and this scent isn't cloves. I look into the locker room from the hall as we walk by. They're set in an island in the middle of the room, twenty back to back, and another forty against two walls.

The smell of cigarettes is in that room. As if someone who recently smoked had walked in. No one is visible, but I don't like it.

"I want to double-check these windows while we have time," I tell Joel casually. "Can you go up and get my locksmith box? I'll wait here."

"You'll call me if something happens?"

"Of course." I watch him leave, going up the stairs. Once he's out I go up and lock the door behind him. I don't know that Don is here, but *if* he is, I don't want him escaping. I also do not want Joel down here in danger. If I told him I was going to check this out, he wouldn't leave. Back on the basement floor, I feel for my Sig Sauer in my back holster. Bob has my Glock.

I take the Sig Sauer out. By the time Joel comes back I'll have reassured myself what's going on.

I walk quietly towards the locker room. I have to use my kinesthetic sense. I move along the inside near wall of the locker room to the right. Turn the corner and move along the island of lockers. Looking over the locker doors for something open, something not right.

The space cushion around me expands, as Master Chiang had told me. My own aura extending from my body to sense others, to sense where they are and what they'll do.

I feel the change as I come up to the end of the island. I turn around quick. The metal bar, a barbell without weights, is aimed at my head but catches me on the right shoulder. The gun falls out of my hand.

∞

Joel has passed by Bob in the lobby, spoken to him briefly, and is now on the elevator going back up to the tenth floor. He checks his phone that no one has called or texted. Being in the elevator makes him nervous, he wants to get back to Gabriel. When the doors open, he jogs to Michaela's door, and Jim lets him in.

"What's going on?"

"He's checking windows in the basement, needs something." Joel finds the bag Gabriel brought with him yesterday. Finds the toolkit. He asks Veronica, "Do you see anything?"

She turns to look at him where she's sitting on Michaela's sofa, watching the laptop. "No. But I don't like him sending you up here. Is Bob in the basement too?"

"No, in the lobby. What do you think..."

"I don't, just being cautious. He's not himself entirely. Jim, take over watching this thing, and just don't answer the door. I'll be back in a minute."

Jim trades places with Veronica, and Michaela locks the door behind them as they leave, Joel moving even faster now.

"Don't panic," Veronica says, taking Joel's hand in the elevator. "We're just being sure."

∞

Don swings again, making a dent in the metal lockers. Objects fall off around us. When he tries to swing a third time, I grab his right wrist before he can draw the bar back. Using leverage, I twist his arm to make him drop the bar. He shoves against me from his right side. We lean into each other, struggling.

My gun is somewhere off to the side. I can't let him get it. Or to anything else he might have on him.

We can see each other close up. I see his raw face and eyes with no pretense. I know his only intent is to kill me, painfully if possible. He grabs at me with his left hand, and digs into my arm to gouge out flesh. Our strength is evenly matched—barely. He's strong, terribly strong. Everything I have keeps him just enough away from me. As I push against him, he spits in my face. To make me jump back. I don't react. He tries to bite at me, gets his teeth in my shoulder. I use my knee to slam into his left leg. He lets go of my shoulder and grabs for my eyes.

Although I block his hands, the action separates us. I come back at him right away. I feel his left then right fist throwing at my face. I duck that and come up smashing my right below the belt.

We're too close for punches to be effective, but he's trying for a blitz attack. His fists swing at me continuously. I have nanoseconds to decide to block or punch, using my hands as Chiang taught me to, aiming for the more vulnerable areas. His throat.

I catch him on the side of his neck with my hand, slowing him for a second. He coughs. I follow up with my foot to his leg; he jerks back.

Don's anger increases. He throws himself at me. His hands go for my throat. His fingers cut into me. I try to pull at his fingers but the grip is too strong. I stumble backwards feeling my breathing cut off. *Don't fall down. You cannot fall down.* He tries to drive me off balance. If I'm down, I'm dead.

I shove forward and ram the heel of my hand into his nose, breaking it. Blood sprays on both of us. He lets go of my throat, and his right comes up and hits the left side of my jaw. I feel my teeth crack, drive into my tongue. More blood comes out of my mouth.

Don tries to catch my other side, and I block it with my arm. He's still able to hit my jaw again. He tries to batter his head into my face and I grab his hair, using that to force him away. He tears away from me, leaving bits of hair.

For a second time freezes as we both back away, locked in a gaze.

And we come at each other again. My fury streams out now. We're ripping at each other like fighting dogs. This isn't a fistfight, this is a mutual attack, an annihilation. Blood and sweat flies through the air, splattering the lockers and floor.

∞

Joel and Veronica arrive at the basement door. It's locked. "What the fuck," Joel says, his voice rising. Veronica is already calling Danny.

"No one went in," He says.

"Gabriel locked the inside door."

Joel is pounding on the door. "Gabriel! Open up."

"Let me check this door," Danny tells Veronica. From outside, he pulls on the back door. "It's still locked."

Joel is pulling at the doorknob. "Something's going on..."

His phone goes off. It's Jim. "Nothing from the back door, but the camera set to the locker room has some movement. I can't see what it is."

"Fuck it. Call the police. He's here," Joel tells him.

He looks at Veronica.

"Back door," She says.

On the way out, she tells Bob, who follows them rushing to the parking lot.

They see Danny waiting against the outside basement door.

Veronica says, "He has the key and we don't. Do you have a crowbar?"

Danny runs over to his Jetta, pops the trunk and takes out a wrecking bar.

Then they hear a scream from inside.

"No." Joel slams his fists on the door. "No. No. No. No!"

∞

I make Don circle with me to carry him forward by momentum, and in a split second while he's off balance, I strike him in the chest with a roundhouse kick.

It connects with his ribs. I hear his gasp. Something broke.

But he's not stopping. We shove against each other. Our blood is mingling, running off our bodies. He backs off to try to grab my gun and I kick it away. He picks up the barbell and swings at me again. I grab it, my hands sliding in my own blood.

The bar shakes between us. I push as hard as I can against the bar, then suddenly let go, jump back. Don stumbles forward. In that second, I snap my foot at his right knee and hear it crack.

It makes him cry out briefly. The pain should be intense. He tries to remain standing but can't, and goes down to the other knee.

Don isn't going to walk right for a while, but he's still dangerous. He snatches the barbell and swings at me savagely. The bolt on the edge of the bar catches me on the arm going over, and the leg coming swinging back. More blood flows. I'm able to kick the bar out of his hand.

He lunges for me, to pull me down with him. I grab his arm and twist it, letting my weight slam his arm down on the floor. Another crack inside his left arm. He tries to get his up injured leg around me. I lift my body up and slam down on him again, cracking his pelvis. I lean on his injured leg and hold him down by his shoulders. He's breathing hard.

"You can't do anywhere *near* what I did," he hisses. "They screamed. They begged. They suffered, pissed themselves."

"Not anymore."

"You going to kill me? You people who "do good" are pathetic. I liked *beating Leonard to death.* Fucking coward that he was. And Charlotte. She couldn't believe I'd hurt her; she thought she could talk her way out of it. Like I'd listen to what some bitch says."

Don's fighting to stay conscious from the pain of the broken bones under my pressure. He's still trying to get to me.

"I don't care what you are. You're nothing."

He spits at me, more blood flying over both of us. "Because you're better than me? You're a fucked-up excuse for a man. These women, your *friend* included, they all should be dead. They can't even take care of themselves. You have to do it for them."

I can see in his eyes every woman he's ever brutalized. Giselle. Charlotte. The women in Devanović's scheme. Sara. The women in Wildemore, on Caraway Road. Ones we may not know about. Never know about. He would do the same to Michaela.

He sees my feelings and digs in. "Fucking *cunts*. I killed the last couple *because of you*...You like knowing that? As smart as you think you are, you couldn't stop that. You have a trail of bodies.' He tries to smile. "And I especially got off killing Giselle —because *she liked you*."

I should be done here. Getting up, retrieving my gun, calling someone. I hear pounding on the outside door. It might be human; it might be demons.

My hands go around Don's throat.

∞

"Stand back."

Danny jams the bar in the door and leans on it. Bob hands the Glock to Joel, and helps to brace, until it pops open.

Joel starts to push past them, and Danny holds him back. "We need to see where he is."

He and Bob and Veronica group around Joel to go inside.

Inside, they can hear sounds to left, down a hall.

"The lockers," Joel says.

Joel holds the Glock out and moves quickly down the dark hallway. The others are with him up to the door of the storage room, where they stop. The scene is like a nightmare of the id.

Two men on the ground, covered with blood, one choking the other. They almost can't tell who's who.

Veronica turns on the light. "Stop him!"

Danny's already moving, seeing what's going on. He wraps his arms around Gabriel, dragging him back. Don stares at them, sputtering through blood, unintelligible words.

Danny has to hold Gabriel with all his strength, backing up towards the far side of the room.

Joel still holds the gun, wide-eyed, shaking. Bob gently takes it from him. He starts to walk around Don. Don glares at him.

Gabriel struggles to break out of Danny's arms.

"Get him out of here," Veronica tells Danny. She picks up Gabriel's Sig Sauer off the floor.

Danny hauls Gabriel out the room. Joel finally sees Gabriel clearly, and almost drops from shock.

"Can you watch him for a moment," Veronica asks Bob.

"Yeah. He isn't going anywhere. Right, asshole?"

Don is racked with coughing, but manages to mutter, "Fucking cocksucker junkie," He tries to spit at Bob.

"The only reason I don't finish you off like he tried to, is that I care about him more." Bob smiles then, enjoying the broken body in front of him.

∞

Twenty ♦ 40 Deliverance (Xiè)

Water over Mountain: The storm is gone, the sky becomes clear. Working together still remains important. The sixth line is moving (six/yin). The person in his wisdom has tamed some predatory evil.

∞

Tuesday, January 11, Continued
Newark, NJ, 10:30 pm

THE POLICE NOW HAVE a guard over Don, who's in intensive care. Zack Rossarian, the investigator with the state police task force, stopped in the emergency room to tell me that much while I was being worked over by the doctors and nurses et al.

I'm on a gurney in an ER exam room, waiting to see what they want to do with me. The third ER visit in seven months. I'm thinking I should write a Michelin Guide to ERs and police interview rooms.

Joel has managed to argue his way back here. Now, he's looking at the bruises and cut areas on my face. I'm feeling the places where my teeth are broken in spite of the morphine that's kicking in. And feeling like an animal that survived a fight with another predator.

Joel takes my hand gently, but he can't keep his eyes off my face. I'm trying to hold an icepack against my jaw. I haven't looked in a mirror, but I catch enough reflections in shiny surfaces to get the idea I look like shit.

Joel holds the ice pack for me. "Why did you lock that door?"

I see he's serious, and getting angry as he looks me over. It burns off him, and it shakes me to see that. And makes me subdued, defensive. "I did it to protect you. No one else—"

"Don't give me that bullshit, "no one else." You've lost perspective. Jesus, Gabriel, you were willing to be killed for this. You were willing to kill *him*. And would that have helped anyone? Would that have gotten Sophie out of jail, or brought Giselle back to life?"

That hurts, but he wants it to. He's the only person I'm really afraid of, and that's a fear he'll leave me. I stare down at my other hand, lying bandaged and useless on my legs. My protector mode has gone back in hiding, and I'm exhausted.

Joel puts a hand on the side of my head. "I can't even find a place to touch you where you're not hurt...I understand for the most part, because you're suffering, and you're not healed, not really. But your fucking stubbornness makes you take it on alone."

The door opens. It's not a doctor to save me, just Bob and Danny.

"Hey," Bob says. "You don't know what I had to promise a nurse to get back here. And he is *not* good-looking."

His terrible joke almost eases the tension. Until Danny stops to look at my face. "Holy fucking shit."

He's never seen me this bad, and we've been in dozens of fights. Even in July, when three men beat me on the street, I didn't look so bad.

"Are those finger marks?"

Joel turns away from me. "Don tried to claw his face off. But he didn't need us there."

"Joel, you giving him a hard time?" Bob tries to make it sound light.

"Yes. He fucking deserves it."

I see Danny agrees with Joel, maybe not as vehemently.

"Give him a break," Bob says. "This isn't the time. I know Don and what he's capable of. Gabriel was doing what he thought best."

Joel explodes, startling us all. "I don't care how much skill he thinks he has! It was just luck Don didn't kill him and escape, or come back and kill Michaela. Or if he killed Don, he'd be in jail now. What the fuck good would it do? What would that do to us?"

His fury leaves the room silent in its wake.

I put the icepack down. "Joel, I didn't know he was there. I *didn't.* I'm not lying to you. I just wanted to be sure, but I wasn't going to have him use you against me. And when he jumped me, I didn't have a chance to let you know."

Veronica has found the exam room. She comes in and gives them a dirty look. "I could hear you from outside. Michaela wanted me to make sure Gabriel's okay."

"I'll go talk to her." I get up. I hadn't seen Mikki since I was taken out of the basement, put in an ambulance, and interviewed by police. I know she's safe but I want to see.

I lean on Veronica, trying to walk out.

She holds me back. "I don't think you should do this. She's all right. Jim is here with her; they're in the waiting room. You need to rest—you're about to pass out...if you all say *one* more word to him, you'll have to deal with me. You don't want to do that."

Even Joel gets quiet at her command. I still want to leave, but my legs are not working well. I feel gray. I don't want to fall on her. But I'm losing it. She tries to hold me up. Other arms catch me. At least, I don't remember hitting the floor.

∞

Wednesday, January 12
Newark, NJ 12:43 pm

I wake up in a hospital bed. Bandaged and in pain. I had a dream about Chiang trying to treat my wounds, saying, "*You follow Avolokiteśvara. This bodhisattva embodies compassion. But just as that bodhisattva has moves from male to female it also has another form, a duality. A wrathful form —Mahakala. Four-armed or six-armed, this is the persona that protects followers. Avolokiteśvara engaged in this persona because such thing is necessary. If you're going to have anger, this is how it's directed.*"

I try to sit up and get a sense of what time it is. Midday, by the light.

My hand touches something by me. I look down to see Joel curled in a chair by the bed, his head on the mattress beside me. He's frowning in his sleep, which I don't like. But he's here. I can see as well I have clean clothes on, my own. He's gone to the apartment, come back here and dressed me. Regardless of his anger, he's here.

My hands are still wrapped in bandages. My fingers are free, and I can touch the tips to his head. Feeling his hair. The warmth of his scalp. And I know when he wakes under my hand, although he doesn't move or open his eyes.

But his hand, next to his head on the mattress, digs into the sheets.

I try to formulate what to say. What will comfort him, what will give him confidence in me.

"Baby, I love you. No matter what."

He pushes himself up, then slowly gets on the bed with me. He combs my hair with his fingers. I see how tired he is.

He talks while he touches me. "When I was 16, and first hustling on the street, I got beat up in a hotel in the Bowery. Punched in the face and whipped with a belt. This guy would have kept on doing it, but Jennah knew something was wrong, and tracked me to the room. She scared the trick away. I was on the bed; I could barely move. I looked like you do now. But she didn't leave me. She cleaned me up and took care of me. I should have died in that room. It would have been clearly the most logical end for me, to be killed by some anonymous sadist. But I wasn't. When I look at you, I see me."

"Don't. This is different. I told you why."

"Okay. I don't want you upset. I want you to leave today. The doctor was worried about your head. You had a concussion. They won't let you out if you're upset... I'm not angry. Bob was going to tell me all kinds of horror stories about what you and him used to get into, but I decided I didn't need to hear it."

"Is Don under arrest? Do you know?"

"Yeah. Rossarian helped with the whole thing. I think he's happy he can prove your prosecutor buddy is an incompetent fuckhead—apparently they used to work together, but not pleasantly. I don't think Don is talking."

His expression is troubled.

"Joel...I know you don't like what you saw down there. I know I lost control."

"You did. And it scared me. Your anger always bothers me. Because it's you and not you. Wherever it comes from, it's not the you I'm in love with."

"I'm lucky, as you said. I'm not apologizing for what I did to him. It keeps him down while we prove his guilt. But this did not go the way I intended. He was hiding down there, maybe all day or maybe just before we turned the cameras on. I reacted to the situation as it was."

"Yeah. It's something to deal with. Either you let me help you more, or you find a way to back off from the anger."

"We'll talk about that. Is anything else going on with the investigation?"

"They've gone to his apartment. Must be something there, because it's in the news. You're in the stories."

"Wonderful."

"Clark called. He wants to talk to you. He's not the only one." Joel takes my personal phone out his pocket and puts it on my lap. Scrolls through it. "Three texts and two calls from Alex."

"Delete them."

"You do it. Or you can answer, I don't care. I have you, that's what's important."

I go through my phone. Alex isn't the only one. I'm surprised by how many people have heard of this, including Raymond's nephew Adam, who I text back right away, and a couple of old boyfriends.

"You haven't given up on me," I say while I write.

"I'll never give up on you, but I will not let you do this again. I went to your place and told Archie what happened. I told him he could piss on your shoes if he wanted."

I almost laugh at that. "Speaking of which..."

He moves to let me up out of bed. I realize I'm going to have trouble with my hands.

"I'm not going so far as to hold your dick. You're on your own."

"I'll manage, Florence Nightingale."

When I come back from the bathroom, he's still on the bed. "The doctor will be by soon. I'll get you something to eat, and we need to go back and talk about work. At the apartment; you're not going out like this."

"I don't care."

"*I* do. People will think I did it. You will go to one place, Chiang's. He wants to talk to you too. I called him."

∞

Saturday, January 22
Alphabet City, Avenue A, 5:33 pm

"Gabriel, I'm glad to see you look pretty much as beautiful as you did before all that happened."

I have to smile at her. Geneva is trying out our new chair. Frustrated from staying in most of the week, I ordered two new side chairs for the living room, with Joel and Veronica's help. Geneva has come over tonight to talk a little about her case, and also to just hang out. She and Veronica are preparing to take over Joel's Chelsea apartment. Geneva has a couple months left in her lease but is moving her stuff over gradually.

"I bought them the same chairs," Joel says. "They'll be delivered Monday."

"Mr. Generous," I tell him. "That was very nice, even if you didn't check with their personal taste."

He doesn't bother to answer. I'm on the couch, and he's curled against me. His arms around me and his head on my chest. This, this...is how it's supposed to be.

"Do you feel okay," Geneva asks me.

"Yeah, much better." Wednesday, I went in to start crowns to my teeth. I've also been on meds to fight infection in the wound in my back, which isn't that serious, and also to reduce swelling. And Chiang found me some helpful herbs, after he lectured me for two hours. He was not as upset as Joel thought he would be. Chiang is not like that. I'm pretty sure he's had similar experiences in the part of his past he doesn't speak about. But we did discuss ways to improve how I handle things.

Meanwhile, over the last couple days, Joel's told Geneva about Senator Derek Baker and his daughter.

"So what do you think is the next step with this?"

"You need the original birth certificate. We need to know more about the circumstances. I would suggest a lawyer to get this straightened out in court—get the papers right. Jim can help find one. I'm already sorry for you about that."

"I just don't know if I can go there to Rochester...to talk to him..."

"Geneva, we've come this far. I could go there on your behalf. Feel them out."

"That seems like too much to ask."

"It's not. We want to get some resolution for you. Confronting them is the only way. If you are reluctant to do it, that's perfectly understandable—I don't see the point in giving yourself unnecessary pain in a difficult situation. Joel and I can handle the initial part. Also, it's our responsibility to finish the case by seeing him."

∞

Monday, January 24
Pittsfield, NY, 1:30 pm

Joel and I have gone to Rochester, flying this time, and arriving in the early afternoon. In the morning I had called the Union County medical examiner to give her some contacts Herrmann had found for me, people who could help identify the women if they were from the Balkans. Then we took a flight out of JFK for the forty-minute trip to Rochester.

The former honorable Senator Baker doesn't have an office. I had called his residence Saturday, and arranged an appointment to see him at his house in the more expensive part of Rochester, Pittsford.

All he knows is we need his help on an important matter regarding an old crime in the city. Hopefully he doesn't have bodyguards or Dobermans to chase us out Mr. Burns-style.

A middle-aged woman, not his daughter, greets us as the door. She's in plain white clothes; not exactly a uniform, not exactly not. "I'm Maria; I'm the Senator's assistant. I'll take you to his office."

She leads us to a large old-fashioned library-style office with shelves of books going up ten feet.

The former Senator himself is settled in a red leather chair behind a massive oak desk. He's a generic old man; mostly bald and somewhat puffy, in a good suit that's meticulous. I have the impression he's dressed up for us. His eyes are what's important. And his are sharp. Tired, cynical, carrying fifty years of political bullshit, but sharp.

I watch him evaluating us as we shake his hand.

"What is this about?" His voice is sharp as well. No shakiness or hesitation. He interrupts himself to ask Maria to get us coffee, then turns back.

"I had you checked out," he adds, looking at me. "You once worked for a lawyer in town who has a good reputation. *Your* reputation is mixed, I hope you know that."

"That happens when you have to stand up for people."

He doesn't comment on that. "This isn't about those bodies in New Jersey?"

"No sir."

He looks at Joel. "I couldn't find anything on you at all."

Joel shrugs. "I don't have a business."

"What do you do, then?"

Joel matches his tone. "I help *him*."

Baker frowns at him. I move on. "Senator, we're here to see if you can shed some light on a family matter."

"Whose?"

"Yours."

Maria comes back with coffee. He stiffens and indicates for her to hurry and leave. She shuts the door. His expression has gone cold. "Exactly what are you trying to do?"

The coffee is ignored. I lean forward towards him. "Get the truth. My client was born here 35 years ago, and got into the hands of Bernadette McCabe—or almost. Caught in her black-market baby operation. You're no doubt heard of it. That baby was most likely your daughter's."

And the look I've seen many times. When something thought long-buried has suddenly erupted.

He manages to go through the mental perambulations and not stroke out.

"What do you want?"

"The precise thing I want is my client's original birth certificate. If you have access to that or can help us get to it, it would be nice."

"Why?"

"My client is entitled to it. The adoption wasn't exactly legitimate."

"Why do you keep saying "my client?" Doesn't he have a name?"

And here is the next part. "*She* does. And if her family is interested in being in contact with her, she is with them. I know what you're thinking, Senator. Before you tell me she can't be your grandchild, my client is transgender. She transitioned from male to female not long ago."

He needs some time to digest this, and moves his hand for the coffee. He can't pick up the milk very well, and Joel gets up to help him in a way that makes me think of Jan, the man he took care of in Amsterdam.

Then we wait. He doesn't ask questions, he doesn't repeat anything, he doesn't deny.

After some time thinking, he's ready. "So he—she —needs the birth certificate."

"Yes." I explain the legal situation. "She doesn't have an identity now. She has the one she gave herself, but she's in a legal limbo. This is not her fault. She was given away at birth and was swept up in a criminal enterprise. The people who raised her, you might want to know, were good people. They took care of her very well. She's a good person."

"I don't understand this at all..."

His voice sounds angry, but it's an outburst rather than a proclamation. He slumps down and stares at us.

"A good person. What does that mean? What does she do?"

"She restores posters and similar artwork. She was also military."

"How did *that* happen?"

"It happens, Senator. She was in the military before she transitioned."

He thinks some more.

Joel puts his hand on Baker's desk. "She's a friend of mine. If you are at all interested in a grandchild, you know, she's one to be proud of."

Baker's face is unreadable. I can't imagine what's going through his head. But this is his situation, what he created. Then he comes out of his reverie. "Do you have a photo?"

Joel has his phone out, and finds pictures of Geneva to show him.

We stop time, so to speak. He's absorbing the last 35 years and considering them. We can see that. Measuring what to do in the last years of his life.

Baker's hands are shaking when he gives the phone back to Joel. He tries to pick up the coffee cup, and has trouble. Joel catches his hand and helps him with his previous sensitivity. I can see Baker, 20 or 30 years ago, would never allow himself to be in this situation or to accept this type of help, but now appears grateful.

"Excuse me a moment." He gets up and leaves the office for several minutes. When he comes back, he's more focused, but also graver. "My daughter is coming over. Can you wait?"

"Sure." I look at Joel. He's watching Baker, who is watching him in turn.

"Could I see the photos again?"

"If you have a computer, I can print them out."

"I have a computer, Mr. McFadden. I'm not a dinosaur yet."

Joel smiles. "I'm not making assumptions. You can call me Joel. I don't like being called Mr. McFadden."

Baker retrieves his coffee. "I sense you're an interesting person, Joel."

"You have no idea."

Baker points out where a computer is hidden in a roll top desk near him. By the time Joel has managed to get the photos printed, Brenda Baker has arrived. Maria shows her into the room.

Brenda Baker is a thin dark-haired woman in her early fifties. She has deep lines around her eyes and mouth that make her look like she has frowned her entire life.

Her expression is not friendly now, either.

She barely acknowledges her father. He waves impatiently for her to sit. Between them we can sense the decades of a tense relationship.

"What is this about?" Her voice is terse. I can see Geneva's resemblance to her in her eyes.

Baker regards her and then comes out with it. "These men are private investigators hired by your child."

She drops the purse she was carrying and grips the arms of her chair. "You have the nerve to just *drop* this on me?"

"You wouldn't have come here if I told you on the phone."

She looks at us again and this time her expression is pure hate. "You have no right."

I keep my voice calm. "I'm sorry you feel that way, but *your* child does have a right."

She shakes her head furiously. "I don't have a child. That was given up a long time ago. You need to leave here, and leave me alone."

"Brenda, you can't control the situation. We might have realized this would happen. We could consider if we're going to communicate with her..."

"*Her?*"

Baker stops. He doesn't know what to say.

I take over. It doesn't matter, she's already hostile. "Your son transitioned to female a couple years ago."

"I don't have a son. Or any child, *whatever* you're trying to pull over on me.

"Brenda, honey. This has gone on long enough. This might be fate's way of giving us a chance."

"Fate? You screwed that up for me long ago."

"You still have choices." He's embarrassed as more of his life is open in front of strangers.

"No, everything had to be for *you*. And now you tell me about this obscenity."

She glares at me but Joel responds with an anger that gets all our attention. "Your *child* is not an obscenity."

She gives her hateful look to him. "Who are you to say that?"

"I'm her friend. Don't be so fucking judgmental, when you all decided you were going to give her to a criminal."

She points at her father. "That was him..." Then she stops and gets cold again. "This is not your business."

"It's our business now. You can't treat children like an inconvenience once they're born. Something to pay someone to take care of."

"That was him!"

"Brenda, I was trying to do the best for us..."

"For *you*. It didn't benefit me at all."

Joel hasn't stopped; he gets out of his chair. "You're both responsible. An abortion is one thing—it's a choice. But if you have a kid, what the fuck do you think you're doing giving her to a black market criminal? You take care of the kid, or let her be adopted the *right* way."

Baker looks stunned and beaten down by Joel's words. I don't jump in. I know where he's speaking from.

Baker speaks haltingly. "This was a different time. 1975. Brenda's mother wouldn't let her terminate, and if anything had come out through a regular adoption, it would have been used against me."

I respond to that. "You don't understand, sir. It *is* coming out, regardless. She has a right to her identity, and if it has to go to court you'll have to live with the results."

Now Brenda looks horrified. "You can't—you can't let this happen." She goes to her father's desk. Pounds on it. "You can't let this happen!"

Joel is still angry. "It's *going* to happen."

She whirls around and slaps Joel across his face.

That makes both Baker and I jump up. Joel would never hit her back, but I'm afraid that she might go berserk with rage. I step between them. Baker moves around the desk and takes her arm. "Brenda, stop."

I take Joel's arm in turn and move him out of slapping range.

Brenda jerks away from her father. "Stay away from me. I want nothing to do with this. With *that*." She points at the picture on the desk. "Keep it away from me!"

Joel moves against my arm, and I hold him. Brenda isn't going to change. She's a lost cause. "Let her leave."

Her father still tries. "Brenda... please consider differently..."

"The hell with you."

She slams out of the room, shoving past Maria, who checks that Baker's okay. He waves her out.

Baker sits down again, staring at his desk. I stay standing with Joel, making sure he's calming down, but we're all unnerved from the encounter. I'm glad Geneva didn't have to hear this. Next to me, I feel Joel shaking.

I see Baker looking up and over at us.

"Does she want to meet me?"

"I think she does, as long as you're not going to be hostile like your daughter."

He rubs his eyes. "I didn't think I could go through with it, I wasn't sure. But...she would come up here?"

"Yes."

"I want to see her." A shadow crosses his face. Regret, sadness.

"What about her birth certificate?" I start to go back to my chair.

He taps his desk and looks at me. Then at Joel, when Joel moves over to his desk and stares down at him. I grab Joel's hand and take him back with me to the chair.

"Give me a minute." Baker gets up and walks, less steadily than before, out the room.

Joel watches him go. I pull him over to me. "Hey."

He turns his fierce eyes on me.

"Come on. It's okay now." I put my hands on his sides. "It's okay now." I touch his head, and leave my hand there. He closes his eyes briefly, easing in his posture.

"I got so mad."

"Understandable."

"What do you think he's doing?"

"Something to help, I think. He's realized life isn't black and white. He wants a grandchild and he's not going to waste time now."

Baker comes back. Joel moves to his previous chair. Baker has changed. It's subdued, but he has a glint in his eyes. Maybe he had a drink. I couldn't blame him.

He has a very old envelope he gives me. "Look at it, but I want to see her first to give it to her. To be sure."

I take out the paper. David Baker. No father listed. I memorize the details just in case, then take out my phone. "You mind if I take a picture?"

"Go ahead."

"To be sure about this, you can have a DNA test. I have her DNA profile with me. It'll be necessary for a court order."

"Yes, I can see that. Look, my daughter...she's had difficulties in life."

"So have we all. Everything Joel said holds true for me. Geneva is not at fault for yours, or your daughter's, actions and decisions. Don't let her terrorize Geneva."

"Geneva." He glances at the photo.

"Do you know the father?"

"Met him, no. Who he was, yes. I'd rather not go into that now. It was a bad time all around."

"I understand that, but information is vital. I can ask on her behalf. In case she can't."

"I'm not lying that I want to see her, Mr. Ross. My intentions aren't hostile."

"Many a slip, if you know what I mean."

"While I believe you, right now your evidence isn't here. So I'd be giving you confidential information."

"Information I'll find out. I'm good at that, or I wouldn't be here. In fact, we almost didn't get here. A man tried to kill us over this."

He looks shocked. "What man?"

"Arthur Knox, who used to work with McCabe. I don't know if you met *him*, but he's still around, and an arsonist on top of whatever he used to do for her. He tried to burn us to death. Didn't you see it in the news?"

He's stunned into silence.

"So, Senator, you'll perhaps understand how we rather feel entitled to the information that we almost had to die for."

"This is true?"

"Right here in Rochester. I'd give you more details, but it's a confidential matter."

He sighs. "Don't be so sardonic, Mr. Ross. Geneva's situation can be fixed, and I'll fix it. Let me have the report or whatever it is."

"Let's have the name."

"You don't quit do you? If you cause trouble for me unnecessarily... I hope you won't. I'll call you when I have the results and arrange for her to come up here...yes, I see your expression. The man's name was Karim Gemayel." He pauses to take off his glasses and think. "Is anything being done about Knox?"

"The police are looking into it. But he hasn't been caught."

∞

Twenty-One ◆ 61 Sincerity (Zhōng Fú)

Wind over Lake: Here is where the great skills help others. Trustworthiness, confidence, sincerity. Sincerity comes from within and is often not visible, but shows through the actions of others when needed to transform, when needed for harmony. The fifth line (nine/yang) is moving. A union of mutual sincerity is present for a relationship, a bond.

∞

He's going back to Cafétière Malífice. He wants to say hello to Nicolas, the barista who helped him figure out what happened to Raymond—he never followed up on that after finding Raymond dead. And when he walks in, he sees Raymond at a table, with two cups of coffee.

"I was waiting for you, Gabriel."

And he's so overwhelmed, he can't speak.

"Please join me."

He sits across from Raymond.

"The keeper of the secrets," Raymond says. "You saw me at my worst."

"No one should go through that."

"You may not believe you helped, but you did. You found out the truth. You did something about it, and you still are. Isn't that what matters?"

"I hope so. But I lost you."

"I tell John this when he feels he lost me." John, Raymond's boyfriend. "You didn't cause someone to kill me. There's nothing you could have done to know what would happen. So no way you could have done anything to stop it."

"Okay. Why are you here for me?"

"Not all dreams are bad, Gabriel. I have some things to tell you. Sometimes people show up in your dreams because you're doing right by them. Not to torture you, but just to visit you."

He sits across from Raymond, who smiles. "Tell me what you're doing now. Tell me how you're making your life worthwhile."

∞

Monday, January 31

GENEVA IS READY to meet her grandfather. He *is* her grandfather; Baker had the test done last week and received expedited results. Geneva has asked us if we would go with her, and Joel and I both thought being with her was the right thing, to support her in this difficult step on the journey. The trip up is conducive to talking about life, as we take turns driving.

Joel at one point asks me, "Did you have a coming out experience?"

I laugh. "Not with my father. He called me a fag, or fucking fag, to be exact, since I was seven and wouldn't play football like he wanted. He wouldn't say it in front of Mom or Dominic, but he didn't stop until I was 16 and capable of taking him on. Then I was upgraded to merely a disappointment."

Geneva squeezes my shoulder from the back seat. I look at Joel. He had it worse. But he doesn't seem to be thinking that. "When did your mom know?"

"For sure when I was 16, because Dom caught me somewhere I shouldn't have been. Danny ratted me out to him. He thinks I don't know he did that. That time with Mom and Dominic was awful, not because either one was angry about me being gay. They couldn't be. But because they proceeded to give me the 'talk.' Safe sex, basically. I was horrified about them saying anything about my sex life. I had quite a mouth back then, and I told them to mind their own fucking business. Dom came close to slapping me."

"I'm glad you've changed since then," Joel says drily.

"You and Bettina seem to think I have issues. That whole night Dominic grilled me about what I had done, which I wouldn't tell. And telling me about condoms and the dangers of hooking up with strange men. I was doing this slow burn, hoping the ceiling would fall on him. He never gave up though, so some of it got through. I didn't tell my mom about who I was involved with until I was in college. Yet she dealt with it better, to just talk about relationships. No one I met was good enough for Dom, so I didn't do that much with him. Mom was afraid to be judgmental of me...and on my own, I got involved with some people I shouldn't..."

I think about the older boy from New Jersey I used to hang out with my first year in college. The one who stole cars and drove us around the back roads of Union and Passaic Counties. And then we'd park somewhere isolated, smoke weed, and get physical. We spun apart eventually; he was lost in his own turmoil.

When I look at Joel, I know life has worked out for the best. "Dom wasn't an ogre, just protective. He would have loved you. I know that."

"Really?"

"He would love your art. He loved beauty. And he would recognize your soul. We were alike that way."

"I see that," Geneva says. "He worked on you, because you weren't meant to be a bad person but you could have been corrupted."

"Yeah, my anger could have corrupted me. It still fucks me up."

"Instead you have compassion. I see that in how you're helping me. You don't pity or patronize me. That's valuable to a person who has to be careful who she talks to about her state of being."

"Thank you. That's exactly what I want to be. Pity is the bottom level of compassion. I always believed in the dignity of humans.

"To search for pity is to have lost human dignity," She says.

Joel is staring at me.

I glance over at him. "Okay, what are you thinking? Do you want to talk more about coming out, or something?"

He shakes his head. "It was irrelevant to me. I didn't come out, I was thrown out. I was reminded of it when we went to see Bob for the sketch. But I like to hear about other people's experiences. Especially things that are transformative. You mentioned butterflies were symbols of transformation. I was going to work that imagery into something for Geneva. Geneva is beautiful as a transformation."

She leans over the back seat and kisses the side of his head.

"But it's also transforming from living to dead, hidden to discovered. Relationships are transformative that way. Except for the dark side, like what you had to do with Don. You mentioned some character in your sleep, *Mahakala*. You dream some real supernatural shit. I looked that name up. It's everything I felt I saw when you were like that in the basement. Scary. Dark blue with three eyes and six arms. A giant knife and a skull with blood."

"Gabriel, that's a pretty strong spirit to carry inside you," Geneva says.

"It's what happens anger manifests, I suppose. But it's going to be under control."

∞

Maria shows us into Baker's office. He's standing next to his desk. His eyes lock onto Geneva. He doesn't know what to say.

She keeps her former military bearing. We flank her in support.

Baker decides to acknowledge us first. "I didn't expect you. I told you I wasn't going to do anything to hurt her."

Geneva speaks firmly. "I want them here."

"All right." He glances a Joel, who gives back his fierce expression. "Mr. McFadden...no, Joel, you want to be called Joel, I remember. I am not going to do anything you need to be worried about. I invite you to sit down. Geneva?"

He holds his hand out, and she hesitantly walks over to take it. Their eyes go over each other, seeing flesh and blood for the first time.

Baker still doesn't know what to say. He must have thought about this over and over, and yet all of it may seem insufficient now. Probably Geneva feels something similar, as well as caution. She sits in a chair directly across from him.

Baker asks us about our drive up. We describe the trip and the weather. It doesn't break the ice that well.

Geneva forges ahead. "Well, Senator. I'm willing to answer those questions you may have. Not because you have a right to ask them, but because I'm just willing to do so. I just want you to understand that."

The Senator looks uncomfortable. "Well, I wasn't going to ask you anything you didn't want to answer. I can't pretend I understand your situation, but I'm willing to try the best I can, because I don't have much family left. Your friends described you quite eloquently. You sound...like a person to be proud of. So I would like to know more about you. Can you tell me about your parents?"

Geneva then describes her mother and father, what they did, how they were good to her in her childhood in Long Island. How they died. Her mother died first, before learning that her child wanted to express her true gender.

"Dad found out when he went through Mom's stuff. I had some bins up in the attic, and Dad thought these were hers. But the sizes were different, and I had pictures in the bins as well. This was stuff I had after I left the military and was going to school. My secret stash of women's items.

"Dad suspected I was gay, but he never abandoned me. What he didn't know is that I had decided to go ahead and live as a woman, with the goal of sex-reassignment surgery. At that time, I was consulting professionals and support groups, and I had actually started hormone therapy when Mom suddenly died. See, I needed the process of "real-life experience," where I documented how I lived as a woman, in order to establish I was ready to do so the rest of my life. Because I wanted the operation, the vaginoplasty, 12 months of RLE was required."

She's blunt with him, perhaps to see how he'll take it. He rolls with it.

"Document? Like a diary?"

"Much like a diary. I described in a journal what I did, when I'd go out. How I dressed. How I interacted with others. What I did at home. It was invasive, and at the same time it was empowering, because I could see how I was being myself. By this time, I had graduated college and decided to live and work as a woman in New York City, because Mom and Dad would not be able to visit as often, and I could gradually explain what was going on. But Mom's death interrupted that, or rather, accelerated it."

Just that much is a huge amount to tell this stranger. We watch both of them. Geneva has told these stories before in therapy, but this is so different.

Baker switches subjects for the moment. Asks about her Army career, what she learned, how she trained.

"Translation. I speak Arabic. I did very well. I had been in combat first, then intelligence. What happened was, someone reported to my commander that I was gay and having an affair with another specialist. This wasn't true, but they found pictures I thought I had hidden. Where I was in women's clothes. I was discharged —not dishonorably, but so that I could still take advantage of VA and GI Bill. The GI was the most helpful. Getting anything from the VA is a joke, and still is."

I like Baker's next question. "How did you...choose your name?"

Geneva beams, appreciating the importance of her chosen name. "I was stationed in Artillery Kaserne, in Garmisch-Partenkirchen, Germany, before going to Afghanistan, for some training. It was close to the Austrian and Swiss border. Once some friends and I drove to Geneva. I really loved it there. So beautiful and romantic. Lennon, I chose because I love John Lennon's music. I thought perhaps it would give me some magic, you know?"

Baker nods. "Actually I was a Beatles fan myself. You're surprised? I was young once. Geneva...how did you know...about yourself? How did you deal with it?"

"It's not a realization. It just is. It's what I gravitated to. I only realized it in a sense because for others, it wasn't what was supposed to happen. Okay, you know. This is *boys'* stuff, this is *girls'* stuff. You can't play with both, and you can't play with the opposite sex's stuff. And especially in what to wear. When I was really young it happened in places like Target. I'd want a dress, some Mary Janes, a necklace, and my mom would rush me away when other people would stare at me for rummaging through girls' clothes.

"You get the idea pretty soon in grade school what boys are supposed to act like and what girls are supposed to act like. Some girls were tomboys and that was okay, but feminine boys were called faggots and set upon. No one wants that. So even though I wanted to be with the girls and do girl stuff, I over-compensated by being rough with the boys. I even beat up a couple boys. I feel bad about that— what we'll do just to avoid being targeted.

"I learned sports but I also followed my mom and tried to copy her in my mind. I'd pretend I was her in my room —how she walked, how she talked, her movements. How she'd do her hair. She and her friends were so beautiful. I took pictures of them. They thought it was a hobby, but I studied those pictures."

"Your voice sounds very...feminine."

"Part of that is the hormones. Part of that is training. Hormones don't change the voice completely, so I had to work at it. I met with a professional voice coach who works with transgender persons, to learn to speak more feminine."

She drops her voice for a moment. "See, this is more what I sounded like before."

Baker looks surprised. She is not ashamed of who she is. Or what she was before. She will be herself, but will not cover up all aspects of having been biologically male, because she must be accepted for everything. "Cesare was me, just not the complete me."

"You're happy, right?"

"With who I am? Yes. Doesn't mean it's easy. Okay, I have a nice body structure to be a woman, but at first it took time for hormones to work. There're certain features in men that are more difficult to feminize. People could tell. In restrooms. But I've had people yell out me to get out of the ladies' room, call managers on me, saying I'm a pervert and should be arrested."

Because she's his granddaughter, because he's trying, I see the change in him. Feeling her pain on her behalf. I see it. We might wonder what he'd feel if she wasn't. Probably wouldn't be on his radar. Like a politician who 'evolves' because he or she knows LGBT persons. Nonetheless, at least Baker *is* apparently on her side.

"This isn't TV, where people like me are a joke, a throwaway comedy line—the transsexual next-door neighbor. People think crossdressers and transgender persons and drag queens are all the same. They don't care. If it's serious, not for laughs, they're horrified."

Baker seems to want to process it. "Why is that?"

Geneva looks at me. She's telling her own tale and does it well. "Senator...it's a difficult thing to say. There are so many reasons for people to be hateful and prejudiced. Simple and complex."

"You don't have to call me 'Senator.' You can call me Granddad, if you want. We need to get to know each other. But I want to do that. I'm sorry what happened to you, the parts of your life experience that caused you pain."

Baker looks at us. "You two understand her very well, I think."

"We appreciate her. We've been through prejudice and seen its effects. I've heard plenty of people say, "I'm okay with gays, but these people...""

Geneva nods. "Some women, even feminists, will tell me I'm not a *real* woman, to stop trying to move in on their space."

"It's all about privilege, Senator. There's always somebody who wants to marginalize others, to exploit privilege to put themselves in a judgmental position."

"Oh..." he draws back. "Oh, I see. Geneva, are you involved with someone?"

"I was, but a year ago he said he couldn't go on. He couldn't introduce me to his family. That was why I moved out of the city."

Baker is visibly distressed over that. I'm amused in a sense.

"I'm not tragic, Granddad. It's what happens. Life isn't fair. We're in a position where we have to protest whether we want to or not. I may have someone else...we'll see."

Joel and I smile about that, this someone else being Jason. She and Jason hit it off at the Christmas party, with their mutual interest in books. She's told Jason about herself, and he was not affected. He has suggested meeting up with her. She's being very careful in starting something new, and we're trying to help by staying out of it.

"I want to help you, Geneva. Where do we go from here?"

"Well, Granddad, I need that birth certificate. It's going to be some trouble to begin with to have a court declare I'm that person. See, I have to already argue to the Department of Health that I have a right to change my gender. They don't just give these out. They make you defend yourself. It's the most frustrating kind of bureaucracy. But it's worse because I have to prove my original identity in the first place, and I'm now forced to explain what happened to me. I'm not humiliated, but I have to explain this to people who aren't going to be like Joel and Gabriel —or like you are trying to be."

Baker gets up and opens a desk drawer and takes out the paper, handing it to her. She's seen it from my phone, but holding it is different. She stares at it in wonder. The first step to reclaiming identity. This is who she was, now she has to integrate it with who she is.

"Do you really think you need to go to court?"

"Government agencies aren't very helpful whenever something is out of the ordinary." She sounds unsure, looking at me.

"She can try. We could also contact a transgender law clinic. They might have some ways of dealing with the DOH —maybe a contact."

"I know some attorneys here in Rochester. Surely, they can help."

I lean forward. "With all due respect, Senator, if these attorneys are not specifically sensitive to trans issues, they may not be effective."

"It should be an issue like other. It's what they're paid to handle."

"People have prejudices. Prejudices affect their work."

She looks at me again. "What do you recommend?"

"Let me talk to Jim and Juanita. Remember them from Joel's birthday? Juanita has probably had to get legal assistance for the kids at some point. Jim can also help."

Baker shifts around in his chair. He wants to help, he wants to draw upon his contacts and powers to make something happen, but this is out of his league. Or maybe it isn't. Money can make prejudices disappear.

"If you need more help on this, let me know," he says to me.

"I will, Senator."

"Have the police found the man who set those fires?"

"No, but a friend of mine says his mother has been questioned, and is being charged with accessory." I wonder how Arthur's sister is handling this, finding out that Arthur is finally being investigated full force.

Baker invites us to lunch, and we stay for a couple hours. Then leave them alone to talk some in private.

We end up staying overnight in Rochester. Geneva stays at her grandfather's house; we're back in the Best Western. I can use the rest. I'm not 100 percent back to myself yet, a little off, a little tired.

The next day Joel and I track down Bettina to visit, and she gives me some flak for being in yet another fight. Especially when I seem to be more subdued than she'd like.

Bettina tells us before we leave her office, "The police received some threatening phone messages about how people were going to pay for Arthur's mother being arrested."

"I'd think it was funny, but it isn't. We know what he does when he thinks someone has insulted his mother."

I'm thinking of checking out the Knox homestead, just to see if Arthur's around. I'd rather do that instead of wait, since I'm concerned Knox might go after Senator Baker.

Geneva calls to update us on her day, and I tell her my plans. "I know an agency in town who can send over a couple of bodyguards on the fly. I'd feel better that they're there."

"Okay, I stay here and wait for them to show, but I'll come over and help out with recon for you."

I give her Mama Knox's address, and we take off.

∞

It's around 11 pm. We park a block down from the house and approach cautiously. No lights are on.

Joel asks, "You think she's there?"

"She's still in jail. She hit a cop; they don't care for that."

"She hasn't made bail, then."

"I'd be happy to testify at the hearing—to keep her ass locked up." We walk around the back of the house to the door. Looking in, I see it leads to the kitchen. I take my lock picks out, and have the door open in a matter of a minute.

Inside Terry's house, everything looks generally undisturbed—as far as we know. I'm not here to criticize housekeeping.

We go to the basement first, since the door to it is in the kitchen. Joel waits on the stairs for me while I check it out. Nothing, just a residential basement. No areas to hide.

Then Joel and I carefully walk through the kitchen, the dining room and living room, and down a hall off the far end of the living room. One bedroom and a hall closet are to the left, two other bedrooms to the right, and a bathroom at the end.

Only Terry's bedroom appears to be used. The other two bedrooms are sparse and more or less clean. Some have boxes, not from GenWorks. A cursory glance tells me nothing important is in them.

The bathroom is last. It's fairly large with a tub in the center, the curtain drawn.

When I pull the curtain back, Arthur is there standing in the tub with a shotgun.

∞

Knox slams the shotgun against Gabriel's head so fast and hard, Joel doesn't have time to react. Now Gabriel's on the floor unconscious, and Knox has the shotgun pointed at Joel.

"Well, well. It's Mr. Smart Guy and The Bodyguard," Knox says. He glances down at Gabriel's prone body. "You're not so smart knocked the fuck out, are you?"

He looks back at Joel.

Joel is frozen in place. "What do you want?"

"I know you have a gun. Take it out, and your phone. Put it on the floor outside." He steps out the tub and over Gabriel's body, keeping the shotgun pointed at Joel.

Joel carefully lays the Glock on the hall floor, along with his phone.

"Now drag him out."

Trying to remain calm with the two black barrels staring at him, Joel moves over to Gabriel, picks up his arms, and pulls him into the hallway. Knox indicates for him to stop.

"I know Mr. Smart Guy has a gun too. Take out his phone and gun, put 'em with yours."

"He's not trying to do anything to you." Joel takes out Gabriel's Sig Sauer from the belt holster. He removes Gabriel's work phone from his jacket. Gabriel has his second, personal phone in another pocket. Joel leaves that. He knows the volume is off.

"Well. He's in my mother's house, and he shouldn't be. She's in *jail*." Knox gestures with the shotgun for Joel to hurry up.

Joel sets down the gun and phone. "He knows people who can help your mother."

"He and I will talk about that. He likes to go places. So we're going to go to some place to talk. You, Mr. Bodyguard, get in the bathroom."

Joel backs up inside. Knox pulls the door closed. A few seconds later he hears a chair being pushed under the door.

Knox says, "Now you just stay where you are, all quiet-like. I'm taking Mr. Smart Guy to have our talk. I'll be back for you."

Joel can hear the sound of Gabriel's body being dragged away. The front door to the house opens and closes.

Then Joel backs up and kicks at the door. It takes a minute to break it sufficiently and knock the chair away.

He snatches up the guns and phones still in the hallway, and runs to the front door. Outside, he doesn't see Knox anywhere. But he does see Geneva in a Lincoln, parking in front. She sees Joel and jumps out the car.

"What happened?"

"Knox has Gabriel. Did you see anything?"

"A van was going around the corner when I pulled up a minute ago."

"That was him. I'm taking the Camry and tracking him."

"I'll go with you."

They get in the Camry as Joel checks his phone. "He's going north somewhere. I have an app in both our phones to track each other if necessary."

Joel dials 911 and tries to explain the situation while driving. "What the fuck do I have to tell you? Arthur Knox has kidnapped my boyfriend, and he's going to kill him."

The voice on the other end tells him to be calm, and police will be on the lookout."

"Fuck that!" Joel hits nearly 80 on the streets, weaving around the few stray cars on the road this time of night. Joel calls Bettina as they reach the north end of the city out of town. He tells her what happened. "Is there anyone you can get to listen? The Goddamned 911 operator is just opening a case file. I need action."

"What do you need?"

"People to track that van—get a roadblock, a helicopter, for Christ's sake. Before he stops."

"What do you think Knox is doing?"

Joel is processing this, in the part of his brain to stay cool. "Knox is going to set him on fire."

"Oh my God, let me see what I can do."

But it isn't fast enough for Joel. While people are asking questions, Knox is carrying out his plan.

Bettina calls back in a few minutes. "Someone's called in about a chemical spill just outside of town, in the north area. They're blocking it off."

Joel looks at the GPS. "My ass. Knox called that in. He wants to kill Gabriel. Because of his Goddamned *mother.*"

"Okay, I believe you, but..."

"Try to convince *them*, Bettina..."

The GPS device tries to keep up with the turns.

"*Recalculating. Keep straight.*"

At the main road out of town, a rural area leading northwest, a cop next to a squad car holds his hand out to stop him. "You need to turn back, sir. There might be a hazardous spill nearby. This area is going to be under evacuation until it checks out."

Joel briefly debates trying to explain the situation to the cop. Then knows it won't be worth it. He shifts gear and backs up slowly, politely, lifting a hand to wave at the officer.

A hundred feet back, he shifts back into drive, and jams on the gas, swerving across an empty field with the lights out. The officer runs after him, but he isn't fast enough to catch up with Joel, who's gone back up to 90 mph to get the Camry to the road at the other end of the field. *Please don't let anything puncture the tires...*

"*Recalculating.*"

Geneva takes it in stride, holding on. She checks the phone again. "Anstel Road..."

Joel speeds down the road looking desperately for that sign.

"Joel, over there!" Geneva points to their left. A group of old brick structures and a factory-type one. "That building is burning."

They get out of the car. Fire surrounds the entire perimeter of the building. It's not raging yet, but it's gathering strength. They can see that the inside of the first floor is burning as well. Joel switches the GPS off and calls Gabriel's phone.

∞

Blackness. Gabriel's in a warehouse. It's the warehouse in Westchester again. It seems bigger this time, filthier. He can smell mold, feel the dirt on his hands and feet as he makes his way through the building.

He's been brought back here, because he knew it never ended. He has to live it again. Find Joel, rescue him for good this time. He can do it, because Joel knows he loves him.

More stairs than he remembers. Very disconcerting, because he can't see or hear anything. He tries to find his phone, flashlight, gun, something. He has nothing. He's just in a t-shirt and jeans, barefoot. Walking a black corridor. Coming to a large room. The wood under his feet creaks.

He steps in the room.

Ethan Nelson waits on a small chair in the middle of the room.

"Well, Gabriel. Did you miss me?"

"Why are you here, Nelson? Why do I have to see you again?"

Nelson smiles in that obsequious way he had. "Why? Because you're in *Hell*. You knew that, didn't you? Did you seriously think you'd escape it? Like you're different than I? You let me be killed, Gabriel."

"You were going to kill Joel, and me too. You killed so many people for your own gain, your own amusement. I'm nothing like you."

"But *you took my life*."

"Zest made the choice, not me."

"Don't fuck around with semantics. You knew what you were doing."

"I had to. You made your own choices too, that led you here."

Nelson leans forward. "And yet you are here with me. How do you explain that? Because the gods don't care. They just have their moral checklist. So you're the same as me. And that means I can finish the job." He stands and knocks the chair to the side. Gabriel sees Joel on his knees again, his back to Gabriel, his head bowed, hands behind him.

"You see, Gabriel, this is my domain. I can kill him, bring him back to life, and kill him again. Over and over and over. And you'll see it each time." He takes a gun from somewhere and puts it against Joel's head. "Watch."

"No!" Gabriel throws himself at Joel's kneeling figure. Ethan's gun goes off in the back of Gabriel's head. He hears it, feels it, falls to the floor. *I'm dead*, he thinks. *Don't let anything happen to Joel, please...don't let it be for nothing.*

And then he hears nothing, sees nothing. Joel isn't there. Nelson isn't there. He's alone.

∞

I must be so tired that I just fell asleep on the floor. But it doesn't smell right. It's not my place. Dirt. Mold. A buzzing somewhere. It won't stop.

My eyes open. I'm on tile. Blackness around me. I don't see anything. At first, I look for Ethan Nelson, from my dream. But I can't see anything. I struggle to get on my knees, my head swimming. The room is cold and smells abandoned. The strangest feeling something's shocking my side. Buzzing over and over. I fall to the floor, in the black dirt and grime. Sudden fear rises in me, alone in the darkness. What happened?

Buzzing. I reach to my side. And touch a phone.

∞

"Answer, Goddamn it." He hangs up and calls again. "Come on, come on. Jesus. Please answer."

Then the call goes through. "Joel..."

Relief and horror. Gabriel's voice is strained. "Gabriel, where are you? Are you in the building?"

"I don't know. I don't know. What is going on? There's a window...."

Joel hears him moving somewhere, maybe crawling.

"Oh, God..."

Gabriel sees the fire.

Joel's internal frenzy rises. "Hold on, we're here. We'll get you out. What floor is it? Gabriel?"

"Oh, Jesus, I can't..."

"Gabriel, what floor? Can you see another building?"

A pause. "One...just next door. I see the fourth floor. I must be on the fourth floor."

Joel is looking at the building next to this one. It's also four stories high.

∞

Four floors down I can see it. The fire. It's growing, and surrounding the building. I know he's set it to trap me inside.

Looking at the fire, starting to crawl up the ground floor to the second, I'm frozen. I'm back in the trailer with my Mom.

"Gabriel! Come with me now, we have to get out."

She's not here.

A part of my mind says get up, find an escape, but I'm so terrified I can't move. Like in the bar, but now I'm so much more frozen. The fire is going to catch me.

∞

Geneva is on her phone, trying to get an emergency response. Joel is still trying to calm Gabriel as well as his own panic.

"Joel...I'm scared...I'm going to die in here."

"Baby, hold on. Don't lose me now." Joel realizes he has to take over. He takes in the precious few feet separating the buildings. Not much time before they can't be even this close.

"I'll jump. I'm not burning to death."

Joel sees him on the fourth floor, at the window. "No! Go to the roof."

He turns to Geneva. "What can he do?" He goes around to the trunk of the Camry. Geneva follows. She takes instant stock of everything Gabriel has for emergencies. "He could rappel, but the fire at the bottom...No, we could do this—" She points up at the roofs of the two buildings. They're almost the same size. "Get the rope across. Can he do it?"

"Yes." Joel speaks to Gabriel again. "Go to the roof, baby. Get up there no matter what and come over to the same side where you are now —but *stay* there, okay?"

Geneva is taking out the rope and the clamps in the trunk. She runs for the other building with Joel right behind her.

"Do you hear me? Go to the roof and wait for me. I know you're scared. I'm here with you, okay?"

Joel hears Gabriel calling for his mother in a whisper voice. God no. He's going to lose it. Joel makes his voice harsh, like he imagines Chiang does. "Gabriel! Wake the fuck up. You know better than this!"

It cuts through the fugue. "Okay. I'm going. I'm trying. The hallway is so dark..."

"Baby, get the fuck to the roof!"

"All right."

"Don't hang up. Talk to me and tell me what you're doing." They're on the third floor.

"I'm putting on the speaker, hold on...I'm on the next floor. The last door is here." Joel can hear him pushing at the door. It pops open. Gabriel's voice sounds like he's trying to stop shaking as he goes up another flight of stairs. "It's the top. The roof."

"Wait for us." Joel is at the roof door to the other building, and finds it stuck. He and Geneva both slam against it and force it open. The air is again cold, and the smell of the fire is strong. "Why aren't the fire people here?"

"The fake evacuation." Joel pulls the rope off Geneva's shoulder. He sees Gabriel twenty-five feet away, staring across.

The fire is on the second floor, and the heat is mixing with the cold, throwing off surreal light.

Geneva quickly ties a clamp to one end of the rope. "Good."

Joel leans over the roof ledge. "Gabriel. Catch the rope. Stay with me."

Gabriel looks over the roof down to the fire. Joel figures he's not acting right, from the blow to his head.

"No, I said stay with me!"

Gabriel looks up again. Joel begins swinging the rope in a circle above his head, and tosses it across.

The weight of the clamp carries the rope across the chasm. Gabriel catches it, and then looks over at them.

Joel gets the phone. "Hook it to a pipe."

The fire gets loud. A bit of flame flies up. Gabriel freezes.

"No!" Joel is yelling across the roof. "Hook the rope!"

Gabriel backs up with the rope, and hooks it to a pipe next to him. When he's done, Geneva already has the other end tied to a clamp in a transport knot, and wrapped tight around a pipe.

Gabriel looks across at him. "What is this?"

Joel takes a deep breath. "You need to come over here." From where he is, he can see the fear.

"I can't do that."

"Of course you can. You're strong, you can hold yourself up. Geneva will talk you over. You need to do it now, and don't think."

He sees Gabriel stare over the side. "I'm not going to make it. I can't get across this."

"Yes, you can. If you don't, I'll come over there. And if you try to jump, I'll jump as well."

Gabriel stares at him across the chasm. "You can't do that."

"I will. I swear to Jesus, if you jump, I'll go right with you. We'll die together." Joel gets on the edge of the roof, on his knees, to make his point. Geneva gasps behind him.

Gabriel's eyes go wide and he grips the edge of the roof. "No!"

"Then do it. Get the rope."

Gabriel steps back, his eyes on Joel. Then his hand goes to the rope. "Okay."

Geneva talks over Joel's shoulder as he steps back. "Gabriel. Do not look down. You're going hand over hand, monkey crawl, you won't see the ground. Just listen to me and don't look down. Lie on the rope, hold it, and tuck your feet around. Get a good grip and swing around. It'll sag a little but hold. Keep your heels crossed over the rope."

Gabriel tests the rope, curves his feet around, and eases backwards. His head is over the roof. Joel encourages him. "You can do it. Hold tight."

Geneva speaks firmly, reassuringly. "That's right. Move your hands back. Pull with your hands and arms...now push with your feet. Don't look down, just look up. Now push again with your feet."

He's off the roof. The rope holds. His body drops in the middle and he struggles to stay with the rope, which seems so thin. They can hear Gabriel exhaling hard and then breathing fast. Geneva talks quickly so Gabriel won't think about the drop. Joel is concerned that the fire, creeping up the building, will burn the rope before he gets over. Geneva keeps coaching him. "It's a good rope. You're fine. Keep your head up, doing great. Hands pulling, feet pushing. That's it. You're halfway. More."

Joel looks over the edge. "If the rope snaps, hold on. Do not let go." Gabriel is breathing loud, mumbling to himself, his mother, whatever God he believes in. Joel interrupts. "Do not let go, Gabriel. Keep your feet on the rope. Answer me, baby."

"I'm not letting go."

Joel can see his face contorted in pain, maybe with the effort straining his body. "Come on, baby. Come over." Adrenaline courses through him. He wants to reach out, pull Gabriel in but he's not close enough. Gabriel is at a slight angle to them heading down. Geneva is still coaching. "You're almost here. You're fine, you're doing it. Almost here."

More sparks are flying up. A random spark hits the rope, and makes it smoke. Gabriel is fifteen feet away. Ten. Joel and Geneva both hold the rope, ready to pull him when possible.

The rope sizzles and catches fire. Then it snaps as Geneva yells, "Hold on!"

They can't do anything to cushion his impact, but the five-foot drop it isn't enough to make him let go. They can hear him grunt from the shock of hitting the building. The rope itself is burning right beneath his feet. He struggles to pull himself up.

Geneva and Joel reach down and begin hauling up the rope a foot at time. Gabriel struggles to catch his feet on the building for leverage.

"Hold on. You're here. You're here."

Geneva braces a foot against the roof and pulls while Joel grabs Gabriel's arms and yanks him over the lip of the roof. They all fall back in a tangled mass. A moment of shocking relief, kicking away the rope that's still burning.

Joel holds on to him. He doesn't want to let go. He feels Gabriel in shock, trembling against him.

They can hear the fire trucks in the distance—finally.

"Come on, before this place goes too." Geneva pulls at Gabriel's shoes, which are smoking, tossing them aside. "Get him out of here —we can't stop now."

The building they're in is now has caught fire as well, but only on the one side. Joel gets to his feet, bringing Gabriel with him. He can barely stand. They both circle him, move him out the door and down the stairs to the first floor, away from the side close to the fire, out a window on the far side, then down the street to where the Camry is.

Gabriel can no longer remain upright, and collapses in their arms. His head is bleeding.

Joel eases him down. "You're okay, baby."

Gabriel is breathing hard, in pain. His hands are bleeding along with his head. His feet look like they have some burns. But he's alive. Joel sits on the street by the car, holding him.

Geneva places her hand on his arm, and Gabriel reaches up and clutches her hand.

The fire trucks finally arrive, an ambulance a minute later. The EMTs, in a repeat of an hour ago, ease Gabriel out of the car, and on a stretcher, pulling an oxygen mask over his face. Joel keeps hold of his hand. "I'm going with him."

"Sir, you're getting in our way, you can follow. I can't have you in here."

The tech, looking at Joel, knows. He asks Gabriel, "Do you need him with you, sir?"

"Yes," Gabriel says through the mask. "Please."

"Just do it." The tech waves his hand at the EMT, who gives up and gets in the front seat to pull away.

Geneva's behind them. "Where are you going to?"

"Memorial. Genesee and Thomas." The same hospital they were in before, after being locked in the bar.

Joel gives her the keys before the tech closes the door.

∞

I hear voices cutting through the blackness. I struggle to pay attention to them.

"There's news people outside. Keep them away from here."

Then later. "I'm sorry, you need to stay in the waiting area."

"I told you, I'm his health care proxy. I want to see him right now."

Someone else sounding gently amused. "Mr. McFadden, do you think I'm lying? He's going to be okay. Wait here."

I slip away, then awaken again when the doctor is finishing whatever she's doing, which hurts. Looking at a clock on the wall, I realize I've been out of it for God knows how long. And then as I feel the pain, the day starts coming back. The doctor smiles down at me. I hear a faint Caribbean accent. "You with us, Mr. Ross? How is your pain level?"

"Ten out of five." I cough. "My throat hurts really bad."

She smiles again. "It will ease up in a moment. We ran an MRI on your head and a bronchoscopy on you while you were sedated."

"What's a bronchoscopy?"

"A tube in your nose to look at your lungs. We wanted to make sure the smoke didn't hurt you. There may be a little inhalation, so I want you to have a few days of oxygen therapy to make sure you don't have permanent damage."

I remember why smoke is an issue. I feel my feet bandaged as well. I have to look around again to see if I'm actually here. Is the doctor real? She catches my look. "Relax, now. You're okay but I want to be sure, since this is the second time we've treated you for this. And apparently, you've had multiple concussions. You'll be taken care of. Your man out there will have our heads if we don't. You don't know what it took to keep him out of here." She laughs.

I have a hard time believing her in my surreal state. For all I know, I'm dead and in a waiting room somewhere in the afterlife, and without my Book of the Dead. I turn my head to look out the glass window of the room, and see Joel watching. His face is intense. Because he's dead too? No, I'm in pain, and pain can't exist in the afterlife. Everyone says so.

He realizes I'm looking at him and smiles, holding a hand up against the window. I try to lift my own, but it's a strain. He mouths through the glass. *I love you.* I mouth the same to him.

The doctor smiles. "He shouldn't be there. But no harm done, as you're being sent upstairs now. He's a powerful force, that one."

"He saved my life."

"Yes? You are blessed, then."

"I am."

"You remind me of my daughter and her boyfriend, can't keep their eyes off each other. Let me get an attendant."

She leaves the room —and the door open.

He doesn't even wait for her to turn the corner before he's inside. His arms go around me. I feel his hair against my face. His chest heaving against mine. I smell the smoke and ash clinging to him.

"How're you feeling?" It's muffled, from being buried in me. I reach up to run my fingers in his hair.

"I'm fantastic." I laugh, or try to. "What else could I say, being alive? With you here, most of all."

He checks all the evidence of medical procedures, all the bandages. They don't seem that bad, yet I see I've inherited my mother's scars on my feet now. Going through the fire.

"What would I do without you? I guess I know the answer to that."

He pauses to meet my eyes. "It didn't happen."

"Like it didn't happen last time."

He takes my hand. "So we take care of each other. Right?"

The attendant shows up with a stretcher. I find out I need it; the strain or sedation has left me shockingly weak. Joel walks alongside without comment from the hospital staff. I get the idea he's made his presence known.

I look up at him. "Are you okay? Did you and Geneva get hurt?"

"No, we're good. You just relax now. All hell has broken loose, but you're out of it for the time being until the cops find out you're awake."

"Why? Oh, yeah, I guess that makes sense."

"The Senator feels terrible what happened to you, but I calmed him down." His mouth curls wryly. "I also called people on your behalf. Danny's probably coming up."

I realize Joel's holding my knapsack, and he sets it on my legs. As we wait in the elevator, and Joel starts charming the attendant, I open the bag and see my work phone.

"The other one fell out when you hit the building. I've canceled it and ordered another."

I look up at him. "Already?"

"I'm a master of efficiency. You have no idea. It kept me calm while I couldn't see you."

I turn on the work phone. A zillion messages. He takes it from me gently. "*Please*. Don't even test me. Anyone has to go through *me* to get to you."

I try to laugh and end up coughing.

We end up on a higher floor, passing a nurse's station. One of the nurses frowns. "Visiting hours are over."

"I'm not a visitor."

I have to laugh again. It still hurts. But I do it anyway.

∞

CHAPTER TWENTY-TWO ♦ 30 RADIANCE (Lí)

Fire over Fire: *Like a phoenix, arising from ashes of turbulence to victory over misfortune, progress over evil. Out of the darkness, two are attached. The radiance comes from the bond between them. The sixth line (nine/yang) moves in this reading. Cultivating virtue brings happiness.*

∞

From the New York *Herald-Standard*, February 1
Arrests in NJ Human Trafficking Ring — by Clark Ahn

Two men were arrested Tuesday in connection with what Elizabeth, NJ, police describe as a long-term human trafficking operation in Union County. The men, identified as Aridian Meksi and Peter Bardulla, were taken into custody in a rented house on the south side of Elizabeth. Police say that six women were being held hostage in the house, and likely had been forced into prostitution. The women were not identified, but were in the US undocumented. They are currently under medical treatment and being interviewed by federal authorities. Meksi and Bardulla were found with several illegal weapons, cash, and some narcotics.

Sources close to the investigation tell the *Herald-Standard* that these arrests are part of the ongoing investigation into the 19 women found murdered in Union and Passaic Counties. The murdered women are in the process of being identified, with help from European humanitarian organizations. The bodies were discovered in Black Mountain State Park, and off Caraway Road in northern Passaic County. Private investigator Gabriel Ross and his associates found the bodies in the course of investigating the murder of Leonard Mathers. Sophie Faulkner had been arrested for that murder in September, after Mathers' body was found buried in her backyard, and her DNA found on the alleged murder weapon.

Mathers' brother, Don Mathers, is currently under custody in St. Vincent's hospital in Newark, a suspect in the murder of the 19 women and also of being the ringleader of the trafficking operation in Elizabeth. Don Mathers was severely injured in a fight with Ross, after Mathers allegedly attempted to stalk and attack Sophie Faulkner's attorney Michaela Connor at Connor's home. Authorities say that statements by Meksi and Bardulla implicate Mathers in the both the trafficking of women now and of some women several years ago. Both men are being held in protective custody in the Elizabeth jail, as are other men suspected of helping Mathers. An affidavit by a former business associate of Mathers, Nikolai Devanović, has added further evidence of Mathers' involvement according to Ms. Connor. Devanović is due to be deported from the US after finishing a prison term in New Jersey on a fraud conviction.

Although initially arrested for trespassing and assault, Don Mathers has since been charged with several counts of murder, for the women and for the murder of his brother Leonard. Ms. Connor is in the process of petitioning the court to have Ms. Faulker released. Ms. Connor said that further tests have shown Ms. Faulkner's DNA to be too old, questionable, and degraded to tie her into the murder. In addition, Don Mather's DNA was found to be on the weapon.

Shockingly, Don Mathers has been positively identified by DNA obtained through Ross's investigation as working for the last year under a false identity —that of Frank Carlson, deputy director of a human trafficking nonprofit, the Women's Freedom Network. Don Mathers is also now a suspect in the recent murder of Ms. Faulker's friend Giselle Greenspan, and the 2000 murder of Charlotte Merical, former director of the Network. Police are looking into Mathers' past as Carlson, and his alleged nonprofit humanitarian work.

Ms. Connor told the *Herald-Standard* that she was pleased the investigation demonstrated Ms. Faulkner's innocence, and also brought to an end the trafficking activities of Mathers and his cohorts. "Even more so, that these long-missing women may be identified and brought back to their families. My investigator, who deserves the credit for discovering these women, and I have been working with local, state and international agencies to properly take care of these victims."

Ross was contacted for comment, but unavailable as the story went to press. His associate, Joel McFadden, said that Ross had been part of an arson investigation in Rochester, and had been injured when a suspect in that case had attempted to trap Ross in a burning building.

∞

A knock at his door while he's engaged in Dao-yin shen t'i yoga. When he opens it, Leonard Mathers is in the hallway.

"Do you mind if I come in, Gabriel?"

"No, I hoped you would visit."

Leonard walks in. "Thank you. Not many people understand me, but I know you do. I want you to take care of my posters, my relics. Can you do that? Not much of me is left in your world...I'm in a different realm now. Maybe it's the one I was meant to be in. I'm seeing so many beautiful things. I wish I could share them with you."

Leonard sits on the ottoman.

Gabriel takes the sofa, watching Leonard. "Tell me about them."

And Leonard begins playing opera music on his old portable stereo, and drawing things in the air.

Gabriel can see these things as Leonard draws. They look like the carved images in Joel's sculptures. The drawings become animated.

Gabriel thinks to himself that this is not the dream he believes it to be —that Leonard is *really* visiting him. Inside his head, perhaps, but still really there.

"It was a long way to get here, Gabriel. Do you know why you see me?" Leonard's still drawing.

"I hope it's because I did right by you."

Leonard stops. "It was never about me. It was the women. You did right by them. You understand *rasa*. I do too. Don't lose that. It's our connection."

"I won't. I hope to hear more from you."

∞

I'M HAVING A STRANGE REPEAT of childhood. After the trailer fire when I was 10, I was in the hospital with my mom for a couple days, on oxygen therapy —just as I am now. It brought me an early fear of helplessness, and a distaste of hospitals exacerbated decades later by my mother's death. I'm a little hoarse and irritated, aching in the chest and head, from the smoke. My smoking history hasn't helped —the doctor is worried about carbon monoxide levels, and the fact I was somewhat out of it when I first arrived at the hospital, and short of breath. So she had me wait 48 hours to see what my blood levels of poisonous gases would be, and insisted on this tube in my nose.

The blow to my head complicated my condition, as I was already recovering from the concussion that occurred in the fight with Don. I've had several over the years. I worry about the cumulative effect on my mind, like what happens to football players. So far it's okay. I'm under instruction to quit smoking now, while I can undo the damage reasonably well. And to avoid fights. We'll see what happens, considering my karma.

Joel and Bettina and Geneva are in my room pretty much constantly while I'm here, making the concept of a private room moot. But I'm not complaining.

I get updates on all "hell breaking loose," even after being interviewed by Rochester police and fire investigators. Arthur's activities are a big story in Rochester. Arthur was finally found at his mother's house and fought with the cops when they arrested him. He had to be tasered. Now he and his mom are both in jail.

On the third day of my stay, Danny comes up from NYC with Veronica, to be helpful by sitting by my bed and talking, giving us a chance to return to how we used to be. This interferes some with Joel's attempt to set a command center in the room; that consists of him being on the phone constantly, talking with Chris and Isabella, and trying to forbid me to use the phone at all.

Veronica is still handling the business for us while I'm out. I arrange, or rather, have Joel arrange for her to get set in the micro office space I rent. We upgrade the part-time cubicle rental to a small office. She and Geneva will share that, as well as their new living arrangement in Joel's Chelsea apartment. And Veronica's going to train Geneva in some investigatory techniques, and Geneva will train her in weapons. All of this to happen when Joel and I go on vacation, which he tells me we're going to do very soon after I recover. I don't argue about that at all. The idea of not working will be strange, but I'll get used to it.

Carl Mankiewitz calls me for a long-distance interview. I half-suspect he's never going to be satisfied about what happened in the Booth case, and wants to keep reporting on me in case something else about it breaks. But he's also a decent person who takes investigative journalism seriously. Clark Ahn is a good guy as well, and follows up with me in Rochester to get more on the story of Knox.

Alex hears of what happened, of course. Joel had shown me Clark's story. Alex calls my work phone while I'm being examined in my hospital room. Joel picks up the phone, looks at it a long time, then hands it to me. I don't answer. The message Alex leaves doesn't help. He says he's sorry I got hurt, he's sorry over our break-up and thinks we should talk, because I'm trying to kill myself through my work. It makes me uneasy, and I delete the message without comment. Someday I'll try to speak to him to get beyond the anger we had. Not right now.

After four days I'm considered safe to leave on Friday. It becomes a crowded send-off with Bettina, Geneva, and Senator Baker all converging at the hotel in Rochester to see us off.

And then we begin the drive back to New York City; since Danny flew in to Rochester, he rides back with us. In a sign the end times are coming, the conversation between the three of us on that six-hour ride is actually pleasant.

∞

"Gabriel. Let's listen to your breathing."

Chiang and I are sitting across from each other in his loft. We both breathe. He watches me. "Fire. It is a natural element, but can only be touched briefly. You got in it, tasted it. We knew the Narakas would be visited again; I didn't think *literally*."

"Neither did I. This duality is freaking me out."

"You're living life once in reality, and once in metaphor. You need to balance out the fire by being around the other elements in a calming fashion."

"I'm planning a vacation, if that's what you mean."

"It would probably help. You are in the news again. Are you making the best of this?"

"To bring attention to what has gone on in New Jersey, to work on uncovering the human trafficking operation, yes."

"That gives you in turn good karma, I would hope."

"I think so. The man who helped me with the Women's Freedom Network is leaving to run another nonprofit that deals with trafficking, and he wants me to help as a consultant."

Chiang smiles. "It was a roundabout journey, but you can really help more people. Protect them. I'm thinking your destiny is unfolding."

"I want to do this. One of the local reporters is really on my side for whatever reason. He's calling me all the time."

Chiang listens to me breathing for a while. "Stay with your positive people. Many negative people await, because trying to do good is like creating a path —and people will try to knock trees across that path. To fuck you up." He smiles at my reaction to his profanity. "Wait here, I'll give you a regimen to help your lungs."

∞

Friday, February 11
Alphabet City, 7:43 pm

Michaela's come over to fuss over me. Well, she kind of has to compete with Joel over that. He is reluctant to leave us alone. Not that I'm really alone these days. Joel has managed to ensure since we returned a week ago that either people are over here all the time, or we're over somewhere with people. Helping Veronica and Geneva decorate. Explaining more of the I Ching to Chris. Watching Isabella make Joel show me a couple of paintings—his show is happening this month. Sitting in with Jason's band. And getting used to chewing gum constantly to get off cigarettes.

But anyway, Michaela's also here. She's been seriously busy with her cases. The publicity helped her, too.

I was worried though, that she would withdraw from me. She's here to prove otherwise. "You look okay," she says doubtfully.

"I'm not that bad off." I cough then, just to be wicked.

She sits with me on the sofa, absently playing with Archie. "I wanted to be sure we're still cool."

"Why wouldn't we be? You're treating my girl Veronica okay, right?"

"Nothing to worry about there. But you, it was tough for me, seeing you like that. With Don. But I think I understand. How are you doing?"

"He's fine."

Michaela turns to Joel, who's sitting on the arm of the sofa like a watch cat. "Baby, you are *hovering*. Things *have* changed."

He folds his arms. "I have to look out for him."

"Good. But from me? What *exactly* am I going to do to him?"

"Nothing." He now looks sheepish.

I laugh. "It's not that. He just wants to remind the world he owns me. I'm glad you're here. I wanted to ask something."

"Shoot."

"You still have some of Leonard's stuff that was going to be evidence for Sophie's trial."

"Yeah. I guess technically it's not evidence anymore, as Sophie's case is dismissed. I think Don's attorney has some of it, and the police have other parts of it...but I think a lot of it is still there in the basement of Wildemore."

"Do you think we can recover it? What's left?"

She shrugs. "If it's not needed for evidence, probably. The new prosecutor on Leonard's case probably has some props for you, since trying Don is going to put her in the spotlight. I know here, I can ask."

"If there's no problems, I would like his stuff."

"You want old posters?"

"Geneva will fix them up. I just feel Leonard had a legacy; it shouldn't be forgotten and just thrown out. Also, a historical society might be interested in the older items."

Joel speaks up. "Maybe Sara will want them."

I put my hand on his leg. "You see why he's around? He thinks about things that need to be thought about. We'll fix up the stuff and have Professor Wheatley ask her about it."

∞

Bettina feels the need to call me every few days, and I feel the need to do the same.

She updates me on what's going on upstate. "Arthur's apparently having a hard time of it, never having been arrested before. He's under suicide watch."

"I don't know how to feel about that. I suppose it's gratifying that besides the arson charges, he has a count of attempted murder. It's hard to get over someone trying to burn you to death. His sister emailed me. She's having a hard time dealing with this too, but she's glad he's in jail. Her, I feel for."

And I sometimes wonder how many legal documents my name is in, including Arthur's indictment. Now Joel gets to have that fun as well. We'll have to go to court in Rochester as well as Elizabeth.

Back in Elizabeth, Don isn't talking—assuming he's more than semi-comatose from painkillers. I hope. Devanović has been shipped back to Serbia, without the necessity of a welcoming committee. He doesn't deserve to be that peaceful, but that's a sacrifice so a greater monster can be off the street.

I get a call from Edward, thanking me for helping Sophie. When Mikki gets a judge to release Sophie from Jail, Bob is with me to meet her and drive her back to her house. Edward comes out to meet up with Bob, and talk about Leonard.

Joel has started testing his version of Tor for the Tertullian Project. In the meantime, I've been writing out what I want to say in the videos, and what might possibly serve as evidence. Hoping to crowd source people getting interested. And we finally get the legal stuff taken care of, wills and all, despite my discomfort.

Herrmann has some input on the Tertullian project as well as other issues. We have started to develop a bond by me listening to his experiences, and asking questions to frame the stories. We also talk about what to research next with the Tertullians.

∞

Monday, February 14
Alphabet City, 5:12 pm

I'm almost home, having returned from a day visiting people to make up for lost time. One person was Nicolas from Cafétière Malífice. He helped me with Raymond's case. I owed him an apology for not seeing him after Raymond died. And Raymond's nephew, Adam, whom I'd promised to keep in touch with. I'd called his great-aunt to check on him, and was invited over to spend some time. He'll spend more time with me tomorrow, on my birthday.

In the car, I'm listening to Freddie Mercury and Warren Zevon. Two great artists taken too soon; songs that carry so much meaning in appreciating life while you have it.

Now I call Joel. "Where are you?"

"I'm here in your place. Where did you think I'd be? It's Valentine's Day. I'm waiting for you, with the cat."

I park, and go upstairs, practically slamming through my door. I can't get there fast enough.

He turns around from the bookshelf, where he's reading something. "Hey. Didn't know you were so close." His smile has changed to something different, better. More relaxed and confident in us.

"Come here."

He tries to tune into me. "Okay..." He starts to walk over, but I can't wait. I'm already rushing over to him, to grab his head and kiss him.

He inhales from surprise, surprise at my ferocity. I break away for a moment to look at him.

"I want you to know it's always like this." I kiss him again, and in that overarching impulse, move him down to the floor. I can practically feel the adrenaline in him responding to my feelings.

"Yes. Tell me."

"This is always you and me." I want to envelope him, protect him with my desire, my love.

On the floor we're in a tangle. A fight. A giving. An attempt to crawl inside and be part of the other person.

I tell him, "I'm going to show you what it means to be loved..."

"I'm going to show *you.* You have no idea..."

CODA

From The *New York Scene's* Thin Blue Line column, by
Carl Mankiewitz
April 18, 2011

Hidden Killers —Discovery ID
Season Three premiere episode
Mask of Sanity —Don Mathers, the New Jersey Demon

PBS *Frontline*
Garden State Slavery

These are two programs about events reported on in this
column, that took place in our sister state and involving a
friend of the *Scene*, Gabriel Ross. But the programs have very
different perspectives. Both of these programs carry heavy
Biblical references, and push the Cain/Abel metaphor.

The heavy-handedness of the Discovery ID series narration is
balanced by the occasional voiceover of Gabriel Ross —the
private investigator who brought down Don Mathers. The
backstory of this is interesting. Ross didn't want to participate
in the Discovery ID crime show about the Mathers killings, but
ultimately did so because, of course, the show was going to
be broadcast anyway. His participation is more evident in the
Frontline documentary, which also includes some information
on global human slavery, and a brief comment by a noted
author of a recent book on sex trafficking.

One of the more interesting side notes in this case is the appearance of two well-known true-crime writers. Tom Freeman, whose last book was plagued by some legal issues due to the convicted con artist who both assaulted him and tried to sue him, and Walter Cleveland, a more high-toned but controversial writer whose essays are often in *New York* Magazine. These writers are competing for Ross's story, but of course with what has happened with Ross recently (see our previous columns) in Wayne, NJ, I imagine he has other things to worry about now.

Anyway, back to the shows. What's a little ironic, perhaps, is that the horror of human trafficking sort of takes a backseat to the story of the man who discovered Mathers' victims, and other collateral characters. Sophie Faulkner, the woman with the multiple personalities who knew Don Mathers, and her best friend Giselle Greenspan, who dated Mathers —thinking he was another person. We don't really know the identities of the women who were found being held hostage as prostitutes in Elizabeth, nor do we really know the women who Mathers killed. These women seem lost and faceless, as they must have felt while trapped in this situation. And how women across the globe must feel when lost in anonymity of unlawful sex work…

∞

EPILOGUE

And so, while this is the end of this story, it is really the beginning. The beginning of Gabriel and Joel's story. We hope that you will come along on this journey with us.

THE END OF TWO-FACED WOMAN.

GABRIEL AND JOEL WILL RETURN IN THE BOOK OF JOEL.

Author's Note

Sex trafficking slavery is happening across the world in countries such as India, Nepal, Italy, Moldova, Albania, the Balkans, Thailand, and the US. Women and children and enslaved by deception, sometimes repeatedly sold to other slavers. Sometimes returning to sex work when no other prospects exist. Sometimes families are complicit in the slavery, and sometimes former slaves become recruiters or complicit in slavery themselves. Men can be trafficked as well.

Human trafficking involves more than forced sex work. It can also be forced labor. Arrests and convictions are shockingly low. The economics of the trade keeps it growing.

The health effects are devastating, including the risk of HIV and other sexually-related diseases, depression, and suicide.

Globalization and the global economic crisis have contributed to the continuing demand in trafficking, despite greater awareness.

More information can be found from Nonprofit organizations such as FreetheSlaves.net and the Polaris Project and in books by Kevin Bales, including *Disposable People: New Slavery in the Global Economy* and Siddharth Kara, including *Sex Trafficking: Inside the Business of Modern Slavery.*

If the past doesn't kill you, the present will.

One of the unique qualities of the Gabriel's World stories is that each features the same characters (NYC private investigator Gabriel Ross and his boyfriend, Joel McFadden) in a natural progression of personality and relationships, and each has a stand-alone theme and style: *The Hanged Man* was a dark conspiracy thriller concerning the price of doing the right thing. *Two-Faced Woman* was a slightly surreal, psychological take on duality in life, and what how far one must go to protect others. In *The Book of Joel*, the story is a departure from the focus on Gabriel's cases—Joel's life becomes the case for them.

For Joel, his initial success as an artist is shadowed by his need to confront his parents, who threw him out at age 15. Joel finds his mother is anxious to reconnect with him, but his father is still hostile. After discovering Joel's father is involved in a corruption scheme, a shocking turn of events follows that reverses Gabriel and Joel's roles. As they investigate further, they are pitted against a notorious New Jersey killer for hire. But perhaps more dangerously, they are also stalked by a former police detective —the man who first abused Joel — and who has a twisted endgame in mind.

In this story, the current investigation is intertwined with a continuing excursion into Joel's history, capturing the ordeal of how the past and present can strengthen you —or break you. Joel might be moving past what's haunted him lifelong, or he might be about to fatally collide with evil. *The Book of Joel* features the necessity of facing the past to overcome it.

Read ahead for a sample of The Book of Joel

Friedrich Wilhelm Nietzsche said, *He wonders also about himself—that he cannot learn to forget, but hangs on the past: however far or fast he runs, that chain runs with him.*

C.S. Lewis said, *"For the present is the point at which time touches eternity."*

∞

P R E L U D E

Wednesday, January 26, 2011
Hackensack, NJ 7:33 pm

CARSON SMITH ARRIVES at his apartment, his mind still on his job even after picking up some take-out dinner and having a drink at the bar of the restaurant. Carson is an auditor for the New Jersey Comptroller's Office; he's been reviewing the State Division of Development. As per protocol, he had first brought the information he discovered to the chief procurement and land use officer in the DoD. But he's still thinking of who else may need to be approached, as he's sure there's serious corruption involved in what he found. He hasn't yet discussed the matter with his supervisor.

Carson tosses his keys on an end table and brings the take-out bag to the kitchen without turning on any lights. His mind is too deep into his situation. A very small kitchen light is already on and giving some faint illumination. He leaves that one on all day to discourage housebreakers.

It's only when he comes back into the living room to check his home phone for messages that he becomes aware he's not alone.

Someone is in a chair in his apartment living room. A huge figure, blurry in the darkness. No, blurry because he's in black and has a hood on his head.

Carson freezes halfway across the room. The figure gets up slowly. It's like a mythological beast rising from a pit. Carson is 5'10 but this person is much taller. And bigger. In the faint light Carson can barely make out any eyes showing through the holes in the hood. The hood is squareish and large, and drapes over the man's shoulders.

"Ah...ah..." Carson can't think of what to say. Is this a home invasion? Does it work like that?

The figure lifts a pair of glasses to the hood and fixes them to his face. As if he's about to read something. Then from somewhere in the black clothing he produces a gun. A very large gun—it looks like two feet in length. Carson doesn't know it's a WTS .50 BMG pistol and utterly impractical to use in a home invasion or anything other than stopping a tank coming at you. He only sees it's a large, large gun pointed at him.

The man speaks slowly. "If I shot you, you'd bleed out in 30 seconds. But most of your internal organs would be destroyed anyway."

"What do you want?" Carson tries not to sound scared or aggressive. He has no idea how to handle this.

The giant seems to stare down at him. "I like to look at them bleeding out," he says contemplatively.

Carson imagines that he will in fact be shot. Something in the man's posture gives the impression that he really, really wants to do this. Carson tries to reconcile to dying. *It's okay*, he thinks to himself.

"Just tell me why."

The man tilts his hooded head as if he doesn't understand what Carson is saying.

"Why you're going to kill me. I have a right to know."

The man moves the gun up and down in his hand. "You don't have to die. Listen to this. You have one chance, one opportunity. You won't see me the next time. You'll just see the blood and brains bursting out of your mouth before you hit the sidewalk. Do you understand?"

"Uh, uh, what? What am I supposed to do?"

"Stop looking into things. Stop asking questions. Just do your job like a good bureaucrat. Keep quiet. Put in your twenty and retire. That doesn't sound so bad, right?"

The man moves closer to Carson. Close up, he blocks out everything, becomes a black void. He puts the gun to Carson's head. "What do you say?"

"Yes...whatever. *Whatever.*"

"Down on your knees."

Carson sort of edges down to the floor. He looks up at the gun. The man nudges him with the large rounded end of the barrel.

An impossible time goes by with the man just touching the gun to Carson's head and staring at him. So it seems behind those glasses.

Finally, the man moves away. "Just so you know, this applies if you tell anybody, *anybody,* anything about your recent investigations. About tonight too. I still kind of hope you fuck up. I'd like to see if this would make your head actually explode. Or your chest. The head would be better for visuals, but the chest—it would be large enough to *see* through. Yeah, you could put your hand through the hole before you die."

The man chuckles to himself. Then he moves away. Carson hears the door of the apartment open and close.

It takes him ten minutes to be able to stand. He has to use an ottoman and another chair to drag himself upright while shaking uncontrollably. Then he runs to the bathroom and throws up. He can no longer eat; the to-go bag stays unopened on the kitchen table.

Every time Carson thinks about who he might call for help, he pictures the big man coming back. And his blood exploding from him in the graphic way the man described.

At two in the morning he composes a resignation note for his supervisor.

∞

Tuesday, February 1, 2011
Wayne, NJ 1:00 pm

Gloria McFadden, a blonde in her late fifties, sits across the table from the older, taller man. Larry Meese, a longtime family friend. She's pleased to see him. Although she's an attractive woman, his demeanor towards her is nothing less than proper and respectful.

"Gloria, it's been some time. I'm glad to have a chance to talk to you."

Her smile is slightly higher on one side of her face, a quirky charm. "Larry... I hope it didn't bother you that I asked you not to tell Ken."

"Of course not."

They're interrupted by the waitperson and give him their orders. Then Gloria says, "I had a couple things I wanted to talk you about."

"Certainly."

"Ken is worrying me. He's been difficult lately. I think something is wrong at work. He won't talk to me about it...does he ever mention anything to you?"

Meese has years of experience in not letting anything show in his eyes or his face, except what he wants others to see. "No, not that I can think of, Gloria. But you know, as I know, working for the state has its pressures."

"I guess...but still, he's drinking more and that's saying something. I try not to be one of those ex-alkies who are judgmental, but he's really sunk into himself. I'm afraid he'll crash."

"Let me see if I can find out."

"Thank you, Larry. The other thing...well, it's so strange..."

"I've heard it all as a cop. I *still* hear strange things in the Sheriff's Office. Don't be worried; you can tell me."

"Well...this is another thing I can't talk to Ken about right now. You've read the stories about the dead women who were found in Union County? The serial killer?"

"That guy Mathers, yeah. Glad it's in Union; my office doesn't have to handle him. It must be a pain."

"Larry...when I read the stories about the private investigator who found these women...Joel was involved."

Meese face changes. So subtly, Gloria can't see it. It's as if the last 17 years fell away just hearing the name. " *What?*"

His voice is off, but she doesn't notice. "He seems to be some kind of *assistant* to this New York City detective. I looked for more about it online...he was working with this man in upstate New York too. Something about an arsonist in Rochester."

Meese puts on a sympathetic expression; his mind is still reeling. "My God, Gloria. To see that after all this time..."

"It *has* to be him in the stories. Larry, since I started recovery, I've had some time to think. John Dell helped me a lot with that. I want to find Joel. His birthday just passed—he's 33 now! I want to tell him I'm sorry. Even if he doesn't care, just to tell him. Look what he's doing—he and that detective. He may have made something good out of his life."

She has a hint of a smile on her face. In her handbag is a picture from a *New York Herald-Standard* story, in which Joel is standing next to Gabriel Ross. She's been taking it out during the day and looking at it, when Ken isn't around. Thinking of the picture makes her smile.

Meese smiles too. But he's thrown. His mind clicks and whirs. He almost grabs the tablecloth in his fists. "Gloria, I know what you must feel. But now...Joel...he did that terrible thing to you and Ken back when. I didn't approve of Ken throwing him out—you know that. But he was on his way to being a criminal. And I have to warn you— private investigators are sleazy. They'll pretty much do anything to make a buck. I wouldn't think this New York PI is some kind of hero."

Gloria draws back at his tone of voice. "Larry, he's my *son*. I want to know what Joel is doing, who he is."

Meese immediately adjusts his attitude. "Sure, sure. You're being a mom. Look, I can check some of my sources, see what I can find out. Just take it slow right now. You don't want to rush into anything and get hurt."

"Okay," she accedes. "I appreciate it. I just want to move forward in life now. It's why I want to know what's going on with Ken, too."

"Of course, of course. Just—as a friend who cares, don't do anything without checking with me first, right? On either of these things."

"Yes, I'll hold off until you find something, Larry."

After lunch, which Meese rushes through, he goes back to his SUV and just sits for a while absorbing the news.

He's not sure what he feels but he knows he must, *must* get a look at Joel.

ABOUT THE AUTHOR

Alex Fiano is a bi/genderqueer writer, teacher, artist, and LGBTQ+ advocate (particularly for youth) living in New York City. Read more about Alex here: https://gabrielsworld.com/gabriels-world/about-the-author/

The books in the *Gabriel's World* series are:

The Hanged Man
Two-Faced Woman
The Book of Joel
Dead for Now
Hardcore (2019)

[Cover images in part from dead_brushes/brusheezy.com]